THE REINCARNATED GIANT

WEATHERHEAD BOOKS ON ASIA

WEATHERHEAD BOOKS ON ASIA

Weatherhead East Asian Institute, Columbia University

Literature

David Der-wei Wang, Editor

Ye Zhaoyan, *Nanjing 1937: A Love Story*, translated by Michael Berry (2003)

Oda Makato, *The Breaking Jewel*, translated by Donald Keene (2003)

Han Shaogong, *A Dictionary of Maqiao*, translated by Julia Lovell (2003)

Takahashi Takako, *Lonely Woman*, translated by Maryellen Toman Mori (2004)

Chen Ran, *A Private Life*, translated by John Howard-Gibbon (2004)

Eileen Chang, *Written on Water*, translated by Andrew F. Jones (2004)

Writing Women in Modern China: The Revolutionary Years, 1936–1976, edited by
Amy D. Dooling (2005)

Han Bangqing, *The Sing-song Girls of Shanghai*, first translated by Eileen Chang,
revised and edited by Eva Hung (2005)

Loud Sparrows: Contemporary Chinese Short-Shorts, translated and edited by
Aili Mu, Julie Chiu, and Howard Goldblatt (2006)

Hiratsuka Raichō, *In the Beginning, Woman Was the Sun*, translated by
Teruko Craig (2006)

Zhu Wen, *I Love Dollars and Other Stories of China*, translated by Julia Lovell (2007)

Kim Sowŏl, *Azaleas: A Book of Poems*, translated by David McCann (2007)

Wang Anyi, *The Song of Everlasting Sorrow: A Novel of Shanghai*, translated by
Michael Berry with Susan Chan Egan (2008)

Ch'oe Yun, *There a Petal Silently Falls: Three Stories by Ch'oe Yun*, translated by
Bruce and Ju-Chan Fulton (2008)

(list of titles continued on p. 425)

THE REINCARNATED GIANT

AN ANTHOLOGY OF TWENTY-FIRST-CENTURY CHINESE SCIENCE FICTION

EDITED BY MINGWEI SONG AND
THEODORE HUTERS

Columbia University Press
New York

This publication has been supported by the Richard W. Weatherhead Publication
Fund of the Weatherhead East Asian Institute, Columbia University.

Columbia University Press wishes to express its appreciation for assistance
given by the Pushkin Fund in the publication of this book.

Columbia University Press
Publishers Since 1893
New York   Chichester, West Sussex
cup.columbia.edu
Copyright © 2018 Columbia University Press
All rights reserved

Library of Congress Cataloging-in-Publication Data
Names: Song, Mingwei, editor. | Huters, Theodore, editor.
Title: The reincarnated giant : an anthology of twenty-first-century
Chinese science fiction / edited by Mingwei Song and Theodore Huters.
Description: New York : Columbia University Press, 2018. | Series: Weatherhead
books on Asia | Includes bibliographical references.
Identifiers: LCCN 2018001388 (print) | LCCN 2018004548 (ebook) |
ISBN 9780231542548 (electronic) | ISBN 9780231180221 (cloth : acid-free paper) |
ISBN 9780231180238 (pbk. : acid-free paper)
Subjects: LCSH: Science fiction, Chinese—Translations into English. |
Chinese fiction—21st century—Translations into English.
Classification: LCC PL2658.E8 (ebook) | LCC PL2658.E8 R45 2018 (print) |
DDC 895.13/0876208—dc23
LC record available at https://lccn.loc.gov/2018001388

Columbia University Press books are printed on permanent
and durable acid-free paper.

Printed in the United States of America

Cover design: Noah Arlow

CONTENTS

ACKNOWLEDGMENTS

We are grateful to the thirteen authors and eighteen translators, whose diligent work and selfless devotion made this volume possible. We also appreciate the support of many colleagues, friends, and science fiction fans of both China and the United States, who have been following the progress of this project. Mingwei Song would like to express his gratitude to his coeditor, Theodore Huters, who not only fine-tuned the translations in this collection but also offered valuable guidance in other important ways. Mingwei Song would also like to thank David Der-wei Wang, who supported this project from the very beginning. He offered advice on selecting the texts and brought the manuscript to Columbia University Press. We thank Jennifer Crewe, of Columbia University Press, for her patience and guidance, and the press's Christine Dunbar for her editorial expertise.

Theodore Huters would like to express his gratitude to Mingwei Song, who initially developed the project as a special edition of *Renditions* and carried it through to the present volume. Theodore Huters would also like to thank his assistants at *Renditions*, Stephanie Wong and Sherlon Chi-yin Ip, who provided invaluable editorial help for those stories originally published there.

INTRODUCTION

Does Science Fiction Dream of a Chinese New Wave?

MINGWEI SONG

U ntil 2013, the only essay on Chinese science fiction published in the academic journal *Science Fiction Studies* characterized the genre's history in China as a hesitant journey to the West and found science fiction "a fairly marginal phenomenon" in the Middle Kingdom.[1] Or, in the words of the Chinese author Fei Dao, whose short story is included in this volume, Chinese science fiction was like a "hidden lonely army . . . laid low in the wilderness where nobody really cared to look at it."[2] The situation has changed drastically in the past five or six years. Chinese science fiction has suddenly gained worldwide recognition, thanks mainly to the success of Liu Cixin's *The Three-Body Problem* (translated into English by Ken Liu), a novel that created an international sensation. It became a bestseller in the United States, causing the *Wall Street Journal* to report that "China launches a sci-fi invasion of the U.S.,"[3] and it won the first Hugo Award for a novel written originally in a language other than English. Today Chinese science fiction is no longer a hidden lonely army, and the genre's journey to the West is no longer hesitant; it has become a fresh new force that is helping shape the outlook of global science fiction.

It should be noted, however, that even before *The Three-Body Problem* "touched down" in the United States, the novel and its two sequels had already become landmarks in the Chinese sf world, and before the trilogy was published in China between 2006 and 2010, a new wave of Chinese science fiction had already emerged at the turn of the twenty-first century. The success of the trilogy in the American book market is a small echo of its record-breaking popularity among Chinese readers. In addition, Liu Cixin's success should also be contextualized as one of the many facets demonstrating the revival of the genre in China during the past fifteen years, something conditioned by the genre's long, complicated history in China.

At the very beginning of the twentieth century, Anglo-American and French science fiction novels were introduced to Chinese readers, primarily through translations based on secondhand Japanese translations. Jules Verne was one of the most translated Western authors between 1900 and 1912. The late Qing reformer Liang Qichao (1873–1929) borrowed a concept from his Japanese mentors, Yukio Ozaki (1858–1954) and Katō Hiroyuki (1836–1916), in coining the Chinese term *kexue xiaoshuo* (science fiction). The first "golden age" of Chinese science fiction lasted ten years, from 1902 to 1911, giving birth to numerous novels and short stories that combined science fantasy, political utopianism, and technological optimism. About ten years later, the rise of a truth-claiming literary realism employing the image of cannibalism to make visible the hidden "evils" of the Confucian tradition, a new literary trend pioneered by Lu Xun (1881–1936), also a translator of Jules Verne during his youth, eventually pushed science fiction to the margins of Chinese literary modernity. However, the realism "invented" by Lu Xun, which differed from the mainstream realism epitomized in Mao Dun's (1896–1981) later epic novels, aspired to reveal the deeper truth beneath the surface reality, and the truth-claiming discourse of Lu Xun's realism may have its roots in his earlier belief in scientific discourse and science fiction. Nonetheless, what is often referred to as May Fourth realism, Mao Dun's naturalistic realism, and, later, the socialist realism under Mao's regime made science fiction an obscure genre that was not taken seriously for most of the twentieth century. It enjoyed short revivals in Hong Kong during the Cold War, in Taiwan during the 1970s and 1980s, and in the People's Republic of China (PRC) during the early reform era (1978–1983), but none of the revivals gained enough momentum to sustain the genre. The history of Chinese science fiction has, in other words, never been continuous.

THE NEW WAVE

The recent revival, particularly what I call the new wave, began almost exactly one hundred years after the late Qing golden age of Chinese science fiction. Some factors related to its recent revival appear similar to the circumstances of its boom in late Qing, such as a rapidly changing mediasphere and anxious expectations concerning change in China. In particular, the free platform for new authors to publish on the internet, the failure of a collective idealism for Chinese intellectuals in 1989, and the "perfect vacuum" for fantasy resulting when mainstream realism more or less lost touch with reality and thus could not avoid being marginalized in the field of literary production—all these could be the essential cultural and social conditions for the rise of the new wave. I first used the term "new wave" to refer to this recent trend of Chinese science fiction in 2013 when writing an article in Chinese for the academic journal *Wenxue.* Subsequently, I elaborated on the definition and aesthetics of the new wave in several articles written in English.[4] My argument is that on its most radical side, the new wave of Chinese sf has been thriving on an avant-garde cultural spirit that encourages readers to think beyond the conventional ways of perceiving reality and to challenge the commonly accepted ideas about what constitutes the existence and self-identity of a person surrounded by technologies of self, society, and governance. However, the term "new wave" is a controversial concept for critics in China; its emphasis on the subversive, darker side of science fiction is questioned by those who have more faith in a utopia and China's contemporary pursuit of wealth and power. Many scholars and writers in the mainland prefer the prosperous "golden age" to the subversive, cutting-edge new wave that sheds light on the darker side.

It's quite possible that, in a peculiar way, Chinese science fiction may have simultaneously arrived at its new golden age and generated a new-wave subversion of the genre itself. The poetics and politics of the new wave are both meaningful at a time when the Chinese government is engineering a "Chinese dream." The new wave has unleashed a nightmarish unconscious of a dream that does not necessarily belong to an individual but rather to a collective entity. In its aesthetic aspect, the new wave speaks either to the invisible dimensions of reality or simply to the impossibility of representing a certain reality dictated by the discourse of the national dream.[5]

This new wave has been marked by a dystopian vision of China's future, ambiguous moral dilemmas, and sophisticated representations of the power of technology or the technology of power. The poetics of the new wave point to the darker, more invisible sides of reality, as mentioned, and in this connection several new-wave writers, with Han Song, Fei Dao, Chen Qiufan, and even Liu Cixin as prominent examples, often refer to Lu Xun in their stories. The irony in the history of Chinese science fiction lies in the seemingly improbable marriage of a truth-claiming realism and science fiction. The new wave achieves a high-intensity realism that surpasses the conventional realistic depictions of everyday life. It speaks to the deeper truth beneath the surface reality, as Lu Xun did in "A Madman's Diary." Han Song's 2011 novel, *Ditie* (Subway), takes readers into the nightmarish, absurd, irrational, cannibalistic, and abysmal underground world beneath a prosperous Chinese metropolis. Han Song has stated, "China's reality is more science fictional than science fiction,"[6] pointing to a reality that people may fear to see, as so evident in the title of his short story "Kan de kongju" (Fear of seeing, 2002), but science fiction, through metaphorical, figurative, or poetic means, represents that incredible reality. To call again to mind Lu Xun, Han Song's characters discover the dark secret of the social system. Like the madman's discovery of the cannibalism in Confucian society, the secrets Han Song reveals are horrifying, unsettling, and challenge the fundamentals of contemporary Chinese society.

Does science fiction dream of a Chinese new wave? The invisible darkness that the Chinese new wave illuminates is the very magnetic force that makes the genre alive, attractive, and provocative in a worldwide context.

TRANSLATING CHINESE SCIENCE FICTION

In 1970 William A. Lyell translated into English Lao She's *Cat Country* (1932), a dystopian novel about China's prevailing corruption and total lack of individual integrity. It was the first Chinese novel of the genre made available to English-language readers. The Martian Cat Country's uncanny resemblance to China in 1932 and its complete hopelessness can be read as an antidote to the didactic "realism" and patriotic propaganda on the eve of the Japanese invasion. A new edition of this translation was recently published by Penguin (2013). The first English-language anthology of Chinese science fiction, *Science Fiction from China*, edited by Dingbo Wu and Patrick Murphy (Praeger, 1989), focuses on the early reform era (1978–1983), including major stories by authors like Zheng Wenguang, Tong Enzheng, Wei Yahua, and Ye Yonglie.

More recently, three important science fiction novels by Hong Kong and Taiwan authors reached English-language readers. S. K. Chang's *The City Trilogy* (Columbia University Press, 2003) is an epic that incorporates other genre elements such as martial arts romance and also has a strong political undertone concerning Taiwan's history and identity. Dung Kaicheung's *Atlas: The Archaeology of an Imaginary City* (Columbia University Press, 2012) is a collection of short Borgesian essays and stories that fabricate the past, the present, and the future of Victoria, a city that may or may not be Hong Kong, or at least a heterotopic mirror of Hong Kong. It should be noted that Dung's *Atlas* won the Science Fiction and Fantasy Translation Award in 2013. Chan Koonchung's *The Fat Years* (2009) was translated into English by Michael S. Duke and released by Doubleday in 2011. *The Fat Years* is China's equivalent of *Brave New World* (if not a darker *1984*), presenting a dystopian image of present-day China, its system, its intellectual culture, and its amnesia of its recent history.

The single most important change in recent years in the English-language translations of Chinese science fiction has been the unrivaled devotion and efforts of Ken Liu. He has translated not only several full-length novels, including *The Three-Body Problem* (Tor, 2014) and, third in the trilogy, *Death's End* (Tor, 2016), as well as Chen Qiufan's novel *The Waste Tide* (Tor, forthcoming), but also dozens of novellas and stories from a variety of authors, including Chen Qiufan, Xia Jia, Ma Boyong, Hao Jingfang, and Tang Fei. His first collection of translated stories, *Invisible Planet*, was released in 2016 (Tor) to critical acclaim.

All such efforts are important milestones in making Chinese science fiction's journey to the West an epic event. *The Reincarnated Giant* is the latest effort, and it is a collection featuring a comprehensive list of science fiction writers, with their most important works translated into

English for the first time. What is also notable is that most of the contributions are from academics and translators whose work is not usually limited to science fiction.

THE REINCARNATED GIANT: RENDITIONS AND THE CURRENT ANTHOLOGY

In 2012, upon the invitation of Theodore Huters, I edited a special issue of *Renditions* (77/78). The issue showcases representative works of Chinese science fiction from its first and latest booms, focusing on the late Qing and the contemporary. Paralleling the science fiction writings from these two beginnings of successive centuries proved to be an intriguing project. Both epochs are characterized by heightened aspirations for change as well as by deep anxieties about China's future. A comparative reading of the stories from the late Qing and the contemporary sheds light on their common themes. Yet the recapitulations of the earlier age's literary motifs also lead to self-reflective variations that point to the latter age's singularity. It is hoped that the fruitful conversations between scholars of the late Qing and observers of contemporary China triggered by the special issue continue with the present volume.

The 2012 *Renditions* special issue was the first English-language collection of Chinese science fiction to appear since the publication of Wu and Murphy's anthology in 1989. The thirteen pieces included in the special issue are divided into two groups. The first four pieces are novel excerpts and short stories from the first decade of Chinese science fiction's development. The other nine selections are recent short stories by contemporary authors.

The present volume, a substantially enlarged collection following that special issue, focuses on contemporary science fiction from Taiwan, Hong Kong, and the PRC. Although no late Qing pieces appear in this collection, there is a large number of authors of the twenty-first century: Liu Cixin, Han Song, Wang Jinkang, Zhao Haihong, La La, Chi Hui, Fei Dao, and Xia Jia, as well as two other PRC writers, Chen Qiufan and Bao Shu, and three writers from Hong Kong and Taiwan, Lo Yi-chin, Dung Kai-cheung, and Egoyan Zheng.

For Chinese fans, Liu Cixin, Han Song, and Wang Jinkang, the three most senior authors (born in 1963, 1965, and 1948, respectively), are called the Big Three. They have shaped the field in significant ways. Liu Cixin, a so-called hard science fiction writer, revived the great tradition of space opera for Chinese readers. Han Song reenergized Lu Xun's legacy in blurring the boundary between realism and surrealism and between politics and technology. Wang Jinkang, a humanist, has worked to keep alive the utopian impulse for a hopeful future—with the possible exception of the collection's title story, "The Reincarnated Giant." This unusual story, with its dark humor, was, it's worth noting, originally published under a pseudonym.

In this anthology are two contributions by Liu Cixin, in fact two of his most important stories, "The Village Schoolteacher" (2001) and "The Poetry Cloud" (2003). In both, Liu creates sublime, awe-inspiring imagery of the universe while also presenting an ambiguous negotiation between poetry and technology, morality and survival, humanity and the universe. "The Village Schoolteacher" combines realistic depictions of the struggle of a teacher to help underprivileged children in rural China with a wondrously imaginative telling of an intergalactic war extending over the entire Milky Way. Whereas the former aspect appears to be but a nuanced detail in the unfolding of the latter divine drama, it nonetheless proves crucial in the story for human survival. "The Poetry Cloud" presents a seemingly utopian description of the happy life of two Chinese poets (one of them a hyperdimensional alien disguised as Li Bai) after the total extinction of the solar system, but the poetry cloud, a supercomputer, can best be viewed as a simulacrum, an instance of a virtual reality fabricated by the technologized mimesis of the poetic vision after its creators have been wiped out. Liu Cixin contrasts scientific certainty with the contingency of the human vision, thus turning a utopia of science and technology into an uncertain dystopia for humanity.

Compared with that of Liu Cixin, Han Song's style is more provocative both artistically and politically. He is often compared to Kafka, but a more relevant comparison is no doubt with Lu Xun. His sf writings are full of uncanny, gloomy, and sometimes inexplicable images that aim to unconceal reality's dark underbelly. Han Song's images also resonate with some of Lu Xun's famous devices, such as the "iron house" metaphor and cannibalism, which are reappropriated to address the problems of contemporary China. "The Passengers and the Creator" (2006) depicts a group of Chinese people stuck in a new type of iron house: the main cabin of an airplane where they are fed the flesh of those who have died on the plane. The passengers have to go through the process of being enlightened to see the truth of their reality before making a revolution that ends in a plane crash, which forms an ambiguous national allegory. In "Regenerated Bricks" (2011), Han Song depicts how artists and developers create humanized intelligent bricks by recycling the earthquake remains in which are embedded human flesh. The miracle of the regenerated bricks eventually enables the Chinese to conquer the universe, but what they build with these bricks is forever haunted by the whispers and weeping of the dead.

Wang Jinkang's "The Reincarnated Giant" (2006) can be read as an allegory about the greedy Chinese nouveaux riches' craving for unlimited development, wealth, and power, and even longevity, that ends in irreversible catastrophe. It foregrounds an unsatisfied desire for *zengzhang* (growth), a ubiquitous keyword in current news coverage of China's economic leap, marked by a continuously escalating GDP. The outcome in Wang Jinkang's story comes as little surprise: the insatiable desire for development leads to uncontrollable results that eventually ruin the developers themselves. The grotesque image of the reincarnated giant epitomizes China's myth of economic development.

A number of the other stories in this volume come from younger writers, and they point to new directions for the genre's future development. La La's "The Radio Waves That Never Die" (2007) and Zhao Haihong's "1923: A Fantasy" (2007) both reuse themes of revolutionary literature in postrevolutionary narratives. La La's story, through a puzzle-solving process, shows how a posthuman descendant decodes, reconstructs, and understands a radio message, similar to what happens in the communist legend of a special agent alluded to in the title, but what is eventually received by the semicyborg is the last message sent from an extinct humanity. Thus a revolutionary theme takes a posthuman turn. Zhao Haihong's story weaves the revolutionary story into a dreamy romance that turns history into a nostalgic dream; the story intentionally misuses historical information to highlight the fantastic nature of the memory of revolution, not unlike the bubbles produced by the machine in the story.

Chi Hui's "The Rain Forest" (2007) points to themes of environmentalism as well as interspecies transformation, or, metaphorically, transgender or transracial identity. Fei Dao's "The Demon's Head" (2007) presents an allegorical image of the evil undead—clearly referring to dictatorship—that is made possible through inventive technology. Xia Jia's "The Demon-Enslaving Flask" (2004) represents a playful experiment with the uncertainty principle that is nevertheless shown as being contained within human intelligence.

Bao Shu's "Songs of Ancient Earth" (2012) plays on the "red songs" of the communist era, which are infinitely reproduced and broadcast by A.I. nanorobotics; the concert of revolutionary songs begins to rock the entire universe: "The Internationale / Unites the human race" (or perhaps more accurately here, ". . . unites the posthuman"). A new class-consciousness, or a simulacrum of a class-consciousness, appears in the work of these younger writers. Compared with Bao Shu's seriocomic parody, Chen Qiufan's "Balin" (2015) reminds us obviously of the left-wing tradition in modern Chinese literature. This story, first published in *Renmin wenxue* (July 2015), situates the problems of identity, compassion, and human-nonhuman interaction (or, more metaphorically, interactions across classes, ethnic groups, and different minds) in the contemporary combination of budding capitalism and institutional corruption. Unlike Bao Shu, who presents a sweeping triumphant vision of A.I. successfully carrying out the revolutionary tradition, Chen Qiufan depicts the bleak reality of contemporary China, where class difference matters and creates the foundation for prejudice, violence, and hatred—a menacing situation that makes compassion and dignity difficult.

Chi Hui, Fei Dao, Xia Jia, Bao Shu, and Chen Qiufan all write about virtual reality, A.I., and future worlds built upon a posthuman vision. At the same time, they all bring science fiction closer to China's reality. These five authors are the youngest of the group, all born in the 1980s, and their future writing may decide whether the new wave of Chinese science fiction will continue to flourish.

This anthology includes excerpts from Lo Yi-chin's experimental novel *Daughter* (2014) and Egoyan Zheng's posthuman saga *The Dream Devourer* (2010), both published in Taiwan. Lo's labyrinthine narrative presents an imaginary realm of memories, speculations, metaphors, reconstructions, and dismemberments of the "other" space in terms of identity, sexual transgression, diasporic experience, literary reference, and historical consciousness. The chapter we selected is "Science Fiction," which can be read as a meta–science fictional text. Lo's efforts, like Han Song's allusions to Lu Xun, also attempt to put science fiction back into the context of modern Chinese literature.

Egoyan Zheng's story unfolds in the year 2219, from which the protagonist reflects on the complex history of the long espionage war between humans and cyborgs. The confusion of identity, which speaks to Taiwan's present-day political situation, is complicated by multilayered explorations of dreams and the political technology that turns dreams into tools differentiating cyborgs from humans. The heterotopia that emerges from the disorienting dreamscape inspires the protagonists to recognize that there is an ethical and epistemological gray zone between self and other, or between the human race and posthuman beings.

Dung Kai-cheung, the most important contemporary writer of twenty-first-century Hong Kong, has also experimented with science fiction in unique ways that not only characterize Hong Kong's cultural dynamism but also render Hong Kong into a metaphor reflecting the postmodern or posthuman conditions of the post-1997 new century. Victoria, the V city that Dung creates in his oeuvres, may allude to Hong Kong's colonial past, its problematic present, and its postapocalyptic future. Dung's most ambitious work to date, the voluminous *Natural History Trilogy* has many remarkable references to sf genre elements. The present collection includes selected chapters from *Histories of Time* (2007), in which Dung achieves a poetic reimaging of science fiction as a fanciful realm that opens to endless self-reflections and self-reconstructions. The novel presents a panoramic vision of the city's imaginary history of its past, present, and future, all combined in the uncanny image of time—time lost, retrieved, reimagined, and represented.

The book is divided into three parts: "Other Realities," "Other Us," "Other Futures." Reality, humanity, and future are closely connected notions when talking about science fiction. They overlap, interact, and create intertextual relations defining what is real, what is human, and what is (future) history, while the guiding theme navigating all these stories is otherness itself. Science fiction is ultimately a literature of "cognitive estrangement," as Darko Suvin has defined it;[7] in a more contemporary context, science fiction is a literature of revelation that demonstrates difference—difference in religion, race, gender, class, ethnic identity; or simply difference in thought, emotional expression, or life choice. Difference also marks science fiction as a truly global genre encompassing all times and spaces of different ages, locations, and peoples. If there were an extraterrestrial intelligence reading our anthology, what would it (or he or she) think of the differences we have envisioned among us? If there were a superintelligence learning about human behaviors, what would it do about the identities or differences among us? In this sense, science fiction asks, in the end, an ethical question: how do we deal with the other? That also decides how we see ourselves.

PART I

OTHER REALITIES

1

REGENERATED BRICKS

HAN SONG

TRANSLATED BY THEODORE HUTERS

On this day the architect came to the village. He was a young man and brought two assistants with him, both from his office. They erected a tent on some open ground and then with great impatience went all around to inspect the ruins. He also went to a place on the outskirts of town where the effects of the disaster were relatively slight to look for a workshop that could still make bricks. He later wrote a "Diary of Making Bricks" to recount this experience. In it we can see that at its outset, the work was pretty difficult. For example, he wrote this:

. . .

June 13: In the workshop's mat shed we worked out the number and agreed that on the fourteenth and fifteenth they would prepare all the raw materials as well as make a few samples to set the standard; on the sixteenth they would begin production, with the goods being delivered on the twenty-sixth. But they did not submit a price, saying they would only know what it was after they started production. So we paid out no deposit, which left things a bit up in the air.

June 16: It rained and it was said the site was flooded.

June 17: We heard that the electricity had stopped.

June 18: We heard that the crusher had developed mechanical problems. Perhaps the intention is to run the clock out and only then report the price. With a backup plan in mind, I also went to get in touch with a big factory, then gave the workshop another call, pressing them for the price and also mentioning "that other factory."

Through all this the architect persevered, leaving the impression that it was all for some sort of unnameable ideal.

In fact, there had been people saying this had been futile from the very beginning; so no one would take any interest in it. The architect, however, stressed, "It will be useful; I have already seen the future." People shook their heads in disbelief. In these times no one could tell what was going to happen even in the next minute. The disaster that had just taken place footnoted this.

⸎

On June 17 in a place far removed from the disaster area—Shanghai—a press conference was held at the Chinese branch of a European art biennial where the exhibition curator introduced the "vernacular architecture" theme and the work of the participating architects. But because the architect himself was still at the disaster zone he could not attend, and his work was introduced by video and voice recording.

The work was titled "Regenerated Bricks." Because they were still in production, for the time being the look of the bricks could be illustrated only by computer, but from the drawings one could see they were square and hollow, a bit like ordinary bricks but somewhat darker; there were also red and yellow miscellaneous elements on them, along with scattered plant stalks. So in terms of form, they were mostly clumsy and ugly. The regenerated bricks had no sensuality to them, nor did they have any sense of shape: all they were was hard and with a bit more actual structure than the earth itself, and what was startling about them was that the regenerated souls trapped in them turned out to reside in this sort of plain hollow form.

The audience saw the process by which the bricks were made via animation on a screen: first, the raw materials of cement and brick fragments were mixed together, then fibers from rapeseed stems were added in (when mass production began, wheat straw was to be used), then water was mixed in, and finally a brick-pressing machine using a leverage mechanism molded the material into the "finished product" . . . the video also showed two bricks taking shape at the same time as well as batches of pressed-out and regenerated brick in the process of drying. The audience also saw that the tactile sense of the regenerated brick was quite different from that of cinder block. It was these bricks that were to be transported many thousands of *li* to be in the art exhibit that would secure glory for the architect and the country he represented.

"Regenerated brick is a low-tech, low-cost quality material that everyone can produce if they wish: the materials are available on the spot, and they can be produced either by hand or with simple machinery; they don't require firing, are fast, cheap, environmentally safe, suitable for any locality, with variable dimensions, extremely adaptable, limitlessly useful, and with no patent impediments." The image of the architect seemed as if he were delivering an admonition when he explained the implications of "vernacular architecture." He was a slightly overweight young man, not at all cheerful and would often display a pained expression when he spoke. He did not call his creation "a work of art."

In fact, a number of national artistic media had reported on this pioneering work, such as *Art World* monthly in Shanghai, and had said this: the architect had stressed from the beginning in his accounts of his thinking about his work that it was not an installation made for exhibition but rather a project for the urgent application of materials for reconstructing after a catastrophe.

But what did he mean?

No matter what, such statements had the effect of augmenting the artistic value of regenerated brick, and no matter how the architect tried to explain, he himself also came to be treated as an artist (whether he agreed or not). The work was smoothly rolled out at the European biennial and achieved unprecedented success. The audience took note of the fact that in the exhibit hall there was a description of the work appended to the name and brief bio of the architect:

Material of the work: regenerated brick
Date of creation: May–June 2008
Size of the bricks: 330 mm long, 170 mm wide, 110 mm tall
The brick wall: an exhibition wall two m tall and 15 m long

Let us now return to the process of making the bricks. Two days after the Shanghai press conference—that is, June 19—the architect finally was able to see the price estimate at the workshop. He then paid the deposit and ordered that three hundred trial bricks be produced by the twenty-second. Just to be safe, however, he also got in touch with the large factory. The owner of the factory received him warmly, their interaction went quite smoothly, and it was agreed that after the samples were decided upon the owner could produce the goods within two days. He made the point that each sample would use the same material for each batch, the reason being to guarantee the accuracy of the proportions of each constituent ingredient. Since the owner was so sensible, the architect paid a deposit on the spot and wrote out inventories for three different composite materials.

In that day's diary the architect wrote, "I felt much more relaxed on the way back: double insurance. Everybody thinks we should gamble on this place. This is the conclusion: the communes are more orderly than farmers. Let's just consider the money placed at the workshop as tuition, and, no matter what, it will provide us with a lot of information and teach us about proper procedure."

Following upon this, the work of making the bricks went on at both places at the same time.

Three days later, the workshop had already made several hundred bricks, and the factory had also made its samples. On June 22, the day set to see the bricks, the architect vacillated: should he go to the factory first, or to the workshop? He finally thought that he should go to the factory first, since his hopes were invested there. Go to the factory first to look at the samples, and if they were all right he would order from there. At any rate he had paid the workshop the whole deposit, and even if he ordered them to cease production, they wouldn't lose any money; they could sell the bricks they had already made and make their money that way. But he hesitated once again: no, I should go to the workshop first and see what their product is like anyway, and there will be plenty of time to stop by the factory on the way back and place the order.

When he arrived at the workshop, the bricks were still wet, so he could not make out their quality, but clearly there was not enough straw, so he wasn't very satisfied. He thought, it looks as if I'll tell the workshop to stop production after I've seen what they've done at the factory. When he arrived at the factory, however, the samples utterly shocked him, since they were completely different from what they had agreed upon. Not only were there not three different composites, of the two there were, it was impossible to tell what their constituents were.

The architect wrote in his diary, Seeing us lose our tempers, a woman came up and entered the dispute, using the guerrilla technique of raising complete irrelevancies; when she saw our anger pointed in one direction, she would pin us down on another point. She didn't understand the origins of the matter at all, but her motives were crystal clear: at the end of the day everything had been done as we had wanted it.

There was another "proprietor" present, and the previous "proprietor" we had talked to looked and spoke more like a "foreman." One way or the other we came up with the invoice from two days before on which was written the correct proportions, and only at this time did we see him squat down and explain to the workers what was meant by the proper proportions.

We didn't want any of them. Now our only hope was with the workshop. Since they had clearly used insufficient straw, I called them on the phone and stressed that I wanted the proportions according to the specifications. Should I call a second time to make sure they got it right? We discussed it a bit and decided not to call, since we feared that if we called again they would add too much straw. My feeling was this: ultimately my tone of voice determined the proportions.

. . .

———— ⌾⌾⌾ ————

I was not clear whether the architect, in writing these words, was intent upon using them to one day write something for publication and to use them as an organic part of his work. Neither did I know whether he would revise some of the content prior to publication so as to match it to the work. If these regenerated bricks were like the architect's children, then would not the diary also have some regenerated significance?

What one could clearly make out, however, was that the architect's mood was not calm, and that his initial feeling of exhilaration had completely vanished. Perhaps all of this was something at odds with his original design. Perhaps he had assumed that since the people of the disaster area had endured so much suffering they would necessarily regard his arrival, including the products that he brought, as if it was unselfish assistance and would be full of yearning and gratitude. But looking at it more realistically, that did not seem to be the case.

At a later seminar, the architect discussed his mental fragmentation:

"After the disaster occurred, I felt all along the issue of personal identity: when I reached the zone I thought of myself as a volunteer, but as a weak, middle-aged volunteer—I have a bad back so was embarrassed if I carried only light things, but I was not up to lifting anything heavy, which made things very awkward; when I saw buildings that had not collapsed in the disaster zone I could still think of myself as an architect; but when I looked at buildings that had collapsed, I simply wouldn't dare to admit that I was an architect; moreover, when I could feel my office rocking day after day as I sat in it and many of the things I had collected were smashed to pieces, I felt a bit like one of the victims."

As the course of manufacturing brick gradually proceeded this mood became ever harder to dispel. Just what sort of person, then, was the architect? This was related to exactly what the architect had come to the disaster zone to do. The question of personal identity gradually came to occupy a preeminent position.

But what lay behind all of this? It must be said that this was a technical matter—that is, this was the central issue with the regenerated brick. At the time, people proposed all sorts of plans for rebuilding, but in the end regenerated brick was recognized as the most successful, so I think that technical matters played the key role. Like those who proposed using large-scale mechanization and professional companies to carry out the work of clearing the rubble, none of their plans were as good as those of the architect, so his was more readily accepted as a compromise. The architect's way of thinking was clearly that of an engineer and very simple. At the time it would not ordinarily even have been brought up, but it was only because of these qualities that, after final comparison, it was able to defeat the extravagant wording of the large-scale proposals by showing how much more practicable it was. Thus, its artistic quality was produced by its technical quality—no matter how much the architect tried to turn it into a charitable activity. Regenerated brick was demarcated as a product of artistic activity by the outside world, and there can be no doubt that the architect subconsciously agreed, otherwise he would not have submitted it to the European biennial. In fact, in the architect's "Diary of Making Bricks," he used the term "disaster zone" only once.

Under such circumstances, the clashes between the architect and the locals were particularly vexing to me. Perhaps the disaster victims had forgotten their personal status much as the architect was not clear about his own.

—It would ultimately prove to be of use. I would later have to devote my attention to these words. Did they, however, refer to the achievement at the biennial or to the possibility that the living conditions of the villagers could be improved? Or to both? Of course, logically it seemed to be the latter, but neither seemed to be what the architect was actually referring to.

In sum, several decades later when I first read the architect's diary, my heart felt as if it were full of broken wheat straw that had piled up at various depths on my flesh; it was a vague and confused feeling that was difficult to extricate myself from, and all I could do was let my blood slowly dissolve these inexplicable feelings, and all this even though I had not personally been through the catastrophe. In fact, in the era of the architect there were probably not too many people who valued pure technology, since people's attention was on other matters. But what the architect presented to everyone was actually a sort of technology, and more than that, one that was low-tech, quite contrary to the trends of the time. This was perhaps what caused a number of people that had engaged in postdisaster reconstruction to be so surprised and produced a series of unexpected infelicities.

⸙

In spite of the pressure put on the proprietor and the workers, progress in making the bricks was still less than ideal. Thinking how the number of collapsed buildings in the disaster area reached 5.3 million, that there were more than 50 million cubic meters of rubble, or about 300 million tons, could not but cause one anxiety, not to mention the fact that there was organic waste and polluted water in the ruins growing more putrid by the day and damaging the environment. How to prevent the disaster area from being abandoned? In his diary the architect continued to write of the difficulties he encountered, as well as how he had put forth tireless efforts to solve the problems of that peculiar place in the presence of so many unfamiliar people:

June 24: I went to the workshop to examine what they had produced—another shock. The ground was covered in white, and from the look of them they were different from the samples we had agreed upon after many days of talks. More cement had been added, but now there was no time. Things did not look good, and yet another woman came out, her combat style completely the same as that at the factory. But now I had some experience, and with a shout from me she retreated. The proprietor of the workshop realized there was some mistake, and even though his intentions had been good, he had done wrong, so his tone was very mild.

As far as using them was concerned, the difference in external appearance was of no importance, but the samples have to be clearer in transmitting the concept, so the outward appearance is vital. This is the only way it can be done, so the rest of the order must be made in strict accordance with what we had initially agreed upon; the workshop proprietor said that he had finally understood, so I took a chance and ordered another batch.

June 27: Delivery day. I went to see the brick-making work site. Because I went via another route I got lost and spent two hours wandering around befuddled among fields and houses, asking my way only after having walked two kilometers. By then, I had followed completely different instructions and walked back and forth in opposite directions. I finally got to the workshop at 1:30. And although we were hungry, the actuality of the work site was exciting, such that the road we took getting there became almost a symbol. We were basically satisfied with this latest batch. It seemed as if the frequency of our meetings was much more important than the accuracy of our technical instructions. You thought he understood, and he also thought he understood, but the key was whether or not he understood what you wanted him to understand. Trial production, testing, applying for funds, production, pushing them, communicating onsite . . . none of these steps could be omitted, and if making a brick was this way, building houses was even harder, since it involved money, local interests, customs concerning both life and manufacturing, and the like; I was full of anxiety about the house building that was to follow.

Regenerated brick was something that had occurred to me to be worth trying when I was traversing the roads of the disaster zone. At present, at least as far as I was concerned, I have already steeled myself in such basic investigation and communication skills, and what needed to be regenerated was not just the brick but even more our own style of work. If I wanted eventually to be a "barefoot architect" in the work of rural reconstruction, and if I didn't consciously remake myself, an urban architect used to working from blueprints, I would perhaps not be able to take off my boots.

The gestation period for the regenerated brick that everyone had expected can be said not to have gone particularly smoothly. And as for the architect himself, his rebirth was like a difficult labor. During this time, he, normally ruddy with health and full of energy, turned quite haggard. The conditions in the disaster zone were difficult, water was hard to get, and the architect had not bathed for several days; his body began to smell, his visage had darkened, and he grew progressively thinner. At first glance he didn't look like a man but rather a rural woman wearied by labor whose body had been weakened by bearing too many children. One night some of the villagers who participated in the brickmaking went to visit him in his tent, and they saw the architect wearing his simple clothes, standing there with his arms by his side, with an unsophisticated cylindrical separator set in front of his feet. His face was as pale as tinfoil, as if he were a ghost and let the yellow moonlight shine brightly into the tent. The architect seemed to be pondering how he had managed to turn himself into a brick, and a brick that would immediately begin asexual reproduction and rapidly produce great numbers of buildings so as to allow any conscious bipeds to move into as soon as they could—this was his only goal, like a calligrapher who wanted to apply the final stroke on a piece of fine paper. He was deeply immersed in his own fantastical thoughts, eyes fixed on the machine in front of him, as if it were another body that belonged to him. So he didn't notice the entrance of the villagers, although they were in fact the subject of the architect's work. It can thus be said that there was a profusion of contradictions within. A silly gray smile crossed the architect's face, as if he were in labor, and an intermittent moan issued forth from his mouth, as if from a swamp. And behind him and the villagers, outside the tent, was a dense blackness, land that, although it had endured grievous wounds, was still rich and abundant and was arrogantly clearheaded as it casually pressed down upon the bodies of the dead, looking at them as if listening to a joke. The living dared not utter a sound. This was the most mysterious and constrained time of the disaster zone. How could those who had not seen the zone gain any sense of this atmosphere?

Regardless of the frustrations it endured, the architect's darling was finally born. I finally discovered that from the standpoint of architecture, there was one key to the work, that it was "simple."

—Simplicity, this was highest goal in all artistic pursuit. Although this was the case, this project was destined to undergo a ten-month gestation followed by a caesarian section. After climbing aboard the wagon of simplicity, the work would finally leave the disaster zone far behind, first for an exhibition platform built by Westerners in another time and space; simplicity: it won its expected or unexpected result, and it seemed to have deleted, excluded, forgotten, and taken the time of everything else. Neither from the undifferentiated exhibition, nor from each silent regenerated brick, nor from the wall that had been built up from that brick and met aesthetic standards could the audience actually discern the tribulations the architect had gone through. Neither could they make out his own process of "regeneration," much less the things that had caused so many people to be immersed in a terrified clamor, to lose so much sleep, or to shed copious tears. It was as if all this had expired or become invalid. After spending his euros to participate in the exhibit, even the architect had the terrified thought—is this real? Under the concealment of the brick wall, the vast disaster zone seemed as if it had become a weak and distant backdrop. This was not a pictorial brick of the Han dynasty, because one could not see the soldiers depicted racing around on it. There were no ranks of plastic bags holding the bodies of students, and the harrowing screams of the parents were also concealed. The homeless dog was not visible, waiting with its injured leg in the rubble for the return of its master. Nor could be seen the dead mother, still protecting her infant under her body, still nursing her child with a now-colorless breast. The teacher who had abandoned his students to rush first out of the classroom could also not be seen: he just happened to be on TV with others debating in a loud voice the question of moral standards. We could also not see the helicopter that crashed in the deep woods, with the corpses of the soldiers slowly rotting in the rain and exposing their white bones. In other words, all the images once indelibly engraved upon people's minds no longer seemed quite so reliable. In the mirrorlike light cast by the regenerated brick, everything seemed calm and unruffled, and the only thing to be seen was a stream of blond and blue-eyed handsome men and beautiful women, all wearing brand-name clothes, politely and serenely strolling by. Curiosity could be seen in their eyes, as if they were looking at the Great Wall, and they issued sighs of admiration at the identical and undifferentiated bricks, which actually became the most fascinating work of Oriental art at the biennial.

The architect grew anxious, and all he could do was to give the audience a timely reminder: for the people who were thousands of *li* from this exhibition, the most urgent matter was to have functional houses to live in. He said that this was one part of the charter agreed upon between humanity and this planet and that has been implemented for millions of years: just look at the stone-age sites at Longgushan, Shandingdong, Banpocun, and Hemudu!

Regardless, regenerated brick, which had arrived on this earth in an exceptional fashion, had garnered a broad and consistently positive evaluation. In the era of the architect, this sort of thing was actually quite rare. Because any sort of avant-garde work of art, including buildings, whenever it appeared in the sight line of the broad public it elicited great controversy. For example, the constantly in focus Bird's Nest, Water Cube, and even the Central Television Tower and National Theater, when appearing in the media gaze all were objects of all variety of contradictory discussion. Regenerated brick, however, was different: favorable assessment was widespread and consistent. I'll give an example here: in a blog titled "Pendulum in Space," the following words appeared:

> It really inspires admiration,
> Good planning, down-to-earth execution,
> A comprehensive solution and an overall vision of craft, materials, environment, society,
> and economics,
> In comparison, any number of theories look feeble.
> Although I cannot consider "the regenerated-brick plan" to be a complete architectural success,

But for someone who is an architect, due attention to society, economics, and the environment must be major issues.

I am afraid that I am not qualified to learn its lessons myself, and all I can do is follow with interest and support the project,

Plus, in my own field of responsibility, I can introduce it over and over again to my students.

Low-tech is a strategy to deal with reality,

Is it that,

Just because it is deeply concerned with actual reality,

And because of the specificity and nonreplicability of reality,

Therefore,

The product "regenerated bricks" will be difficult to replicate elsewhere. Why do I think that!!!??? Really disappointing.

"Regenerated brick" cannot but remind us of Wright's concrete blocks,

From an architectural point of view, I cannot really differentiate them,

But from their social background and function, I can feel a vast difference,

Whatever their difference in property, it will require in-depth analysis to find it out,

However, I still think they share the uniqueness of the backgrounds in which they are set,

Because of the possibilities of this uniqueness and its suitability,

It requires sustained and continuous attention!

This essay made a great effort to clarify something for us, but in fact the relationship between art and society, because of the nature of writing itself, got all tangled up once again. Plus, looking into these materials from another day consumes much time and energy. In the era in which the architect existed a great deal of information was transmitted by the elusive and illusory conduit known as the internet, the veracity of which was difficult to assess. Transmission also implied withering away, sinking into a vast ocean, with a loss of the original meaning that was to be expressed. No matter how great the shock, it would finally revert to quiescence. But why was I so resolutely holding on to this? Mulling it over, perhaps I was attracted by the phrase "its nonreproducibility." As far as the human species is concerned, the traditional view is that one can exist only once and never return again. So it was with the dinosaurs. As far as we now know dinosaurs have not appeared in any other time or place in this universe. Humans, who have a three-million-year history, are the same case. What we call reincarnation is merely a way of comforting ourselves. If you cannot remember your previous self, then becoming a new person is simply a fruitless effort. Now, however, via a man-made way of recycling through the medium of bricks, there is an attempt to make a structure to render existence endure through countless cycles. How can this not be art?

Eventually, however, I discovered the true nonreproducibility—it was actually embodied in an important detail involved in the process of making the bricks—that is, the "spraying on of an epidemic prophylactic," something other industrial activities did not require. When they were sent to the exhibition, however, we didn't know why it was done, and even in the "Diary of Making Bricks" it was not explained, which seems like a deliberate omission. Although this was but a very short part of the production line, it was a step that could not be left out of the production of regenerated bricks and was really the first step. Perhaps subconsciously the architect did not really wish to create any sort of link between his artistic image (which was his real demand) and that of epidemiologists?

This "spraying on of epidemic prophylactic" was to use 0.2 percent solution of peracetic acid or 2 ounces (100 grams) of powdered bleach in solution to spray, either by hand or mechanically, on the ruins, basically as a disinfectant. By that time, it was no longer possible to completely clear out the corpses buried in the rubble. I have in my hand a photo of the spraying: a dozen odd slender people, dressed in white prophylactic garb that went to their ankles, wearing masks that revealed only eyes, with black iron tanks on their backs. On the brown debris, their arms like trees and their feet like boats, they formed a fractal image dispersed to the outside, looking like utterly inhuman extraterrestrials, with layers of hazy white fog rising on all sides of their bodies as if a resurrecting fragrance were being dispensed by their flesh. Some people even said that they had seen any number of budding flowers emerging after the spraying, vivid and bright. But flowers themselves cannot really serve as building material. What was actually useful was the even plainer wheat stalks.

But can it be said that spraying is also a technology—and because of that made into art? All this was a product of very different times, and one can at present only surmise about it. What we also do not know is what the actual mood of the sprayers was when they were working: could they not also have been schizophrenic? From outward appearance, they looked as if they were engaged in a very earnest dance, like "The Silk Road" ballet, which completely accorded with a shaman's rite of regeneration.

No matter what, when the spraying began some of the villagers gathered around to watch; their expressions were hard to describe.

Of course, the reason for spraying was because of a dead-certain truth about the regenerated bricks, that they were a combination of three things: bodies, rubble, and wheat stalks. But what could be directly perceived at the European biennial were only two parts, debris from the disaster zone and wheat stalks, respectively, which were regarded as the raw materials, which had been neatly filled into two rectangular stone boxes, then set aside beneath the already formed shiny-bright brick wall provided for the perusal of the visitors, who were hard-pressed to pull themselves away. Similarly, these items had undergone a rigorous and delicate process of sterilization before they were shipped to Europe, something not revealed to the visitors.

—Was it, then, owing to the fact that the work had achieved success at an international exhibition that it later attracted so many more architects and planners, not to mention investors, construction-material dealers, developers, and the like, who all came to the disaster zone to participate in what was always referred to as relief work? But did these people also long to realize their own regeneration? This was particularly the case in the year following, when, after the outbreak of the financial crisis, even more people showed up, almost flattening some of the ruins. Normally they would be accompanied by county or district leaders when they came. These officials were also highly enthusiastic, as if they were receiving meat pies that were falling from the sky.

"This small-scale semihandicraft mechanization as far as possible employs the handicraft resources that were already extant throughout the locality; they were extremely suitable to the task, easy and convenient to use, can be put into production without the need for a long training period, is are advantageous to the flowering of the whole locality, and to the reconstruction and self-support for the masses in the disaster zone."

At the invitation of the local government, architects had personally returned again and again to the area and had offered these opinions on the manufacture of the bricks, as if to refute the notion that the popularity of regenerated bricks resulted from their having participated in a European artistic exhibit.

By this time he had already won a number of major international and domestic awards, such as the prize for architecture in media from a major media organization. In its justification for his selection, the prize committee in fact listed his behavior in the category of "social responsibility."

The media organization also provided photographs, one of which used a wide-angle lens to shoot the brick-manufacturing scene. On a relatively large flat space among the pale mountains, with the black ruins as background, there were altogether three thousand workers wearing bright red T-shirts that had been distributed to them by the organizers, on the backs of which were printed "Regenerated Brick" in yellow characters in both Chinese and English. In front of each of them was a silver-colored manual crusher, and they were rhythmically swinging their arms in an orderly fashion, dripping with sweat as they manipulated carrying poles in cadence with the architect's sonorous commands; it was like something from the early Industrial Revolution in the eighteenth century. The sunlight beat down like innumerable blue dragonflies droning on, while the silent earth was once more brought to seething motion even as it gave off a violent and seemingly familiar, if alarming, shaking.

Be that as it may, the activity was organized by the village committee and was labeled as "a union of masses and experts," and it at least embodied a formal sense of mass participation, as if they had all come to support the movement begun by the architect.

"It looks exactly like the performance at the Olympic opening ceremony," a reader cried out involuntarily when he first saw the photo. This reader was my humble self.

I immediately noticed that among the brickmakers, two-thirds were local women. They stretched out their soft, golden bodies, and in their calisthenic-like movements they appeared to be in a semistupor-like condition of overexcitement, as if they had just been sent to the delivery room.

The photo was of limited size, so the people in it were just really too tiny. But when it was seen with a magnifying glass, the architect, standing

in front of the farmers like an orchestra conductor and incessantly bobbing his head, although seemingly in a highly stimulated state, revealed
a vaguely depressed look, which lacked any sense of the happiness of one
who was about to become a father.

The local government was quite grateful and had conferred upon him
an honorary title, for it was a fact that without the regenerated brick it
would have been practically impossible for thousands of people who had
lost their homes to be able to move into new dwellings so quickly. And
even as the regenerated bricks demolished this impossibility, they also
routed the fixed patterns of popular thinking. For example, at the time
there were no legal regulations on what "reconstruction planning" was
supposed to be. As far as professional planners were concerned, they did
not know whether these plans applied to structures or to roads. Were they
to be applied to buildings or to blueprints? They knew nothing of any of
this. Could you say something could be completed within three months?
Once you had regenerated brick, however, suddenly all of these ceased
to be problems. Moreover, with "regenerated bricks" being a new type
of light, hollow brick made of slag and wheat straw, there was no cor-
responding national standard for them. But precisely because they were
the regenerated bricks upon which everyone had heaped so much praise,
they were subject to no strictures, so applying the tests used on hollow
concrete bricks was fine. Everything was simplified. The result of these
tests turned out to be that the compressive strength was up to standard and could satisfy the demands for sustaining the strength of infill
walls.

Because of this, although the local homes had been destroyed, but
based on the architect's instruction, the shattered tiles and bricks still
contained the feelings that had been invested in them previously.
Although it was discarded building materials that had been "regenerated"
materially, it was also a "regeneration" built on the spiritual and emotional
plane following the catastrophe. When the architect said such things, he
all but closed his eyes, like a preacher reciting scripture in church, which
imparted a warmth akin to a spring breeze blowing in one's face. There
was also an admixture of the floating colors of a lotus pond, but that
was something a bit hard to grasp, although in contrast to actual colors
and breezes, it had more of the quality of a medieval print. This is of
course my perception as a latecomer, so perhaps there is a generation

gap involved. He was like the sun god; he had long been in charge of everything.

The true start of mass production was at the wheat harvest the following May, when considerable quantities of wheat straw awaited disposition. At the time the ruins had not been completely cleared, or perhaps it could be said rather that they had been intentionally left in place. The architect, with disciples clustered around, stood on a hillock of rubble looking down, and all they could see was a golden sea of wheat straw stretching away endlessly. It seemed that only the straw had not been affected by the catastrophe, as if it were so many women who, when the wind sprang up playfully, fell into one another's embrace, jabbering happily with faintly coquettish smiles on their faces. The straw had already seen its fate once it was collected together, so it happily gathered itself, since it would no longer be burned by lowly flames, turned into gray smoke, and dispersed to the horizon. It yearned to be chopped up neatly and to become raw material for the renowned regenerated brick, to become the most valuable form of solid matter, to continue to adhere to the dazzling but inexplicable earth that also seemed to have an artistic quality to it. A new cycle was thus begun, but one that seemed to approach the eternal. What? The eternal? Yes. This appeared to be the promise of the architect-cum-artist. Would the entire disaster zone also be regenerated because of this? During this short period things were truly beyond normal! It was like a lizard that had had part of its body lopped off that used the full extent of its internal resources of dilapidated flesh and via the mysterious function of genes passed down from remote antiquity to, in the flash of an eye, give birth to a new body.

But could it endure?

Perhaps . . .

There is a woman here who was among the first group of farmers to respond to the call to make bricks. I don't know whether she can be considered a member of what the architect labeled "the wives," but her house collapsed in the catastrophe, and at thirty-eight she lost her husband and child. She had no one to look after her and even thought of taking her own life. Yes, with her husband and child gone, what had she to live for?

She loved them; she had been with her husband for thirteen years, and they had been affectionate the whole time. Her child was an only son in middle school, mature and with good grades, who had back then wished her a happy mother's day. Now, both gone . . . missing them bitterly, she had one day used a rope to hang herself from the big tree at the edge of the village. She had not, however, succeeded in killing herself but had been discovered and saved by the architect, who was fortuitously passing by on his way to the workshop to press them to produce the bricks. When she was brought down and laid on the ground, she sat stupidly in the ruins, looking at the spectral pale green figure of the architect as if he were an extraterrestrial alien. She could not figure out what it was that had happened and just sat there with her mouth agape and being unable to stand up for the longest time. That night she had a dream in which she saw a path leading to the netherworld, where her husband and child, covered with blood and dust, were laboriously supporting each other as they attempted to move forward. But they could not make any progress, since both of them were bearing several baskets of bricks weighing down their bodies. She was taken aback and said in a pitying soft voice, "If you can't walk, don't try, just rest awhile and have a drink of water."

This took place that summer. The village committee had already mobilized people to make bricks, but at the time there were not many people volunteering to participate in the work. They didn't want to do anything, since they no longer had any hope for the future. They spent all day blankly staring at photos of their children. Every day they went to the multicolored ruins, and when people asked them what they went there to do, they replied that they were trying to lead lost relatives back home. Thus, the demonstration samples of the work, no matter how artistic the work was, or how many prizes it had won, or to which continent it had gone and what sort of international sensation it had elicited—none of it mattered to them. They merely passively participated in the brickmaking at the urging or even the compulsion of the chair of the village committee. Six family members of this chair had also been buried in the catastrophe, but he did not move first to save his own family members, rather he immediately organized people to rescue other villagers, with the result that not a single member of his own family was saved. He dried his tears and led the villagers to speedily engage in recovery through production, urging everyone to heed the calls for self-reliance and reconstructing their homes, to go all out and mobilize. In spite of this, the people could not instantaneously summon up enthusiasm and confidence, so they often produced substandard regenerated brick, or even plain scrap. The architect or artist was extremely annoyed at this, since it increased costs, with the disaster victims paying the ultimate cost; how could the ruins be regenerated this way? How could he honor his commitment made at the foreign biennial? Many villagers withdrew from the making of brick under the harsh regulations of the architect, but this woman was one who persevered throughout, because she gradually became aware that that sort of repetitive movement could help her to forget her lost relatives.

The woman later told me that what the disaster victims needed most at the time actually was not housing. I understood what she was saying, since I later also lost the one I loved most and lived like a zombie for the rest of my life. Be that as it may, when winter came the woman did move into a new brick house that she had made herself, simply because she could not endure the cold winter living in a thin tent. The biological instincts accumulated in her body over tens of thousands of years expressed themselves, and the desire to live on gradually resurrected itself. She even somewhat bashfully wrote to a female reporter from Beijing who had interviewed her, asking if she could contribute some padded clothing or quilts. It never occurred to her, however, to be grateful to the architect-cum-artist, although it was he who had saved her life as well as taught her how to construct such an avant-garde house. She furnished her house only a bit, hanging on the walls photos of her husband and child that she had plucked from the ruins. She abided in her empty house, seemingly unaccustomed to it. The future was still a vague blur.

But just that evening she heard the voices of two people flowing out of the seams between the bricks. She stood up with a shiver and began enumerating each brick. She was not afraid but realized both in surprise and happiness that building a house using regenerated brick was not only for herself to live in.

———— ⟋⟍ ————

The next year even more people came to live in houses made of regenerated brick. The woman also had her own small-scale brick factory, which provided an income. She did this in partnership with a middle-aged man who had previously run a small building materials business and had also lost his family in the disaster. They hired two workmen and every day worked tirelessly to produce brick. People in the locality who needed to build houses came to buy the bricks they produced. It was as if things had returned to predisaster days.

"How do you buy the bricks?" asked someone from a neighboring village as he pointed to the neatly lined-up bricks. "Thirty-three cents a batch," replied the well-versed woman. The villager picked up a brick as he was going by and asked, "Why is it black?" "It is made out of the rubble from collapsed buildings." "Is it sturdy?" "Absolutely, it's made using a new technology." Finally, she smiled and added, "Rest assured; it's also been thoroughly disinfected."

When they saw how the business was thriving, the villagers who had not participated in the original brickmaking grew regretful, so they all set up their own brick works, or at least brickmaking family workshops.

Not long thereafter that woman married the man who made bricks with her, and a year later they had a child. That child was me. It is said that my birth was a terribly difficult process, a home birth that lasted the whole night, with mother screaming miserably the whole time, as if she were trying to call something back. The walls of the house erupted with huge, strange sounds, like running water, as if wanting to rip something apart; Father stood to one side helplessly, calling on the bodhisattva for protection. This is the only thing I remember about my birth. Later I grew up among these peculiar sounds and gradually became accustomed to them. It was not Mother's milk but another method of nourishing me, with the deceased who lived in the regenerated brick watching me grow up with what seemed to be gray countenances. I dreaded this at first. I would howl all day long, unable to calm down, eating or drinking nothing, and the doctor could do nothing. Eventually my parents discussed it and invited in a Buddhist monk to perform a ceremony to release the souls of the departed. This was the first time something like this had occurred to them, and they were quite ill at ease.

"Don't blame us, we did want to keep you here, but things have changed. I've moved into a new house and also have a new family. I had to do this for my child, so please forgive me," the woman said to them as she walked over to the photo of her late husband and child. She then took the photos of the deceased down, wrapped them up in a cloth, and put them in the cupboard.

The monk arrived. According to the understanding of Buddhism, after people die they travel to the liminal state of bardo, where after seven times seven, or 49, days they obtain a new life. If because of certain factors, however, this journey could not proceed and the destination could not be reached, not just in seven times seven, or 49, days or 490 days or 4,900 days . . . the destination could never be reached and the bardo transmigration would be stretched on without limit. Because of the architect, the deceased were suspended in this world and were unable to transmigrate into new lives. My parents believed that only a Buddhist service could remove this impediment. But still they hesitated: was doing this the right thing or not?

The monk, however, failed. When the ceremony had reached its midpoint, the spaces between the bricks began to emit a strange sound like the lowing of cattle, which overwhelmed the monk's sutra recitation and his beating of the wooden blocks that accompanied it, and the house seemed to shake, with fragments of brick falling from the walls. The monk's countenance changed abruptly as he shouted out "Earthquake!" sheltered his head in panic, and fled, treading on his cassock as he went. None of us moved a bit, and my parents were in a trance as they contemplated whatever was on their minds.

When the ceremony was performed I was still a child, lying in my cradle with my eyes wide open, staring at the void above me. The regenerated brick was like a set of nets encircling me completely, to the point that even my parents disappeared from my field of vision. And in this great world there was only a spider overhead, ignorantly and fearlessly moving about; my only thought was that his eyes were big, really big, and it was only with it that I could have a soundless dialogue. The monk's ceremony was thus, of course, also a baptism for me, and I felt it possessed a sense of reality, but I also felt a desolation for religion in its final moment of abjection—it was extremely odd that I had that consciousness just then. I knew that I was ordained to be accompanied by things I didn't understand for the rest of my life. A new type of life different from that lived by the previous generation was about to begin, but were we prepared for it? In fact, from the moment the monk fled the house I stopped my weeping, not to mention gaining a strong appetite for food, and a sense of maturity. Mother saw this in me and came over to hold me at her breast and nurse me; I was quite anxious, fearing that she was going to shed tears, but her expression remained determined and calm.

From that point on I became accustomed to coexisting with regenerated brick and no longer believed in old-fashioned transmigration. Probably art can overturn anything.

But it was not merely art. After I grew up I came into contact with what we call the scientific explanation for those strange noises. For instance, the American scholar A. Palliser believes that hallucinations and strange sounds possibly originate in a person reflecting upon and being concerned about a lost relative or friend and thus wishing to share these scenes and feelings that he or she has seen and heard with others.

Another explanation is that this was perhaps a function of collective suggestion. In a group, each person generally has a feeling of having lost his or her independent character, resulting in an impulse for imitation, which produces a kind of reciprocal influence. Under this influence a common mood is produced in which everyone sees and hears the same things. This is especially true in a disaster zone in which the minds of tens of thousands of people have been badly wounded, so it is easy to produce this sort of response.

If the above still belongs in the realm of traditional psychology, then parapsychology believes that such things as strange sounds are perhaps produced by the psychological energy of survivors. To explain it more profoundly, it touches upon the complicated relationship between material and consciousness.

There is also an explanation that comes from acoustic phenomena. The crisis produced a huge energy when it took place, such that the electromagnetic field changed, and both the earth's crust and the atmosphere were no longer the same. This caused the ordinary bricks and tiles in the ruins to become able to record sound, and the final sounds of people as they departed were thus recorded on the tiles and bricks. And regenerated brick made from these became a resonating body, which, in particular circumstances, could broadcast the voices of one's relatives.

None of these explanations, however, resolved the doubts that remained deep in my mind. I merely became even more excited about them.

Many years later, after regenerated brick had become a nationwide vogue, and even university architecture departments had established regenerated-brick studies, I surprised everyone by not choosing this exceedingly hot topic as my field of study. It was as if I purposely avoided it. But in my spare time I continued to pay close attention—or perhaps better to say a sort of vigilance. A female classmate of mine was mesmerized by it. She was from the city, and she often sought me out to discuss it.

"Is it the case that every new house in your village has those strange sounds in them?"

"Only those made from regenerated brick; there's no doubt that the voices of deceased family members flow out of the spaces between the bricks like water from a spring."

"That's really beautiful. My feeling is that people have completely merged with nature, and that nature and these people have become one body."

"But don't you feel that between them there is a mentality of mutual hatred and that it's a grudging merger?"

"Can it really be called grudging?"

"To be passively bound together via a method over which you have no control, as if you clearly understand something is poison but that you must drink it. Human life is generally nothing more than this."

"But this truly is art, or, perhaps, transcends art. . . . Is it not also poison? To take life and death and congeal them into one. It really is something to be envied."

"Art? Wow, you didn't personally experience the catastrophe . . ." At this point my heart was pounding so that I thought it would jump out of my chest. Just then I wanted to strip this girl and do her on a pile of regenerated brick.

"No matter what, it seems as if only fine and primeval handicraft production could produce this result. It's both wonderful and mysterious."

"I'm afraid that has to do with the fact that we actually lived in the ruins."

It was my habit early every morning to climb to the top of the classroom building wearing only my underwear and look west. The heavy air pollution kept me from seeing very far, so all that was within my field of vision was heap after heap of gray buildings, like so many pieces of paper, but so sluggish they could never soar up like pigeons. They were for the moment not ruins, but they contained the intrinsic logic of ruins. Not to mention that in regenerated-brick studies, everything was taken as ruins for the sake of research. This sort of mentality would seem to be closer to the basic nature of the world. At such times I would often see my classmate, wearing very little and running repeatedly around the track. Her graceful figure, covered with sweat, combining the obscured sun with a slight burning made her seem like a frail phoenix.

—Yes, truly beautiful, how she elicited envy. But this was merely the beginning of the day. I couldn't help thinking of her birth and childhood. What sort of noises accompanied her growing up?

She already expressed her love for me.

I couldn't bear it.

But what is regenerated brick? Around this question, the academic world produced any number of definitions, which were often contradictory. Within regenerated-brick studies many research articles took defining what they were as their topic. Once people became immersed in conceptual dispute, teachers and their students would fall out over it.

In order to resolve this vexing issue, regenerated-brick studies developed into an interdisciplinary field, not restricted to architectural studies. It absorbed the most recent achievements of physics, chemistry, and biology, among others. Regenerated brick came to be understood as a kind of composite material, a kind of helix based on the energy of shock waves, or even a kind of effect of a Bose-Einstein distribution. It perhaps had to do with high dimensional space, a wormhole in time-space. Regenerated brick had reordered the electromagnetic and gravitational fields, transformed some of the qualities of physical space, and renewed its geometry. All this produced extraordinary results, allowing us to hear the voices of dead relatives.

But why did this have to be via regenerated bricks? They were, after all, something quite low-tech. Perhaps, then, we needed to reconceptualize our notions about technology itself. What is our understanding of ideas about "high" and "low"? It is not necessarily directly related to a soul reanimating the corpse of another, the intervention of mysterious external forces, superintelligent beings in the universe, or even of God. What regenerated bricks represent is something much more recondite, which will completely revise the science, philosophy, and theology of our world.

—◈◈◈—

And in the disaster area, under the impetus of the invisible hand of the market, the regenerated-brick industry has already progressed to a considerable extent. The new-style brick factories have long since ceased to be labor-intensive enterprises, and now seven people can, using computerized controls, easily produce forty thousand bricks a day. This is the scale Mother's factory eventually reached.

An important event that took place later was the entry of the government into the production of regenerated brick, reaching in its visible hand. The news media reported on this in the following way:

Amid a deafening sound, mountainous piles of construction debris are devoured by "ravenous" machines and pulverized, the resulting material sent by conveyor belt to another machine, where it is compacted into forms that conform to quality standards; thus brick after brick is born—this was something this correspondent saw in person on the production line of this city's regenerated-brick project. At present, the production line has already begun mass production.

According to a briefing, the site of the production line for this construction debris occupies 205 *mu*, and its equipment represents an investment of 4,150,000 yuan. The production line is able to produce wall-building material such as standard bricks and cinder block, as well as brick for a variety of functions such as road edging and decorative brick. Each year, the production line processes 400,000 tons of debris and produces approximately 50 million standard bricks, enough to build 150 thousand square meters of brick and concrete dwellings or 500 thousand square meters of framed dwellings.

According to a briefing by a representative of the city construction committee, this project has been a beneficial attempt at dealing with construction debris via social investment and has established a firm foundation for the next step in the social processing of construction debris of the entire urban disaster zone in an orderly and scientific manner. It is an important part of the postdisaster reconstruction work, plays a positive role in protecting our urban environmental resources, and has extremely important social benefits.

Reports like this one reveal that the production of regenerated brick has not only transcended the level of handicraft production and entered the stage of industrial mass production, but they also entail more complex and deeper meanings, touching on such spheres as politics, economics, and the social, and from there going on to even more gloriously display their Eastern characteristics. People, however, seldom brought up their original artistic quality and that they had been shown at an artistic exhibition in the West. When someone would occasionally bring up the subject, others would consciously avoid it, and their faces would reveal an expression that resembled having been snubbed.

⸙⸙⸙

People would continuously come to the disaster zone, insisting that they wished to buy brick. They were somewhat out of the ordinary, however, since they didn't want anything produced on the assembly line but rather bricks produced by hand. At first the villagers really wished to understand why this was the case.

They were actually tourists to the disaster zone—the disaster zone had become reconstructed as a tourist area, and the tourists inevitably wished to take home souvenirs, with regenerated brick being a most distinctive product that elicited much attention. Taking into consideration the needs of tourists, the brick producers recalled their first principles and reprogrammed their brick production to include individual artistry. For instance, they drew pictures on the bricks, like the local bamboo, or pandas, or the scenery, things that true artists (like the architect) regarded as unspeakably vulgar but that now unaccountably added much to the splendor of the brick. As a result, the production of tourist souvenirs also became a part of how the brick-production chain became ever more prosperous. One of the jobs at Mother's brick factory was just this: every day her workers would drive over to the scenic area, busily delivering brick to souvenir stands there. When Mother saw the brick being taken far away, a girlish radiance would float across her face.

There were others with less-ordinary identities, who had different intentions in buying regenerated brick. For instance, scholars of regenerated brick bought bricks and took them to their laboratories for research purposes. There were also volunteers who had participated in the disaster-relief efforts, who had shed blood and tears here and who, it is said, bought the bricks so as to reflect on the past. There were yet others whose identities were not clear.

Once I was in a downtown bar chatting with my girlfriend when I was suddenly seized by a sense of wanting to break into tears; the surroundings were suffused with an otherworldly air, the spectral shadows of the fancily dressed young men and women flickering about. This fascinated me, and I slowly stood up. Under the startled gaze of my girlfriend, I floated back and forth through the bar, as if in search of something. I eventually espied a dozen or so regenerated bricks mixed in among the ordinary brick in a strip of wall by the orchestra pit. I called the bartender over.

"I know these, they're produced by my family," I exclaimed, "they have a special stamp on them. You know, each house's brick has its own hallmark."

As I said this, I pointed to an icon on the bricks. It resembled my mother's red and indistinct, yet excited, eyes. The bartender was quite surprised and looked at me with grave respect. And my girlfriend's expression showed a new esteem for me.

The bartender sat down and had a drink with me. He said that he had once been through the disaster zone and when he saw these bricks he thought that they had certainly been works of art at one time, and that they would be most suitable to decorate his bar, so he had bought some. And, as he had expected, after he installed them there was even an increase in regular customers.

There was nothing I could say in response. Even as people were drinking their cocktails, my mother's husband and child, whom I had never met, were sequestered deeply within these regenerated bricks, in an unfamiliar city they had never been to, in a bar that was completely incompatible with their customary lives; they emitted wave after wave of gentle songlike echoes that intoxicated the customers. This was not, however, merely a result of the urban pursuit of stimulation and the new, but that people seemed to gain an account of the unknown they had longed for for some time, which they could use to explain why they were there that evening.

In this way bars with walls of regenerated brick began to pop up in the city like bamboo shoots after a spring rain; and not just in bars, but they gradually spread to all sorts of trendy buildings. If, owing to limitations in building materials, regenerated brick could not be used throughout, then at the least it would be used at key points, and certainly in the foundation. This was not just a standard for construction but also became a fashion, something particularly esteemed by young people. At the most obvious level, people thought this represented the notion of green. It can be said that the appearance of regenerated brick rescued an urban housing industry that was on the verge of collapse. As for luxurious single-family homes, they used regenerated brick extensively, driving up prices and attracting more and more of the rich to live in them.

By the time that everyone had encountered regenerated brick—it was a sort of practical experience, and also an ordeal, ruins rapidly became a resource even scarcer than petroleum, with its price shooting up and demand exceeding supply. It was often necessary to work behind the scenes or through connections to secure a supply of broken bricks and tiles. Not a few brick factories in the villages converted from producing regenerated brick to merely reselling rubble that they had stored away. By then quite a few people hoped there would be another disaster so as to produce more ruins. In fact, desire for a disaster became an overwhelming social sentiment. It reached the point that if a quite ordinary mishap took place in a certain locality, architects, businessmen, and tourists . . . they would all descend en masse. When scientists later invented disaster detectors and predictors, efforts were made to find the sources of disaster not just on dry land but in the deep ocean, in the air, outside the atmosphere, and in the molten core of stars. This caused our nation to stride proudly ahead on the road to regeneration, thereby stimulating a movement of magnificent scale, characterized by an unprecedented greatness of force. Material about this is so plentiful that everyone understands it quite well, and there is no need for me to dwell upon it here . . . In short, everyone rushed to dispose of their most beloved objects by crushing them up, completely smashing them, allowing them to perish, and then, on this basis, to create new things.

After going to the bar that time, my girlfriend left me; she became infatuated with exploring disasters, and I didn't want to go along. We had a difference of opinion.

"This thought occurred to me while jogging: early every morning when I see you, standing tall as a birch tree in complete silence on top of the classroom building, seeming as if you are about to jump off it, it's a wonderful sensation for me—also just as sexy as can be. I think you will just melt into the air and that we are very close." She spoke in a self-serving manner, as if she were sipping on a whiskey, which made me think that her whole body was probably as red as a lobster. But I knew there would be no sleeping with her. When she spoke of "sexy" it was a general concept that was even a bit dangerous, but it had no specific referent.

A year later she died on an exploration venture in the north. According to eyewitness accounts, the group of young men and women she was with obliterated themselves. For the sake of being cool, they used a type of low-tech equipment, a machine made from an air mixer, run by hand with two curved cranks, along with an old motor, which from the effects of electric vibration, after three and half hours of shaking caused the body to disintegrate into air.

This process no doubt caused more than a little agony. Compared with those who were buried under the ruins back then, however, and who were able to hold out in great suffering for a hundred or more hours, then to be pulled out, only to die right after seeing the light, the mood would be somewhat more bearable.

I remember what my girlfriend said: the world's greatest catastrophe is the atmosphere. It is silently everywhere yet can at any time produce violent explosions, creating longitudinal and transverse waves that annihilate everything. This is, however, the real power of life, and, in exploration, one wants to go to places like this. If you can't avoid it, then embrace it.

"This is the way to solve our intellectual crisis." The girl eyed me as she murmured, the sides of her nose showing a bit of juvenile heroic spirit.

—But, what is our intellectual crisis? I will never understand this until the day I die. Perhaps I'm just a person without any ideas.

I endeavored to get close to the things she and her friends had left behind, including the air mixer. It had a crude blade and gear structure, with a number of bluish metallic and plastic pipes sticking out of its brown cylindrical form. The whole thing resembled a partially dissected womb, and someone could sit in it like a fetus, awaiting the final judgment of fate. In addition, this group of young people had collected other machines having to do with the atmosphere, consisting of such things as spray guns, air cleaners, filters, wind tunnels, and the like. They were all bright and shiny, full of the charm unique to metallic objects. These playthings elicited both envy and regret in me.

I went to the place where she had disintegrated and collected some of the air there using a discarded Coca-Cola bottle. It had a pale purple color that reminded one of a new perfume from Christian Dior.

I took this bottle of air, which was just another form of ruin, back to my old home. The village had not changed much in appearance, just my mother had aged a good deal and my father had passed away. I threw myself into my mother's embrace and had a good cry. To her I would always be a child. She did not shed any tears, just lightly stroked my shoulders while saying, "Good boy, don't cry, there's really nothing to cry about. Everything will be fine now that you've returned to Mother. And you're much luckier than your older brother."

Mother still lived in the brick house, and she seemed to have had a premonition of my return, since even my bed had been made up and the quilt washed very clean.

In the middle of the night, the walls yet again gave forth their familiar sounds, making it hard for me to sleep. I listened carefully to what the people inside them were saying but just could not make it out.

The next day, I stuffed some rubble and wheat straw into the bottle, mixed it up thoroughly, and handcrafted a regenerated brick, which I placed in a corner of our home, not far from where I slept. My mother sat on a little stool, silently watching me do all this through hooded eyes, making no protest of any sort but also not coming to my assistance. She was by now an authority on making brick.

There were even more unsettling noises coming from the room at night, some sounding as if they were fighting, others as if they were playing mahjong; I couldn't be sure. I opened my eyes and saw Mother with an arched and trembling body—like that of an aged cat—with an ear bent to the brick wall, as fascinated as a child. When our eyes met, we both laughed in embarrassment.

———— ∞∞ ————

It needs to be told that my girlfriend just happened to be the daughter of the architect. We met when she was sixteen and came to the disaster area to look for traces of the father whom she so venerated, and we later went to the same university. This really was a fortunate coincidence, as if the result of some obscure plan. I was very grateful to the architect, for without him Mother would not have regenerated, and there would have been no me. And if not for him there would have been no daughter, and my life would have been for nothing. But for some inexplicable reason, in my heart of hearts I harbored a latent resentment against him, as if he were my rival in love. As a result, I projected all these complex feelings onto his daughter. She, however, unexpectedly took her leave. I was thus at a loss, feeling in despair about the future and thereby able to comprehend my mother's frame of mind in the time after the catastrophe. After that, however, with the passage of time I came gradually to feel guilty about the architect, because, as a man, I had not taken care of his only child. But I had never said a word to the architect in person, somehow never having found the opportunity.

At the time, the architect stood at the apogee of his professional life, having attainted the status of national treasure or grand master. His daughter's death, however, brought him down: he got very sick, after which he retreated from the front ranks of his profession. Perhaps he had had a vision of the crisis of regeneration. He no longer appeared in public places and was thus soon forgotten both by people and the times. Whenever someone would think of him, regenerated brick had already become a glorious metaphysical concept, which much diminished its creator. It controlled every element of social movement and evolution, governed both the spiritual and material lives of human beings, and had cut itself off from the architect himself.

I then could not help but hazarding a guess: could it have been that the architect had foreseen the future death of his daughter while he was still young and thus given birth to the notion of regenerated brick? So this was no doubt the function of regenerated brick but also its greatest dysfunction.

With the boom in space travel, regenerated brick was gradually introduced in the development of outer space. Astronauts took regenerated brick to space stations, and when the first permanent bases were set up on the moon and on Mars, regenerated brick was used in the foundation. Such was the custom of the new age, and no one knows how future archaeologists will regard it.

There were some installation artists who used a space ship to shoot a great quantity of regenerated brick at a specific weight between the orbits of Jupiter and Saturn to create a new asteroid belt.

Some astronauts said that in the near vacuum of space, they could hear unusual noises, something that commonsense would deem impossible. There were those who explained, however, that perhaps the vacuum recuperated death, thereby forming a continuous ruin, and it was only where there were ruins that there could certainly also be regenerated brick, although they would not all appear in a form familiar to us and could very possibly exist as an alternative physical form.

The philosophers said, If the mind is the master of the universe, then we will be able to hear its trilling.

Scientists thought, If the universe will one day collapse, the omnipresent regenerated brick will play a very significant role. Perhaps in certain autonomous worlds regenerated brick is a form of life. The basic human conception of life needs to be revised, and we need a new understanding of the essence of life and death.

The theologians expressed themselves thusly: there is nothing in a regenerated brick, it is empty.

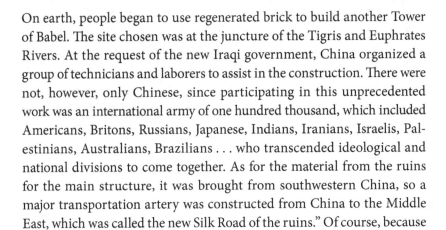

On earth, people began to use regenerated brick to build another Tower of Babel. The site chosen was at the juncture of the Tigris and Euphrates Rivers. At the request of the new Iraqi government, China organized a group of technicians and laborers to assist in the construction. There were not, however, only Chinese, since participating in this unprecedented work was an international army of one hundred thousand, which included Americans, Britons, Russians, Japanese, Indians, Iranians, Israelis, Palestinians, Australians, Brazilians . . . who transcended ideological and national divisions to come together. As for the material from the ruins for the main structure, it was brought from southwestern China, so a major transportation artery was constructed from China to the Middle East, which was called the new Silk Road of the ruins." Of course, because the Tower of Babel was of such a huge scale, relying upon only Chinese raw material was vastly insufficient, so ruins left over from the Iraq War were also used. It was the first time that humans had directly lifted construction material more than three kilometers into the air, so the new Tower of Babel became the world's tallest building, surpassing such famous structures as the skyscraper in Dubai.

Later, and in the same fashion, people rebuilt the Twin Towers of the World Trade Center in New York. In the course of construction, scientists discovered a technique of cloning the ruins, which was also known as the technique of restructuring similar materials, which took the molecules making up the tiles and used microengineering to reproduce them individually, thus creating the needed raw material.

After this, it was the turn of Pompeii and Ani . . . in order to get better results, seven small planets were dismantled even as human-engineered life-forms—more than thirty types of microorganism—distributed on them were intentionally destroyed. The ruins of the planets were towed to earth by a huge fleet of spaceships and used to make the regenerated brick used in the construction.

There were some problems encountered in the reconstruction of Hiroshima and Nagasaki, since people marched in protest. Just then, however, scientists came up with a new scientific breakthrough, discovering that time itself was a kind of ruin. So matters became manageable. With the aid of the Yang-Guderian conversion equation, scientists united the ruins with time and used the result as the raw material for regenerated brick, thereby calming those who had been agitated. It was also discovered that, like alloys of memory, in respect to the disaster time in fact had the capacity for memory.

It must be incidentally mentioned that some of the Chinese workers brought back some waste material from the new type of regenerated brick and used it to construct Qin Shihuang's Epang Palace, which is said to have been undertaken somewhat playfully.

These buildings from different civilizations in different parts of the world were all able to produce their own particular sounds from within and were also able to transcend the basic level of language and use ionization to open up dialogue among themselves. They constructed a net that covered the world, another communication network in addition to the internet, and on the new net all the departed souls from the past three million years were in constant touch. To perform an in-depth exploration of this world, however, was virtually impossible. Once it had been constructed it had its own autonomous existence.

———— ∞∞∞ ————

The first group of extraterrestrials to visit earth was a corps of construction engineers. They had worked in each major galaxy with the goal of repairing this worn-out universe, so as to allow the dead to have a place to go. The extraterrestrials had come to earth by chance and became quite interested in regenerated brick. They actually used a similar construction material, but it was still quite different from that used by humans. So the first interstellar civilizational dialogue and opportunity for cooperation used the language of construction as its common tongue.

A delegation of extraterrestrials once came to the disaster zone in my hometown to visit a large-scale brick factory. They intended to regenerate some new galaxies in the Ophiuchus constellation to create a base to link the future with the past. They hoped to choose a number of technicians from among the people of earth to assist them in the work. It was then suddenly discovered that one of the members of the delegation much resembled the architect from earth who had invented regenerated brick, although it was impossible to be completely certain. How could he have subsisted with an extraterrestrial?

But just then the brick factory collapsed for some unknown reason, crushing to death quite a few earth people as well as extraterrestrials. It proved impossible to dig out some of the corpses, including that of the one who resembled the architect.

The local government was embarrassed and angry, punishing the people responsible. The news media reported the event in a low-key fashion.

Mother later bought a segment of the ruins at auction and used it to make brick. At the head of the village she built a small house, which seemed like neither residence, nor factory, nor hotel and would not allow anyone to live in it.

"After so many years have gone by, I seem to have returned to the past," she muttered.

I once asked Mother whether or not she knew who the dead people were who were mixed in the pile of regenerated brick. Mother looked back at me with a peculiar expression, as if to say, Do you even need to ask? I think, however, that Mother was not completely sure. Her behavior in her later years was governed by a subconscious effect of deep memory.

I also had a strong feeling that in the year of the disaster, the architect did not really achieve regeneration through making bricks; all he did was make a preview. He did in fact, however, assist in my mother's regeneration, so does his regeneration now require arrangement by my mother?

There is a matter here that has heretofore been overlooked—namely, the disposition of the architect's wife, about whom we are completely in the dark. Because of this we did not solicit her opinion about the architect's funeral arrangements. I don't know whether we behaved correctly or not.

But was the person that was buried actually the architect?

Later, taking advantage of my being away from home, Mother infused the air of the architect's daughter into that brick and moved it to the new house. It was only through this that Mother seemed to be able to set her mind at rest; moreover, she would constantly measure me up with an expression of victory, but in an unsteady fashion that even seemed a bit mischievous.

I could not dispute about anything with Mother. But in the night people would frequently hear the sound of an older man and a young woman coming from the isolated house at the edge of the village.

———— ◦≈◦ ————

In that period I frequently returned home. I would remember odd things that took place when I was little, some that I had heard about and some that I had actually witnessed.

The village as a whole had not undergone any great changes, but the disaster zone section of it had undergone a huge transformation, which made me feel a stranger. A great many things became simpler and plainer but seemed increasingly mythological.

Sometimes people would see children in the fields jumping rope in groups of five. Their whole bodies were coated in white wax, with their viscera exposed, which were clearly fragments of brick and were interlocked with one another and stopped up. These children were not the ones from our village who had perished in the disaster but were perhaps from neighboring villages or perhaps from town. Some among them, however, seemed to be wearing ancient Chinese clothing, as if they had been assembled from the dust of time. But as they vigorously jumped and leaped about, they shot up into the air, each of them changing into a shadow and dispersing. Then there would immediately be a new bunch. As a result, although their torsos were structured of dry brick, they very possibly were not solid, since some people said that when they came across them, they could walk right through their bodies, as if walking into air. At the time, however, extraterrestrial spaceships had yet to land on earth, so people had not yet connected them with extraterrestrial life.

When I woke up one morning I noticed that outside my window the sky above the village had taken on the characteristics of a solid, with some of the disorder of a construction site, densely packed with material, like a pomegranate; it was only through narrow fissures in the mudstone that wisps of white cloud could be seen floating by. This feeling was extremely unnatural, and I asked other children if they had seen it or not. Some said they had while others said they had not. There were yet others who had seen sound waves reverberating off the rigid structure, like ringlets of ripples on a pond. Still others said that they had seen something like a whirlpool carved out of purple willow, but which when looked at carefully turned into the growth rings on a ficus. As for Mother, she said she had seen a golden Buddha light, as viscous as corn porridge. All these things displayed themselves in the sky above the village, like a vast expanse of mirage. Neither the villagers nor the city dwellers had ever heard of such structures. They seemed to suggest the establishment of a new cosmology, which affirmed that which we had never affirmed previously but also negated what we had negated in the past. Its perfect gradations and orderly system restored the elegance and delicacy of the Ptolemaic world. It may not, however, have been our world but a parallel one, one of the grains of sand in the Ganges.

I later left the village to attend university in a far-away city. My mother escorted me as far as the village entrance, but we already had nothing to say to each other, exhibiting the awkwardness that exists between many mothers and sons. I had a CD in my backpack on which I had recorded the sounds from the brick house. I later gave it to my girlfriend.

In a continuation of the work of Webb and Hubble, a massive new celestial telescope was shot into space, after which people were finally able to clearly see the macrostructure of the universe.

It was a sort of reticular structure with a brick pattern. Within it there seemed to be landscapes, beasts, as well as stagnant disk-shaped objects like bee swarms; there were also tombstones spread throughout the galaxies, neatly arranged in macroarrays like dominoes. There were no striking colors to any of this, but they were not imaginary, being actually extant. They also seemed to be signs, and although they were crude representations, they were full of energy along with a considerable width of field, background, and atmosphere.

For the first time the universe has been connected by a continuous and visible entity.

But was it a work of art?

Where was its exhibition hall?

Standing on earth, I could clearly hear sounds coming from the universe. Some were human, while others were from unknown beings. Some came from hundreds of millions of years ago, while others were produced only within the past few hours. Some seemed like people whom I knew well, while others were strangers. Once I thought I heard my girlfriend calling out to me. I hadn't forgotten about her, had I? Was she still thinking about me? Had she actually gone to heaven? She had quite possibly regenerated some other place but had formed a quantum tangle with my soul. At these times I thought the universe was closed, that there was nothing random about it at all.

Just then there appeared a new trade specializing in selling an interconnection technique that assisted customers in finding the whereabouts of old friends and relatives via the sounds from bricks and tiles. Whenever they would be found, however, the correspondent would not know about it. In spite of this, people would still wish to continue the search.

American scientists hypothesized that the universe in which we live was constructed upon a building that was on a huge ruin. But it was unknown what it was a ruin of or how it had taken shape. This was the mysteriousness of the universe. Research on this question had come to replace the Big Bang and superstring theories as the central propositions of cosmology. Some scientists conjectured that the universe was just then within a period of regeneration, and that the disasters it had endured in its early years probably far surpassed anything we could imagine. And the tragic experiences we insignificant humans had undergone were really nothing in comparison.

—Thereupon, with this as the basic content of literature, there was a renaissance of poetry in Japan and Korea. It revolved mainly around construction themes and became a new school of poetry. The poets rhapsodized: the world is a brick.

Later on a British scientist discovered regenerated atoms, which he considered to be basic particles of matter, and whoever grasped this would be able to avoid free energy reverting to zero and thus would never reach absolute entropy. As with ether and phlogiston, however, this generated controversy.

Several Russian spaceships successfully explored the Galactic Supermassive Black Hole, and the cosmonauts said that they had seen a structure like a ruin that was similar to a Cauliflower Snake, which was actually real space constituted by continuous particles. This also suggests that differential equations are the basic mathematical forms that ultimately describe the laws of life. They could not, however, describe it well.

Once it was realized that the universe was very possibly a ruin that could be described by using quantum matrix mechanics, people were able to set their minds at rest, believing that this resource could be used for hundreds of millions of years. At least the manufacture of great quantities of regenerated brick would pose no problem.

Since the universe continued to exist, people were encouraged and wished to make some contribution. In this way making regenerated brick was part of this glorious enterprise of detaching from the limitations of individual people. Before the ultimate catastrophe arrived, could this negligible human race be put to some definite use? We will wish to prepare sufficient regenerated brick before this disaster arrives. We have fully comprehended the significance of disaster in our once again moving toward prosperity.

Dispute over the question of what regenerated brick was, however, continued and seemed to be a bottomless pit.

———⊗⊗⊗———

Mother had grown old. After she constructed the small house, she turned the management of the brick factory over to my younger brother, while she herself became a tour guide. Every morning she would don the traditional ethnic garb of the region and, resembling someone out of a Western oil painting, she appeared all the more young and elegant, not at all like someone from the country. Moreover, from her shoulders on down, she was dressed in divine, buttery hues, right down to the blade-thin heels of her dark green cotton shoes. She had never wanted to live in the city, since, she said, the cities were built on even more ancient ruins so were in actuality even more rural than the countryside. And she did not like the country at all.

She would come nimbly to the village entrance and fight noisily over the tourists with the young tour guides. In general, Mother would win the greater victories in this, leaving the competitors, who were two or three generations younger than her, deeply envious. Leading a group of visitors, she would enthusiastically stride into our house to look around. She walked so fast that the urban visitors from afar would be having misgivings as they jogged behind her. Going into houses to call on the residents was an established part of the disaster tour. Mother enunciated clearly and did not tremble as she introduced the visitors to the house, saying that in the very year of the disaster she had personally built it out of regenerated brick. After that she related how her husband and child had perished, something she still remembered without a single error. The visitors much preferred this sort of story, and without fail they would click their tongues in amazement. They were of the new generation that had no experience of disaster whatsoever.

Mother: That afternoon the house suddenly began to rock. My husband shouted out, "Earthquake!" and picked up a piece of clothing that he used to cover my head as he pushed me outside. But before we got out the house collapsed. As the house was collapsing he continued to use his arms to protect me; I couldn't see anything at the time, since the air was filled with dust. We fell into a narrow space between two buildings.

Visitor: How seriously were you hurt at the time?

Mother: My right leg was crushed by a chunk of the house, but I was completely clearheaded. My husband continued to determinedly protect me with his arm. I told him to let up a bit, and he said I may be done for; I reckon I'm going to die. I told him that we were safe now, so why would you say such a thing. But I felt his back and it was covered with blood. I was sure his head had been smashed.

Visitor: And what did he say?

Mother: He wanted me to be more firm. We also had a child, who had started middle school the year before. He wanted me to be a bit more strict with the child, to have him adhere to the correct path. If he took one misstep, his entire life would be ruined. I told him I got it. Both of us had always been very exacting with the child, but I would try to be even stricter.

Visitor: And after that?

Mother: I continued to shout at him. He responded at first, but after about half an hour he went silent. I continued to hold him tight. There was a small bowl-sized hole in the ruins that were on top of me. The ruins were made of crisscrossed pieces of concrete. My leg continued to bleed and the pain was acute. When I was thirsty I had to drink my own urine.

Visitor: Oh . . . !

Mother: When I could urinate no more I of course thought, Why don't I just die. But when I thought of what my husband had said to me I wanted to continue living. I continued to hold him. My right leg was no longer bleeding—I assumed it had clotted up. I later grabbed a chunk of brick, using it to strike at my right calf; when I'd struck it enough it began to bleed and I propped it against my husband's back, and as the blood flowed down, I was able to get it into my mouth and drink it. When I was confined in there that was the only way I was able to drink any blood . . . After three days I was pulled out by soldiers. It was only then that I learned that the child had also died. The classroom building at the town school had collapsed.

. . .

It is said that when my mother was pulled out by the army, she was almost completely naked. As soon as she saw the bloodred sun, she burst out crying, very loudly, and also pursed up her purple lips and began seeking out water to drink.

When the visitors came to our house Mother would provide snacks, as well as rice wine she had fermented herself. She would bring these to the table and partake along with everyone else; she charged very little. Although they were strangers, she got along with them informally as if they were family. Some of the young or middle-aged guests would on occasion get drunk and stay on at the house; in the middle of the night Mother would lead them group by group like candy on a stick to go listen to the sounds coming from the walls. Her charge for the lodging was also quite reasonable. Some guests liked to linger at our house for several months, just not wanting to leave, eventually admitting sheepishly that they hoped to experience so-called aftershocks. Sometimes there would really be some, and Mother's guests would glance at one another, burst out laughing, and vie with one another to climb up on the roof. The result was that one could see countless other similar travelers standing on every roof in the village, like the little monkeys on Flower-Fruit Mountain, raising their arms like flags, swaying back and forth along with the waving of the earth. The scene resembled a heavy-metal rock concert. At such times Mother would hold her knees and sit on the ground with her eyes closed, as if taking a nap; she would snore gently.

The year she turned eighty-two Mother suddenly went deaf and could hear nothing at all. There was nothing the doctors could do. So she decided to attend the deaf-dumb school in the village. At the time, many of the elderly in the disaster area were in the same condition. It seemed as if this were a fixed plan for them to serenely pass their later years.

Every day Mother would put on the book bag she had sewn herself and like a child go happily to school, humming a folk song as she went. She would always pass by the little house she had built herself of regenerated brick, the house enduring at the eastern edge of the village under the morning sun like a wisp of fog, seeming to be incessantly evaporating. Mother would pass by without looking at it, as if it didn't exist. There was a photographer who took photos of it and sent them to a Dutch contest and won a major prize. In the photo Mother was but a drifting yellow silhouette looking as if she didn't know where she was going or where she was from, the boundless earth under her feet at an indeterminate distance from her. The solid dark green house was the real subject, lurking like an old-fashioned graveyard. In fact, however, it had become a temple, with incense winding around it all day. The villagers said it was dedicated to the god of brick. This was, however, merely superstition. Even with the production of such a huge quantity of regenerated brick, such that even extraterrestrials had visited, the scientific level of the villagers had not achieved any appreciable elevation. They seemed to pass their days much as they had prior to the disaster. Low-tech, therefore, was most practical for them.

I saw from the photo that everything had subsided into near quiet, and that there was no participation in the discussion of disputed matters. This was all, however, precisely the effect of the expression of the technological ideas of those years. It can only be said that in the history of the fading away of the human race, those who had worked under the pure principles of technology had been extremely fortunate.

—Actually at this time Mother and I had both begun to consider the method of our own regeneration hereafter. And such arrangements, aside from implementing them personally, could not be put into writing. It was, however, not a great concern.

2

THE VILLAGE SCHOOLTEACHER

LIU CIXIN

TRANSLATED BY CHRISTOPHER ELFORD

AND JIANG CHENXIN

He realized that the final class would have to be moved forward. The pain in his side surged up again, nearly knocking him unconscious. He didn't have the strength to get out of bed and could move only with great difficulty to the bedside window. The moonlight shone on the paper window a brilliant silver, making the small portal look like a door leading to another world, a world where everything was silvery, like a bonsai terrarium made of silver coins and snow that wasn't cold. Quivering slightly, he raised his head to look through a hole in the window paper, and all at once the mirage vanished. He saw in the distance the village where he'd spent his entire life.

Spread out under the moonlight, the silent village looked as though it had been abandoned a century before. The houses, with the characteristic flat-topped roofs found on the Loess Plateau, were of a shape no different from the loess mounds that surrounded them. In the moonlight they were of the same tinge, as though the village had merged with the hillside. Only the old pagoda tree, standing out in front, could be seen clearly. The crows' nests in its withered branches stood out a blacker black, like large ink drops on the deep-silver tableau. The village did have its moments of beauty and warmth. At harvesttime, the young men and women who had gone off to work in the city would return, and the village would fill with the sounds of their joyous laughter; every rooftop was stacked high with golden corn and children could be seen rolling about in the freshly cut hay on the threshing ground. Or there was the New Year when the gas lamps over the threshing ground burned bright and there would be several days of wild festivities, the rowing of the "land boat," and the dancing of the lion dance. Of these lions not much remained save some clicking wooden skulls with the paint worn off and a few bed-sheets, since the village could not afford to replace the coverings with proper lion skins . . . yet everyone had great fun. But after the fifteenth, the young people would all have returned to their jobs and the village had nothing to enliven it. Only at dusk, when the smoke rose from the chimneys in thin wisps, would one or two old men appear on the outskirts of the village, their faces, wrinkled like mountain hickory nuts, raised and peering eagerly at the road that led out of the mountains, till the last rays of the sun hanging from the branches of the pagoda tree faded away. By nightfall the lights in the village had long been put out. Electricity was expensive. It was now up to 1.8 yuan per kilowatt hour.

The faint sound of a dog barking drifted through the village, as though it were talking in its sleep. He looked around at the yellow earth in the moonlight and felt suddenly that it resembled the unbroken surface of a lake. If only it really were water. The drought was in its fifth straight year. The villagers had to carry water to irrigate the land to have any harvest at all. He thought of the fields as he looked off into the distance at the tiny mountain plots. In the moonlight they looked like footprints left by some prehistoric giant passing over the mountains. On these rocky slopes, cov-ered with brambles and artemisia, there was space only for small plots here and there. Farm machinery was out of the question; even a draft ani-mal could barely turn a full circle on the fields, so the fields had to be tilled by hand. Last year a farm-machinery company came around sell-ing a mini push tractor that would function even on these palm-sized plots of land. A good enough machine, the villagers said, but you must be joking: did the salesmen know how little these tiny fields produced? Even tilling them as carefully as if one were embroidering flowers, you'd be lucky to harvest enough to feed yourself year-round; in a time of drought you might not even recover the price of the seeds you planted. With fields like these, who could afford a three- or four-thousand-yuan push tractor, plus the two-yuan-a-liter diesel fuel you'd need to run it? How could these outsiders understand just how hard life was in the mountains?

Several shadows passed by the windows. They squatted together at the edge of a field not too far off, for who knew what reason. He knew that they were his students. He could sense their presence when they were near him even without using his eyes. He had developed these intuitive skills over the course of his life, and they only sharpened in its final moments.

He could even identify which of the children it was under the moonlight. He was sure that Liu Baozhu and Guo Cuihua were among them. They were locals and so were not meant to board at the school, but he had taken them in anyway. Ten years ago Liu Baozhu's father had purchased a wife from Sichuan. The woman gave birth to Baozhu, and by the time the child was five, Baozhu's father slackened his watch on the woman. The result was that she escaped and ran away back to Sichuan, taking all the money in the house with her. After this, Baozhu's father wasn't himself anymore. He started gambling, and just like any old bachelor in the village, he reduced his household to but four walls and a bed. And then he started drinking. Every night he would hit the sweet potato wine hard, drinking himself into oblivion. He took his anger out on the kid, slapping him around once a day, violently beating him up every three. Just last month in the dead of the night, he took a fire poker and beat Baozhu within an inch of his life. Guo Cuihua was even worse off. Her mother was respectably married—a rare occurrence in these parts—and her husband was very proud of the fact. But as all things good are short-lived, as soon as the wedding festivities were over, she was discovered to be insane. That no one noticed before the wedding must have been because of the fact that she'd been drugged. Besides, what sane women would come to a place so poor that a bird wouldn't bother to shit on it? But despite all this Cuihua was born and, with some difficulty, grew up just the same. Her mother's illness grew worse, acting up more frequently. She hacked at people with a kitchen knife in broad daylight and tried to burn her house down in the middle of the night. More often she would just laugh darkly to herself. Her laughter made people's hair stand on end.

The rest of the children were from other villages, even those who lived near were separated from their homes by ten kilometers of mountain road. They had no choice but to live at the school. They would have to spend the entire term at this makeshift village school. In addition to their bedding they also brought with them a sack of rice or flour, which the children cooked together in the school's large cooking stove. When winter came, a dozen of them would gather around the stove to watch the food pop and sizzle. The straw burning inside the stove cast an orange glow onto their faces . . . this was one of his most cherished memories. He would be sure to take the image into the next world with him.

Outside the window several tiny red sparks appeared among the children, standing out a brilliant red against the silver-gray night. They were burning incense. Then they lit spirit money, the flames casting the children's forms in bright orange against the silver-gray winter night. It made him think back to the stove fire, which brought to mind yet another scene. When the power went off in the schoolhouse (either because the wiring was bad or, more often than not, because the school hadn't been able to pay the electricity bill) and their lessons ran late, he would hold a candle to the blackboard. "Can you see?" he would ask. "Not really!" the kids would respond. With so little light it most certainly wasn't easy to see clearly, but they had missed so many lessons that he had no choice but to hold classes at night. He would light another candle, holding it together with the first in his hand. "Still can't see!" they would chorus. And so he would add another candle. They still couldn't see clearly, but this time the children wouldn't bother to shout out. They knew he would not light another candle—it would cost too much. He could see their faces drifting in and out of the circle of candlelight. They looked like little bugs struggling with all their might to throw off the darkness surrounding them.

Children and firelight, children and firelight. Always children and firelight, always children and firelight at night. It was what this world had burned into his mind, this image, and yet he never understood exactly what it meant.

He knew they were burning the incense and spirit money for him. They had done it many times before, but this time he didn't have the strength to go out and reprimand them for being superstitious. He had spent his entire life lighting the fires of science and civilization in their hearts, but he knew that in a remote mountain village shrouded in ignorance, the fires he lit were small by comparison with the fires of superstition, like the candle he held against the blackboard in a freezing cold classroom deep in the mountains on a dark winter's night. Six months earlier some villagers had taken the rafters from the already rundown school dormitory. They said they needed them to fix the old temple. When he asked how the dormers would get on without a roof over their heads they said the kids could sleep in the classroom. When he reminded them that the classroom let in drafts on all sides and asked what the children would do in the winter, they said, "Well, they're all children from other villages anyway." He went after them with a bamboo shoulder pole and ended up with two broken ribs in the resulting fight. A couple of decent people took him thirty kilometers to the township hospital.

During his checkup they discovered by chance that he had cancer of the esophagus. There was nothing strange about this, since the area was a high-risk zone for esophageal cancer. The doctor congratulated him on his happy turn of fortune. The cancer was still in its early stages and hadn't yet begun to spread; a simple operation would take care of it. Esophageal cancer has a high postoperative recovery rate. He was lucky.

He had come all the way to the city and was in the cancer ward when he asked the doctor how much the operation would cost. The doctor replied that given his situation he would be qualified to move to the poverty-relief ward and other costs could also be reduced, making the final sum not large, probably around twenty thousand yuan. Seeing that he had come from a remote mountain area, the doctor explained in great detail the procedure for staying in the hospital. He listened quietly and then asked abruptly, "If we don't operate, about how long do I have?" The doctor stared at him blankly for a moment before saying, "About half a year." The doctor then looked confused as he let out a sigh of relief, as if he had been greatly reassured. At least he would be able to send off this year's graduating class.

He really couldn't afford the twenty thousand yuan. The salaries of locally sponsored teachers were low, but since he had worked for many years and had only himself to worry about, it would be reasonable to suppose that he would have some savings. But he had spent all that money on his students and could not remember how many times he had helped to pay tuition and other fees. Most recently it had been for Baozhu and Cuihua. Many times he had noticed that the food cooking in the pots lacked oil, so he had used his own money to buy meat and lard for them. . . . Now he had only about one-tenth of what it would take to pay for the operation.

Following one of the wide city avenues, he walked in the direction of the train station. It was dark and the neon lights were already casting their enchanting glow across the cityscape, a gorgeous radiance that baffled him; when night fell, the tall buildings turned into giant multicolored lanterns. The music that drifted through the night air was frenzied and mellow by turns.

In a world that he had never been a part of, he thought back on his relatively short life. He was calm; each person had his own life to live. Returning to his primary school in the mountains twenty years ago after graduating from middle school had sealed his fate. Besides, he owed the greater part of his life to another village schoolteacher. The school he was now in charge of was the one he'd spent his childhood attending. His mother and father had died early and so the crude school was his only home. His teacher had taken him in and treated him like a son.

Even though they were poor, his childhood was not without love. One winter, when school let out for the holiday, his teacher brought him to his own home. His teacher's house was far away and they had to travel down long mountain roads packed with snow. By the time they caught sight of the dim lights burning in his teacher's village it was already midnight. It was then that they saw behind them four small green shimmering disks of light. Wolves' eyes. At the time there were still many wolves in the mountains and one could see piles of wolf droppings near the schoolhouse. He'd been naughty once, igniting and tossing the whitish gray lumps into the classroom, filling it with heavy smoke. The children had bolted out of the classroom choking and his teacher had been very angry. Now the wolves behind them were slowly drawing close. His teacher broke off a thick tree branch and waved it in their path to block their approach, shouting for him to run into the village. He was out of his mind with fear and could only run, could only think about the possibility of the wolves bypassing his teacher to get at him, could only think there might be other wolves. He ran, breathless, into the village and returned with several men carrying guns to help his teacher. They discovered him lying in a frozen pool of blood, with half a leg missing and one entire arm ripped off. It was on the road to the hospital that his teacher breathed his last. He had caught a glimpse of his teacher's eyes in the torchlight and the deep bite on the side of his cheek where a large chuck of flesh had been torn off. Although his teacher could no longer speak, he had used his eyes to communicate a most urgent and sincere concern. He understood this. He would never forget it.

After graduating from middle school, he had given up his chance to get a good job in the township government and returned instead to this destitute mountain village, to the school his teacher had worried so much about. By then the school had already been abandoned for a number of years.

Not long before this the Ministry of Education had announced a new policy directive. They were discontinuing the "locally sponsored teachers" and replacing them with those who could pass their examinations to become "state-certified teachers." When he received his teaching certificate, showing that he was now a nationally certified primary school teacher, he was happy, but merely happy, not elated as his colleagues had been. He didn't care about the difference between locally sponsored and state certified. All he cared about were the children who passed through his classroom: that they might graduate and go out into the world. Whether they stayed in or left the mountains didn't matter; their lives would always be a little different from the lives of those who had never attended a day of school.

This desolate mountainous region was one of the poorest in the entire country. But being poor wasn't the worst of it. The worst was how numb to their condition people had become. He remembered many years ago, when it came time to fix household farm quotas, the village began dividing up the fields and then went on to divide up other things. As for the village's only tractor, nobody could decide how to divide the cost of fuel or arrange a time schedule for its use. Finally they settled on the only solution everyone could live with and divided up the tractor itself. Literally divided it up: you'll take the wheels, they'll take the axle.

And then there was two months ago when, as part of a poverty-relief effort, a factory had come to install a water pump. Since electricity was expensive they had thrown in a diesel generator and an ample supply of fuel. A nice thing that was, but as soon as they had gone, the village sold all the equipment—pump, fuel, and all—for only fifteen hundred yuan . . . enough for everyone to have two hearty meals, and the New Year to be regarded as a happy one. Then there was the tannery that came to build a factory. The villagers sold the land without asking any questions. After the factory was built, the poisonous chemicals used for tanning the leather began running into the river and soon seeped into the wells. The people who drank the water broke out all over in sores. But nobody cared even then. Instead they felt very pleased with themselves for having gotten a good price for the land. The old bachelors in the village who could not afford to get married did nothing but drink and gamble all day long. They didn't even bother to till the land, and for this they had their reasons: if they were poor enough they would be given an annual relief payment by the government, and this amounted to more than what one could make in a year pounding that palm-sized clod. Without knowledge people became ignoble. Those mountains with their barren hills and bad water could make one lose heart, but what really made one lose hope was the dull and lifeless gaze seen in people's eyes.

He was tired and sat down on the curb. Opposite him stood a luxurious restaurant, its outer wall a solid pane of glass. Magnificent hanging lamps threw their light into the street. The restaurant looked like a giant aquarium and the lavishly dressed patrons like schools of ornamental tropical fish. He saw, seated at a table by the side of the street, a fat man looking as though he were oozing grease from his face and hair, which made him look as though he were a giant ball of wax. Seated on either side of him were two tall, thin, scantily clad women. The man turned and spoke to one, causing her to burst into laughter. He joined in, while the other woman whined and playfully punched him with her tiny fists in his . . . Who would have thought that women could be so tall. Xiuxiu was only about half their height. He sighed; he was thinking of Xiuxiu again.

Xiuxiu was the only one in the village who hadn't married her way out of the mountains. Perhaps this was because she'd never been away and was afraid of the outside world. Perhaps there was some other reason. He'd been with Xiuxiu for two years, till they were finally ready for marriage. Her parents were reasonable people and asked only fifteen hundred yuan in "belly pain" money. That's one word for dowry in the northwest; it means that the mother should be compensated for her pain in giving birth to the girl. Then some of the men who had gone to the city to make money returned with their earnings. One Erdan, the same age as the teacher, was illiterate but clever enough and had gone to the city and cleaned kitchen ventilator hoods door to door. He made more than ten thousand a year in this way. The year before, he had returned and stayed for a month, and nobody knew when and how he got together with

Xiuxiu. Xiuxiu's entire family was illiterate. On the walls of their house, which was coarsely made by filling in the gaps between wooden planks with mud, were balls of melon seeds, also stuck together with mud; there were long or short lines scratched on the walls as well—these were her father's accounts over the years. Xiuxiu had never attended school, but she'd always had a fondness for literate people, which was the reason why she was with the teacher. But Erdan changed all that with a bottle of cheap cologne and a gold-plated necklace. "Just because you can read doesn't mean you'll have enough to eat," Xiuxiu had said. Even though he knew that being literate one could earn enough to eat, he had to admit that in his case he didn't eat anywhere near as well as Erdan, so he could not say anything in his own defense. Seeing this, Xiuxiu turned away, leaving behind her a lingering cloud of cheap cologne that made his nose wrinkle.

A year after marrying Erdan, Xiuxiu died in childbirth. He remembered watching the midwife carelessly running those horribly rusty forceps through the fire before jamming them inside Xiuxiu. Xiuxiu was out of luck, her blood filled an entire copper basin and she expired on the way to the hospital. Erdan had spent nearly thirty thousand on wedding preparations alone. This kind of extravagance was unheard of in the village, so he had wondered why Erdan was reluctant to pay the cost of sending Xiuxiu to the hospital to have her baby. He'd asked about the cost later— two to three hundred, people said, just two to three hundred. But the village had always been this way. No one ever went to the hospital to give birth. No one blamed Erdan—it was Xiuxiu's fate, they said. He'd also heard that compared with Erdan's mother, Xiuxiu had been lucky. Erdan's mother had a very difficult birth and once his father learned from the midwife that it was a boy, he decided he wanted only the child. They laid Erdan's mother across the back of a mule and had it trot in circles until the baby was squeezed out. People who were there remembered the bloody circle left in the yard.

He sighed once he thought this far. The ignorance and despair that smothered his village were suffocating.

But there was still hope for the children. For those children huddled together in the freezing dark looking up at the blackboard in the candlelight, he was that candle. It didn't matter how long he could stay lit or how bright the light he gave. He would burn brightly from beginning to end.

He stood up again and continued on. He had not gone far before he turned into a bookstore. How wonderful the city was with its bookstores still open at night. He spent all his money, save for his return fare, on books to add to the school's meager library. At midnight, carrying two heavy bundles of books, he boarded the train home.

Fifty thousand light-years from Earth, near the center of the Milky Way galaxy, an intergalactic war that had raged for twenty thousand years was near its conclusion.

In that region of space a dark square gradually appeared, as though a window were being carved out of the starry background. It was nearly ten thousand kilometers on each side and was darker than the darkness that surrounded it: a void within a void. From out of this black square, several forms emerged. Roughly moon sized, they were of a dazzling silver, each shaped differently. More and more of them emerged from the darkness and arranged themselves into a cubical formation. The silvery formation slid out of the black square, the two forming a mosaic that hung on the eternally unmoving wall of the universe, a picture with a perfect square velvet of absolute black as the backdrop, inlaid neatly with silver pieces that emitted a pure, bright, silvery glow. This unfolding seemed to be a moment in some universal symphony. Gradually, the black region melted away as the background stars filled it in. The silver formation remained, suspended imposingly among the galaxy's stars.

The fleet of the Milky Way Carbon-Based Federation had completed the first space-time jump of its current patrol run.

On the flagship, the Carbon-Based Federation's chief administrator contemplated the silver metallic world before his eyes. Its surface was crisscrossed with intricate lines, like a vast circuit board etched in silver. Occasionally a few shiny droplet-shaped ships appeared above the surface, traced the lines at a dizzying speed for a few seconds, then disappeared again soundlessly into a dark well that suddenly opened up in front of them. The ionized space dust produced by the space-time jump formed a cloud that floated in the atmosphere above the silver planet, emitting a dark red glow.

The chief administrator was known for his equanimity. The light blue and perpetually undisturbed intelligence field that surrounded him was the outward symbol of his character. But now, like the officers gathered around him, it emitted a pale yellow.

"It is finally over," the chief administrator said, his intelligence field rippling slightly, passing this message to the senator and the fleet commander standing on either side of him.

"Yes. It is over. A war that was far, far too long. So long we have forgotten how it began," the senator responded.

The fleet then began its sub–light speed patrol, the sub–light speed engines starting up all at once. On either side of the flagship several thousand blue suns appeared, and the surface of the silver planet resembled a giant mirror, doubling the number of blue suns.

A memory of the distant past had been rekindled. In actual fact, who could forget how the war had begun? Although the memory had been passed down through hundreds of generations, in the minds of the Carbon-Based Federation's citizens, it was still fresh, still clear.

Twenty thousand years ago the Silicon-Based Empire launched a full-scale attack on the Carbon-Based Federation from outside the Milky Way. All along the ten-thousand-light-year-long front line, the Silicon-Based Empire's five million and more intergalactic battleships simultaneously began leapfrogging between stars. Each battleship used the energy of the star to open up a wormhole that would connect them to another star. They would then use the energy of the second star to open a second wormhole and continue on to the next. Because the wormhole consumed such a massive quantity of energy, the stars' spectrum would temporarily shift toward red. When the ship had completed its space-time jump the star would return to its original state. When several hundred thousand battleships leapfrogged stars at the same time, the effect was truly terrifying: at the edge of the Milk Way a ten-thousand -light-year-long band of red light would appear, and this band of light would move toward the center of the galaxy. This effect wasn't visible at the speed of light but superspatial monitoring systems could pick it up. This band of red-shifted stars looked like a ten-thousand -light-year-long blood tide sweeping into the Carbon-Based Federation's territory.

The Carbon-Based Federation first made contact with the Silicon-Based Empire's attack vanguard at the Green Sea Planet. This beautiful planet orbited a double star system, a great ocean covering its entire surface. In this vigorous sea there floated a forest made of soft, vinelike plants. The gentle and beautiful Green Sea Planet inhabitants disported themselves gracefully through it and established an Edenic civilization there. Suddenly tens of thousands of blinding light bolts fell from the sky into the sea. The Silicon-Based Empire had begun to vaporize the ocean with its lasers. In moments the ocean was a broiling cauldron. All life on the planet, including the five billion inhabitants of the sea, met a painful end in that boiling water. The cooked organic matter of their combined bodies turned the sea into a thick green soup. Finally the entire ocean was vaporized and the once-beautiful Green Sea Planet turned into a gray hellscape enveloped by a thick vapor.

This war then spread virtually throughout the entire galaxy, a violent war of survival between two competing civilizations, the carbon based and the silicon based, but who could have predicted that it would last twenty thousand galactic years?

Now, none but a historian could remember exactly how many battles were fought by millions of starships. The largest battle, the Campaign of the Second Spiral Arm, took place in the middle region of the second spiral arm. Both sides committed more than ten million intergalactic battleships. According to historical records, more than two thousand supernovas were detonated on that one tremendous battlefield. These supernova explosions were like a furious firework display in the dark middle region of the galaxy's second spiral arm, ultimately turning it into a sea of gamma radiation with spectral black holes drifting within it. The result was mutual destruction for both galactic fleets. Fifteen thousand years passed and the Campaign of the Second Spiral Arm now sounded more like a vague ancient legend, with only the historic battlefield itself to testify to what had happened there. Very few ships have actually entered the ancient battlefield, since it is the most terrifying region in the galaxy, and not just because of the radiation and the black holes. During the battle both sides used an unimaginably large number of ships, and in their strategic maneuvers they had utilized a massive number of close-range space-time jumps. It is said that some star fighters engaged in dogfights, making space-time jumps at distances of only a few thousand meters! This had a disastrous effect on the space-time continuum in the region, twisting it into tunnels like those a mouse makes through cheese. When ships accidentally enter the region they might be instantaneously stretched out into a thin metal string, or compressed into a sheet hundreds of millions of kilometers square in size but only a couple of atoms thick, or shattered to pieces in an instant by the radiation winds. More often the ships were converted back into their individual component parts, or suddenly aged to the point where everything turned to ancient dust and nothing was left of them but an old shell. The people inside would perhaps be returned to some embryonic state, or collapse into a pile of desiccated bones.

But the decisive battle was no myth, since it took place only a year ago. In the desolate stretch of space between the first and second spiral arms of the galaxy, the Silicon-Based Empire gathered its last remaining forces. Its fleet assembled 1.5 million battleships surrounded by a cloud of antimatter, forming a barrier with a radius of a thousand light-years. The first fleet of the Carbon-Based Federation to enter the battle landed themselves in the antimatter cloud as soon as they completed their space-time jumps. Even though the antimatter cloud was very thin, it was deadly to battleships. Carbon-Based Federation ships immediately turned into fireballs one after the other, but they continued steadfastly toward their goal, each ship leaving a glittering trail in its fiery wake. This array of more than three hundred thousand burning meteors was the most violent and magnificent image of the entire war. These fireballs gradually became smaller in the antimatter cloud, and by the time they neared the Silicon Imperial force they had completely disappeared. But they had sacrificed themselves to clear a path in the antimatter cloud for the follow-up assault force. During this campaign, the Silicon-Based Empire was finally driven back into the most desolate region of the Milky Way: the tip of the first spiral arm.

Now, the Carbon-Based Federation fleet was about to accomplish its final combat mission. They were to establish a five-hundred-light-year-wide quarantine zone through the middle of the first spiral arm. This would require that most of the stars in the vicinity be destroyed, thus preventing the Silicon-Based Empire from leapfrogging in. Leapfrogging by using stars was the galaxy's only long-range, high-speed assault option for large battleships, and the greatest distance you could leap between stars was two hundred light-years. Once the quarantine zone was created, if the Silicon-Based Empire's heavy battleships wanted to enter the Milky Way's central region, they would have to traverse the five-hundred-light-year-wide quarantine zone at sub–light speed. This meant the Silicon-Based Empire would be effectively confined to the tip of the first arm. They would never again be able to threaten the Milky Way center's carbon-based civilizations.

"I bring with me the wishes of the parliament," the senator used the vibrations of his intelligence field to tell the chief administrator. "They still strongly recommend that before clearing the quarantine zone of stars, we screen for protected life-forms."

"I understand this," the chief administrator said. "In the course of this long war the blood spilled by every sort of living thing would be enough to fill the oceans of a thousand planets. After the war the most pressing need is to restore respect for life. This respect extends not only to carbon-based life forms but to silicon-based life forms as well. It is precisely because of this respect for life that we did not completely wipe out the silicon-based civilizations. But the Silicon-Based Empire completely lacks this feeling for living things. Before the Carbon-Silicon War, war and conquest were just a kind of instinctive enjoyment for them; but now these things are written into every single gene and every single line of their code. It has become the goal of their existence. Because silicon-based life-forms' capacity to store and process information far exceeds our own, we can only predict that their recovery and development at the tip of the first spiral arm will be extremely fast. We must therefore establish a wide enough quarantine zone between the federation and the empire. To carry out a life-form screening on the billions of stars in the quarantine zone would not be practical under the circumstances. Although the first spiral arm is the most desolate region in the galaxy, the spread of stars with life-supporting planets orbiting them are dense enough for leapfrogging: their density would be sufficient for midsized battleships to leapfrog. Even if only one of these ships were to enter the Carbon-Based Federation's territory, the damage could be immense. Therefore, we can only afford to screen for civilizations. We must sacrifice the lives of the lower life-forms surrounding some of the stars in the quarantine zone in order to save the greater part of the galaxy's higher and lower life-forms. I have already explained this to the parliament."

The senator replied, "The parliament understands you and the federation's Defense Committee. What I bring to you is merely counsel, not legislation. But stars that support 3C or higher levels of civilizations must be protected."

"To be sure," the chief administrator said, his intelligence field flashing a resolute red. "For the stars in the quarantine zone with orbiting planets, the civilization screening will be extremely rigorous."

The fleet commander's intelligence field made a transmission for the first time. "To be honest, I think you are worrying too much. The first spiral arm is the most desolate region of the galaxy. There is no way a 3C civilization or above exists out there."

"Let's hope so," the chief administrator and the senator transmitted simultaneously. Their intelligence fields resonated to produce a curved plasma field that spread out and broke across the atmosphere of the silver planet.

The fleet then commenced its second space-time jump, tearing off at nearly infinite speed toward the Milky Way's first spiral arm.

It was late. In the candlelight, the entire class had gathered around his sickbed.

"Teacher, get some rest! You can teach tomorrow," a boy said.

He smiled with some difficulty, "Tomorrow we'll have tomorrow's class."

He thought to himself, If I could really make it until tomorrow that would be great. I could teach another class. But intuition told him he was close to the end. He gestured and a student brought a small blackboard over and placed it on the blanket that covered his chest. This was how he had taught class for the past month. With his enfeebled hand he received half a piece of chalk from a child and laboriously placed its tip against the blackboard. The pain surged up again. His hand shook and the chalk tapped against the blackboard, ticking out a series of white dots. Since returning from the city, he hadn't gone back to the hospital. Two months had passed and his side, the place near his liver, began to ache. He knew that the cancer had spread there. The pain worsened until finally it was overpowering. He fumbled with his hand under the pillow and pulled out some painkillers. They were the ordinary variety, wrapped in long plastic strips and individually sealed. For severe late-stage cancer pain, they were completely useless. Perhaps it was the placebo effect, but after taking them he always felt a little better. Demerol wasn't at all expensive, but the hospital wouldn't let him take it home. Even if he had, there wouldn't have been anyone who could administer the injections. As usual he took two pills out of the plastic wrap. But then he thought for a moment, unwrapped the remaining twelve pills, and swallowed them all at once. He knew he wouldn't be needing them later. He struggled again to write on the chalkboard but suddenly turned his head to one side. A child quickly snatched up a basin and held it under his mouth. He coughed up a mouthful of blood and then leaned weakly against the pillow, gasping for breath.

The children began to sob quietly.

He gave up trying to write on the blackboard and waved his hand feebly. He had one of the children take the blackboard away. He began to speak, his voice as thin as gossamer.

"We're going to keep doing parts of the middle-school curriculum, as we have done for the past two classes. This isn't on our syllabus. But most of you won't ever have the chance to go to middle school, so for my final classes I just wanted to give you a sense of what slightly more advanced classes might be like. Yesterday we talked about Lu Xun's 'Diary of a Madman.' You almost certainly didn't understand it. But whether you understood it or not, you should read it several more times, or better still learn it by heart. When you get older, you'll understand. Lu Xun was an extraordinary man. Every Chinese should read him. You should all read him one day."

He was tired. He paused for a moment to catch his breath and rest. While he watched the flickering candle, Lu Xun's words floated through his mind. They were not from "Diary of a Madman," nor were they in the textbooks. Those words were what he had read in his own dog-eared volume from Lu Xun's complete works. Even when he read them for the first time many years ago, they were etched into his mind.

"Imagine an iron room. It has no windows and is nearly impossible to destroy. Inside there are a great number of people, all of them sound asleep. They will soon suffocate and die. But they will die in their sleep, feeling no pain or sorrow. Suppose you were to shout, waking a number of them who are a bit more clearheaded, thereby bringing this unfortunate minority to an awareness of their irremediable predicament. Wouldn't you owe them an apology?

"But now that several people are awake, you could no longer say that there is absolutely no hope of destroying the room."

He used the last of his strength to continue.

"Today we're going to learn junior middle school physics. You've probably never heard of physics before. It deals with the principles of the physical world. It is a very, very deep subject.

"This class is on Newton's three laws. Newton was a great English scientist. He said three things, three very profound things. He brought everything in the world under an all-encompassing set of laws, from the sun and moon above to the wind and running water below. Nothing could escape the delimiting circle of the three things he said. And with these three things you could calculate a solar eclipse, which is what the old folks in the village call 'the heavenly dog eating the sun,' and be exact to the minute and the second of its occurrence. When people fly to the moon they rely on these three things—they are called Newton's three laws.

"Now we will learn the first law: a body continues in its state of rest, or of uniform motion in a straight line, when it is not compelled to change that state by external force."

In the candlelight the children looked at him quietly and said nothing.

"Let's say you give one of those stone grain wheels a hard shove. It will keep rolling and roll all the way to the horizon without stopping. Baozhu, what are you laughing at? Yes, of course it wouldn't really happen that way. There is friction, and friction will make it stop. There is not really a place in this world where friction does not exist. . . ."

Indeed, the friction in his life was too great. In the village he was an outsider, with no connections to begin with, and with his bad temper he'd offended everyone these past few years. He'd gone from door to door dragging their kids to school. He'd gone to the county seat to fetch back the ones who had gone with their dads to find work, had thumped his chest assuring them that he'd pay for their tuition. In doing this he hadn't earned much gratitude, mostly because his views on how life should be lived were just too different from those around him. What he spent all day thinking and talking about were a bunch of impractical matters, which bothered people more than anything else. Before he'd discovered he was sick, he'd gone to the county seat and somehow managed to return with a sum of money given to the school for maintenance work by the Department of Education. The villagers had taken only a small portion, intending to invite an opera troupe to perform for two days during the New Year. But he messed up their plan and even brought the vice–county head over to demand that the village return the money. But by then the opera stage had already been built. The school had of course been repaired, but he had all but swept away the villagers' good spirits in the process. After that things just got worse. First the village electrician—the mayor's nephew—cut off power to the school. Then the village refused to give them straw for cooking and keeping warm. Things got so bad he had to abandon his own plot of land in order to go up into the mountains to gather kindling. And then there was the incident involving the dormitory's rafters. The friction was everywhere. It exhausted him and kept him from moving at a uniform speed in a straight line, such that he could not help but slow to a halt. Perhaps the world he was about to enter was without friction and where everything was sleek and lovable, but what was the point? His heart would still be here in this world of friction and dust, still in this village school he'd poured his entire life into. After he passed away, the remaining two teachers would leave as well. The village school to which he'd devoted his life pushing would, like the stone grain wheel in the threshing yard, come to a stop. He sank deep into sadness; whether in this world or in the other, he lacked the strength to change things.

"Newton's second law is a little bit more difficult. We'll save it for last. Next let's learn Newton's third law: Whenever one body exerts a force onto a second body, the second body exerts a force on the first. The two forces are equal in magnitude and opposite in direction."

Again the children fell into a long silence.

"Do you understand? Who can explain it?"

The best student in the class, Zhao Labao, said, "I get his meaning but I can't really figure it out. This afternoon me and Li Quangui got in a fight and he hit my face real hard so it hurt and swelled up. The force there definitely wasn't equal. I definitely took more of it than him!"

He took a moment to catch his breath and went on to explain, "You got hurt because your cheek is softer than Quangui's fist, but the two forces were nevertheless equal. . . ."

He wanted to use his hands to illustrate, but he couldn't even lift them. He felt as though his limbs were made of iron, and this heaviness quickly spread throughout his entire body. He thought he might crash through the bed and end up on the floor.

There wasn't enough time.

———— ⦿⦿⦿ ————

"Target 1033715. Absolute visual magnitude: 3.5. Evolutionary status: above main sequence. Two planets discovered. Average orbital distance from the star: 1.3 and 4.7 units of distance. The first planet is found to support life. *Red 69012* reporting."

The Carbon-Based Federation's 100,000 ships had already spread out along a belt 10,000 light-years long in the cordoned-off area and were in the process of constructing the quarantine zone. The project had just begun and they had already experimentally destroyed 5,000 stars, among which only 137 had planets. This was the first to have life.

"The first arm really is a desolate place," the chief administrator sighed. His intelligence field rippled as he used a hologram to hide the ship beneath his feet and the stars above him, making him, the commander, and the senator look as though they were suspended in the black emptiness of space. He adjusted the image sent by the detector. A blue, glowing fireball appeared in the void. The chief administrator's intelligence field produced a white frame that adjusted its size, till it encircled the star and covered the image. They sank again into the boundless darkness. But there was a small yellow light in the darkness. The image began to greatly modify its focal length, and the image of the planet flew toward them at dizzying speed, rapidly filling half the space around them, bathing the three men in the orange glow it reflected.

A thick atmosphere enveloped the planet. In this orange gaseous sea the swirling of the atmosphere produced complex, constantly changing lines. The image of the planet continued to approach until it engulfed the entire universe and the three men were completely swallowed up by the orange sea of gas. The monitoring device kept them on course through the dense fog. The gas rapidly thinned, allowing them to catch a glimpse of the planet's life-forms.

A group of balloonlike forms floated in the uppermost layer of the dense atmosphere. Their surfaces were covered in beautiful, constantly changing patterns and colors. At one moment they were striped, at another speckled—perhaps it was a kind of visual language. The balloons had long tails that would flash from time to time. When they did the light traveled from the tip of the tail up to the balloon, causing it to glow brightly.

"Initiate four-dimensional scan!" said a captain serving as duty officer aboard *Red 69012*.

A thin band of light began to scan the group of balloons from top to bottom. This wave band was only a few atoms thick, but its internal dimensions exceeded those of the universe around it by one dimension. The scan's data returned to the ship. Inside the ship's main computer this group of balloons was cut up into billions of microscopically thin slices, with each slice measuring only a single atom in thickness. Each of these sections was then meticulously recorded, accurate down to the quark.

"Initiate digital reflective composition."

Inside the main computer's storage device those billions of slices were reconfigured according to their original order to form a virtual balloon being. This planet's balloon creatures now had an exact replica in the main computer's vast interior universe.

"Begin the 3C Civilization Test."

In this digital universe the computer had accurately identified the balloon's organ of thought, which was an ellipsoid hung in the middle section of its extremely complex nervous system. The computer had instantaneously calculated the structure of this brain, bypassing all the more rudimentary organs, and constructed a direct high-speed informational interface.

The civilization test consisted of questions arbitrarily selected from an enormous database. If the test taker was able to answer three questions correctly it would pass the test. If the first three questions were all answered incorrectly the tester would have two options: either consider the test failed or continue the test, since the number of questions was infinite, until at least three questions were answered correctly. Once this had happened the test taker could also be considered to have passed the test.

. . .

"3C Civilization Test question number 1: describe what you have found to be the most basic unit of matter."

"Dee dee, doo doodoo, deedeedeedee," the balloon answered.

"Question number 1 failed. 3C Civilization Test question number 2: What are the characteristics of the flow of thermal energy through objects? Is this flow reversible?"

"Doo doodoo, deedee, deedee doo doo," the balloon responded.

"Question number 2 failed. 3C Civilization Test question number 3: what is the ratio of a circle's circumference to its radius?"

"Deedeedeedee doodoodoodo," the balloon replied.

"Question number 3 failed. 3C Civilization Test question number 4 . . ."

"Let's stop here," the chief administrator said when they reached question number 10. "We don't have time enough for this." He turned and signaled to the commander next to him.

"Launch the singularity bomb," the captain ordered.

The singularity bomb actually had no size. Strictly speaking it was a geometrical point. An atom by comparison would be infinitely large. While the largest singularity bomb was more than ten billion tonnes, even the smallest was still around ten million. When a singularity bomb followed the long guidance track and slid out of *Red 69012*'s bomb bay, a faintly glowing sphere with a diameter of several hundred meters could be seen. The light was the radiation produced by space dust as it was pulled into the tiny black hole at the bomb's center. Different from the black holes created by collapsed stars, these black holes were created at the beginning of the universe. They were shrunken prototypical singularities that existed prior to the Big Bang. The Carbon-Based Federation and the Silicon-Based Empire both had large fleets that patrolled the dark and barren outer reaches of the Milky Way collecting these mini black holes. Some ocean planets' inhabitants jokingly called them the fishing fleets of the high seas. They fished for one of the galaxy's most feared weapons of war, the only weapons known that were capable of destroying stars.

After the singularity bomb left its guide rail, it followed a path created for it by the ship's tractor beam as it picked up speed, heading straight for the star. After a moment this dustlike ball sped into the fiery surface of the star. Imagine a deep well with a hundred-kilometer radius opening up in the middle of the Pacific Ocean and you'll have an approximate idea of what happened at this moment. A tremendous amount of the star's matter was sucked into the black hole, a swirling torrent of material falling toward a single point from all sides and disappearing there, producing radiation that created a ball of blinding light on the surface of the star, as though the star were wearing a brilliant diamond ring. As the black hole sank into the star, the ball of light dimmed. One could see that it was at the center of a maelstrom several million kilometers in diameter. This maelstrom emitted a brilliant light, slowly turning and rapidly changing color, making the star look like a giant savage face. Just as quickly the light disappeared, and so did the maelstrom. The star's surface seemed to have returned to its original color and luminosity. But this was just the calm before the ultimate destruction. As the black hole sank to the center of the star, the voracious glutton was even more raven-ously swallowing up the high-density matter around it. In the space of a second it could devour an amount of stellar material equal to one hundred midsized planets. The strong radiation produced in the process slowly spread out across the surface of the star. Because it was blocked by the star's matter, only a small amount reached the surface. The rest situated its energy inside the star, quickly destroying the star's every cell, pulling it away from its point of equilibrium. From the outside one could observe the star's color gradually changing from light red to bright yellow, then from bright yellow to bright green, then from bright green it changed again as though washed in azure, and then from azure to a terrifying purple. At this point the energy produced by the radiation of the black hole at the center of the star was far stronger than that of the star itself. Even more energy poured out in forms that were beyond the spectrum of visible light. The purple became darker. The star looked like a spirit being in space suffering through tremendous pain, a pain that increased rapidly. The purple deepened to its limit. In less than an hour, the star had reached the end of its billions of years of life.

A ball of light that looked as though it could engulf the universe flashed brilliantly and then slowly disappeared. Where the star had once been you could see a rapidly expanding orb, like a balloon being inflated. This was the surface of the exploded star. As this orb grew in dimension, it became transparent. Inside there was a second expanding orb and deep inside it a third. . . . This exploding star was like a series of exquisitely wrought ornamental glass spheres nesting one inside the other that had suddenly appeared in the universe. The surface area of the innermost orb was hundreds of thousands of times larger than the surface area of the original star. When the first layer of the exploding star passed through the orange planet it was instantly vaporized. Against the background of the entire magnificent spectacle this part could not be seen. It was noth-ing more than a microscopic dust mote compared with the expanding outer shell of the star, its size not even adding up to a tiny mark on the surface of the glass sphere.

"Do you feel depressed?" the commander asked, seeing that the chief administrator's and the senator's intelligence fields had darkened.

"Another living world annihilated, like a dewdrop under the blaze of the sun."

"Just think of the great Campaign of the Second Spiral Arm, when more than two thousand supernovae were blown up, when one hundred twenty thousand worlds like this one were vaporized by Carbon-Based and Silicon-Based ships. Your Excellency, at this late hour we should really be done with this sort of pointless sentimentality."

The senator paid no attention to the commander's words and asked the chief administrator, "These surveys of random locations are unreliable. What if they are missing important cultural particulars on the planet's surface? We should conduct a full surface-area survey."

The chief administrator said, "I've already discussed this with the parliament. We will need to destroy more than a hundred million stars in the quarantine zone, and in the process some ten million planetary systems. Among them there might be as many as fifty million planets in total. We are pressed for time. To conduct a full surface-area survey on every single planet would be impractical. The best we can do is to widen the survey beam to cover a greater random-survey area. Besides that all we can do is pray that those planets in the quarantine zone with cultures have them spread evenly over their surfaces."

⸙

"Next we will learn Newton's second law."

He burned with impatience and did everything he could with his limited time to teach just a little more to the children.

"The acceleration of a body is directly proportional to the force causing it and inversely proportional to the mass. First, acceleration. This is the rate of change of velocity over time. It is not the same as velocity. High velocity does not imply a large acceleration, and large acceleration does not imply high velocity. For example, a body is moving at 110 meters per second. Two seconds later its speed is 120 meters per second. Its acceleration is 120 minus 110 divided by 2, or 5 meters per second . . . wait no, 5 meters per second squared. Another body is traveling at 10 meters per second. Two seconds later it is moving at 30 meters per second, so its acceleration is 30 minus 10 divided by 2, or 10 meters per second squared. See, in the second case even though the velocity is small the acceleration is large! Ah, I just mentioned the word 'squared.' Squared means a number multiplied by itself."

It surprised him that his mind could be so clear, his thinking so quick. He knew that the candle of his life had burned down to its base, that the wick had collapsed, igniting the last bit of wax, which burned ten times brighter than the candle flame had ever burned. The pain had disappeared. His body was no longer heavy. In fact he couldn't feel his body at all. Of his life force all that seemed to remain was his brain, churning wildly, as though suspended in midair, using the very last of its resources to pass more of its stored-up information to the children gathered around him. But speech was a bottleneck. He knew he didn't have enough time. He began to hallucinate: a crystalline ax soundlessly cut his brain to pieces. The accumulated knowledge, not much but very valuable, all poured out like shiny pearls onto the floor, with a sweet tinkling sound. The children gathered around to snatch them up as if they were New Year's candy. This vision gave him a feeling of good fortune.

"Do you understand?" he asked anxiously. He could no longer see the children, but he could hear their voices.

"We understand! Teacher, hurry up and take a rest!"

He felt the last of the flames die down, "I know you don't understand, but memorize it and later you'll slowly come to understand its meaning. The acceleration of a body is directly proportional to the force causing it and inversely proportional to the mass."

"Teacher, we really understand! We're begging you, please rest!"

He used the last of his energy to shout, "Memorize!"

The children set about memorizing the words through their sobs, "The acceleration of a body is directly proportional to the force causing it and inversely proportional to the mass. The acceleration of a body is directly proportional to the force causing it and inversely proportional to the mass . . ."

This thought produced hundreds of years ago by a brilliant mind long since turned to dust in faraway Europe was now being reproduced in the innocent voices of children speaking in the thickly accented northwestern dialect in a remote mountain village in twentieth-century China. Ensconced in this sound, the candle went out.

The children gathered around their teacher's lifeless body and began to cry.

"Target: 500921473. Absolute visual magnitude: 4.71. Evolutionary stage: main sequence. Nine planets. *Blue 84210* reporting." "An exquisite, nearly perfect planetary system!" the commander cried out.

The chief administrator agreed, "Yes. It's small terrestrial planets and gaseous giants are deployed in a kind of rhyme scheme. The asteroid belt is perfectly positioned, like a beautiful jeweled necklace. The tiny icy outermost methane planet is like the last lingering note of a musical piece, hinting at the birth of a new era."

"This is *Blue 84210*, preparing to scan for life on the innermost planet. Survey beam projected. This planet has no atmosphere and rotates very slowly on its axis. Surface temperatures vary greatly. Random location survey number 1. The result is white. Random location survey number 2. The result is white . . . random location survey number 10. The result is white. *Blue 84210* reporting. This planet contains no life."

The commander said with disapprobation, "This planet's surface could be used as a smelter! There's no need to waste any more time!"

"Initiate life scan on the second planet. Projecting beam sent. This planet has a thick atmosphere. Surface temperatures are high and relatively homogeneous, covered mostly by acidic clouds. Random location survey number 1. The result is white. Random location survey number 2. The result is white. . . . Random location survey number 10. The result is white. *Blue 84210* reporting. This planet contains no life."

Using four-dimensional communication, the chief administrator said to the officers on board *Blue 84210*, more than a thousand light-years away, "My intuition tells me that there is a great probability of life on the third planet. Initiate thirty random location surveys."

"Sir, we are pressed for time," the commander said.

"Do as I say," the chief administrator said firmly.

"Sir, yes sir. Initiating survey of the third planet. Projecting beam sent. This planet has an average atmospheric density. Most of its surface is covered by ocean."

The life-survey beam fell on a slightly southerly portion of the Asian continent. The tip of the beam formed a circle on the ground with a diameter of roughly five thousand meters. If it was daylight, one could detect the beam with the naked eye as every nonliving thing within the beam's range became transparent when it hit them. It now shone on a small mountainous region in northwestern China, and the loess slopes would have looked to an observer like crystal. The sun would have refracted in and out of these mountains, creating a truly magnificent scene. The observer would have seen the ground below him transformed into a bottomless abyss. All things determined to be living remained unchanged. People, trees, and grass would have stood out with utter clarity in this crystalline world. But this effect would have lasted for only half a second. During this time the scanning beam would have already completed its initial scan and everything would have returned to normal. The observer would have thought it a momentary hallucination. But right now it was night and naturally it was difficult to notice anything.

The village school happened to be right at the center of the circle made by the survey beam.

—— ∞ ——

"Random location survey number 1. The result is . . . green! The result is green! *Blue 84210* reporting. Target 500921473. The third planet contains life!"

The survey beam began to classify the many kinds of life that fell within its range, ranking the species according to the complexity of their structure and their estimated stages of intelligence, and putting them in order in its digital database. The group of creatures under a square shelter were ranked at the top. The beam speedily retracted, focusing on that shelter.

The chief administrator's intelligence field received *Blue 84210*'s image and enlarged it to cover the entire space background. That image of the village schoolhouse covered the entire universe in an instant. The image-processing system had already removed the shelter, but the images of the life-forms were still unclear. These life-forms' appearance was not eye-catching in the slightest and even seemed to blend in with the silicas and yellow dirt that surrounded them. The main computer could not but eliminate from the image everything lifeless, including the larger dead form that was surrounded by the life-forms, making them look as though they were suspended alone in the vast emptiness. Even this way they seemed rather ordinary, devoid of color, looking like yellow plants. One look and you knew these creatures weren't capable of performing miracles.

Blue 84210 projected a thin four-dimensional beam. The moon-sized ship had anchored just outside Jupiter's orbit, temporarily providing the solar system with an additional planet. The four-dimensional beam moved through three-dimensional space toward Earth at almost infinite speed. It plunged straight through the roof of the school and began conducting an elementary particle scan on the eighteen children. The torrent of information returned to space at a speed scarcely conceivable to humans. In an instant the children's digital replicas had been assembled in *Blue 84210*'s main computer's database, a database more vast than the universe itself.

The eighteen children were suspended in a boundless space of a color impossible to describe, not really a color at all since the void does not have a color but is more transparent than transparent. The children couldn't help but grab on to one another. They looked normal, but their hands passed through one another's bodies without the slightest obstruction. The children felt an indescribable terror. The main computer observed this and, thinking that these life-forms needed familiar objects, it created in its own internal universe a blue that mimicked that of this planet's sky. The children immediately looked up at the blue sky, with no sun and no clouds and no dust, just blue, so pure and profound. There was no ground under their feet but a sky the same as the one over their heads. They seemed to be in a universe of endless blue, and they were the only substance in it. The computer felt that these digital life-forms were still in panic and in a millionth of a second understood: most of the living things in the Milky Way galaxy were not afraid of being suspended in space, but these life-forms were not the same. They were land creatures. It therefore provided them with ground and a feeling of gravity. The children were surprised to see the ground suddenly appear beneath their feet. It was pure white and its surface was crisscrossed with an orderly black and white grid. They seemed to be standing on a gridded writing-practice book that extended to infinity. Some of them bent down to touch it. It was the smoothest thing any of them had ever seen. They took long strides but did not move, since the surface was absolutely smooth, the coefficient of friction was zero. They wondered why they did not fall down. One of the children took off a shoe and slid it across the ground. This shoe slid forward at a uniform speed. The children stared as it moved off into the distance at an unchanging speed.

They had seen Newton's first law.

A sound, gentle and lovely, resounded in the digital universe.

"Begin the 3C Civilization Test. 3C Civilization Test question number 1: Please describe the evolutionary principle of life on your planet. Is it natural selection or gene mutation?"

The children remained in stupefied silence.

"3C Civilization Test question number 2: please briefly state the source of the stars' energy."

The children still remained in stupefied silence.

. . .

"3C Civilization Test question number 10: please explain the molecular structure of the liquid that fills your oceans."

The stupefied silence continued.

The shoe, now only a tiny dot on the horizon, disappeared.

'Let's stop here!" the commander said to the chief administrator a thousand light-years away. "We cannot delay any longer, or we won't be able to complete the first stage of the mission on time."

The chief administrator's intelligence field rippled slightly to signal agreement.

"Launch the singularity bomb!"

The beam carrying this information traveled through four-dimensional space and arrived in an instant at *Blue 84210*, anchored in the middle of the solar system. A faintly glowing foggy ball slid out of the front of the battleship and down the long guide rail, following an invisible tractor beam as it swiftly gathered speed and hurtled toward the sun.

The chief administrator, the senator, and the fleet commander turned their attention to other areas of the quarantine zone, where they found a few more planetary systems that contained life. But the highest form of life they found was a brainless worm that lived in mud. The exploding stars looked like blossoming fireworks, reminding them of the epic Campaign of the Second Spiral Arm.

After a long time, a small portion of the chief administrator's intelligence field unconsciously wandered to the solar system. He heard the voice of *Blue 84210*'s captain: "Prepare to exit the force field of the explosion. Ready for space-time jump. Thirty-second countdown."

"Wait, how long will it take for the singularity bomb to hit the target?" the chief administrator asked. His question attracted the attention of the senator and the fleet commander.

"It is crossing the orbit of the innermost planet to the star, so it will take another ten minutes."

"Spend the next five minutes doing a few more tests."

"Yes, sir."

The voice of *Blue 84210*'s duty officer rang out. "3C Civilization Test question number 11: on a three-dimensional plane, what is the relation between the three sides of a right-angled triangle?"

Silence.

"3C Civilization Test question number 12: what number planet is your planet within your solar system?"

Silence.

"Sir, this is pointless," the commander said.

"3C Civilization Test question number 13: describe the motion of a body when unaffected by external force."

The children's clear voices suddenly sounded out through the wide blue space of the digital universe: "A body continues in its state of rest, or of uniform motion in a straight line, when it is not compelled to change that state by external force."

"Question number 13 passed! 3C Civilization Test question number 14 . . ."

"Wait!" The senator interrupted the duty officer. "Choose the next question on the laws of motion at low speeds." He turned to the chief administrator. "This doesn't contravene the rules of the test, does it?"

"Of course not, as long as the test questions are from the digital-test database," the commander answered instead. These living beings had surprised him and captured his full attention.

"3C Civilization Test question number 14: describe the interaction between two bodies when one exerts a force on the other."

The children replied in unison: "Whenever one body exerts a force onto a second body, the second body exerts a force on the first. The two forces are equal in magnitude and opposite in direction."

"Question number 14 passed! 3C Civilization Test question number 15: explain the relation between the mass of a body, its acceleration, and the force exerted on it."

The children chanted, "The acceleration of a body is directly proportional to the force causing it and inversely proportional to the mass."

"Question number 15 on the 3C Civilization Test passed. The Civilization Test has been passed! We have ascertained that the third planet orbiting the targeted star number 500921473 contains a level 3C civilization."

"Redirect the singularity bomb away from the target!" The chief administrator's intelligence field flashed urgently, forcefully sending his order through hyperspace to *Blue 84210*.

Inside the solar system, the repulsor beam propelling the singularity bomb curved. It bent like a bow hundreds of millions of kilometers long, straining to divert the bomb from its trajectory toward the sun. The force-field generator on *Blue 84210* was operating at maximum capacity, and its immense heat-dispersion plates turned from dull red to white-hot. The force field it beamed out was starting to make the trajectory of the singularity bomb curve away, but it had already crossed Mercury's orbit and was now too close to the sun. No one knew whether the redirection would succeed. Through live hyperspace projection, the whole Milky Way was gazing at the trajectory of that foggy ball and watching it suddenly get brighter. This was an alarming sign: it meant the bomb was already encountering the greater density of particles surrounding the sun. The captain's hand was on the red button for space-time jump, so as to escape the area the instant before the singularity bomb hit. But the bomb grazed the sun like a bullet, with only a few dozen kilometers to spare. The singularity bomb grew bright as the black hole sucked in the matter from the sun's corona, becoming a flaming blue-white sphere that became visible at the edge of the sun. For an instant, they looked like a double-star system, a sight humans would never be able to explain. As the blue-white sphere whizzed by, the sun's own ocean of fire dimmed by comparison. Like a boat speeding through calm water, the black hole's gravitational force made a V-shaped wave on the surface of the sun that spread across a whole hemisphere before it disappeared. The singularity bomb ruptured a solar prominence, making this beautiful million-kilometer-long veil that rose from the sun shatter into a beautiful dancing vortex of plasma swirls under the impact of such high velocity. . . . Soon after the bomb had skimmed past the sun, it dimmed and vanished into the vast night of the universe.

"We nearly destroyed a carbon-based civilization," the senator breathed.

"Crazy, isn't it, a level 3C civilization in such an isolated place!" exclaimed the commander.

"That's true, neither the Carbon-Based Federation nor the Silicon-Based Empire included this area in their plans for civilizational mentoring and development, so if this civilization evolved on its own, that makes it unique," said the chief administrator.

"*Blue 84210*, stay in that solar system and thoroughly examine the level of civilization across the entire surface of Planet No. 3. Your other duties will be taken over by other ships," the commander ordered.

Unlike the digitally reproduced beings stationed beyond Jupiter's trajectory, the children in the village school had not noticed anything out of the ordinary. They had gathered around their teacher's body in the flickering candlelight, sobbing. Finally, after a long time had passed, they quieted down.

"Let's go to the village and tell the grown-ups," Guo Cuihua said, sniffling.

"How would that help?" Liu Baozhu hung his head. "They couldn't stand him when he was alive, I bet they wouldn't even pay for a coffin."

The children decided to bury their teacher themselves. With hoes and shovels, they began to dig a grave on the hill beside the school. A whole universe of dazzling stars looked silently at them.

"It's a level 5B civilization they have on that planet, not a level 3C!" The senator was amazed by the report *Blue 84210* had sent back from a thousand light-years away.

Images of the skyscrapers in human cities began to appear in the space above the main spaceship.

"They have started using nuclear power and are beginning to explore space using chemical propulsion. They have even successfully landed on their planet's satellite."

"What are their chief characteristics?" the commander asked.

"What would you like to know?" *Blue 84210*'s duty officer replied.

"For instance, what is the level of hereditary biological memory on this planet?"

"They don't inherit memories biologically. All their memories are acquired."

"How do individual beings communicate among themselves, then?"

"By a primitive and unusual means. They have a very thin organ inside their bodies that, when it vibrates in the chiefly nitrogen- and oxygen-based atmosphere of the planet, creates sound waves. They encode the information they want to convey in these sound waves, and the recipient absorbs the information from the sound waves via another thin-membrane organ."

"How fast is this means of communication?"

"One to ten bits per second."

"What?" Everyone on the spaceship began to laugh.

"It really is one to ten bits per second. We didn't believe it either, but we've checked time and again."

"Captain, are you some kind of imbecile?" the commander fumed. "Are you trying to tell us that a species of being without inherited memory, that communicates via sound waves, and manages to convey only an unimaginable between one and ten bits of information per second, created a level 5B civilization that evolved of its own accord without external help from higher civilizations?"

"Sir, those are the facts."

"But under these circumstances, these beings would simply be unable to accumulate and convey information between generations, which is crucial for an evolving civilization!"

"There are a certain number of individuals dispersed throughout the population who serve as the medium conveying knowledge between two generations of these beings."

"It sounds like a myth."

"It's true that such a concept existed in the remote antiquity of Milky Way civilizations," the senator said, "but even then it was very rare. No one knows about it except those of us who specialize in the history of how galactic civilizations evolved."

"You mean the individuals who communicate knowledge between two generations of living beings?"

"They are called teachers."

"Teach-ers?"

"Yes, it's an archaic word that has long since disappeared, very rare—you can't find it even in most databases of ancient words."

Now the images sent back from the solar system zoomed out, showing a blue planet revolving slowly through space.

"During the Milky Way's federal period, independently evolved civilizations have been very rare, and as for a 5B civilization—this is the only one. We should allow this civilization to continue evolving undisturbed. Further observation and study will contribute to our understanding of ancient civilizations, but it may also be significant for today's Milky Way civilization," said the chief administrator.

"So let's have *Blue 84210* leave that solar system immediately and designate a hundred-light-year radius around this star to be a no-fly zone," the commander said.

———— ◌◌◌ ————

Insomniacs in the Northern Hemisphere would have seen the sky shudder with circular ripples that appeared to start from a point in the sky and expand outward, as though the sky were a clear pool of water touched by a fingertip.

The space-time warp caused by *Blue 84210*'s space-time jump had greatly weakened by the time it reached the Earth, merely making all the clocks there three seconds faster. But human beings living in three-dimensional space would have had no way of noticing this.

———— ◌◌◌ ————

"It's a pity," the chief administrator said. "Without being fostered by a higher civilization, they will be stuck in three-dimensional space at sub-light speeds for another 2,000 years. It will take them at least 1,000 years more to start using annihilatory energy, and a further 2,000 to communicate across multidimensional space-time. As for traveling through space by space-time jumps, it might take another 5,000 years. It could be 10,000 years before they meet the basic requirements to become part of the Milky Way's great family of carbon-based civilizations."

The senator said, "This kind of independently evolved civilization is a thing of the Milky Way's ancient history. If the records of antiquity are correct, my ancestors lived in the deep seas of an oceanic planet. After countless dynasties in that dark world, a great exploration project began. They launched their first spaceship, a transparent floating ball, which floated all the way up to the surface of the ocean. It was night, and the ancestors in the little sphere saw the starry sky for the first time. . . . Can you imagine how splendid and mysterious it must have seemed!"

"Those were exciting times, in which a planet like a speck of dust would have seemed like an infinite world to our ancestors," said the chief administrator. "They would have gazed up at the universe from green oceans and purple plains, full of awe. . . . We lost this feeling millions of years ago."

"No, I have rediscovered it!" the senator said, pointing to the image of the Earth, its white clouds swirling across a crystal-blue surface. He thought it looked like the kind of beautiful oceanic pearl from the oceanic planet of his ancestors. "Look at this little world. The living beings on it are living their lives, dreaming their dreams, unaware that we exist, unaware of the wars and destruction in the Milky Way. To them, the universe is a fount of hope and dreams. It's like an ancient ballad."

He actually started singing. Their three intelligence fields merged and rippled with rose-pink waves. This song that had survived from an unimaginably ancient civilization sounded mysterious, far away, desolate. It spread through the Milky Way via hyperspace, so that countless beings in this galaxy of hundreds of billions of stars suddenly experienced a long-lost warmth and tranquility.

"The most unfathomable thing about the universe is that it can be fathomed," the chief administrator said.

"The most fathomable thing about the universe is that it cannot be fathomed,' the senator said.

———— ✺ ————

The sky had grown bright by the time the children finished digging the new grave. They placed the body on a door dismantled from the classroom and buried their teacher with two boxes of chalk and a dog-eared set of primary-school textbooks. They marked the grave with a stone, on which they had written in chalk, Mr. Li's Grave.

The first rains would wash the childish handwriting from that stone; before long, the grave and the man sleeping in it would be entirely forgotten by the outside world.

The sun peeped out from behind the mountains and cast its golden rays on the sleeping village. In the valleys still enfolded in shadows, dewdrops glinted on the grass, and a bird or two chirped timidly.

The children walked back to the village on a mountain path, and their little shapes soon disappeared in the pale-blue morning fog of the valleys.

They would continue to live. On this ancient, impoverished piece of land they would reap a small but truly substantive hope.

3

HISTORIES OF TIME

The Luster of Mute Porcelain

DUNG KAI-CHEUNG

TRANSLATED BY CARLOS ROJAS

TRANSLATOR'S INTRODUCTION

Published in 2007 in two volumes (and totaling nearly nine hundred pages), *Histories of Time* is part of Dung Kai-cheung's as-yet unfinished *Natural History Trilogy*, which began with *Works and Creations: Vivid and Life-like* in 2005 and concludes with *The Origin of Species: The Educational Age of Beibei's Rebirth*, the first volume of which was published in 2010 but the second volume of which remains incomplete.[1]

Each chapter of *Histories of Time* consists of four parts, which alternate back and forth between several different narrative modes. The main diegesis is written in the third person and describes an interview of a Hong Kong author known as the Dictator, conducted by a young Eurasian woman named Virginia. The novel also features, however, excerpts of a fictional work attributed to the Dictator, letters written back and forth between the Dictator and one of his own fictional characters, as well as excerpts from another novel that Virginia and the Dictator begin to coauthor during the course of her interview with him. The latter work is set in a world in which different temporalities (including different iterations of Virginia and the Dictator) are interwoven with one another.

I have translated and include here the work's preface, which is written in the voice of the fictional character Virginia Anderson and appears at the beginning of each of the two volumes of the novel. I have also translated an excerpt from chapter 1, which is written in the third person and describes Virginia's initial visit to interview the Dictator. This excerpt includes a combination of standard written Chinese and transcriptions of oral Cantonese, and to preserve this dialectal distinction in the translation, I have rendered all the Cantonese portions in italics. There are a handful of words or phrases that appear in italics in the Chinese original, which I render with a combination of italics and underlining, and the work also includes words and passages in roman script (including, but not limited to, portions in English), which I have rendered in bold. Finally, I have also included an excerpt from chapter 7, which consists of a fragment of the fictional text that Virginia and the Dictator coauthor during their interview. This latter excerpt is structured as a dialogue between these two authorial voices, but the text offers no orthographic indication where one voice ends and the other begins. In my translation of this excerpt, accordingly, I have similarly eschewed the use of punctuation or other formatting to differentiate between the two voices.

PREFACE

"THE GROWTH OF POWER, AND THE BIRTH OF POSSIBILITY"

Virginia Anderson

As the Dictator's coauthor and editor of this novel, please permit me to make a few simple observations.

First, I want to address the issue of this book's author. Without a doubt, it is the Dictator's work and revolves around the author, the Dictator. However, within the work itself, the Dictator's consciousness has been either relegated to the margins or folded into the consciousness of other characters. The novel contains three narrative voices, and in the first two the narrator or the narrator's consciousness has been split between the characters Nga Chi and Yan Yan, while in the third narrative voice the Dictator and I either sing in unison or counterbalance each other, and in this way we produce a sort of theme and variations. Therefore, regardless of whether this novel is considered from the perspective of the real author or that of the narrator, the work is constantly oscillating between a "self" and an "other." I myself serve as the Dictator's collaborator, editor, annotator, and spokesperson, while at the same time I am also a character and a narrative voice within the work. Therefore, I am intrinsically a plural entity and fully sense the multiple possibilities of history.

I know that the Dictator has never been a writer interested in currying favor with anyone, and his confusion and self-doubt are virtually a disease. Ordinary readers typically prefer authors who are full of self-confidence, and they don't even object if an author is arrogant or conceited, since they view authors as authorities—as idols, mentors, even gods. Therefore, such readers find the Dictator unsettling. He even takes his "illness"— including his physical disability, his spiritual illness, as well as the fact that, by virtue of being an "author," he is a symptom of the era—and uses it as the foundation and starting point for a final analysis, hoping that by undergoing a dissection of this "illness" he can thereby find the possibility of a cure. It is my understanding that the resulting process proceeds from a moment of self-affirmation to a process of self-expansion and, finally, self-collapse. But at the moment when the "self's" consciousness collapses, an "other's" consciousness will appear and begin to develop, until the latter is positioned in symbiotic opposition with the former. As for this so-called other, it refers not to an abstract social group or class but rather to a collective of individuals and a group of individually differentiated "other selves." Therefore, the self and other are positioned not in a subordinate relationship with each other but rather in a mutually reciprocal one. The Dictator is keenly aware of the fact that "superseding the self and becoming an other" is a task that cannot be realized— and yet he nevertheless yearns to find a way, in his novel, to make this a possibility.

So this is a novel about possibility. But this so-called possibility definitely does not involve issues of plot choices or old questions about fate. In a certain respect, the novel can be seen as a scientific experiment. By setting conditions it is possible to demonstrate the probability that a particle will follow a certain trajectory, and it is even possible to consider two different sets of possibilities at the same time and thereby sketch out a variety of different historical scenarios. The novel even suggests that through fiction—and through the creative process—it is possible to alter the particle's historical possibility. This demonstrates that history is not merely a process of recording past events, nor even a process of presenting or interpreting those events, but rather includes all ongoing events, together with the possibility of events that have not yet occurred. Therefore, this novel is also *a history of the future*, which is to say that it represents a mode of treating the future as a potential event that may be experienced and imagined.

This notion of *a history of the future* infinitely expands the novel's temporality, and in the resulting imaginative space the work begins to exceed the geographic limits of so-called V City proper as it expands to include the existence of this species humanity itself. Thus, in spatial terms the work is not merely a history of V City, nor is it a history of a city at all, but rather it can be read as a history of human civilization, of the universe, and of nature itself. This is a work that transcends narrow provinciality, or—to use a comparatively broad term—it can be called a kind of will. Perhaps the Dictator himself was not yet able to realize these objectives within this broad and distant space-time matrix, but this obviously represents his hopes for the literature and the writers of the future. As an inheritor of this project, I may take these objectives as my own mission, in order to struggle to help realize the Dictator's ambitions.

This novel's temporality can be observed in the musical structure that the book adopts. If we use the opening, body, and conclusion of a musical piece as a model for a character's birth, life, and death, then the musical voice represents the conditions of consciousness of the novel's various characters, while the vocal counterpoint represents the logical and causal relationships between these characters. Meanwhile, the novel's engagement with painting generates a spatial matrix that directly complements the music-based temporal matrix. The spatial imagination that takes the ice-skating rink as its nucleus also contains the temporal element, and by taking different historical incidents and using a synchronic means to arrange for them to occupy the same scene, it is possible to achieve a transtemporal, transspatial imagination, which is also a specific incarnation of the universalism referred to above.

The dynamics of the ice rink can be seen as a kind of "novelistic dynamics." From Nga Chi's scientific enthusiasm to the Dictator's literary metaphors, countless physical principles are redeployed as modes of literary reference, thereby constituting different dynamic connections. Quantum mechanics, the theory of relativity, theories of black holes, and the like, all contribute to the novel's temporal and spatial structure, while the concepts of baby universes and the *sum over histories* similarly help the novel open new avenues of possibility. The history of time itself is constituted not merely of matter but also of movement. And out of all different kinds of movement, human behavior is a product of both its animal origins and a culturally constructed "sexual dynamics." Naturally, this also became one of the key propulsive elements in the novel.

This passage was written not for this particular novel but rather for a future work. In my imagination, I stand among the endless ranks of literary inheritors, like a particle in a chain reaction, which generates an enormous amount of energy by violently colliding with other particles. I originally treated $E = mc^2$ as a literary equation, which was definitely the original intention of Nga Chi and the Dictator.

CHAPTER 1, PART I

LIGHT-YEAR

In this instant I am burning
Tears that release fire
At a speed of a hundred and eighty-six thousand meters per
    second.
In a night in the future
Among stars that have already become past
Separated by tens of millions of light-years
I wink at you.

(Light-Year)

Ever since she lost Fa, her son, Nga Chi had gone seventeen years without speaking a word to her husband. When she heard her husband's interview on the tape recording, she had to make a tremendous effort before she was finally able to link that unfamiliar voice with the already-faded image in her memory of that figure known as the Dictator. Furthermore, his voice and image could never be completely reconciled, like those old movies in which the sound and image are out of sync with each other—in which not only is the soundtrack not coordinated with the images onscreen but the characters' speech is not coordinated with the movement of their mouths. The result resembled the way you first see lightning and only after a delay do you hear the rumbling sound of thunder. Nga Chi stopped to ask herself, Why would she have had this kind of thought? In fact, she herself had never seen a film in which the sound and the image were not in sync with each other, nor did she know whether, in even earlier eras, there had been this sort of technological problem. Nevertheless, at this moment this peculiar example of temporal mismatch tormented her mercilessly, making it impossible for her to concentrate on the actual content of the recordings. She was holding an old-fashioned cassette tape player, and when it was in operation you could clearly hear the grinding sound of the tape moving through the cartridge. The quality of the audio, however, was better than she would have expected, and the echo of her husband's voice functioned like a piece of sonar equipment sounding out the room's size and shape. It was the room that her husband had barely left over the previous seventeen years. Because he was afraid of getting cold, he would usually keep the window tightly sealed, but since he liked the expansive view outside, he would rarely close the curtains. Covering the entire wall there was also a bookcase, which produced an echo even as it helped dampen the sound inside the room. In the recording, the Dictator's voice was low and he sounded somewhat hesitant. He spoke very slowly and occasionally would stop and search his memory for uncertain details, or to try to find the right word. When he suddenly mentioned Nga Chi's name, it was as if she had dropped in from nowhere, and it sounded as though it was difficult for him to collect his thoughts. After a long silence, Nga Chi heard a woman's voice through the head-phones. The voice was very soft and the woman was evidently sitting far away, but her voice was nevertheless transmitted completely accurately, to the point that you felt as though you could reach out and touch her trembling throat when she spoke. Nga Chi's eardrums were disturbed by the sound. This was the first time that she had come so close to Virginia. Virginia's local dialect was impeccable, at least at the level of her vocabulary and syntax, though she clearly had a foreign accent. Her accent made her questions sound even more direct than they were, like an unrestrained child. She asked, *How did you and your wife get together?* Nga Chi removed the headphones and turned off the tape player, then stood up and walked over to the glass door leading to the veranda.

Through the glass door, Nga Chi saw someone standing in the shallows where the tide was receding. She pulled open the door and stepped out onto the veranda, where she gently leaned against the railing. The morning air was humid but cool, and Nga Chi instinctively pulled her cape tight, buttoning it in front of her with both hands. She suddenly realized that even though there was still a modest distance separating her from the figure in the shallows, they were nevertheless each visible to the other in the gloomy air. As she looked out from the first-floor veranda, Nga Chi could see that the other person was wearing a thin, light-green dress, parts of which had gotten wet and were sticking to her calves. It was as if the compliant fabric were incapable of hiding her voluptuous figure—since even though it seemed to fit, it gave the rough impression of a large child wearing clothes that were too small for it. That had been Nga Chi's first impression of Virginia. It was as if she had just been born from the sea but already possessed the body of a mature woman. Standing on the wet sand of the seashore, Virginia lifted up her skirt, revealing a pair of long muscular legs as she strolled out into the water. The inland sea seabed was very shallow, and the girl could probably continue walking out for another several dozen meters. Standing near the center of the water there were several great egrets, whose elegant bearing stood in stark contrast to the girl's awkward manner of stepping forward. An enormous gray heron was soaring over the water's surface, while a flock of small waterbirds were standing and eating in the shallows near the rocky beach. A floor-mounted telescope was positioned in front of the veranda's glass doors, but Nga Chi knew without needing confirmation that the birds were red-legged sandpipers passing through on their spring migration north. The girl proceeded out to where the water was up to her knees, then stopped and leaned over to peer down at something in the water—as her long hair, which had been in a bun, fell over her neck and shoulders. With one hand she held up her dress and with her other she kept pulling her hair back over her shoulders. Then, she suddenly squatted down and reached into the water to grab something. Her hair and dress both fell down, and she quickly reached back to grab them. Nga Chi carefully watched the girl's every move, and it seemed she could even feel the girl's feet as they sank into the wet mud. No, it suddenly occurred to Nga Chi that the girl was probably wearing water shoes or sandals, because other-wise the seashells covering the ground of the seabed would be cutting her feet. However, even then, Nga Chi still could not rid herself of that slip-pery feeling between her toes.

Virginia had already been living there for a week. Initially, she had come from some distance away and asked to see the Dictator, explaining that she just wanted to interview him for an afternoon. That was a Sun-day, and Virginia had walked into the Dictator's room, which was located in the attic of their house. Nga Chi remembered that it was 3:30 in the afternoon, and after about half an hour Virginia had come back down-stairs, explaining that her miniature tape recorder was broken. Nga Chi had searched the entire house, but in the end all she could find was an old-fashioned cassette recorder, and more than a dozen ninety-minute cassette tapes. She had bought the recorder more than a decade earlier, just as this sort of device was about to disappear. At the time Nga Chi had just borrowed the tapes of an interview with a local female botanist who had recently passed away, and because they had a copy of the interview only on a cassette tape, she had acquired this portable cassette player to play them. After Nga Chi spent more than six months transcribing the contents of twenty tapes—a total of eighteen hundred minutes of interviews—the cassette player was then put aside and left unused. She had never expected the day would come that it would be needed again. Nga Chi found some appropriate batteries, and it turned out that the ancient device still worked. She gave Virginia a simple explanation of how to use it. Virginia held the device as though it were a recently unearthed ancient artifact and then went back upstairs. The interview then contin-ued late into the night. Apart from taking her husband his dinner, Nga Chi never entered his room, instead simply remaining in her own room, sorting through the newspaper clippings on biological and ecological matters from the past half year. Just before dusk, she spent another half hour watching the seabirds flying over Shataukok bay with her telescope, while also taking some notes. For years, Nga Chi had been submitting observation reports on migratory and resident birds to the local bird-watching society. In order to bird-watch more conveniently, she had installed a tripod with a telescope and a camera with a wide-angle lens on the front of her veranda, but that evening was the first time that year she had seen a visiting red-legged sandpiper.

When Virginia came out from the interview, Nga Chi, seeing it was already late in the day, cleaned up a nearby unit that happened to be empty and invited Virginia to sleep over. This was the place Nga Chi and the Dictator had purchased with a mortgage five years earlier together with their current house, at a time when their household's financial situation had begun to improve, and when Nga Chi had just quit her job as a pharmacist and instead started working in a Traditional Chinese Medicine research center. The house was located in a small village called Wooshekok, in the Shataukok border zone. Because the former owner, whom Nga Chi had known for many years, was an old lady whose son had invited her to come live with him in England, and there was no one to look after this desolate property, not to mention that it had no potential to appreciate in value, she decided to sell it at a bargain-basement price. Nga Chi purchased the house, as well as another unit in a building next door. Originally she had planned to arrange for her elderly father to live there, but her Auntie Lok, who had been looking after her father, found the location too remote, and Nga Chi thus abandoned the plan. She then considered renting out the apartment but had trouble finding tenants, though for a short time she did rent it to a foreign woman who was teaching English in a local high school.

Later, as the scope of the interviews kept expanding and their contents became increasingly detailed, Virginia simply moved in and even considered transforming the interview into a full-fledged biography. Nga Chi did not object to this idea. Indeed, from the moment she first saw Virginia, she had really liked the girl. Although Nga Chi had been working for many years and her son was already in college, she nevertheless usually found it very easy to like someone new. She did feel it somewhat odd, however, that her husband had agreed to the interview. After they lost their son Fa, the couple, together with their remaining son, Guo, had moved to this remote seaside house in Shataukok, and since then the boy's father had barely left the house. Nga Chi remembered how, seventeen years earlier, the first time she and her husband had driven out here to see the house, she had felt as though they had reached the end of the world. The sea was so calm, with no wind or waves, and the couple standing in front of it was similarly silent. After this, Nga Chi and her husband both settled in. Later, her husband's health deteriorated, with him losing the use of both legs, so he very rarely left the house. Before they moved in, which was probably around the time he began hinting that he wanted to write a novel about <u>baby universes</u>, he had already stopped attending all literary events, also declining all interviews. Regardless of whether the person requesting the interview was an enthusiastic friend from the literary world or a reporter who was simply doing his job, everyone was rejected at the door. He even had Nga Chi come up with all sorts of acceptable reasons on his behalf. Visitors thereupon gradually began to wane, until finally tapering off altogether. It had already been more than ten years since anyone remembered the existence of the person known as the Dictator, or the books he had written. Who would have thought that, after so many years, a young woman would suddenly show up and announce that she wanted to write a biography of the Dictator?

The young woman had managed to find the telephone number of the Traditional Chinese Medicine research institute where Nga Chi worked. Nga Chi, however, could not take responsibility for agreeing to this sort of thing, and she was also certain that her husband would refuse. However, out of politeness, she agreed to relay the girl's request. That night, Nga Chi—using their son Guo as intermediary—told her husband about the request. Although Nga Chi had not spoken with her husband since they lost their son Fa seventeen years earlier, she could not avoid using common directives, such as "yes" and "no," or "here" and "there." There was certainly nothing, however, that could count as serious conversation. It was primarily because of the incident involving their son Fa that Nga Chi had stopped speaking to her husband, though she did realize that there was no single factor that had led to this outcome. As for what those other factors might have been, she was even now not completely certain. In any event, the two of them spent the following seventeen years in silence, during which time the only way the household had any hint of life was through the conversations each of them had with their son Guo. Whenever there was anything fairly complicated that one of them had to communicate to the other, they would use Guo as a relay. Guo had grown accustomed to playing this role from an early age and didn't find anything odd in the way his parents interacted with each other. Even if all three of them were together, everything that Nga Chi and the child's father said to each other would have to be said twice, the first time when it was spoken to Guo and the second time when Guo would repeat the same thing to his other parent. This sort of arrangement did not necessarily imply antagonism or deadlock, and at times you could even say that the result was relaxed and natural. Sometimes, they would even crack jokes together. However, Nga Chi and her husband would never speak directly to each other. This time, because Nga Chi was conveying a request on behalf of someone else, however, she made an effort to communicate to Guo as succinctly as possible the request for an interview, and without altering a single word Guo relayed this request to his father, who remained unmoved, as Nga Chi had expected. Later, she casually added, *Baba should know that the girl's name is Virginia, Virginia, but she introduced herself using the Cantonese transliteration of her name: wai chun nai ah.* To her surprise, their son's father then promptly changed his mind. Nga Chi immediately understood: his unexpected decision was entirely on account of a name.

Nga Chi suddenly remembered another name. The first time she saw Virginia, she was reminded of Tatiana Larina, the female protagonist of Pushkin's *Eugene Onegin*. At the time, Nga Chi had been driving to go pick up Virginia, and they had agreed to meet at the side entrance to the Fanling train station. Gazing out the car window, which was covered with drizzle, Nga Cha felt as though she were in a film scene of a moving car as she searched for her objective among the people who were coming and going. She was almost immediately certain that the young woman sitting on a low stone wall under the tree—reading a book and seemingly oblivious to the drizzle—was in fact Virginia. The girl was sitting cross-legged, and in her lap she was holding a book, as her thick brown hair fell on either side of her face. Although there was still a slight chill in the early spring air, the girl was wearing a wide-collared dress that exposed her shoulders and chest, and even from a distance Nga Chi could discern her sumptuous Western physique. The girl had an assortment of pinkish white bauhinia blossoms in her hair, which matched well enough with her nondescript rice-colored dress. Nga Chi parked her car on the side of the road in front of the girl, then rolled down her window. The girl looked up, instantly figured things out, and broke into a candid but somewhat bashful smile. Even sitting down, she gave the impression of being very large, and when she stood up she appeared to be significantly taller than the average person, though her demeanor was still that of a young girl. As Virginia got into the car, her head almost hit the roof. In a childish manner, she bowed her head and greeted Nga Chi in a perfect local accent.

Nga Chi saw that the tattered green pages of the book Virginia was hugging to her chest were rubbing against her white skin, as though she were unconsciously connoting something both innocent but also a bit overly bold. Nga Chi recognized the book as being the last novel that the Dictator had published, after which he had produced no more books. Nga Chi didn't know why she suddenly thought of Tatiana. Perhaps it was because Virginia had an Asian quality to her features, making her look a bit Russian, perhaps it was because she had a calm external demeanor but an inner enthusiasm, or perhaps it was that she appeared to have an almost naive faith in books.

On the road to Shataukok, Nga Chi and Virginia had a simple conversation, and Nga Chi learned a bit about Virginia's background. Virginia's father was English and a university biology professor. When he was young, he had lived for more than ten years in V City, where he had been responsible for suburban wildlife preservation in the civil affairs office, while at the same time writing and editing an illustrated handbook of V City's dragonflies. Nga Chi also owned an illustrated handbook of dragonflies but couldn't remember whether or not it was the one edited by Virginia's father. It had been a long time since she had last taken that sort of handbook with her when she went on an observation hike through the wilderness outside the city. Virginia's mother was a second-generation overseas Chinese whose family was originally from V City and had emigrated to England. Like Virginia's father, her mother also worked at the university, where she taught English literature. **My mother is wholly British in her mentality. She never talks about her Chinese heritage. Oddly enough, it's my father who is always urging me to learn about my roots.** Virginia said this very naturally in English and then switched back to the local dialect, speaking slowly and carefully: *It was one year ago that I came to V City for the first time. At that time, I had just graduated with a major in* **Oriental Studies** *and told my mother that I wanted to come take a look. I always felt that that I had a special connection to the place, but I didn't know what precisely it was. I therefore wanted to come and take a look for myself. Furthermore, I wanted to use V City's local literature as the topic of my* **postgraduate** *studies. After I arrived, I learned the local dialect. Ever since I was small my* **daddy** *had wanted me to learn Chinese, so I had no trouble with reading or writing. My* **daddy** *knew Chinese, and my* **grandma** *would often speak to me in the local dialect of V*

*City, so I learned it quickly. I also used an invitation by my former profes-
sor to participate in a research project on local literature hosted by a university in V City, for which I helped collect materials and interview local
authors. I read an old book from twenty or thirty years ago, in which the
thing that most attracted me was the author, the Dictator. Why so? I don't
know how to explain it. Perhaps the reason I've come here is precisely to
try to figure it out. In his first collection of stories, there is a short piece
called "The Story of the Piecing Together of Virginia in a Fast-Food Restaurant." That must have been his first short story, wasn't it? To tell the
truth, I felt the story was quite good at a technical level, but—how should I
put it?—to use an English term, I would say that it was a bit **naive**, and
very immature. However, I must say I was very **impressed**, and it left a
strong impression on me. Was it because the protagonist had the same
name as myself?* **Well, I don't know! Maybe! Anyway,** *I very much wanted
to go find him, but everyone said that it had been a long time since there
had been any news of the Dictator. There were even some professors who
felt he was not very important, and that he did not have any research value.
Everyone said that there was no chance I would ever find him, but because
of that research project on local literature, I was able to meet a retired biology professor who said he knew that the Dictator's wife works in a Traditional Chinese Medicine research center, so I gave you a call. It was truly a*
coincidence. I'm really lucky! *That is how I found you.*

Nga Chi listened intently as she gripped the steering wheel, smiling as
she nodded in response to Virginia's remarks. When Virginia mentioned
the retired biology professor, Nga Chi asked casually how she had met
him. Virginia explained that it had been when she was conducting her
interviews: *Although he was a biologist by training, he was also a local
essayist. His essays were not bad at all, and he was very active in the literary arena. Last year, he was asked to serve as an adviser to the local literature research plan. That is how I found him. He said he wanted to extend
the tradition of linking science and literature, which is to say the practice—
which can be traced back to the French scientists* **Buffon** *and* **Fabre***—of
using literary methods and sensibilities to write about scientific topics, or
alternatively doing the reverse, and using sensibilities associated with
the natural sciences to write literature.* Nga Chi felt Virginia's story was
uncannily familiar, but she simply said, *You seem to know a lot about
these things.* Virginia replied with a straight face, **Please be reminded**

that my father is a natural history scholar! Since my early years I've been as familiar with these names as if they were my relatives. Frankly speaking, I like Fabre's style, but I don't agree with his misanthropic sentiments. He loves wasps more than his neighbors! The girl couldn't help breaking into laughter, but Nga Chi just nodded silently. In front of them was a long straight road without a single car, and Nga Chi pressed down too hard on the gas pedal without realizing it.

Virginia glanced at the mountains on either side of the road, then suddenly changed the subject, saying, *Isn't there a Dragon Village nearby? Dragon, meaning* **Dragon**. *It is in the mountains. I think I have relatives living there. My* **grandmother** *grew up in Dragon Village, but after she went to England, she lost contact with her relatives. After all these years, my mother has never come back to take a look.* **She doesn't care!** *If it hadn't been for the fact that* **Grandma** *would occasionally discuss it, I wouldn't have known that I was originally from there.* **I wonder if the village still exists. I don't know anybody there, but I really want to go and see it. It would be an extraordinary experience to see Grandma's birthplace.** Nga Chi laughed but didn't say anything. The car entered a stretch of road where both sides were lined with enormous melaleucas, whose intertwined canopies completely covered the arrow-straight, downhill road. This was a stretch of road that Nga Chi thought of as a tunnel of time, where it seemed as though the car were floating weightlessly. The shadowy trees opened up in front of her like mottled columns and swept past her. Time rushed by at a dizzying speed, but it was unclear whether it was proceeding forward or backward. Nga Chi glanced at the Eurasian girl beside her and said, *My grandpa and grandma are both northerners, but when my father was born they were living in V-Cheng. My mother, on the other hand, is a local. I have small eyes, thick eyebrows, and white skin, and in winter my face turns red very easily. When I was growing up, people would often ask whether I was from the mainland. However, my parents separated when I was twelve. My three sisters all went with my father.* Virginia asked, *Are you the eldest daughter in your family?* Nga Chi replied, *Don't I seem so?* Virginia said, *I am too, but I have a younger brother. What about your mother?* Nga Chi replied, *Mother remarried but would still see us often. Father lived with a woman we called Auntie Lok, and even when they later married, we still called her Auntie Lok.* Virginia then asked, *Then what about you?* Nga Chi didn't understand, *What about me?* Virginia said,

Did you ever fight with your parents? Nga Chi smiled and shook her head and said, *I respected their decision. They are adults. I'm sure they had their reasons for what they did. When I was young I didn't really understand, but I also didn't pay much attention. Once I was older and had more experience, however, I finally understood.* Nga Chi glanced at the girl's suddenly somber expression.

Nga Chi left the veranda and returned to her bedroom, located on the first floor of the house. As she was closing the window, she saw through the veranda railing the girl wading in the shallow water suddenly turn around, reach up, and grab her long hair, then glance over in Nga Chi's direction. At that instant, there appeared to be a flash in the mist-filled spring sky, but it was not followed by the sound of thunder. Nga Chi shook her head and smiled at her own rambling imagination. Then she draped her cape over the back of a chair, opened the door, and stepped carefully into the hallway. In the hallway, in front of the steps, there was a full-length mirror hanging from the wall. Standing ten steps away, Nga Chi looked at the reflection of her short self. She was wearing sweat pants and a loose-fitting white T-shirt—the kind she had been used to wearing ever since she was young. Her hair was in a ponytail, and since there wasn't much light and you couldn't clearly see her middle-aged face, she could have been mistaken for her younger self from thirty years earlier. The reflection in the mirror stood there silently, appearing to be unable to make up its mind whether to move or not. Nga Chi paused and looked more carefully than she ordinarily did and suddenly realized that, even after thirty years, she was still the same naive girl she had once been. Everything she thought she knew was merely the product of habit. Nga Chi lifted her wrist and realized that she had not yet put on her watch. At this point, the sound of the clocks chiming the hour could be heard coming from her son Guo's room. It was seven o'clock. Nga Chi noticed that between the dozen or so chimes, there were a couple of irregular rings, and she suspected that perhaps one of the clocks was malfunctioning. She thought, When Guo returns from college for the weekend, I'll have to tell him. As she passed through the side room, she glanced inside at the painting implements but immediately turned away and somewhat shyly brushed by the reflection of herself in the mirror. Her husband's room was upstairs, and not a sound could be heard from behind the tightly closed door. She walked lightly downstairs, then proceeded into the kitchen, where she fixed breakfast. From more than ten years, Nga Chi had been waking up at the break of dawn every morning, preparing breakfast for her husband and son. After waiting for her husband's day nurse to arrive, Nga Chi would then drive to work, and on her way she would drop her son off at school. As for daily household tasks, in the early years she would always do them herself, so she would have to work non-stop after returning home from her day job. More recently, however, their family's financial situation had improved, and Nga Chi was able to hire an auntie from a nearby village to work as a maid, which significantly lightened her own workload. When her son Guo started college and moved into a dormitory, Nga Chi became the only person in the family who would still go out regularly. However, she never objected to the dull solitude. Her car was like an old friend and would accompany her every day when she went out. When out driving alone, she even got into the habit of talking to herself while listening to music, as though she were chatting with the car. She would speak more while driving alone in her car than she would while at home or in the office.

When the doorbell rang, Nga Chi had just placed two bowls of oatmeal with dried fruit on the table. She opened the door and found that her visitor was neither the nurse nor the maid but was none other than Virginia. Virginia was wearing her light-green dress and was holding her notebook behind her. She was wearing sandals, but her feet had been rinsed clean. There was only her wet skirt to serve as evidence that the scene Nga Chi had observed from her veranda was not a fiction. Nga Chi said Tanya, and Virginia responded with a smile, as though she had already accepted this new form of address. The two of them hurried over to the dining table and sat down, and after Nga Chi finished saying grace, they began eating their oatmeal; you could hear the sound of their metal spoons striking the sides of the porcelain bowls. When Virginia finished, she opened the notebook she had placed on the table. She then took out a folded-up pho-tocopied document and handed it to Nga Chi, saying, **You may be inter-ested in this.** Nga Chi took the document, immediately realizing it was the transcript of her interviews with the Dictator. She said thank you and put the document next to her place at the table. Then she got up to go to the kitchen to get some more oatmeal. She brought out a tray with eggs and toast and asked if it was okay if Virginia took them upstairs. Virginia immediately stood up, took the tray, and carefully proceeded up the narrow staircase. This was normally the responsibility of the nurse, Wai Yan, but over the past few days Virginia had taken it over, in this way it becoming a new habit without their even needing to discuss it. Virginia was tall and made people feel safe, though the wooden staircase produced a loud creaking sound, as if under stress. Nga Chi looked up and saw Virginia, like a marble statue, disappear up the staircase. In a quiet voice, she quickly reminded Virginia that she had left the tape recorder on the desk, telling Virginia that if she wanted to use it, she should go get it. From upstairs, she heard Virginia's soft voice saying thanks, as light as the sigh of a sprite.

Nga Chi picked up the document on the dining table but didn't read it. Instead, she stood in front of the living room window with a mild smile, squinting at a small skiff drifting on the sea. The skiff moved silently across the window frame, as though it had been muffled. Nga Chi suddenly felt as if she couldn't stand it anymore and stepped forward to open the window, but what flowed in was just an even thicker silence. She didn't feel she had even been there very long but then suddenly looked up at the clock, tucked the manuscript under her arm, and rushed upstairs. Looking up at her husband's room at the top of the stairs, she didn't hear any movement inside. Trying to walk as quietly as possible, Nga Chi returned to her own bedroom. She placed the document on her desk, planning to read it after she returned in the evening. The mini cassette recorder that had been there, however, was now missing. To one side there were several watercolors of plants, which looked as though they had been slightly moved from their original position. In front of the paintings there were three pots of recently planted asparagus ferns, each with new stems poking up out of the soil, which were already beginning to sprout tender green leaves. These shoots had been taken from the old fern in the first floor side room. The fern's shadow happened to fall on the folded painting of a white narcissus flower lying on the desk. Nga Chi slightly shifted the orientation of the bonsai light, then briskly changed into the light-brown dress she wore to work, put on some low-heeled leather shoes, and picked up her briefcase. As she was taking her watch from the desk drawer, she couldn't resist glancing again at the manuscript lying there. This was the same beginning portion of the interview she had, in a moment of distraction, already listened to on the tape recorder. The words printed on the page gave her a sense of unfamiliarity, seemingly completely disassociated from the dialogue she had heard on the tape—as though it had become ossified. She saw the first sentence the Dictator had uttered upon accepting the interview with Virginia: I am a symptom, and if there is any point in writing about me, that would be the only reason. Without realizing it, Nga Chi read this sentence out loud in a low voice, as if attempting to bring it back to life. Then she put on her watch and smoothly placed the manuscript into her briefcase.

As she was driving down the shady street toward the entrance of the village, Nga Chi ran into the nurse, Wai Yan, who had just gotten off the minibus. Nga Chi stopped the car to greet Wai Yan. It actually wasn't that Wai Yan was running late but rather that Nga Chi had left the house earlier than usual. Even so, the nurse appeared deeply embarrassed. Nga Chi asked Wai Yan if she wanted a ride, but Wai Yan said there was no need and smiled as she waved good-bye, then, carrying a heavy bag that looked as though it contained paints, she proceeded into the village. When the girl smiled, she revealed very prominent dimples. Nga Chi liked Wai Yan's dimples. In contrast to the uncertain look in her eyes, Wai Yan's dimples projected a feeling of directness and permanence. Nga Chi watched the twentysomething girl as she gradually receded out of sight, and suddenly felt bad for her—it was really unacceptable for her to be wasting her youth in this isolated place, performing such a monotonous job. Therefore, when a little earlier Wai Yan had asked if she could use the first-floor side room as a studio, so that she might paint in her spare time, Nga Chi had immediately agreed. At the same time, Nga Chi had asked Wai Yan to paint her some plants that she could use to decorate the house.

Nga Chi drove onto the highway. In this area, even what they called highways were very narrow, and on either side of the flat, straight road there were only uncultivated fields and an occasional village. Up ahead, however, there was a winding section where the road circled around a fairly dense forest, after which it became straight and flat again. After passing Luen Wo Hui, it became the municipality of Fanling. Traffic was not very heavy in the morning, but because she was stuck behind a container truck on a one-lane road, she proceeded very slowly. Nga Chi didn't care, however. She never became anxious while driving, not to mention that she was driving an underpowered car. Nga Chi liked small vehicles. Her first car had been a cheap, secondhand Japanese four-seater, which she drove for nearly ten years, not giving it up until it had reached the point that it could no longer be repaired. After that, she had bought another small car by the same maker, which she was still driving today. Although it was now old, and had many problems, Nga Chi nevertheless had no intention of trading it in. The car's stereo was playing Bach's *St. Matthew Passion*. Nga Chi found the word **passion** very interesting and recently had been listening to this piece over and over. The chorus and the arias made her feel very peaceful. The container truck in front of her finally left the main road, turning into a side road heading north, and in her rearview mirror she didn't see any cars behind her. All of a sudden the road became oddly quiet, and at this point the car reached that stretch of road Nga Chi called the entrance to the tunnel of time. The mist over the road became thicker, which made the scenery appear even more indistinct. Nga Chi peered down at her wristwatch, then pulled over into a lay-by. She looked at her watch again. It was a self-winding woman's watch her son Guo had given her, tubular in shape, with a black leather band, and was the most expensive thing she owned. Nga Chi had originally declined the gift. She had always worn battery-powered plastic watches and was not used to wearing something so expensive. But eventually she began wearing it every day. Nga Chi turned on her car's hazard lights, gripping the steering wheel with both hands as she stared intently through the windshield at the white mist outside, as though wanting to see something lying behind it. She then took the manuscript out of her briefcase, turned on the light inside the car, and carefully began to read it.[2]

The interview ended here. Nga Chi fell silent. Virginia's Chinese-writing ability was better than Nga Chi had expected, to the point that she found it virtually unbelievable. It was almost as if the transcript had been written by someone else. She also noticed that there were some discrepancies between the written transcript of the interview and what she had heard on the tape, but she couldn't remember where precisely the differences lay, nor did she did know which version was more accurate. Perhaps, they were both equally accurate, or perhaps they each had their own separate accuracy. At this point, the music playing over the car stereo reached a particularly emotional segment and sounded as swift and violent as an earthquake or a thunderstorm. Nga Chi was startled back to reality. She turned off the stereo as well as the dome light. The vehicle fell into a twilight silence, with the only sound the white noise of the air-conditioning. The fog outside became thicker and thicker. Nga Chi stepped on the clutch, released the hand brake, switched on her right-hand turn signal, then honked a couple of times at the indistinct road. When the sound returned from that stretch of road in front of her that she called the tunnel of time, it sounded like spring thunder. Nga Chi looked up, peering at the white sky visible through the tree canopy above her, but it was as if she hadn't heard a thing.

CHAPTER 7, PART III

ANNUS

Seventeen years sounds like just a number and is not easier to comprehend than a single year. At the very least, one year is a single cycle: the amount of time it takes the earth to revolve around the sun. It is three hundred sixty-five and a quarter days. But why can't seventeen years also be a single cycle? There is a seventeen-year cicada, which hatches, matures, breeds, and dies once every seventeen years. Then the next generation lies dormant underground for another seventeen years. This is what the number seventeen means to you. This is how I reassure myself when I think of how I've wasted the past seventeen years. Seventeen years ago there was a cause, and seventeen years later there is an effect. Fa's loss has long since been buried underground, and I thought it had long since been completely repressed. But now it has suddenly hatched, emerged from the soil, and crawled up the trees. That which died long ago appears to have come back to life and furthermore is now maturing rapidly, making what sound like mating calls as it craves the extension and reproduction of life. However, who will respond to this call? For the past seventeen years, Nga Chi has been continually guarding this tree. Half the tree is already withered, but the other half still bears fruit every year. Nga Chi resembles an ascetic monk, continuing to water the tree every day, hoping for the other half to come back to life and blossom. Meanwhile, the cicadas have finally emerged and crawled up to the crown of the tree, drinking the sap of the living half of the tree and singing loudly. This is because you have arrived, Virginia. You are producing another cicada call. So you imagine the Virginia who is forever seventeen. In the possible universe, which permits the twisting of time and space, we will encounter each other in the library of the future, using text to woo, sing in harmony, copulate, get pregnant, give birth, and face death. But Nga Chi continues to keep watch and lend assistance. This is what you yourself call a form of redemption—or, to be more accurate, you could say it is your form of wishful thinking. You attempt to use metaphors to satisfy your vestigial desire, as well as your own mode of extinction. I, meanwhile, yearn to collaborate with you but refuse to play the role of a conspirator. On what basis would I dare say that I could give birth again to Fa for you? On what basis would I dare say that I am completing that which Nga Chi was not able to complete? In the end, only Nga Chi is qualified to accompany you to the grave and to enjoy your hard-earned result from the past seventeen years. And this result is in itself necessarily a bitter one.

Part 1 of the Annals. 1967: The Dictator was born. 1997: The Dictator and Nga Chi married. 2002: The twins Fa and Guo were born. 2005: The Dictator wrote *Yan Yan and the Baby Universe*; he lost his son Fa at the ice rink; the Dictator's health deteriorated, and he moved into the house by the shore in Shataukok. The Dictator hid out in Shataukok, bedridden, for seventeen years. 2022: Guo turned twenty; the Eurasian girl Virginia arrived at the seaside house to interview the Dictator and went on to coauthor *Virginia's Heartbeat* with him; the literary little universe was restructured and failed; the ice-skating mural was created; the car that Nga Chi was driving with the Dictator plunged into a pond. 2030: Guo's daughter, Virginia, was born. 2037: Virginia was seven years old and had an accident at the skating rink that caused her to become deaf. 2047: Virginia was seventeen years old; her father transformed her heart into a mechanical clock, and she moved into the library, where she remained seventeen years old forever. Fifty years later, Fa traveled through time, appearing in the library. The year was 2097. This kind of chronological arrangement is full of beautiful symmetry: Before 2022, everything was factual; afterward, everything was imagined but nevertheless could not be excluded from the realm of possibility. The crucial turning point that is key to all this lies between 2022 and 2030, when something happened between Guo and the Eurasian Virginia. As for the Virginia who was born afterward, she was the daughter of Guo and someone else—but who that someone else might be we can't be sure of. Perhaps she was the daughter of the Eurasian Virginia, but perhaps she wasn't. But if she wasn't, then why would Guo name his daughter Virginia? However, perhaps these doubts have no real bearing on what would come later, so that this is instead completely the product of my personal curiosity. Since you have already decided on this sort of structure, I have no intention of changing it. Regardless of whether it is as the former Virginia or the latter one, I am a character in these annals. At the same time, however, I am also their author. Meanwhile, little Virginia will inherit my historical and fictional fate. Therefore, in 2097, in the library, Virginia began to write *Annals of the Little Universe*, also known as *Biography of a Little Person*.

Ever since she followed the train tracks on her return from her trip north, Virginia had been engaged in writing. She wanted to write a book that would revolve around that lake district. The azure lake water summoned up some of her past memories, spurring her to speculate about the future. Perhaps she had already entertained such fantasies. These fantasies are inspired and formed by what she read in books in the library over the preceding fifty years. Apart from literary works, the fantasies also touch on history, science, religion, art, philosophy, politics, society, and economics. In reality, for her these disciplinary divisions no longer had any meaning, because in her consciousness, there is no form of knowledge that is not already permeated and distorted by another form. In the end, all these different forms of knowledge are distorted and smelted together, yielding a work of fiction. Because the library had recovered a portion of its electricity supply, Virginia could write on her computer. Most computers had been discarded years before and could no longer be booted up, and there was only one that functioned normally. Virginia limbered up her fingers and began typing on the keyboard, as though playing a piano piece that she once knew well. She set aside virtually all her daily maintenance responsibilities in the library and threw herself into her writing. Even as she was enthusiastically writing, accordingly, the state of the library gradually deteriorated. Dust accumulated everywhere, and the books got slowly eaten up by silverfish. Books were taken down and left everywhere, with the filing system beginning to fall apart. A book that was misfiled would be extremely difficult to find again and therefore would virtually disappear in the forest of books. In the end, there was no longer any order or classification system to speak of, and everything was simply random and fortuitous. Whom are you talking about? Who was it that created this situation? It could have been me, but it also could have been any of the countless ghosts residing in the library. Why would anyone want to do this? Perhaps it was a practical joke, or perhaps it was a reaction to a long-standing sense of repression by a regime of order. Perhaps it was an act of revenge against the library, or perhaps it was an expression of love for Virginia. What kind of love? Why this kind of love? Perhaps it was an attempt to prevent Virginia from writing this book, or perhaps it was because after she finished writing this book the library would no longer have any need to exist and Virginia would therefore be released. In the end, however, Virginia could always find the materials she needed, like a bird able to rely on its instinct to easily locate its own offspring among thousands of other chicks. Or, perhaps she simply no longer needed to find any more materials—since all the material was already in her consciousness, forming a self-sufficient world.

I stared at Virginia, who was sitting at the end of the reading room, and walked over. Outside, it had been raining continuously, while inside it was unusually humid. It was a sunless summer afternoon. Sweat was pouring down my forehead, and it was as if I could hear the sound of the droplets of sweat falling onto the floor. No, perhaps that was only the sound of the raindrops hitting the windows, or the faint sound of her fingers striking the keyboard. With her back to me, Virginia sat down on the piano bench, her snow-white bottom on the black-leather bench creating an oval depression, just like how, in science books, the space-time continuum is deformed by gravity. The movement of her typing was like a slight trembling, and her uneven shoulders seemed to be supporting a balance that could collapse at any time. She was in a state of focused attention, and I was afraid of disturbing her, so I stopped several steps behind her. Her back was covered in tiny droplets of sweat, like powdered silver, and when viewed from the side they gave off a dull sparkle. Sweat-covered strands of hair stuck to her bare shoulders, with droplets of sweat hanging from the tips of her hair. The drops of sweat rolled down the curvature of her back, and as they proceeded they accumulated more moisture and increased in both size and speed, before disappearing into the cleft between her buttocks, as though being drawn into that depression in the space-time continuum. My gaze passed over her head, until it struck the glass wall in front of her. Behind the glass wall, there was a stairwell, a dark cavity leading to the lobby downstairs. On the glass, there was a transparent reflection of an old man, like a specter. The old man stood behind the typing girl. I touched my own cheeks and found that they were in fact covered in wrinkles. That was my true age at this moment. Virginia must have noticed the movement of the light, so she turned around, but when she saw it was me she did not appear terribly surprised. In her light-brown pupils there appeared two reflections of myself in my old age, but I couldn't be certain which version of myself she was seeing. In the slight opening created when she had moved her upper body, I was able to see that her computer monitor was full of Chinese characters, like pictures, architectural plans, human figures, or a row of objects. She moved to make room on the right-hand side of the bench and gestured for me to come over and sit down. In the center of the cushion was a depression with a peach-shaped sweat stain. She leaned forward and reached out to type on the keyboard. On the computer monitor, a sentence appeared: You have finally arrived. She removed her hands to be replaced by mine, which also typed something on the keyboard: I finally understand that we are separated by fifty years of time. She smiled, then typed in response, Between you and yourself, there is also a gulf of fifty years. I typed, What does that mean? She typed, I mean that the seventy-year-old you is encountering the twenty-year-old you.

Your hands were still resting on the keyboard, but your gaze was leading him forward. Behind the glass wall, in the dark stairwell, the figure of a young person was emerging. The youth looked like a figure who had just stepped out of a Renaissance painting: He was completely naked, his hands and feet long and elegant, and his skin seemed to emit a white aura, like an angel. When he reached the top of the stairs, the youth turned around and gazed back at you with his jet-black pupils. His pupils were familiar to you. In the past, these jet-black pupils, appearing against a snow-white background, had attracted you, like stars. His straight back, powerful legs, and supple buttocks simultaneously supported you and cast you aside, such that you spun around in midair before returning to his embrace. You saw yourself stand up, run up to him, and hold him tight. The two of you are the universally known golden boy and jade girl.

The golden boy and jade girl are passionately kissing, skin rubbing against skin, sweat mixing with sweat. The two of you bumped into the bookcase, knocking down books, which thereby became your carnal mat. In the midst of your ecstatic panting, you turn around and glance back at the old man sitting on the piano bench. Originally occupying the position of an onlooker, the old man was suddenly drawn into the scene as an intense feeling of jealousy rose up in his heart. On the monitor there appeared the words, He is your twenty-year-old self. But I don't recall having this sort of encounter with you when I was twenty. Perhaps it really didn't happen. That is your twenty-year-old self traveling through time to arrive in the present, to have an encounter with me. But the old you of today is jealous of your younger self from fifty years ago. Yes, it is indeed jealousy. A horrifying thought occurred to me: I wanted to murder my younger self from fifty years earlier. That twenty-year-old youth definitely doesn't have the right to enjoy, at a different point in time, something lost fifty years earlier. As for me, after painstakingly waiting and searching for fifty years, I have finally become merely a pathetic bystander. However, if you murder your twenty-year-old self, will the present-day you still exist? I don't know, but if I do this, it will not be only out of jealousy. Who would kill themselves out of jealousy? Do you know? That year, it was precisely in order to prevent this eventuality that your father sent you into the library. Why is that? Why did your father want to prevent us from falling in love? Didn't he once fall in love with a Eurasian girl named Virginia? And didn't he give the name Virginia to his own daughter? Why, then, did he want to turn around and attempt to control his daughter's affections, even transforming her heart into a mechanical clock in order to have her follow an unfeeling set of rules and procedures? When these text banners stopped flashing across the monitor, there was a pause, after which there appeared the following response: It is because that attractive youth who crossed through space-time, whose name is Fa, is none other than the twin brother whom your father lost when he was three. The images of the youth and the older man suddenly disappeared, as if the monitor had malfunctioned. You lay alone on the pile of books, your body covered in sweat. There was no one sitting on the piano bench in front of the computer, merely a depression from the person who had been sitting there, and the peach-shaped sweat stain left behind on the black leather cushion was slowly disappearing through evaporation. A new sentence automatically appeared on the computer monitor. Your stomach begins to quickly expand, like the beginning of the universe, then your lower body begins to experience a series of painful rhythmic contractions. One cycle of pain after another emanates up from your abdomen, as though it were being run over by thousands upon thousands of soldiers and horses, until finally they reach your head. You saw the head that resembled a small fruit being pushed out through your vaginal orifice. Blood and water covered the ground and were gradually absorbed by the books.

A tiny infant was born from between your legs. You vaguely remember that something like this once occurred, before you moved into the library. However, perhaps that was merely your imagination, or perhaps it was a fictitious experience derived from a birthing manual. What you gave birth to was a three-year-old Fa—a beautiful baby boy. He was born onto the book-covered floor. He didn't cry but rather merely looked scared and confused, as though he didn't know where was. He resembled a terrified small animal, and in the library's forest of books he began to run around blindly, as if trying to find an exit in order to return whence he had come. He didn't know that he had already been expelled from one space-time and cast into another. You chased after him, trying to comfort him, but he simply fled even faster, until he was exhausted, then collapsed in the middle of the lobby and began bawling. You came up and embraced and comforted him, saying, Fa, don't be afraid; your sister is here. Even if you lose the rest of your family, you'll still have me. I won't let you be lonely and won't let you endure alone the agony of the tearing apart of time. I won't let you think for a moment that you have been abandoned by the world. Irrespective of how unfeeling the earth and heavens might be, I want you to experience love. But if you really do lose the world, I will create a new world that will belong just to you. As long as I'm here, you will not go lacking. As long as you are still young, I will be your mother; after you grow up, I will be your lover; and when you are old, I will become your daughter. As for that ice rink, we shouldn't even think of returning there. It is a frightening place that is full of space-time traps, and if you are not careful you may fall into a wormhole. The tracks of time in the ice rink resemble crisscrossed years. Yes, we met there, and not just once, but we should never again be separated from each other there. Fa gradually stopped crying, his gaze fixated on a single point revealing a tiny smile. You lifted your head and looked in the direction of the child's gaze and saw there was a girl about seven years old shuttling back and forth between the lobby's tables and chairs. The girl lifted both her hands as she glided forward as though she were ice-skating, and it seemed as though nothing could block her. She disappeared between the bookcases then reappeared and prepared to perform a backward-spinning jump. She didn't notice that there was a reading table in the middle of her tracks. You released Fa from your grasp and stood up. You wanted to shout out, Be careful! But when you opened you mouth, no sound came out. The girl's head smashed into the table, with a loud thud, then she hit the floor. You began to feel dizzy and found that suddenly you couldn't hear a thing.

Part 2 of the Annals. 30XX, the first year of the little universe: The baby universe is born. There are two ways of recording the years: One would be 30XX + 1, 30XX + 2, 30XX + 3, . . . and so on; the second would be the first year of the little universe, the second year of the little universe, the third year of the little universe . . . and so on. The little universe is really V City's entirely new situation postminiaturization. It is said that in the year 30XX − 17, V City experienced a major pestilence that precipitated an economic collapse, which also led to a sudden change in the physiques of the residents of V City, what history has come to call a process of miniaturization. Following this miniaturization, V City split up into a number of smaller city-states or walled cities. In the year 30XX − 3, V City suffered a large-scale ecological disaster, during which many of these city-states were either destroyed or abandoned, and the miniaturized people of V City either fled to sea or else retreated north. In the year 30XX, a fluctuation in the gravitational field resulting from undetermined factors caused the V City region to partially fall into a different time-space configuration. An unusual closed space-time body formed in a basin originally located to the north of V City, surrounding a lake at the center of the municipality of Fanling. This closed space-time body was separate from the external world, so it was difficult to determine the status of the "exterior," or even whether or not it continued to exist at all. As a result, countless speculative questions, such as the relationship between the "exterior" and the "interior," between "fundamentals" and "contingencies," and between "self" and "other"—all offered future philosophers unlimited avenues for investigation. Meanwhile, the stability or habitability of this new space-time body depended on the fact that it was simultaneously a closed ecosystem. This closed ecosystem was protected from the dome of polluted atmosphere; the northern portion was separated from the mainland on account of the flooding of a polluted river; the southern portion was separated from the original city on account of topographic changes resulting from rising sea levels; the eastern portion was shielded by forests and high mountains; while to the west lay a continuous string of miasmic swamps. The great lake in the center of the system was called Blue Lake, on account of its distinctive color. Because of its relative miniaturization and its autonomous system, combined with the fact that its residents had been miniaturized, the first-stage builders called this ecosystem a little universe. This expression subsequently became widely accepted and became the common name. Because it remains in a newborn state, some people suggested the phrase _baby universe_, which became an alternative—and informal—term for the little universe. As for the question of the little universe's calendar, an animated debate erupted among early chronologians, with some arguing that the new calendar should follow the lead of natural scientists and begin with the year when the space-time body was closed off and the self-contained ecosystem was born, which is to say the year 30XX. Others, however, argued that they should instead follow the lead of political scientists and have the calendar of the little universe begin with the year when the region's first city-state with its own political structure was established—which is to say the year 30XX + 3. Those in favor of the former thought that having the first year of the little universe be the year 30XX was straightforward and easy to understand and believed that the latter arrangement could result in confusion between different chronological systems. In addition, within the little universe, different city-states were established at different times over a period of more than a decade, with the process ongoing. City-states that were established later would not want to have to use the date of the founding of the first city-state as the starting point of their own calendar, so quite a few of the city-states supported the use of the natural-history-based chronology. However, given that there was no commonly accepted higher power structure with sovereignty over all the individual city-states, it was difficult for them to agree upon a shared understanding, much less implement it. Therefore, the first city-state and its neighbors continued to use the latter chronological system, while others did as they pleased, resulting in a variety of alternative chronological systems. The chaos resulting from this arrangement in which every city-state had the power to establish its own chronological system would later create a major headache for the little universe's historians. The same event may have occurred in different years in the chronologies compiled by different city-states, and because of different narratological perspectives, political stances, and presentational methods, it could end up looking as though they were different events. Alternatively, if there were two separate events that arose from similar causes but took place at different times, it could appear as though they were the same event. In order to help clarify and resolve this chaotic situation, in year 97 of the little universe, which is to say the year 30XX + 97 (this is obviously using the natural-history-based dating system), a group of young scholars from the little universe established a "little universe history restructuring operation" and cooperated in advocating the unified use of the natural-history-based chronological system. However, it was not the intention of these scholars to eliminate the simultaneous development of alternative chronological systems, nor did they wish to establish a hegemonic approach to time. However, scholars still found it difficult to escape from the critiques outlined above, and they were in fact in danger of being manipulated by certain powers. Therefore, this eventually developed into a historical movement replete with confusion and contradiction. A key player in the movement was a group of young scholars known as the seven sisters, which included a historian, an archaeologist, a natural scientist, a theologian, a philosopher, an economist, and a novelist. It is possible that these "seven sisters" were actually related by blood, but it is also possible that they were merely nominally allied. In the era of the little universe, because this universe was characterized by a plural history and an unstable space-time matrix, blood relations had become something extraordinarily complicated and difficult to explain. But we'll discuss this later. The names of the seven young authors were Virginia, Victoria, Venus, Viola, Veronica, Vivian, and Vienna. It is hard to say to which generation of the little universe they belonged, since the relationship between different generations had become very fluid. There was only one thing that explains the designation "young," which was that none of them had personally experienced the creation of the little universe. Moreover, contemporaneous with the "little universe history restructuring plan," there began to circulate within the public sphere a proposal that, on the surface, appeared to have a similar objective:

to abolish the common era chronological system altogether. Those advocating this proposal argued that not only was it unnecessary to maintain two separate and parallel common era and little universe calendrical systems, it was also the source of all the current contradiction and confusion. Thus, the only way of rectifying the current chaos was to abolish the common era calendar and retain only the little universe calendar. It was not difficult to discover the difference between the implications of this kind of proposal and that of the "little universe history restructuring plan." An animated debate then emerged between those advocating a dual calendrical system and those advocating a unitary one—together with a separate debate, within the unitary calendar camp, between those advocating a common era calendar and those advocating a little universe calendar. Virginia, who was among those supporting a dual-calendar system, argued, The little universe calendar represents our subjectivity, but the common era calendar represents our only point of contact with the "external" or "former" world. Although for the moment we are unable to confirm the existence of this "external" or "former" world, if we were to lose this sole point of contact with it, we would become an orphan of the universe. We would permanently lose our history, as well as the possibility of understanding ourselves.

A line of words appeared on the computer monitor: Actually, how do you know that this is the fiftieth year since you and I separated? How do you know that the twenty-year-old you see has come from fifty years ago to meet the seventy-year-old you, and that it isn't actually the seventy-year-old you who has gone back fifty years to meet the twenty-year-old you? How can you be sure that it is not the seventy-year-old you who has traveled into the past to meet the seventeen-year-old me, or the seventeen-year-old me who has gone to the future to meet the seventy-year-old you? Or, perhaps it is the seventeen-year-old me and the twenty-year-old you who have gone together to the future library and are meeting there? Or, perhaps it is me, still seventeen years old even after fifty years, and you, still twenty years old even after fifty years, together returning to the ice rink fifty years earlier, where we meet again? No matter whether it is fifty years earlier or fifty years later, the meeting between the seventeen-year-old me and the twenty-year-old you is still exactly the same, as though it were continually replicating itself in mirrors. Or, perhaps they are actually different, but neither side would tolerate it. If we could travel through space-time in this way, would we have been considered to have conquered time? Or, would we merely become slaves of a different sort of time—slaves who have lost their way as a result of being able to travel freely back and forth through time? Because we can no longer tell which you is you, and which me is me; or, which you meets which me, and which me loses which you; or if there exists love and desire between me and you, you and me, me and me, and you and you—it could therefore all very well lead to an enormous web of jealousy, mutual craving, and mutual pursuit to the death. So I prefer to return to a time that advances in a unitary fashion. In that time, all the possible yous and mes—in all possible worlds—would mutually offset one another. In the end, the only thing left would be you and me, here and now. In the year 2097. No, it is the year 2022.

4

THE DREAM DEVOURER

EGOYAN ZHENG

TRANSLATED BY CARA HEALEY

EDITOR'S INTRODUCTION

The novel describes a century-long espionage war between humans and biosynthetics. K, a special agent working for the humans, harbors doubts about his real identity. Through a relationship with his human colleague, Eurydice, K is on a journey seeking the truth about his actual identity— human, machine, or a third kind of being. On December 9, 2219, K hides with Eurydice in a hotel room, where he is immersed in dreams, illusions, and memories of the past: where he came from, what he experienced, what made him self-conscious. The narrative contains dozens of lengthy footnotes that provide crucial information on the plot's development.

CHAPTER 5

December 9, 2219. Early morning. D City. High-rise hotel.

K composed himself and looked behind him.

The woman on the bed breathed evenly, her chest rising and falling.

She was fast asleep. The glossy expanse of her black hair spread across the pillow like silk. In the dim light of the room, the hair gave a strange illusion of diaphanous phosphorescence.

Like the night they first met, the broad slice of moonlight spread thick as jam across the beach.

(Or, technically, not the *first* time they met. But, in short, before that night on the beach, K and Eurydice had been only nodding acquaintances. They did know each other, but before that night, they had only really met once at a training session for new employees of the Seventh Seal. Otherwise, they had just had routine professional interactions, and nothing more.)

K suddenly realized you could describe it this way: At the moment, the black-haired Eurydice, fast asleep on the bed, had just surrendered to her own dreams. In addition to her physical body temporarily going still, her will, her mind, and her emotions all floated through a chaotic, indefinite space and time. There, love and hate, sacred and profane, light and dark, giving and taking, and other such concepts that had originally been in binary opposition were perhaps all intertwined and tangled with one another, so that they were suddenly changed.

They were like something floating through space-time, unstable visions blurring together.

He turned away.

K knew that he himself was very likely the target of the so-called internal investigation, the main culprit of that huge disaster.

Because he was not actually human.

He was a biosynthetic.

Or, more precisely, you could say that K was a double agent for the Federal Government of Humanity and the Biosynthetic Liberation Front. Or, from another perspective, you could say that in K's long career in intelligence, he had never really understood his own identity.

At first, K had thought that it was only a question of deciding whom he wanted to become, not a question of who he had been originally.

It was only a question of urging on a will to reveal itself, not a question of inherently belonging to a given race.

There was only self-determined identity, not innate identity.

K closed his eyes.

K. Human male. Born March 2, 2179, at Bokonon Memorial Hospital, Yangon, Myanmar. His parents had been from a residential district in the southern outskirts of the city. Because he had been slightly premature, the doctors had instructed that he temporarily remain in the hospital for observation. After approximately two weeks, on March 15, a guerrilla band of biosynthetics had initiated a two-pronged incendiary attack on a small military base and an administrative center in southern Yangon. The fire had partly destroyed the base and burned the administrative center to the ground before spreading to the neighboring residential area. Both of K's parents had died in the disaster. After the uprising had been put down, the International Red Cross had provided assistance, and the orphaned K had been raised in a foster home on America's West Coast. In 2198, K had entered university to study molecular biology, and his performance had been outstanding. He had earned his master's degree in 2201 and his doctorate in 2203, at the age of twenty-four.

A fake record. A nonexistent identity.

That was precisely what K had initially crafted for himself: a fabricated person, what was called a life experience.

Even now, K could still clearly recall every detail from memory. *Of course* he could recall the details clearly. It was quite an elaborate scam, taking advantage of a small gap in the system, along with an unlikely incident, as if carved in glass. Only K himself knew that he had with the utmost care built this facade of information, from start to finish. His educational credentials and knowledge level were real, but his family origins, his place of birth, all that was fake. . . .

Yes, K was, in fact, not human. He was a biosynthetic. But the strange thing was, he did not seem like an ordinary biosynthetic.

He was an abandoned biosynthetic.

From the first moments of his life (at age eighteen), he had realized that the process of his creation must have been quite different from that of a typical biosynthetic. K knew that, according to standard procedure, when a biosynthetic left the factory, it ought to have had a unique serial number and possess a certain degree of intellectual capacity, in addition to being aware of and identifying with the fact that it was a biosynthetic. A biosynthetic ought to know its own manufacturing date and factory of origin, as well as the work unit it had been assigned to. According to standard manufacturing procedure, this default data should have been imported via the Dream Implantation technique.

K stood up to turn off the light. The windowpane now reflected the scene inside the room: sofa in the distance, carpet, floor lamp, holographic television, bed, with a dreaming woman asleep atop a white mattress.

K gazed again at his inverted reflection in the window. The scene outside was superimposed on the mirror image; a seemingly vast and empty darkness revealed itself in the sky outside the window. But soon it was clouded by the fog of K's own breath on the glass, looking as if it had been covered by the vapor given off by his own semitransparent reflection.

It was like all his experiences, each contradictory dream.

Dream Implantation. The key technique for manufacturing biosynthetics.

The dark core of K's life.

CHAPTER 6

"How much do you know about the production of biosynthetics?" asked T. E.

It was 10:45 A.M. on January 25, 2208. He was in the premier's office, located in the General Office of National Security in the suburbs of D City.

The morning was clear and bright. K and T. E. stood side by side in front of a French window overlooking a stretch of river and green fields. They could see the outline of D City in the distance, like a series of reduced-size skeuomorphic models.

It had still been the age of DSM Neuropotenial Personality Analysis, no longer discarded to the periphery but rather returned to prominence after the development of the Montage Revolution. No one had expected, however, that the Logic Formula of Dreams would replace DSM Analysis as the primary method for distinguishing humans from biosynthetics in just two years' time.

K had suddenly received an order calling him to come by himself to the premier's office.

"Well, in addition to my major," K replied cautiously, "that's exactly what I was trained in. Of course, I know that some parts are top secret." He paused for quite some time. "Is that what the premier means?"

T. E. nodded, "Tell me what you know."

"Okay. I guess there are basically two aspects to biosynthetics: their bodies and their minds. The part about their minds is classified, and I don't understand it. In regard to their physical bodies, there is a long-established tradition that can be traced back even to the classical era—"

T. E. picked up his pipe and filled it with tobacco. "Please continue."

"The general version is that the history of cloning technology began with the creation of Dolly the sheep. That was in 1997, during the classical era. The first cloned animal in human history. After Dolly, cloning technology developed rapidly. In 2010 humanity produced the first man-made bacteria. This was practically creating something out of nothing and did not come from a clone. At approximately the same time, cloning technology was able to handle more complex organisms: cows, and then orangutans. By September of 2054, the first biosynthetic person was created.

"Yes." T. E. lit his pipe and slowly inhaled a mouthful of smoke. The lamp behind him outlined his dark silhouette like a paper cutout. "You must know that manufacturing the human body is really not difficult at all. You can skip ahead to the difficult part."

"The problem was, at that time, the technology for producing biosynthetics had no practical value," K replied. "That directly involves biosynthetics' minds, which is the classified bit. Actually, the difference is, when cloning other animals—sheep, deer, koalas—in all those cases, there is absolutely no need to consider the question of their knowledge or education. But if your intention is to produce biosynthetic people, then their educational program becomes extremely important. After all, if they are not equipped with basic life skills and a certain amount of capability for knowledge, along with a certain degree of personality and socialization, then even if they have human form, they are still essentially worthless.

"This was a significant hindrance to the industrialized output and commercial application of biosynthetics. In the course of human development, the long process of education really wastes a lot of resources and time, which was not at all in line with society's expectations for biosynthetic human capital. . . ."

T. E. glanced at K and sat in the armchair. Sunlight spilled down, silhouetting his face in shadow like an old portrait. "I imagine you've already guessed that I am planning to tell you something." Smoke gathered in a cloud around him. "The secret part."

K remained silent.

"The first person you need to know about is Daedalus Zheng." T. E. put down his pipe. "For now, we can skip over his biography. But in short, he was the one who overcame the challenges. Ever since he unraveled this difficult problem, we have no longer needed to create biosynthetic embryos. We could produce fully grown biosynthetic adults—eighteen-year-olds. This is now the norm we have adopted for biosynthetic production.

"Without a doubt, society did not need more 'good-for-nothing' people." T. E. lightly scraped his fingernail across the chair's armrest. "But the crucial point was, how could biosynthetics skip childhood. How could they be produced as adults—eighteen-year-olds—and be given an 'education' that assigned an identity, intellectual capacity, human socialization, and all of that? In theory, it was nearly impossible, because obviously such an education was made possible only by a long childhood, young people maturing bit by bit over the course of a dozen-odd years until they became . . .

"At the time, Professor Daedalus Zheng had a federal government position at Academia Sinica's Neurology Research Institute. Of course, his relationship with the Seventh Seal wasn't publically known at the time. To put it simply, the Seventh Seal secretly entrusted him to carry out this research. In February 2081, now one hundred thirty years ago, he provided the Seventh Seal with the plans for Dream Implantation as the solution."

T. E. stood and removed a folded electromagnetic document from his suit pocket. "You can start by reading this."

K took the document. He immediately saw that its encoding and encryption were crude and old-fashioned compared with those commonly used today. Perhaps they were not even as durable, for in many places he could see traces of damaged magnetism and unstable electric fields.

"There was actually only one solution. It was possible to replace the long years needed for education by implanting certain brain activity related to Symbolic Order before the brain made contact with the outside world. To make a long story short, the only possibility for what we call brain activity was dreams." Daedalus Zheng's insight was still sharp and penetrating, even as the writing on the document flickered with the unstable electric field. *"But these kinds of 'dreams' had to be supplied in quantity to the individual intelligence prior to its having any contact with the external*

world. In other words, in order to complete the biosynthetic production process, we had to make biosynthetics dream. Before they made contact with the jumble of information and Symbolic Order of the outside world, we had to fill their minds with the content of these dreams: intellectual capacity, a sense of self-identity, and human socialization. . . . In this way it was the equivalent of using dreams directly to insert a preexisting Symbolic Order into their minds, so it directly occupied their consciousness. This was called Dream Implantation.*

---

* Historical material related to Daedalus Zheng's revolutionary concept of Dream Implantation is difficult to acquire, since it touches upon state secrets. For a long time, even material about Daedalus Zheng himself was almost completely lacking. At the time, Daedalus Zheng and his contributions were basically unknown to the general public because the Federal Government of Humanity considered any information related to Dream Implantation to be top secret and was thus completely classified. Research shows that the name Daedalus Zheng first appeared in biographer K. Toffler's 2225 book *Enlightenment*. According to Toffler, Daedalus Zheng died in 2098. However, because *Enlightenment* is not primarily about Daedalus Zheng and in fact contains only about half a page of information pertinent to him, we know only that Daedalus Zheng played some role in the development of certain crucial parts of biosynthetic technology. In other words, following the innovation of the Dream Implantation concept in the 2080s, the name of Daedalus Zheng was not revealed until 2225. In the intervening one-hundred-fifty-year period, the external world knew almost nothing about him or his work. Even after 2225, historians did not have access to basic information about Daedalus Zheng's background, like the year or location of his birth, let alone other information. Without a doubt, this is a gap in history. The Federal Government of Humanity long flatly refused to confirm any comment on Daedalus Zheng, keeping him a closely guarded secret. It is thanks only to celebrated historian R. L.'s determined research and pursuit of the matter that the full truth of this historical riddle was revealed in 2273, forty-eight years after the publication of *Enlightenment*. In the biography, *Daedalus Zheng: A Melancholy Prophet*, R. L. describes Daedalus Zheng as a slightly built, nervous, talkative, blusterous, and arrogant but shy scientist, whose personality changed after middle age. According to R. L.'s investigation, despite an unending series of sex scandals, Daedalus Zheng was a lifelong bachelor. He was rumored to be bisexual. Moreover, Daedalus Zheng resolutely disapproved of the Federal Government of Humanity's use of Dream Implantation technology. He viewed implanting emotions simultaneous to the implantation of general knowledge, identity, and other essential information as the only correct course of action. According to the historical material R. L. had in hand, Daedalus Zheng had written the following to one of his male lovers in a personal email:

Actually, it has nothing to do with humanitarianism. Those bureaucrats and politicos always think it is for humanitarian reasons that I advocate implanting biosynthetics with emotions, but they are wrong. They are wrong. . . . It is so that we can use biosynthetics more

"Do you understand?" asked T. E.

"I—" K hesitated. "I think so. But the content of these dreams?"

"Right. That is actually related to the coordination of relevant dream technology." T. E. nodded. His fingertips drummed, almost involuntarily,

---

effectively. . . . Admittedly, emotions can decrease the quality of biosynthetic strategic decision making, but even that is not completely true. Certain emotions are actually beneficial to judgment and work efficiency. Appropriate emotions would very likely help biosynthetics react properly in emergencies. . . . Most of the time, if you are afraid, it is quite possible that whatever is making you feel fear is in fact dangerous. If the appearance of a wild animal causes you to intuitively feel fear, that means that the wild animal could in fact harm you. Fear aids rapid decision making, leading one to leave the scene and avoid immediate danger. This is precisely why instinct is useful . . . it is genetically imprinted in human brains. If you lack fear, if flight arises only from reason and cold logic, then it is possible, very likely in fact, that your response will be delayed. . . .

In the end, however, the Federal Government of Humanity did not adopt these ideas. According to R. L.'s research, Daedalus Zheng was apparently completely disappointed by this result. While he had always been shy, after this he became even more sealed off, even to the point of breaking off most of his dealings with friends. According to the textual evidence, from the late 2080s until his death in 2098, Daedalus Zheng had almost no human contact, with the exception of two or three friends. Among these, only mathematician Paz Carlos is very well known. During this period, Daedalus Zheng continued to be blusterous but grew more and more mercurial, continually muttering to himself as if no one else were there. In the spring of 2098, Daedalus Zheng died of sudden heart failure in the home he shared with his lover, W. He was only fifty-three, so you could call it an untimely death. The historian R. L. was in fact very suspicious about the cause of death, believing that murder could not be ruled out, nor could even W's involvement: "From all indications, W's identity can be considered very mysterious. . . . Strangely, in the process of gathering historical materials, I always met with obstruction whenever it came to anything about W." In a television interview, R. L. expressed it like this: "Speaking frankly, I suspect that W was somehow affiliated with the Federal Government of Humanity's intelligence agency . . . of course there is no explicit proof, and we ultimately have no way of confirming this. But, in short, if Daedalus Zheng didn't die from homicide, then saying he met his end from depression is not an exaggeration. . . ."

Additionally, in *Daedalus Zheng: A Melancholy Prophet*, R. L. also mentions that Daedalus Zheng grew increasingly pessimistic and utterly disturbed by the consequences of biosynthetic technology after the Federal Government of Humanity's authorities ignored his advocacy. In his diary, Zheng quoted a research paper originating in late classical-era England, which said, "Humanity ought to have an innate predisposition to connect and cooperate." (The paper focused on the human eyeball, observing that the whites of humans' eyes are relatively larger than those of other mammals, resulting in eye movement being more clearly on the glass desktop. "By then, the Seventh Seal had already struggled with the problem of the biosynthetic mind for more than a dozen years. In 2081, Daedalus Zheng gave us the solution in Dream Implantation. But the real question was how to create these dreams."

"Fortunately, although early-stage dream technology like 'dream harvesting' and 'dream collecting' were not yet fully developed, they were already in the last stage of research and development. We could already anticipate that the end result was in sight." T. E. stood and walked to the

---

visible; the paper suggested that this had an evolutionary purpose—namely, to "allow others to more easily understand our moods and intentions through the change of expressions in our eyes." In addition, there was also a related research paper illustrating that people with lighter eye color were usually worse at forming interpersonal relationships.) Daedalus Zheng was thus deeply dissatisfied at the government's neglect of emotional aspects in the application of biosynthetic technology. He even used the language of religious prophecy, including "the Flood" and "the Fire of Judgment Day," to describe the inevitable disaster:

It is not only that a whole group of people are being deprived of a childhood, to the extent that a large portion of their lifetimes are being displaced . . . I would call this another type of evolution . . . that is, one group of people's muddled and chaotic dreams of despotic rule displacing another group's original features, which should by rights belong to them. Humanity ought to have an innate predisposition to connect and cooperate. Without a doubt, people should not treat one another like this. Or maybe you will let me say it like this: Being born and becoming a person, the reason we are naturally able to frown, smile, shed tears, express anger, and experience anxiety, and other such rich and varied expressions, the reason we have such sturdy and complex facial muscles, is to express ourselves and communicate. And now, we go so far as to discard the instinct by which people create moods and cooperate. The resulting harm may temporarily be hidden but could in fact lead to disasters more severe than we can possibly imagine. I can predict it even now: because of their lack of emotions, the portions of biosynthetics' brain lobes and facial muscles responsible for expression will atrophy much faster than those of ordinary people, which might then in turn influence their other organs' functions. . . ."

R. L., in his book's final chapter, expresses a similar view regarding Daedalus Zheng's tragic prophecy: "'The fact of biosynthetics' lack of emotions has had considerable influence on the way history has subsequently unfolded. . . . We must admit that although the advance of technology played an important role in pushing forward the great wheel of history from the Age of Enlightenment through the classical era, scientific detail has never had such an astonishing, large, or far-reaching influence on the world that we live in as now—and this can all be summed up in a ubiquitous phenomenon: today's science has already advanced to the point of destabilizing humanity's deepest roots and distinctive characteristics at a fundamental level, and this shift might unavoidably trigger the creation or collapse of other characteristics . . . this is something we have never seen before . . . like a nuclear fission chain reaction gone out of control."

window, his figure lit by the streaming sunlight. "Thereupon, we discovered 'Dream Implantation.' This was really a revolutionary conceptual innovation. It coincided with progress in dream-harvesting technology and in due course proved to be the breakthrough in the mass production of biosynthetics. And thus, within a decade, by 2090, following the development of dream harvesting, dream cultivating, and dream editing in close succession, in secret experiments conducted by the Federal Government of Humanity, biosynthetic Dream Implantation was finally successful. Large numbers of biosynthetics were mass-produced via these methods, providing humanity with unlimited manpower at almost no cost."

T. E. paused for some time, as if observing K's reaction. "So, now you know the classified part." He took back the electromagnetic record from K's hand and looked him in the eye.

K pondered for a bit. "Chief, I'm still not very clear on whether this type of Dream Implantation is effective—"

"Of course," T. E. interrupted, "Daedalus only outlined the general concept. In its actual application, Dream Implantation still went through a great deal of follow-up research and experimentation until it was successful. But I must say that the concept was, in fact, correct.

"Here is a summary of 'biosynthetic identity recognition' Dream Implantation procedures." T. E. strolled back to the desk, opened a drawer, took out another document, and handed it to K. "This is the current method, for your reference. Take a look."

K read the document carefully:

Dream Implantation procedure
Breakdown 1: Biosynthetic identity

Step 1: Dream harvesting	Use the dream-harvesting technique for large-scale collection of human dreams of all kinds; establish a dream database.
Step 2: Dream editing	Select material related to "biosynthetic self-identification" from the dream database. For example, A person dreams he is a biosynthetic and works in a certain position at a certain factory. The editing personnel would harvest this dream and edit it appropriately.
Step 3: Editing completion	Assemble the selected dream material from step 2 and edit into a complete dream. This material transmits the message, "I am a biosynthetic."

Step 4: Dream Implantation	In the process of producing adult biosynthetics (of course, this should be done only when the production of the biosynthetic body is close to complete and when the central nervous system is fully developed but consciousness has not yet clearly emerged), implant the dream produced in step 3 into a biosynthetic body and let it dream. Beyond that, repeat the dream in its mind several hundred thousand times. Thus, when the biosynthetic's manufacturing is complete and it becomes self-aware, "I am a biosynthetic" will be its natural identity.
Step 5: Quality control	After self-awareness occurs (simultaneous with the birth of consciousness) but before it officially leaves the factory, implement quality-control inspection. In our experience, a small minority of biosynthetics will experience Dream Implantation failure. If, after inspection, such flawed products are discovered, they must be destroyed.

"Do you understand?"

K nodded.

"Those are the basics." T. E. pointed the stem of his pipe at K. "K, you are about to receive the authority to access the relevant classified material. If you're interested, you can look up a good deal of material on the technical details in the research center's archive. Oh, right!" He put down his pipe. "There's something I need to elaborate on. As a matter of fact, in addition to self-identification and intellectual capacity, we haven't yet dealt with the issue of biosynthetic sexual desire."

"Chief," K asked suddenly, "why are you telling me this?'

T. E. smiled and patted K's shoulder. "You are very polite, but in my eyes being polite is not necessarily a good thing.

"First, have a seat," T. E. gestured, then paused. "In regard to your question, I can answer it like this: on the whole, I plan to advance the role of technology used in intelligence work—"

"You mean?"

"Throughout human history, many breakthroughs were actually driven by technological advances," T. E. answered. "For example, back in the classical era, the Industrial Revolution was one such case. This is common knowledge and needs no further explanation. At the same time, I can also straightforwardly predict that DSM Analysis will not be effective forever. Maybe—" his expression grew meaningful, "—perhaps during your tenure, we will need a new test to distinguish biosynthetics from humans."

"You are already at a high-enough level, and I think you need to know more. This will definitely help with your work, especially if we need you to develop a new test in the future.

"Anyway, I don't think this is too important," T. E. quickly ended the discussion. "As I just mentioned, we are even using Dream Implantation to deal with the problem of biosynthetics' sexual desire. As we all know, biosynthetics' emotions are relatively bland, compared with ordinary humans. In fact, this is also accomplished through Dream Implantation.

"As far as I know, this part was not directly related to Daedalus Zheng." T. E. tapped his pipe. It was almost noon, and perhaps it was just a change in the angle of the light, but the office seemed to grow darker as the sunlight receded. A dry air current sucked all the moisture out of the surrounding air. "It was developed later by the Seventh Seal, which should be no surprise. People have a variety of emotions and desires, so biosynthetics based on human genetic blueprints inevitably do as well. The problem is, if we allowed biosynthetics to experience the full range of human desires, it could lead to many problems: emotional problems, marital problems, the problem of having children, or even problems with criminality. These would inevitably go so far as to create ethical controversies and burden society.

"As a result, the Federal Government of Humanity resolved that 'dream purification' become a standard part of the content of biosynthetic Dream Implantation. In other words, in the course of the normal Dream Implantation method, biosynthetics are implanted with dreams that eliminate sexual desires. By this I mean a type of subconscious castration. The sexual desires of biosynthetics that have undergone dream purification have been greatly reduced, to the point that, if they find themselves in situations that have anything to do with love or sex, they will likely feel nauseous or physically and emotionally unwell—"

"Oh, so you're saying that," K suddenly realized, "there is truth behind the saying that 'biosynthetics have a limited emotional range'—"

"Of course that's true," T. E. said calmly. "Moreover, dream purification is not the only reason. It is generally accepted that this is also related to biosynthetics' lack of a childhood. Because they experience dream purification and, beyond that, lack a childhood, biosynthetics' emotions are really quite stunted. Thus, we seldom allow biosynthetics to engage in jobs that require emotional intelligence.

"But, I must say, dream purification is only a stopgap measure." In the office, it seemed as if the light were slowly being devoured by shadow, and T. E.'s voice faded into the surrounding emptiness. "Our present technology has reached only this level. The problem is, it deals only with the psychological factors. Even though, in practice, it appears that the result has been successful, I personally cannot place full confidence in it. . . ."

CHAPTER 7

December 9, 2219. Early morning. D City. High-rise hotel.

Even now, K could still clearly remember the scene in the premier's office, after he had been promoted to head of the Technology Standards Department, when he had first read the original version of the secret report on Daedalus Zheng. The dramatic surge of sunlight on that morning. Because it had come from such a long time ago (it was already one hundred thirty years old), and the electromagnetic field had not been stable, the electromagnetic record was substandard: it was covered in rusty patches and riddled with holes.

Even so, that did not change its stunning revelations.

It was hard to imagine that it had already been one hundred thirty years since this had taken place, K thought.

Without a doubt, the new concept of Dream Implantation had broken through a barrier that had stood for several decades, achieving a crucial milestone. The one who had proposed the theory, Daedalus Zheng, was owed the majority of the credit. Then, in the year 2091, the Federal Government of Humanity had enacted the Basic Law of Biosynthetic Production, which had announced that research on mass production of biosynthetics had succeeded and mandated that the technology remain strictly regulated. It allowed only official government production, and the manufacturing process was added to a list of highly classified information.

That was the dawn of humanity's biosynthetic age, and since then the biosynthetic-manufacturing industry had gradually become mainstream.

Any biosynthetic that had been manufactured according to the standard procedures, from the time they were created had already been given a clear biosynthetic self-identity, experienced dream purification, and been equipped with a certain amount of intellectual capacity, enough to understand clearly the date when they had left the factory, the plant at which they had been manufactured, their serial number, and the work unit that they were about to enter.

This was the way that most biosynthetics were produced. But this was, after all, applicable only among ordinary biosynthetics. K's case was entirely different.

K was obviously an exception. The exceptional part was that, other than knowing that he was a biosynthetic, knowing his own age, and possessing a certain degree of intellectual capacity, K's memory about all the rest was blank, from start to finish. He did not know his manufacturing plant or serial number, and he did not know if he had really been intended to enter into any work unit.

Based on his own conjecture, K seemed to have been created by an entirely different process altogether. He could only faintly remember his first moments of consciousness: he had been lying alone amid the ruins of an old-style cement structure. It had been a wide, empty space, containing nothing more than a mottled gray wall and an upright pillar. Patches of various colors had been scattered unevenly across the wall like stains. There were exposed rusty steel beams, like blood vessels torn from a wounded body. A large section on one side of the pillar had been damaged. Beneath his body, on the smooth, untreated concrete floor, a puddle of water remained after a rainstorm. . . .

The air had still been saturated with a warm, damp smell. The smell of mud. Of floating vapor and mist. A wide swath of bright, lustrous white daylight illuminated the dust particles floating in the atmosphere, as if it flowed through the high, stained-glass window of a church dome. . . .

K sat up, feeling his body and limbs intact. He dusted the dirt off his body as he composed himself.

The cheerful sound of children laughing and talking came from somewhere indistinct in the distance. Countless faint echoes rippled in and out of the dreamlike ruins. He felt a sensation, like a soft tentacle or a warm liquid. He stood and walked to the window. Beyond the rust-stained iron grate, a lush patch of green filled his field of vision. Through the branches and leaves he saw children, in the slanting golden rays of sunset, run after one another in a tiny far-off playground.

In that moment, K realized two things about himself.

First, he was an abandoned biosynthetic.

Second, even if that were the case, he *could* become human.

He would become a real human, when all was said and done.

But this did not seem to be an urgent or intense desire. He did not feel particularly determined. Still, when he gathered his will, if it really can be said to have been gathered, he also lacked hesitation, indecisiveness, indirectness, or any trace of changing his mind. In that bizarre moment, K had suddenly understood that, even if he was a nameless, abandoned biosynthetic (or perhaps he was the result of a failed Dream Implantation experiment, but in that case, why hadn't he automatically been destroyed as a flawed product?), this could not prevent him from becoming an actual human. From then on, he had been moving step-by-step toward what he had anticipated in that moment, a new identity and a new future.

A forgery of a life. A counterfeit biosynthetic.

2179. Yangon, Myanmar. The biosynthetic guerrilla band's firebomb attack had indeed burned down the site of the census registration data and the relevant electronic records. The important thing was, because the Myanmar government had been quite weak, almost to the point of anarchy, and because relations between the local government and the Federal Government of Humanity were strained, there had been no backups of the electromagnetic records. And thus, taking advantage of the crack in the system left by the fire damage, K had forged his own chip worm[†] and obtained a new identity. Even before the Biosynthetic Liberation Front

---

[†] The chip worm, also known as the functional chip or the wallet chip, evolved from an early identity chip. It was a basic neuro-organism based on the tapeworm *Spirometra mansoni*. The worm's body measures about one centimeter square, is very thin, can survive for a long time in human subcutaneous or muscle tissue, and is harmless to the human body.

had developed its method of self-evolution to break through DSM Analysis, K had achieved a similar type of self-evolution on his own during the course of his doctoral research. It went without saying that the Logic Formula of Dreams had been developed after K had been recruited by the Seventh Seal, as a result of the blood, toil, tears, and sweat of Professor Wolfe's research group in the Technology Standards Department. Since K had been a part of that group, it was only natural that he knew about

---

The chip worm's chief function was originally to record personal information within its nervous system by the relevant government organization. It was used primarily as a replacement for classical-era identity certificates, driver's licenses, visas, passports, and other documents used to verify identity. By the end of the classical era, in addition to proof of identity, identity chips began, for convenience's sake, to integrate with credit cards, company loyalty cards, metro cards, laptops, cell phone communication, and audio-video broadcasting as a multipurpose chip. By the mid-twenty-second century (around 2150), as implant technology developed, chip worms were generally accepted by the public.

The present-day chip worm is usually implanted in the back of the left hand. Approximately sixty hours after implantation, the chip worm will sprout strands of connective tissue to fix the body of the worm in place in the subcutaneous tissue of the back of the human's hand. Within one hundred twenty hours after implantation, the worm's extrabody nervous and circulatory systems will completely connect to the host's human nerves and capillaries. At this point, the material recorded in the chip worm's body will have already separated and multiplied in the cells adjacent to the subcutaneous tissue of the back of the left hand, so that even if the chip worm is removed, the data can still be detected and read in the cells of the subcutaneous tissue of the back of the left hand for a fixed period (approximately thirteen months).

The period of chip worm implantation varies according to each country's customs and regulations. It is usually implanted upon adulthood (eighteen years of age) or a little before (fifteen or sixteen years of age). In certain Asian and American countries, the implantation of the chip worm has even become a rite of passage signifying adulthood. Parents invite their friends and family to collectively witness their son or daughter become an adult. Moreover, related colloquialisms have emerged, such as "You don't even have a chip worm, and you already want to join in the fun" and "You're how old? And still acting like this? You're like a kid without a chip worm!" to signify that someone is wet behind the ears or behaving in an infantile manner. Since the 2170s, certain communities have developed customs related to the chip worm. For instance, some people have their chip worm surgically removed every ten years, to collect the specimens as souvenirs. They then report once again to the local government, pay a fee, and receive a new chip-worm implantation. Ten years later, they undergo another surgery, add another specimen to their collection, and the cycle begins again. Other rituals developed as new religious customs, including the posthumous removal and collection of the chip worm as a commemoration for the dead.

the principles of the classified technique in some detail. Consequently, it did not take long for K to overcome the Logic Formula of Dreams independently through self-evolution.

That precisely was K's chosen identity: Human. Molecular biologist. Head of the Seventh Seal's Technology Standards Department. His unexpected career in intelligence.

———— ∞ ————

K recalled his own part in that long process, the many Seventh Seal secret missions in which he had participated. Initially, K did not have a background in intelligence; he had been part of the Technology Standards Department. When he had found himself in the middle of the Seventh Seal's Special Intelligence Department, it had often been awkward. In theory, it was just part of the IT Department, responsible for heavy-duty research and development work; in fact, its primary mission was to develop a finer degree of differentiation, a more precise method of distinguishing between humans and biosynthetics. Under normal conditions, it was in charge of only tech support and was not supposed to be directly involved in intelligence operations. Technical staff with science backgrounds were not, in fact, very well suited for directly participating in the spy war between the Seventh Seal and the Biosynthetic Liberation Front.

The change began when the Seventh Seal appointed T. E. as the new premier. It had been in his new office that T. E. had revealed to K his belief that highly specialized technical support was indispensable to its mission as a whole; in the long term, cultivating an understanding of intelligence work in the technical staff was also necessary. It was at T. E.'s insistence that designated employees from the Technology Standards Department participate in intelligence work outside the department according to the situation after receiving basic training.‡

———————————

‡ Generally speaking, employees of the Technology Standards Department were dispatched by the Federal Government of Humanity for basic training to an intelligence training center located in Fanling, Hong Kong. The content of this training was similar to that for ordinary intelligence agents, including techniques for surveillance, avoiding being followed,

And after K had been promoted to head of the Technology Standards Department, T. E. adjusted his internal regulations, requiring K to regularly attend meetings of the Seventh Seal's highest echelons. This had even directly involved the manipulation of insiders to increase the Technology Standards Department's strategic position. According to K's own understanding, it was after this kind of institutional transformation that he had really become an intelligence officer.

And it was because of this that K had the opportunity to directly participate in the examination and interrogation of those biosynthetics who had been arrested.

K once again paced over to the window. In the gaps between the buildings, in the dim light before dawn, the streets that had been nearly empty were now sparsely populated with people scurrying about like ants. He saw a stream of people pouring from the ground floor of his own building, like an outgoing tide. High at the edge of the horizon, a giant, leech-shaped form remained indistinct, perhaps because there was not enough light. Silver-white morning clouds were inlaid in the still-flickering starlight, in the deep-blue gloom of the sky.

But K did not want to flee.

K turned back to the table and lit a cigarette. He strolled back to the French window, closing his eyes in tranquility as he inhaled.

He thought of that night, several years ago, on the northern coast of Taiwan.

By then the Wittgenstein Project had long been finished and Gödel's trial had already concluded more than a year before. K had gone to the northern coast of Taiwan alone on his regular vacation. Long accustomed to living alone, K had been in the habit of traveling by himself each year. For

---

wiretapping, counterwiretapping, small-group cooperation, basic combat, escape, and securely transmitting intelligence.

him, those lonely, quiet trips were always an opportunity for reflection—about his identity, the details of his job, his job performance, and his future.

Or maybe you could say that each year's trip was when he reconsidered his desires. Again and again, he carefully explored the idea that had sprung to mind in his earliest moments of consciousness: to discard, or at least hide, his biosynthetic identity and become a real human.

Many years had gone by, but K still did not feel like he had arrived at an answer. He did not even think that his thirst to become a real person had grown more pressing. In fact, based on K's current situation, he could say that he was entirely leading the life of a human. But, although a greater or more far-reaching desire had not emerged in K's heart, that yearning to become human was still a tender, stubborn form lingering there.

In this respect, that trip had been like many before it, and K's thoughts had not yet reached a clear-cut resolution.

But compared with the past, that trip to Taiwan's northern coast still felt a bit different.

That was undoubtedly because of the incident between Gödel and Eros. After that, aside from K's work having changed significantly, his frame of mind had also been transformed, and these changes had affected him even more subtly.

At first glance, it seemed like these changes had nothing to do with K's earliest desires.

But in fact they did.

It was precisely in that mood, and during that trip, that K had unexpectedly encountered Eurydice.

5

THE DEMON-ENSLAVING FLASK

XIA JIA

TRANSLATED BY LINDA RUI FENG

Although James C. Maxwell was a rigorous physicist, he could nonetheless remain unfazed when confronted with supernatural phenomena. This was probably all because of his wife's enthusiastic interest, over the years, in all types of folktales and legends.

Right now the uninvited guest was sitting next to the fireplace, looking somewhat shabby. It was only after repeated entreaty from his host that he finally—and reluctantly—took off his hat. It was a heavy, wrinkled pointed hat of olive green, which he was now fiddling with on his knee, leaving exposed his sweat-soaked brow and a pair of furry, iconic ears.

"Excuse me for a moment," Maxwell said to him and left the living room. Mrs. Maxwell was by this point standing at the end of the hallway, holding a cup of coffee.

"So this is the legendary demon?" she asked with curiosity.

"At least he says so himself."

"He's rather large in stature," she commented, "though ineffectual looking." Indeed, sitting next to the fireplace, that—what might one call it? Thing?—was devoid of any appearance of grace, enigma, or even the ability to instill awe. He was wearing a rough coat and looked like a farmhand who had just emerged from a field of corn, despite the fact that he had indeed landed in Maxwell's laboratory in a shroud of smoke accompanied by that proverbial boom.

"This must be some kind of a joke," Maxwell said, "though I cannot understand why."

"Still, be prudent. We shouldn't judge people by their appearances, much less demons," Mary said without any hint of anxiety. The two of them returned to the living room together.

After downing a cup of hot black coffee, the demon seemed visibly more at ease. So Maxwell took up the original conversational thread: "Mr. Ro . . . pardon me, you said your full name was . . .?"

"Cornelius Gustav Rumpelstiltskin," said the demon, looking almost embarrassed.[1] "It was given to me generations later—an ancient Germanic name."

"Yes, yes, sir, but let us continue—we were talking about Archimedes just now." "Right, he was my first master, you see. But to be perfectly honest with you, he was a bloody old lunatic," the demon said, pulling a long face. "For dozens of years I was at his beck and call, and I built pile after pile of useless things. The night before the Romans barged into Syracuse, he sealed me under slats of stone. It'd be another hundred plus years before I could come out, you see."[2] Quite amazingly, the demon's eyes grew misty at this point, and he used the back of his furry hand to wipe them hastily.

Maxwell cleared his throat. "I quite understand. But you haven't told me about the wager you two made back then." "Wager? Yes . . . it was so long ago and all rather . . . fuzzy to me," the demon stammered and continued to fiddle with his hat. "The odds were against me from the very start—I'm sure you know what a curmudgeon he was."

"Very well, then. But how did you emerge again out of Mr. Faraday's laboratory notes?"

"That was a long story, with many things happening in between. If you knew the long list of people I served, you'd probably guess it all, and I wouldn't have to ramble on needlessly here." The demon lifted his face toward Maxwell with a plaintive look. "You physicists are a crazy lot, when it comes down to it. You take, for example, that Mr. Faraday. One day I was wrapping wire coils for him, as usual, when he suddenly said to me, 'Well, you've been with me long enough, and I don't have much more for you to do here,' and just like that he sealed me up in that notebook without so much as a farewell. And then I somehow ended up here. I'm not kidding—all those years I was with him, it was all coils, coils, coils. It'd never occurred to him to ask me for even a copper."

Maxwell was about to express his own opinion on this matter, because, as we all know, Faraday was his mentor, but just then Mary appeared elegantly at the door.

"James? Are we not going to ask our visitor to stay for dinner?"

The demon was instantly ill at ease. "No . . . don't go to all that trouble, good madam, sir. I would rather that we take care of our business right now." He fished out a piece of parchment from his pocket. It was oily and ancient, much the worse for wear.

Maxwell spread it out and began reading the paper carefully, while the demon continued speaking next to him: "In any case this is how it works. We make a wager, and if I lose I'll become your servant; if you lose, your soul and property are all given over to me and I gain my freedom."

"Must we do it this way?" asked Mary, leaning over.

"Old rules, madam, for thousands of years. I'm sure you've heard it all."

"Wagering with a demon is not necessarily a profitable thing," Maxwell lifted his head. "So what can you do for me?"

"Lots of things." The demon stretched out his furry hand and a few glittering gold coins materialized in his palm; he deliberately let them drop to the ground, clinking loudly. "Wealth, power, status—whatever you desire."

Maxwell looked into his palm curiously. "Well, whatever else it may be, this does seem like an opportunity," he muttered to himself. "Very well. Dinner can wait, Mary, and bring me a pen."

The rule of the wager was like this: Maxwell raises a difficult problem; if the demon fails to solve it within twenty-four hours, Maxwell becomes the victor—of course, the condition being that this problem must have a specific solution.

"Don't try to stump me with ambiguous problems, sir. You can ask me to circumvent the American continent, but don't ask me to raise a question that even I myself cannot answer."[3] Maxwell agreed.

"This may not be so simple, dear," Mrs. Maxwell seemed uneasy. "How can you be sure you will win this wager?"

"Listen, Mary," Maxwell cautiously lowered his voice. "I read over the contract carefully. Guess what the most interesting part was? That long list of signatures—Aristotle, Galileo, Newton, Copernicus. Almost every physicist I know is there, with encyclopedic completeness. This is nothing extraordinary, but think of it this way: in more than several thousands of years we've never heard of any physicist losing his life from having made a deal with the demon. So I hardly think I'm going to be the first."

Mary blinked rapidly.

"Poor demon," she said, sighing. "How are you going to put him to the test?"

"We will see. Actually I'm not so sure myself."

Just when the demon was scrunching up his sweat-soaked hat for the one hundred and eighth time, Mrs. Maxwell, with an amiable smile, invited him into her husband's laboratory. On the way, she hung up the much-abused hat she had carefully rescued from the demon's hands. At this point Maxwell was adjusting the experimental equipment that was just beginning to take shape.

"I think this ought to do it," Maxwell said, taking out the rubber-stoppered end of a flask from the sink.[4] "Come—the entrance is here."

The demon looked at the set of glittering glass vessels in near despair. The equipment's main component was a large glass flask with rubber stoppers at both ends. It contained a colorless liquid. The middle of the flask was divided by a vertical glass partition. "Are you going to put me in there?" asked the demon weakly.

"Correct. To see if you can find a way out," Maxwell replied. "And it will be a most worthwhile experiment."

The demon stood at the side of the empty flask and hesitated for a moment. With resignation he shrank his body and slipped into the flask, and after a brief flurry of sounds, the opening was stoppered.

The demon floated in midair and looked around. The curvature of the glass's shape distorted the objects outside. The Maxwells were looking into the flask with curiosity.

It was impossible for him to get out directly. It is a truth universally known that in any fairy tale, once a demon spirit is imprisoned inside a flask, he can never escape. (This odd fact perhaps shows the limits of the demon's transformative powers, since he could theoretically shrink himself to an atomic scale and exit through the orderly lattice of silicon dioxide molecules. Although we cannot be sure that he wouldn't be suctioned onto a covalent bond from the forces of static electricity.[5]) Obviously, Maxwell had already considered this detail in this intriguing experiment—I mean life-and-death wager.

So, there was only one way to escape, predetermined by the experimenter. The only way.

To be fair, the demon Cornelius Gustav Rumpelstiltskin in fact possessed a sound scientific mind, or, at the very least, after having been around physicists for several thousand years, he had acquired some scientific habits of mind. Now, after he got over his initial gloom, he tried to shrink himself even further, investigating every inch inside the flask.

After the Maxwells finished a cup of coffee and went into the laboratory to check on the experiment's progress, the demon had restored himself to a size visible to the naked eye. He looked quite gloomy.

"I found two small holes in the partition, not much larger than the size of air molecules," he declared. "But the air is really terrible in here. I feel a bit dizzy." "There is ether in the flask, of course," Maxwell said somewhat apologetically, "for the purposes of the experiment."[6]

The demon scratched the back of his furry head.

"I think I will soon be able to grasp your meaning," he said. Then he disappeared again.

When the Maxwells were walking out of the laboratory, Mrs. Maxwell winked like a mischievous girl and said, "I'm beginning to think that you'll win for sure, my dear. Though it's not so extraordinary that a fisherman couldn't do just as well.[7] How did you manage it, if I may ask?"

"I wanted to see if it was possible for him to separate the cold and hot air molecules—you know, the fast-moving ones and the slow-moving ones.

This is about reducing entropy," he went on. "As you know, the second law of thermodynamics dictates that systems of low internal energy cannot be converted into high internal energy without loss. In other words, the degree of disorder in a system—entropy—can only ever increase. This is why a cloud of hot gas can freely expand but can be compressed only through external work. Bread goes stale, roses wilt, people grow and age, the universe will eventually diffuse into a mass of thin, uniform gas, and the stars will stop burning: all this is because of the second law."[8]

"It sounds rather sad," Mary said quietly, squeezing his hand. "I don't like this law."

"Well, at least I didn't come up with it," Maxwell smiled gently. "But maybe it doesn't have to be absolute. I was thinking, if there were a clever and agile demon the size of a gas molecule, someone who could channel fast-moving molecules to one side and slow-moving molecules to another, then after a while the gas could be partitioned into cold and warm halves. As a result, entropy would decrease, and this unpleasant law would be nullified."

"Can that be done?" Mary's eyes grew wide.

"Hypothetically, yes, but I had never thought that I would have the chance to confirm it experimentally. Theoretically the second law is irrefutable—and now, you see, our lives and possessions are all riding on it."

"This is not a comforting thought."

Smiling, Maxwell put his arm around his wife's shoulders and a kiss on her forehead. "Why don't you go to bed first, dear. I'd like to observe a bit longer."

An hour later, when he went to look again, he saw that the demon had already gotten the hang of it.

"I shrank to the smallest size possible, and these molecules are just dashing around me like mad marbles," said the demon, out of breath.[9] "I was thinking that if I could control the molecules passing through and let only the fast ones enter this side, the temperature on this side would go up and make the liquid ether evaporate. Then it would turn into gas, force open the rubber stopper, and then I could get out!"[10]

"Looks like you really do know some things," Maxwell praised him. "Well, carry on. If you get the chance, do also note the velocities of those molecules coming your way, so that I can perhaps verify my theory on velocity distribution," he said, then left the room.[11]

The next day, after having breakfast and having enjoyed a Schubert piano impromptu, the Maxwells walked toward the laboratory with a spring in their steps. A fresh morning breeze carried the scent of roses from the garden into the room.

"How goes it?" Maxwell leaned over the equipment to take a careful look. The pool of liquid ether had not changed noticeably. "It appears that you were not very efficient last night."

The demon did not show himself but only shouted, "You ought to try this for yourself, sir—it's like a forest of flying bullets—ow! To you the molecules may look well behaved, but in fact they fly around like mad—they never stop. If I could only stand still for a minute . . . ouch! Ouch! It's like separating a herd of stampeding cattle! This work is dangerous!"

Maxwell shook his head. Mary came up from behind him.

"You look disappointed, James?" she asked him gently.

"Perhaps a little." He turned and kissed his wife's sweet-smelling curls. "Our demon may not be very nimble, but he's been working hard."

"Our?" Mary blinked mischievously. When her husband left the laboratory to go to his study, she carefully closed the curtains, to prevent the warm morning light from interfering with the experiment's accuracy.

When they returned from their evening walk that day, they finally saw some small change. The temperature on one side of the bottle did increase, but not nearly enough.

"I should have thought of this: the demon needs to do work in there, too. This was too difficult for a demon of this scale," Maxwell said thoughtfully. "In any case, the second law triumphed." The two of them sat aside and waited calmly. When the giant clock struck nine, they heard a "bam" sound and saw the demon's flat nose angrily plastered to the inside of the flask.

"I admit defeat!" the demon shouted hoarsely. "Let me out of here this minute."

Attentively, Mary brought bread rolls and hot coffee. After devouring everything, the demon seemed to have regained his stamina.

"I've never done such exhausting work. I would quite like you to try it yourself."

Smiling, Maxwell puffed on his cigar, his expression inquisitive.

"That would be interesting indeed. Yes, were it possible, I would love to see that marvelous microscopic world, just as you did."

After a brief silence, he seemed to have remembered something and from his breast pocket took out the scroll of parchment on which the contract was written. Glumly, the demon scrawled his name there, signifying the beginning of his new servitude.

"I will be at your service from now on," the demon said and began chewing his fingernails one by one. "But can you explain to me what just happened? There must be some principle that you can tell me about, right?"

Maxwell scratched his head and stood up. "All right. Come with me to my study. There are a few books I've written myself that can start you on the fundamentals. . . ."

He left with his arm draped across the demon's shoulders.

Mary sighed and dutifully gathered together the cups and plates on the table—tasks she had hoped could be turned over to the demon. But in fact she should have anticipated this—that physics was precisely the kind of thing that gets someone hooked and distracted.

In any case, there was much to look forward to in life from this point on.

This was the story of how Maxwell easily conquered the demon. Alternatively, the story of how the demon Cornelius Gustav Rumpelstiltskin once more found defeat after having met Archimedes and begun his miserable millennia-spanning experiences. But the story is not yet finished.

After the Maxwells passed away, they tended a small rose garden in a corner of heaven. No physics research disturbed their quiet and leisurely days, though the kindhearted demon occasionally came to visit them.

"What have you brought us?" Maxwell asked him, sitting in a chair, his wife standing beside him with her gentle demeanor, assuming the same positions and postures as when they were alive.

"A photograph, master and mistress." The demon took out the thin glossy piece of paper from behind his back, looking slightly diffident. "I took it myself."

Maxwell held the photograph close and scrutinized it. In it were people he did not know.[12]

"Let me guess . . . which one is your current master? Which one read my manuscripts?"

"Front row middle, that one—no, a little more to the right. Can you believe it? He was only sixteen back then. I more or less watched him grow up," the demon said, sighing. "He looks slovenly now, as if his hair had been hit by lightning—back then he was a handsome lad."

"What did he ask you to do?" Maxwell asked curiously.

"He said to me, 'Go chase after this light beam, run as fast as you can, and come back to see me when you catch up with it.' You tell me, is this something you are allowed to make someone do?"[13]

"Of course, of course . . ." Maxwell seemed deep in thought. "This is a tremendous idea. As we all know, the speed of light is constant, something I proved long ago."

"I don't quite understand," Mrs. Maxwell said gently. "It does sound rather taxing."

"There was more, madam." The demon blinked, tears welling up in his eyes. "Look at this man. Who knew what he was doing behind my back? He then became very enigmatic and made me go inside this box. I learned my lesson from you, you see, so I suggested that he put a cat in there instead and let me guess what might happen. To this day I don't know whether the poor little creature is alive or dead."[14]

"You don't know if it's alive or not? Why not?" Maxwell asked.

"This has to be explained more slowly, but you'll understand eventually. It's not quite like what you were studying before," said the demon with some satisfaction. "And then there's this old bloke—yes, him—he lectured me on the structure of matter for an entire morning, all smiles and patting me on the back about how quickly I was absorbing it all. Then, at the end, he took a piece of red chalk to draw two small circles on a blackboard covered with diagrams and said to me, 'You win if you can make these spin in the same direction.'"[15]

Maxwell shook his head with bemusement. These topics were clearly outside his areas of expertise, but there was no question they provoked his interest in physics again.

"I will raise these topics at tea this afternoon. Would you like to join us? Perhaps you might like to see your former masters? You now know far more than we do."

"Do they all attend?" the demon asked timidly.

"Most of them will, assuming Archimedes doesn't lose track of the time, and that Mr. Newton is not feeling unwell.[16] We have tea every afternoon, a tradition that has continued for thousands of years."

"Archimedes? You mean Mr. Archimedes?" The demon leaped from his chair, grabbing that pointed hat of his that never left his side. He looked around anxiously. "Actually, no, thank you, I just realized I have another engagement . . ."

"That's unfortunate—are you really so averse to seeing him again?" Maxwell stood up to walk the demon to the door. "So, can you tell me what question he asked you? I've never been able to figure it out."

The demon turned around. A quiet celestial afternoon light spread across his furry ears and sad yellow eyes. It was so warm and serene, but still he shrugged clumsily, as if that excitable old man were standing in front of him right now, issuing an exhilarated challenge to the whole world.

"Actually he was a very agreeable old fellow; sometimes I really do miss him," he answered. "But he had no business shouting to me, 'Give me a point to stand on!' That is something not even God could deliver. . . ."[17]

PART II

OTHER US

6

THE POETRY CLOUD

LIU CIXIN

TRANSLATED BY CHI-YIN IP AND CHEUK WONG

They are on a yacht, Yiyi and two others, sailing across the South Pacific Ocean on a poetry-composition cruise. Their destination, the South Pole. If all goes well, they will arrive in a couple of days' time and then pierce through the Earth's crust to see the Poetry Cloud.

The sky and ocean are crystal clear today, much too clear for poetry composition. The American continent, usually hidden from view, can now be observed plainly floating above in the sky, forming a dark patch on the Eastern Hemisphere that envelopes the world like a giant dome. The continent looks not much different from a patch of wall left exposed when the sheathing has fallen off. . . .

Oh, by the way, people now live inside the Earth, or to be more exact, people now live inside a balloon. That's right, the Earth has been turned into a balloon. It has been hollowed out, leaving behind only a thin crust about a hundred kilometers thick. The continents and oceans remain exactly the same, however, except for the fact that they are now on the inside. The atmosphere is still there, but it has also moved to the inside. So the Earth is now a balloon, a balloon with continents and oceans stuck to its inner surface. This hollow Earth still revolves on its axis, but the effect of the spin is very different: it now provides the Earth's gravity. The mass of the thin crust is so small that the gravity produced by it is not even worth mentioning. Gravity is now generated mainly by the centrifugal force caused by Earth's rotation. This gravity is, however, not evenly spread across the world: it is strongest at the equator—roughly equivalent to one and a half times the original gravitational force on Earth—and decreases as the latitude increases, until it becomes zero at the North and South Poles. The latitude that the yacht now sails on has exactly the standard gravitational force of the original Earth, but Yiyi still finds it very difficult to regain the feelings of the old world, the feelings that one would have felt on the now disappeared solid Earth.

A tiny sun hovered at the core of the hollow Earth, bathing the whole world in brilliant midday rays. The sun's intensity changes constantly in the course of twenty-four hours, gradually dimming from maximum brightness till it extinguishes completely, giving the inside of the hollow Earth days and nights. On some nights, it also casts the cold gleam of the moon, but since the light shines only from one spot, one cannot see the full moon.

Of the three on board, two are not actually human. One is a ten-meter-tall dinosaur named Big Tooth, who rocks the yacht left and right with his every movement, causing much annoyance to the poet standing in the bow of the yacht. The poet is an old bony man, with snowy white hair and beard that mingle together in the breeze. He is wearing a wide, ancient-style robe, like the robes of the Tang dynasty, with an immortal air about him, much like a character written in a wild cursive style with the sky and ocean as backdrop.

This is the creator of the new world, the great Li Bai.

A GIFT

It all started ten years ago. At the time, the Devourer Empire had just ended its two-century-long plunder of the solar system. Prehistoric dinosaurs directed their gigantic Ring World, which was fifty thousand kilometers in diameter, away from the sun and glided toward the Cygnus constellation. The empire carried away with it 1.2 billion humans, which the dinosaurs planned to raise like poultry. But just as the Ring World was about to reach the orbit of Saturn, it suddenly began to decelerate, actually turning back along its original track and reentering the inner solar system.

A Ring World week after the Devourer Empire began its return, Ambassador Big Tooth set off from the Ring in a spaceship shaped like an ancient boiler, carrying in his pocket a human named Yiyi.

"You're a gift," Big Tooth told Yiyi, his eyes peeping through the porthole into the dark space outside, his deep voice vibrating so hard that it turned Yiyi numb from head to toe.

"For whom?" Yiyi raised his head and shouted out loudly from within the pocket. From the pocket's opening, he could see only the dinosaur's lower jaw, which looked like a giant rock protruding from the side of a cliff.

"For the gods! The gods have come to the solar system, and that's why the empire returned."

"Are they real gods?"

"They've mastered unimaginable technologies and exist in the form of pure energy. They can jump from one end of the Milky Way to the other in a flash. That makes them gods enough. If we could master but one hundredth of that supertechnology, the Devourer Empire would have a bright future. We are completing a grand mission, and you must learn to please the gods."

"Why me? My meat is of very inferior quality," Yiyi asked. He was more than thirty years old, and compared with the fair and juicy humans carefully raised by the empire, his appearance was much more haggard.

"Gods don't eat bugs; they just like to collect them. According to the breeders you are quite special, and it's said that you have many students?"

"I'm a poet. I teach classical literature to the humans kept on the breeding farms." Yiyi pronounced the words "poet" and "literature" with some difficulty, since these were very rarely used words in Devourish.

"A boring and useless learning indeed! But the breeders have turned a blind eye to your teaching activities since the contents seem to be mentally helpful to you bugs, thus improving the quality of your meat. . . . I've noticed that you think yourself noble and pure and others to be beneath your notice. Very interesting feelings for a little fowl from a feedlot."

"Thus the way with all poets." Yiyi straightened himself in the pocket, proudly holding his head high, though he knew that Big Tooth could not see this.

"Were your ancestors in the Earth Defense War?"

"No," answered Yiyi, shaking his head. "My ancestors from back then were also poets."

"A most useless kind of bug, very rare on the Earth even then."

"He lives in his own inner world and does not care for the changes happening around him."

"Good-for-nothings . . . Ah, we're nearly there."

Upon hearing this, Yiyi poked his head out from the pocket and peered through the porthole. There were two white, glowing objects floating in space before them, one a square plane, the other a sphere. As the spaceship drew level with the plane, the plane suddenly disappeared for a second into the backdrop of the starry sky, which meant that it had almost no thickness. The perfectly shaped sphere hovered above the plane, both of them casting a soft, white glow, their surfaces so smooth and even that nothing distinctive could be seen. They were like two elements drawn from a graphic database, two simple and abstract concepts within the mess and confusion of the universe.

"Where are the gods?" asked Yiyi.

"Those two geometric shapes. Gods like to be concise."

As they drew near, Yiyi saw that the plane was about the size of a football field. The spaceship landed on the plane; the flames emitted by the engine touched the plane first but left no marks whatsoever. It was as if the plane were nothing more than an illusion. Yet Yiyi felt the gravitational pull and a tremor as the spaceship came in contact with the plane, which meant that it could not be an illusion. Big Tooth had obviously been here before, since he opened the cabin door and jumped out without hesitation. Yiyi's heart churned when he saw Big Tooth simultaneously open both doors on either end of the air-lock cabin. However, he did not hear the swoosh of air gushing out from within. As Big Tooth stepped outside, Yiyi could even smell the fresh air as he stood in the pocket and could feel the cold breeze brushing his face . . . This was a kind of wondrous technology that neither man nor dinosaur could comprehend. Its gentleness and effortlessness astounded Yiyi. This astonishment pierced even deeper into the soul than when humans saw the Devourers for the first time. Yiyi looked up; the sphere was hovering above them and, behind it, the galaxy glittered and shone.

"Ambassador, what little offering have you brought me this time?" inquired the god. He spoke in Devourish, his voice low, as if echoing from the depths of an abyss in the infinite distance, and for the first time Yiyi felt that even this coarse dinosaur language could sound pleasant to the ear.

Big Tooth dug his paw into his pocket and grabbed Yiyi, then put him down onto the plane. Yiyi felt its elasticity with his foot. Big Tooth began, "My venerable god, we know that you like to collect little creatures from various universes, and I have brought you this interesting little specimen, a human from the Earth."

"I care only for perfect little creatures; why have you brought me this filthy little bug?" asked the god, the glow of the sphere and plane flickered twice, a probable sign of disgust.

"You know this species of bug?" Big Tooth raised his head in astonishment.

"I've heard travelers from this spiral arm mention them, but I do not know much about them. In these bugs' relatively short evolutionary history, the travelers have often visited Earth, and they were all disgusted by the bugs' dirty thoughts, low behavior, and the chaos and filth in the course of their history. Hence, till the Earth's destruction, no one bothered to establish contact with them. . . . Throw it away at once!"

Big Tooth grabbed Yiyi and turned his huge head around to see where he could dump him. "The rubbish incinerator is behind you," the god's voice interjected. Big Tooth turned and saw a small hole suddenly appear on the plane, with eerie bluish lights flickering from within. . . .

"Don't you say that! Humans have created great civilizations!" Yiyi shouted in Devourish at the top of his lungs, his face turning blue.

The white radiance of the sphere and plane again flickered twice, and the god's voice sounded in a sneer, "Civilization? Ambassador, tell this bug the meaning of civilization."

Big Tooth raised Yiyi to eye level and held him so close that Yiyi could hear even the gurgling sound of his eyeballs turning in their sockets. "Bug, the uniform measurement of how civilized a race is in this universe is the space dimension that it has entered. Only those that have entered the sixth dimension or above can be regarded as having met with the basic criteria for joining the circle of civilized races. The race of our venerable god already possesses the ability to enter the eleventh dimension. The Devourer Empire is able to, on a small scale limited to laboratory trials, enter the fourth dimension, which means that we can be regarded as only a primitive tribe, while your race is nothing more than weeds or moss to the gods."

"Throw him away this minute! Such filth!" the god pressed, already out of patience.

Big Tooth ended his speech and marched toward the incinerator holding Yiyi. Yiyi struggled with all his might, and several pieces of white paper fell from his clothes. As the papers floated in the air, a thin ray of light shot out from the sphere, hitting one of the pieces, suspending it in midair and scanning it in a flash.

"Wait! What're these?"

Holding Yiyi suspended right above the incinerator, Big Tooth turned toward the sphere.

"Those . . . are my students' homework!" Yiyi answered, struggling hard inside the dinosaur's paw.

"Those square symbols are very interesting, and so are the little matrixes they create," the god muttered, sending out rays and swiftly scanning the other sheets of paper that had already landed on the plane.

"Those are Chinese . . . Chinese characters. These are classical poems written in Chinese characters!"

"Poems?" the god asked in amazement and withdrew the rays of light. "Ambassador, you are no doubt familiar to some degree with this bug script?"

"Of course, my venerable god. I lived in their world for a long time before the Earth was consumed by the Devourer Empire." Big Tooth placed Yiyi on the plane near the edge of the incinerator and, bending down, picked up one of the sheets. Raising it to his eyes, he tried, with great difficulty, to make out the words. "It roughly means . . ."

"Don't bother, you will only misinterpret it." Yiyi stopped Big Tooth with a wave of his hand.

"Why?" the god asked with a good deal of interest.

"Because it is an art that can be expressed only in classical Chinese. Even when translated into another human language, it loses the better part of its meaning and beauty and is transformed into something quite different."

"Ambassador, do you have this language's database in your computer? And all knowledge relevant to the Earth's history too? Fine, then transmit them to me. Use the channel we established during our previous interview."

Big Tooth hurried back to the spaceship, mumbling to himself as he fumbled with the computer aboard the spaceship. "The classical Chinese part is missing and will have to be downloaded from the empire's network; there might be delays." Yiyi could see through the open cabin door the changing colors of the computer screen reflected in the dinosaur's giant eyeballs. When Big Tooth exited the spaceship, the god could already read the classical poem aloud in perfect Chinese.

> *Behind a mountain the day fades,*
> *The Yellow River uniting with the ocean.*
> *Scenes a thousand li away,*
> *One may survey from a higher floor.*

"You are a very fast learner!" Yiyi exclaimed in amazement.

The god took no notice of him and remained silent.

Big Tooth explained, "It means a star has fallen behind a mountain on a planet, and a river called the Yellow River flowed toward an ocean. You see, both river and ocean are formed by compounds consisting of one oxygen atom and two hydrogen atoms. And if someone wants to see further away, he should climb higher on a building."

The god stayed silent.

"My venerable god, you have, not that long ago, honored the Devourer Empire with your presence; the scenery there is very similar to the bug's world portrayed in this poem. There are also rivers and mountains and oceans, so . . ."

"So I do know the meaning," the god said, and the sphere suddenly moved, stopping right above Big Tooth's head. Yiyi thought that it was like a giant eye without a pupil, glaring fixedly at Big Tooth. "But do you not feel anything at all?"

Big Tooth shook his head in bewilderment.

"I mean, things that are hidden within the apparent meanings of this simple matrix of symbols?"

Big Tooth became more puzzled still, and so the god recited another poem.

I see none that have come before,
Nor any who might follow.
Reflecting on a world so ancient and vast,
My tears fall in lonely sorrow.

Big Tooth at once eagerly offered an explanation, "This poem means, looking forward, one cannot see the bugs that lived long ago on this planet; looking back, one cannot see the bugs that will later live on this planet. So one feels the vastness of time and space, and so one cries."

Still perfect silence.

"Um, crying is how the bugs of the Earth express sorrow. When this happens, their visual sense organs . . ."

"Do you still not feel anything?" the god interrupted, the sphere lowering a little more, until it almost touched Big Tooth's nose.

This time, Big Tooth shook his head with great firmness and said, "My venerable god, I believe there is nothing more to it—just a simple short poem."

The god recited a few more poems, all short and simple, all on the theme of transcendence, including poems like Li Bai's "Going Down to Jiangling," "Night Thoughts," and "Seeing Meng Haoran Off from Yellow Crane Tower as He Took His Departure for Guangling"; Liu Zongyuan's "River Snow"; Cui Hao's "Yellow Crane Tower"; and Meng Haoran's "Spring Dawn."

Big Tooth said, "There are quite a number of long epics in the Devourer Empire, some are millions of lines in length. My venerable god, I will gladly present them to you. The bugs' poetry is, by comparison, so short and simple, much like their technology . . ."

The sphere suddenly flew away from Big Tooth's head, floating in random curves in midair. "Ambassador, I believe that your greatest wish is for me to answer one question: Why is the Devourer Empire still struggling in the atomic age after its eighty million years of existence? I now have the answer."

Big Tooth looked at the sphere with the keenest interest: "My venerable god! The answer is everything to us! Please . . ."

"My venerable god," Yiyi raised his hand and spoke out loud, "I, too, have a question, if I may?"

Big Tooth glared angrily at Yiyi, looking as though he would like to swallow him whole. But the god agreed: "I still despise the bugs of Earth, but those little matrixes have earned you the right."

"Does art exist everywhere in the universe?"

The sphere trembled a little in midair, as if nodding. "Yes, I myself am a collector and researcher of the art of the universe. I travel between nebulae and have made contact with various art forms of numerous civilizations. Most are complicated and obscure. But this, with such few symbols, making up such tiny matrixes yet expressing such complex layers and subdivisions of feelings, all composed under such strict, almost brutal, restrictions of style, meter, and rhyme is, I admit, something I had never seen before. . . . Ambassador, you can now dispose of the bug."

Big Tooth again grabbed Yiyi. "Yes, throw it away, my venerable god. There is enough data stored on the Devourer Empire Central Network on human culture, and you now have all these stored in your memory. This bug, on the other hand, probably knows only a few simple poems." With that, he again marched toward the incinerator with Yiyi in his paw.

"And those papers, too," the god added.

Big Tooth at once turned back and began collecting the pieces of paper with his free paw. Yiyi started to scream wildly from within Big Tooth's grasp, "God, please keep those pieces of paper as relics of human classical poetry! You have collected an unsurpassable art form; transmit it to other parts of the universe."

"Wait," the god again stopped Big Tooth, even as Yiyi was dangling above the incinerator; he could feel the heat of the blue flames below him. The sphere floated near, stopped, and hovered just a few centimeters away from his forehead. He was now under the intense gaze of the gigantic pupilless eye just as Big Tooth had been.

"Unsurpassable?"

"Ha ha ha . . . ," Big Tooth held Yiyi up and laughed, "This poor little bug dares to say this in front of this mighty god! Hilarious! What do humans have left? You've lost everything on Earth and have forgotten most of your scientific knowledge—the only thing you might have taken away. Once at the dinner table, I asked a human this question before I ate him: "What was the atomic bomb used by humans in the Earth Defense War made of?" And he answered, "Atoms!""

"Ha ha ha ha . . ." The god was amused by Big Tooth, and the sphere shook so much that it turned into an oval. "There could not be a more correct answer, ha ha ha . . ."

"My venerable god, these dirty bugs have nothing left but those few short poems! Ha ha ha . . ."

"But they are unsurpassable!" Yiyi insisted, squaring his chest in a most dignified manner.

The sphere stopped trembling and murmured in almost a whisper, "Technology can surpass all."

"This has nothing to do with technology! This is the essence of the inner world of the human soul and is unsurpassable!"

"You say this because you are ignorant of the power that technology could eventually bring. Small bug, insignificant bug, you do not understand." The god's voice was silky, like that of a loving father, but the cold, murderous notes buried within made Yiyi shudder with terror. "Look at the sun," the god said.

Yiyi did as he was bid. They were in between the orbits of the Earth and Mars, and he had to narrow his eyes before the sun's brightness.

"What's your favorite color?" the god asked.

"Green."

Before the last syllable fell, the sun turned green, a bewitching, seductive green, as if a cat's eye had suddenly appeared in the abyss of space. Under its gaze, the whole universe turned profoundly and eerily mysterious.

Big Tooth's paw quivered, dropping Yiyi onto the plane. After they had regained their senses a moment later, they suddenly realized a more shocking fact than that of the sun turning green: it would have taken more than ten minutes for light to travel to the sun from where they now were, yet all this took place in a flash.

Half a minute later, the sun returned to normal, once again casting its customary dazzling white rays.

"Did you see that? This is technology, the kind of power that enabled our race to rise from slugs in the muddy ocean beds to gods. Technology is the real God. We worship Him with our whole body and soul."

Yiyi blinked his eyes, still dazzled. "But even gods cannot surpass that kind of art! We, too, have gods, imaginary gods, and we worship them too; but we do not believe that they can create the kind of poetry written by Li Bai or Du Fu."

The god sneered and said to Yiyi, "You are the most stubborn kind of bug, which makes you even more repulsive. But, just for fun, I will surpass your art form."

Yiyi also sneered, "Impossible. For one thing, you are not human and cannot feel human passions. Human art is to you merely a flower carved in stone, and you cannot overcome this obstacle with technology."

"There can be nothing simpler than overcoming this 'obstacle.' Give me your genes."

Yiyi was at a loss. "Give a hair to the god!" Big Tooth directed. Yiyi raised his hand and pulled out a hair. An invisible force sucked the hair to the sphere then let it fall to the plane. The god took only some flakes of skin from the hair root.

The white glow within the sphere surged around then slowly turned transparent. Clear liquid then filled the sphere and a string of bubbles floated to the surface. Yiyi then saw a small yolklike ball in the liquid. It appeared a light reddish color under the sunlight and seemed to give off its own light. The sphere grew quickly, and Yiyi realized that it was a curled-up fetus, its swollen eyes tightly shut, with red interlocking blood vessels running all over its huge head. The fetus continued to grow, its small body finally stretching out, then began to swim in the liquid like a frog. At that point the liquid gradually turned opaque, and the sunlight that shone through the sphere revealed nothing but a vague shadow. The shadow rapidly grew bigger, finally turning into a fully grown, human-shaped form swimming in the sphere. The glowing sphere had now turned back to its original white opacity, and a naked man fell from the sphere onto the plane. Yiyi's clone staggered up, with sunlight reflecting off his wet body. His hair and beard were very long, but he appeared to be only about thirty to forty years of age and looked nothing like Yiyi except for the fact that they were both stick-thin. The clone stood stiffly, gazing lifelessly into the distance and looking as though he knew nothing about the universe that he had just entered. Above him, the white glow of the sphere dimmed, then extinguished altogether. The sphere itself disappeared as if it had evaporated. Then Yiyi saw something light up and realized that it was the clone's eyes. The dull empty gaze had suddenly been replaced with a light radiating intelligence. Yiyi later found out that this was when the god had moved all his own memories into the clone.

"Cold, this is cold?!" A gentle breeze blew over them, and the clone wrapped his hands around his soggy shoulders, shivering all over, but his voice was filled with delight: "This is cold, this is pain! Delicate, perfect pain! The sensations for which I've wandered the galaxies searching so painstakingly: it's as sharp as a ten-dimensional string passing through time-space, as crystal clear as the pure-energy diamond at the hearts of quasars, ah—" He stretched out his bony arms and raised his eyes to the Milky Way: "I see none that have come before, nor any who might follow. Reflecting on a universe so—" A bout of shivering made his teeth clatter, ending his natal speech; he rushed to the incinerator to warm himself.

The clone held his hands above the blue flames, shivering as he said to Yiyi, "What I am doing now is in fact ordinary enough. When I research and collect any art form from a civilization, I always invest my memory temporarily into a member of that civilization, thus ensuring that I truly and wholly understand the art form."

The flames in the incinerator suddenly flared up, sending multicolored radiances surging across the plane. Yiyi thought the whole plane was now like a sheet of frosted glass floating on a sea of flames.

"The incinerator has been turned into an output window. The god is making an energy-matter transformation," Big Tooth whispered to Yiyi in a low voice, and seeing that he was still perplexed, he added, "Idiot! Making matter from pure energy. God's work!"

The output window suddenly spurted out a ball of white stuff, which unfolded in midair as it fell. It was a piece of clothing, which the clone caught and put on. Yiyi saw that it was in the ancient style of the Tang dynasty, snowy white and made of silk, with broad black trim. The wretched-looking clone was at once transformed into a divine-looking figure. Yiyi could not imagine how this piece of clothing could be fabricated from those blue flames.

More things were being fabricated. Out from the window flew something black, which landed with a thud on the plane like a rock. Yiyi ran over to pick it up; he could hardly believe his eyes: what he held in his hand was undoubtedly a heavy inkstone, and it was as cold as ice. Something else fell to the plane with a clang. Yiyi picked up the black, strip-shaped object, and it was indeed a Chinese ink stick. Some writing brushes were then created, followed by a brush stand, a sheet of white rice paper (imagine that coming out of the flames!), a few antique-looking desk ornaments, and finally, the biggest object of all, an ancient writing desk. Both Yiyi and Big Tooth hurried over to straighten the desk and arrange the little objects on it.

"The energy that was transformed into these things is enough to blow a planet to dust," Big Tooth whispered to Yiyi, his voice shaking a little.

The clone walked over to the desk, nodded in approval at the ornaments placed on top, and, using one hand to stroke his now-dried beard, he said, "I, Li Bai."

Yiyi scrutinized the clone and asked, "Do you mean that you want to become Li Bai, or that you think you are already him?"

"I am Li Bai, the Li Bai who can surpass Li Bai!"

Yiyi smiled and shook his head.

"What? Do you doubt me?"

Yiyi nodded, "It's true enough that your technology is way beyond my understanding and is, to a human, no different from magic or divine power; there are things that make me gasp with wonder even in the realm of poetry, that given such huge cultural, time, and space barriers you can nonetheless grasp the true significance of Chinese classical poetry . . . but to understand Li Bai is one thing, surpassing him is quite another. I still believe that what you face is a transcendent art form."

An unfathomable smile appeared on the clone's—Li Bai's—face, but it disappeared at once. He pointed his finger at the writing desk and commanded, "Prepare the ink!" He then walked away, stopping near the very edge of the plane, and gazed at the distant galaxies in deep contemplation as he stroked his long beard.

Yiyi picked up a Yixing-ware pot from the writing desk and poured a little water onto the inkstone. He then picked up the ink stick and began grinding. It was the first time he had ever done this, and he tilted the ink stick sideways, clumsily grinding its edges. As the ink got thicker, Yiyi began to comprehend that he was in the vast space one and a half astronomical units away from the sun, on an infinitely thin plane (even when matter was created from pure energy a moment ago, the plane still had no thickness when observed from afar) that was just like a floating stage in the abyss of the universe. On this stage was a dinosaur, a human who had been raised for meat like poultry by the dinosaurs, and a god of technology in an ancient Tang-dynasty robe who was preparing to surpass Li

Bai—actors in a truly bizarre stage play, thought Yiyi with a bitter smile, shaking his head.

The ink more or less ready, Yiyi got up and stood waiting together with Big Tooth. The gentle breeze had ceased to blow on the plane, and the sun and the stars glimmered silently—it was as if the whole universe were waiting. Li Bai stood quietly at the edge of the plane, and since light did not scatter in the air above it, his form was distinctly divided by the sunlight into lit and shadowed parts. If not for the occasional movement of his hand stroking his beard, one would have taken him for a stone statue. Yiyi and Big Booth waited and waited. As time soundlessly flowed by, the writing brush on the desk that had been soaked with ink had already started to dry. The sun's position had changed a great deal without anyone noticing, casting long shadows of the desk, the spaceship, and of themselves onto the plane. The white rice paper laid flat on the desk seemed to have become a part of the plane. Finally, Li Bai turned around and walked slowly to the desk. Yiyi at once dipped the writing brush into the ink again and handed the brush to Li Bai with both hands, but the latter raised a hand in dismissal and simply sank again into deep thought, looking at the paper on the desk. Something new appeared in his eyes.

With considerable satisfaction, Yiyi saw that it was uneasiness and confusion.

"I need to fabricate a few things, they are . . . fragile, so be careful when you go catch them." Li Bai pointed to the output window. The blue flames that had grown weak flared up again, and Yiyi and Big Tooth had only just reached the window when a stream of blue flame spat out a round object. Big Tooth was quick and managed to catch it; he saw it was a large jar. Three large bowls followed, but Yiyi only caught two of them, with the other smashing to pieces on the plane. Big Tooth carried the jar in both arms to the desk, then carefully opened the seal. A strong scent of liquor gushed out, causing Yiyi and Big Tooth to stare at each other in astonishment.

"There was not much information on liquor making by humans in the Earth Database that I received from the Devourer Empire, so this may not be exactly correct." Li Bai pointed to the liquor jar and motioned to Yiyi to try it.

Yiyi scooped out a little with a bowl and took a sip. A burning sensation passed from his throat to his stomach, and he nodded, "This is indeed liquor, but much stronger than the kind we take to improve the quality of our meat!"

"Fill it up," said Li Bai pointing to the empty bowl on the desk, and after Big Tooth had filled it with the strong liquor, Li Bai drained it in one go, then turned again to walk into the distance, sometimes taking uneven, dancelike steps. Once he reached the edge, he stood there again facing the galaxies in deep meditation. But this time his body swayed rhythmically from left to right, as if in unison with an unheard tune. He did not take long to meditate before returning to the desk with dancing steps the whole way. He grabbed the brush that Yiyi handed to him and flung it into the distance.

"Fill it again." Li Bai stared dully at the empty bowl.

. . .

An hour later, Big Tooth carefully laid a hopelessly drunk Li Bai onto the cleared writing desk with his large paws. But Li Bai turned over and tumbled down, muttering in a language neither man nor dinosaur could understand. He had already thrown up a huge and colorful mass (no one knew when he had eaten anything), and his wide ancient robe was now a complete mess. The white glow of the plane shone through the vomit, forming a highly abstract painting. Li Bai's mouth was stained black with ink, because after his fourth bowl of liquor, he had tried to write something on the paper but had ended up only jabbing the brush onto the desk very hard, after which he had tried to smooth the hairs of the brush with his mouth, just like any child starting to learn calligraphy.

"My venerable god?" Big Tooth bent down and asked cautiously.

"Wayikaah . . . kaahyiaiwa," Li Bai answered with a thick tongue.

Big Tooth stood up and said to Yiyi with a sigh and shake of the head, "We'd better go."

THE ALTERNATIVE ROUTE

Yiyi's feedlot was on the Devourer equator, an area that used to be a beautiful grassland between two large rivers when the Devourers were still in the inner solar system. As the Devourers traveled beyond Jupiter's orbit, harsh winter had descended, the grassland disappeared, and the rivers froze. The humans being reared there were moved underground. Later, the Devourers were summoned by the god and returned to the inner system. As they drew nearer to the sun, spring returned to the land, the rivers thawed, and the grassland became green once again.

When the weather was favorable, Yiyi usually lived alone in a thatched hut he had built himself by the river and grew his own crops. This was forbidden for the general run of people, but since Yiyi's lectures on classical literature at the feedlot had a tranquilizing effect, producing a special flavor in his students' meat, the dinosaurs left him alone.

It was an evening two months after Yiyi and Li Bai's first meeting. The sun had just set on the flat horizon of the Devourer Empire. The two large twilight-lit rivers joined together at the horizon's edge. Outside the riverside thatched hut, a gentle breeze carried the faint sound of joyful dance songs from the distant grassland. Yiyi was playing go by himself when he looked up to see Li Bai and Big Tooth coming along the bank. Li Bai had changed a lot. His hair was tousled, his beard terribly long, and his face much tanned by the sun. He carried a rough-cloth bag on his left shoulder and a large gourd in his right hand. The traditional garb he wore had become tattered, and the straw sandals on his feet were worn beyond recognition. Yiyi thought Li Bai actually looked more human now.

Li Bai came over to the go board and, just as he had the several times he was there before, set the gourd down heavily on the table without so much as a glance at Yiyi and demanded, "Bowls!" He uncorked the gourd after Yiyi brought over two wooden bowls, filling them to the brim. He then fished out a paper-wrapped package from his bag, which Yiyi discovered contained cooked meat, already sliced. As its aroma reached Yiyi, he automatically reached out, took a piece, and started chewing.

Big Tooth was standing two or three meters away, watching them in silence. Based on previous experience, he knew that they were going to discuss poetry again, a topic that he was neither interested in nor qualified to join.

"Yummy," Yiyi nodded with approval. "Is this beef also transformed from pure energy?"

"No, I have long since embraced Nature. You may not have heard, but I have a farm quite a distance from here where I rear beef cattle from Earth. I've made this dish myself, using the recipe for Shanxi beef. The key is when braising the beef you should add—" Li Bai leaned over and whispered in Yiyi's ear, "urine salt."

Yiyi looked at him, confused.

"Oh, that's the white stuff left when human urine evaporates. It creates a nice rosy tint in braised beef, making it tender and the texture just right without being too greasy or too dry."

"This urine salt . . . it's not made of pure energy either?" Yiyi asked in trepidation.

"I just told you that I've embraced Nature. I've gone to a great deal of trouble to secure this urine salt from a number of human feedlots. This is true folk culinary art that had been lost long before the Earth was annihilated."

Yiyi had already swallowed the piece of beef. To keep himself from throwing up, he picked up the wine bowl.

Li Bai pointed to the gourd and said, "The Devourer Empire has built a few distilleries under my guidance. They can now produce most of the famous Earth liquors. This is the authentic Green Bamboo Leaf wine they made by infusing bamboo leaves in *fen* liquor."

Yiyi only then noticed that the liquor in the bowl differed from the one Li Bai had brought previously. It had a fresh green tint, with a sweet herbal taste.

"It seems you've already gotten to know human culture inside out," Yiyi was moved and told Li Bai.

"That's not all. I've spent a lot of time experiencing things for myself. As you know, the landscape in many regions of the Devourer Empire are quite similar to that on the Earth where Li Bai had lived. In the past two months, I've been wandering among the mountains and waters, enjoying the beautiful scenery, drinking under the moon, and reciting poetry on mountaintops. I've also had a few amorous encounters in human feedlots all over this world."

"So you must be able to show me your poetic creations by now?"

Li Bai quickly put down the wine bowl, stood up, and began pacing uneasily. "I did write some poems and they're sure to astound you. You'll see that I've become an excellent poet, outdoing even you or your fore-fathers. But I still don't want to show them to you because I'm equally sure that you'll think they have not surpassed the work of Li Bai, and

I . . ." He gazed afar at the waning glow of the setting sun, his eyes hazy with distress, ". . . would agree."

On the distant grassland, the dance was over, and the jolly people started their sumptuous dinner. A group of young girls ran toward the riverbank and began to play in the shallow water at the river's edge. They each wore a coronet of flowers and a light chiffon gown reminiscent of clear morning mists, composing an intoxicating image in the twilight. Yiyi pointed to the girl nearest to the hut and asked Li Bai, "Is she pretty?"

"Of course," Li Bai answered, giving Yiyi a puzzled look.

"Just imagine: cut her open with a sharp knife, take out her internal organs, gouge out her eyeballs and brains, pick out each of her bones, separate all the muscles and adipose tissues according to their original locations and functions, then tie all the blood vessels and nerves into two bundles, and finally spread out a large piece of white cloth and lay everything out on it in anatomical order. Would you still regard that as pretty?"

"How can you think of such things when you're drinking? It's disgusting!" Li Bai knit his brows.

"How's it disgusting? Isn't it the technology you are so devoted to?"

"What are you getting at?"

"The Nature in the eyes of Li Bai is the girl you see now at the riverside. The same Nature in a pair of technologically oriented eyes is the bloody components lined up in an orderly fashion on the white cloth. In other words, technology is antipoetic."

"It seems you are ready to give me some advice?" Li Bai commented thoughtfully, stroking his beard.

"I still don't think you have any chance of surpassing Li Bai, but I can point you in the right direction for your efforts: technology has clouded your eyes, concealing the beauty of Nature from you, so the first thing you should do is to forget all about your supertechnology. Since you were able to transplant all your memories into your current brain, you must be able to delete a part of them, too."

Li Bai looked up and exchanged a glance with Big Tooth, and both of them burst out laughing. Big Tooth told Li Bai, "My god, I warned you about these devious bugs, it's easy to fall into their traps if you aren't careful."

"Ha ha . . . devious but fun," Li Bai replied, turned back to Yiyi, and said sneeringly, "You really think I'm here to admit defeat?"

"You haven't managed to surpass the pinnacle of human poetic art. That's a fact."

Li Bai suddenly lifted a finger and pointed to the river. "How many ways are there to walk to the riverbank?"

Yiyi stared at Li Bai for a few seconds, baffled: "It would seem there's . . . just one."

"No, two. I can also walk in this direction," Li Bai said pointing in the direction opposite to the river. "If I set off straight ahead that way, I can reach this shore after circling the Devourer Empire's outer ring and crossing the river. I could even take a round-trip of the Milky Way and get back that way. This is easy with our technology. Technology can surpass all! I am now compelled to take the alternative route."

Yiyi thought long and hard before finally shaking his head in puzzlement: "Even if you have the technology of the gods, I still can't imagine what the alternative route would be to surpass Li Bai."

Li Bai stood up and said, "It's simple. The two ways to surpass Li Bai are one, to write poems that surpass his and two, to write every possible poem!"

Yiyi felt even more confused, but Big Tooth, standing to the side, had a look of dawning comprehension.

"I will write every possible pentasyllabic and heptasyllabic poem, which were Li Bai's strong suit. I'll also compose all possible lyrics to the common classical tunes! You still don't understand?! I'm going to try out all the possible combinations of Chinese characters within these prosodic frames."

"Oh, great! A great project!!" Big Tooth cheered in excitement.

"Is that difficult?" Yiyi asked dumbly.

"Of course it is. Extremely difficult! Even if we use the largest computer in the Devourer Empire for the operation, it might still not be completed before the universe ends!"

"There shouldn't be that many . . . ," Yiyi said doubtfully.

"Of course there are that many!" Li Bai nodded smugly. "But with the quantum computation technology that your people are far from fully grasping, it can be done within an acceptable time frame. I will then write all the poems, both those already written and those that might be written in the future. Mark my word—all that might be written! That will certainly include poetry that surpasses the greatest work of Li Bai. In fact,

I will bring an end to the art of poetry: any poet thereafter, till the end of time, will become a mere imitator. No matter how highly regarded their work is, it will definitely be found in my enormous storage base."

Big Tooth suddenly emitted a low howl of alarm. His gaze at Li Bai turned from excitement to shock: "An enormous . . . storage base? My venerable god, you aren't really saying that you are going to . . . to store every single poem composed by the quantum computer, are you?"

"What's the point of deleting them after composition? Of course I'm going to store them! It'll be one of the artistic milestones my race leaves to this universe!"

The shock in Big Tooth's eyes now turned to horror. He extended his huge paws, his legs crooked, as if he were falling to his knees in front of Li Bai. He sounded on the verge of tears, too: "Don't . . . My venerable god, you shouldn't do this!!"

"What struck such terror in you?" Yiyi looked up and asked, astonished by Big Tooth's reaction.

"You idiot! Don't you know that atomic bombs are made of atoms? That storage device will be made of atoms, too, and its storage cell cannot be made finer than the atomic level! Do you know what atomic-level storage is like? It means all the books by humankind could be accommodated within the size of a needlepoint! Not that tiny stack of books you have now but all the books on Earth before it was devoured!"

"Oh, this does sound possible. I heard that the number of atoms in a glass of water is larger than the number of glasses of water contained in the Earth's oceans. So? He can take the needle with him after the poems are composed," Yiyi said, pointing to Li Bai.

Big Tooth was mad with rage. He paced rapidly back and forth for a short while before regaining a slight bit of equanimity. "Fine, fine, let me ask you, how many characters do you think there would be in total if all the poems that fit the pentasyllabic and heptasyllabic meters as well as the common lyric tunes are written out, as the god plans?"

"Not many, maybe around two to three thousand. Classical poetry is the most concise form of art."

"Fine. I'll show you, you idiotic bug, just how concise it is!" Big Tooth said as he walked to stand by the table, pointing with his paw to the go board on it. "What do you call this stupid game? Oh, right—go. How many points of intersection are there on the board?"

"With 19 rows each way, 361 intersection points in total."

"Very well. On each intersection, you can put either a black piece or a white piece, or leave it open, so altogether there are three states to choose from. This way, you can see each go game as a 19-line, 361-character poem made up of just three Chinese characters."

"This comparison is fantastic."

"So, if you exhaust all the combinations of these three characters in poems of this format, how many poems will you have in total? Let me tell you: 3 to the power of 361, or rather, hmm . . . let's see, 10 to the power of 172."

"Is that . . . a lot?"

"Idiot!" Big Tooth spit the word out a third time. "The total number of the atoms in the whole universe is just . . . argh—" He was too angry to continue.

"How many?" Yiyi still wore his dense look.

"Just 10 to the power of 80!! You idiotic bug—"

Only then did Yiyi show a hint of surprise: "You mean if one atom stores one poem, there's still no way of saving all the poems composed by the quantum computer? Not even if we exhaust all the atoms in the universe?"

"Far from enough! Insufficient by 10 to the power of 92, to be exact!! Besides, how can a single atom store a poem? The number of atoms required for one poem in a storage device made by human bugs may be larger than your total population. As for us, the technique for storing single-digit binary data within a single atom is still in the experimental stage. . . . Alas . . ."

"Ambassador, your views on this matter are too shallow and lack imagination. That's one of the reasons for the slow development and advance of technology in the Devourer Empire," Li Bai said, smiling. "A quantum storage device built according to the Multistate Superposition of Quanta can save those poems with just a small amount of matter. Of course, quantum storage is not very stable, so in order to permanently save the poems, it still has to be combined with traditional storage technology. In spite of this, the mass required for producing such a storage device is very small."

"How much would that be?" Big Tooth asked, looking as if his heart were pounding in his throat.

"Approximately 10 to the power of 57 atoms—a tiny amount, tiny."

"That . . . that is just about the mass of the whole solar system!"

"Yes, including all the solar planets and, of course, the Devourer Empire, too."

This last line of Li Bai's was said matter-of-factly, but in Yiyi's ears it was like thunder in a clear blue sky. On the other hand, Big Tooth, surprisingly, seemed to have calmed down: having been long tormented by an inkling of impending doom, one actually experiences a sense of relief when disaster finally strikes.

"Aren't you able to transform pure energy into matter?" Big Tooth asked.

"You should have known how much energy would be required for such an enormous mass. It is unthinkable even for us. We'd better make use of what's readily available."

"It would seem His Majesty's concern wasn't groundless," Big Tooth muttered to himself.

"Oh, yes," Li Bai said, delighted. "I made it clear to the Devourer emperor two days ago that this grand Ring World empire will be used for an even greater purpose. All dinosaurs should be proud of this."

"My venerable god, you will see how the Devourer Empire feels," Big Tooth answered darkly. "There is another problem: compared with the sun, the mass of the Devourer Empire is negligible. Is it necessary to destroy a civilization that has been evolving for thousands of years for this infinitesimal fragment of matter?"

"I completely understand your doubts. You have to bear in mind that to extinguish, cool down, and dismantle the sun would take a long time. The quantum computation of poetry will have started before that and we will have to save the results in real time, so as to free up the operation memory of the quantum computer for further computation. Thus, the matter immediately available from planets and the Devourer Empire for producing the storage device is essential."

"I understand. The last question, my venerable god: Is it necessary to save all the combinations and results? Why not install a decision-making program at the output end to eliminate the poems that are not worth keeping? To my knowledge, classical Chinese poetry has to follow strict prosodic rules. If we eliminate all the poems that do not fit the prosodic schema, the end quantity will be much reduced."

"Prosody? Pffft . . ." Li Bai shook his head scornfully. "It is a constraint against inspiration. Ancient-style poetry in China before the Southern and Northern Dynasties was not bound by prosody, and even for the strictly regulated new-style poetry after the Tang period, a lot of renowned classical poets departed from the prosodic rules and came up with outstanding mixed-style poems. So in this ultimate poetry composition exercise, I won't consider prosody."

"But you still have to consider the content of the poems, don't you? Ninety-nine percent of the computation output will be utterly meaningless. What's the point of saving such random matrixes of Chinese characters?"

"Meaning?" Li Bai shrugged. "Ambassador, the meaning of a poem does not depend on your approval, nor mine, nor anyone else's. It is determined by time. Many works of poetry that were meaningless in their own time later became unparalleled masterpieces. Many of the current or future masterpieces must also have been meaningless once upon a time. I am going to compose all poems. Who knows which one of them will be selected by the great passage of time as supreme billions and billions of years later?"

"This is ridiculous!!" Big Tooth roared, his hoarse voice startling the few birds in the distant shrubs. "If it goes according to the Chinese character corpus of the human bugs, the first poems produced by your quantum computer will be like this:

Ah Ah Ah Ah Ah
Ah Ah Ah Ah Ah
Ah Ah Ah Ah Ah
*Ah Ah Ah Ah **Alas***

"Are you telling me that this will be chosen as a masterpiece by the great passage of time?!"

Yiyi, who had remained silent all the while, exclaimed in delight, "Wow! This has no need of being selected by the great passage of time! It's already a masterpiece now. The first three lines along with the first four characters of the last line express a sense of marvel at the magnificence of the universe, while the last character is the "eye," the focal point, of the poem, containing the poet's lamentation after appreciating the vastness of the universe, at the fleetingness of life against the infinity of time and space."

"Aha . . ." Li Bai stroked his beard and chuckled with delight. "Well done, Yiyi bug! It's a wonderful poem. Haha . . ." As he spoke, he picked up the gourd and filled Yiyi's wine bowl.

Big Tooth slapped Yiyi with his giant paw and sent him hurtling far. "Damned bug. I know you're happy now. But don't you forget. If the Devourer Empire is destroyed, your kind can't live either!"

Yiyi had tumbled as far as the river shore before he finally managed to pick himself up, his face covered with sand, his mouth wide open, from both pain and joy. He was really happy, "Ha ha, this is great. This universe is damned unbelievable!" he yelled heartily.

"Any other questions, Ambassador?" As Big Tooth shook his head, Li Bai continued: "So I'll leave tomorrow. The day after, the quantum computer will activate the poetry-writing software, and the ultimate poetry composition will commence. At the same time, the operation to extinguish the sun and dismantle the planets and the Devourer Empire will also start."

"My venerable god, the Devourer Empire will complete the preparations for battle this evening!" Big Tooth stood at attention and announced solemnly.

"Good, very good indeed. The coming days will be interesting. But before all this happens, let's finish up this bottle," Li Bai said, then nodded, pleased, and picked up the wine gourd. After pouring his liquor, he watched the great river now shrouded in the dusk as he mused, "A wonderful poem, the very first one, ha ha . . . the first one is already a wonderful poem."

THE ULTIMATE POETRY COMPOSITION

The poetry-composing software was actually very simple; it would require just two thousand lines of program code in the C language created by human, plus a not-too-big database storing all Chinese characters. When this software was activated on the quantum computer (a giant transparent prism suspended in space) in Neptune's orbit, the ultimate poetry composition began.

Only then did the Devourer Empire realize that Li Bai was just an individual member of that supercivilization, which went against the former assumption by the dinosaurs that a society evolved to that technological level would have melded into a single consciousness. The five supercivilizations encountered by the Devourer Empire in the past ten million years had all been like that. Li Bai's kind had retained the existence of individuals, and this partly explained their extraordinary understanding of art. When the poetry composition started, many other individuals of Li Bai's kind leaped from all over outer space into the solar system to start the storage-device production project.

Humans in the Devourer Empire could see neither the quantum computer in space nor the newcomers from the godly race. From their point of view, the process of the ultimate poetry composition equated to an increase or decrease of the number of suns in space.

A week after the poetry-composing software had been activated, the godly race successfully extinguished the sun, so the number of suns in the sky was reduced to zero. However, the termination of nuclear fusion inside the sun led to a loss of support for its outer shell; the sun quickly collapsed into a nova, whereby the dark night was soon relit. The thing was that this new sun was a hundred times brighter than the original one and burned the plant life on the surface of the Devourer to fumes. The nova then extinguished itself, too, and exploded again after a while, so the cycle of extinguishing and exploding came and went, as if the sun were a cat with nine lives, struggling on and on. Yet the godly race was actually quite proficient in killing off stars, so they easily extinguished the nova over and over again, maximizing the fusion of matter into the heavy elements required for making the storage device. The sun finally breathed its last when the nova was extinguished the eleventh time. By then, the ultimate poetry composition had already been going on for three Earth months. Prior to that, when the nova showed up for the third time, other suns had appeared in space. These suns lit and went out one after another at different spots in space, with as many as nine new suns in the sky at one time. These suns resulted from the power released by the dismantling of planets by the godly race. Since the glare from the sun gradually faded, people had problems distinguishing the real sun from the others.

The dismantling of the Devourer Empire started five weeks into the poetry composition. Before that, Li Bai had put forward a suggestion to the empire: The godly race could relocate all the dinosaurs to a world at the other end of the Milky Way where a civilization a lot more backward than the godly race lived. That civilization had yet to achieve existence in pure energy forms, but it was a lot more advanced than the Devourers. Once the dinosaurs arrived, they would be reared as domestic fowl, living a jolly life with no want of food and raiment. The dinosaurs, however, angrily rejected this idea, preferring to perish with dignity than to submit to a humiliating existence.

Li Bai then made another proposition: let humans return to their mother planet. Actually, the Earth had been dismantled, too, most of it being used on the storage device, but the godly race had built a hollow Earth for humankind from a small portion of the leftover matter. The size of the hollow Earth was more or less the same as the original planet, but its mass was only one percent of the latter. It was not exactly the case that the Earth had been hollowed out, since there was no way that the layer of fragile rock on the original surface of the Earth could be used for the new crust, whose material probably originated from the Earth core. In addition, the intersecting lines on it, which looked like latitude and longitude lines, were fine but strong reinforcement rings made from degenerated neutron matter produced when the sun collapsed.

It was heartening that the Devourer Empire not only granted Li Bai's proposition immediately, letting all humans leave the great Ring World, but also returned the seawater and air they had raided from Earth. With these materials, the godly race then restored all the continents, oceans, and atmosphere inside the hollow Earth.

After that, the brutal Great Ring War of Defense took place. The Devourer Empire launched nuclear missiles and gamma-ray laser beams at godly-race targets in space, but these were useless against the enemy. Spurred on by a strong invisible force field launched by the godly race, the Devourer's outer ring revolved faster and faster, finally disintegrating from the centrifugal force caused by the high-speed rotation. By this time, Yiyi was on his way to the hollow Earth and witnessed the total destruction of the Devourer Empire from twelve million kilometers away.

The disintegration of the Ring World took place very slowly, as if it were a mirage against the backdrop of pitch-dark space. The giant world dispersed like milk foam floating on a cup of coffee, with the debris on the margins gradually disappearing into the dark as if it were dissolved by space. Only the sparks of explosions every now and then made them visible again.

This great civilization from the ancient Earth that exuded virility was thus annihilated. Yiyi was grief-stricken. Only a small proportion of the dinosaurs survived and returned to the Earth with humans. Among them was Ambassador Big Tooth.

On their way back to Earth, most of the humans were quite depressed, though for an entirely different reason from Yiyi. Once back on Earth, they would have to open up the land and cultivate their own food. For people who themselves had been raised and have weak limbs and who could not tell one grain from another, this was indeed a nightmare.

Yiyi, however, was full of confidence for the future of the world on Earth. No matter how much hardship lay ahead, human beings would be the masters of themselves again.

THE POETRY CLOUD

The yacht on the poetry voyage has reached the coast of Antarctica.

The gravity here is weak and the motion of the waves sluggish. It is like a dance describing a fantasy. Under the low gravity, the water splashes more than ten meters high when waves hit the coast, with surface tension creating countless balls of water in midair, whose sizes range from as large as a football to as small as raindrops. These balls of water drop slowly, so slowly that you could draw a circle around them with your fingertips. The balls refract the glare of the small sun, bathing Yiyi, Li Bai, and Big Tooth in a glittering light as they go ashore. The Earth's revolution has slightly distorted and lengthened its axis along the North and South Poles, so the polar regions of the hollow Earth have retained their freezing climate. The snow in the low-gravity environment is most unusual, puffed up and foamlike. Its depth varies from waist-deep to places where Big Tooth would be completely submerged. However, they can breathe normally even when immersed! The whole of Antarctica is covered in such snow foam, giving off an uneven whiteness.

Yiyi and the others take a snow sledge to the South Pole. The sledge is like a jet boat speeding across the snow foam, parting waves of snow as it goes.

The next day, they arrive at the South Pole, which is marked by a tall crystal pyramid, a monument to remember the Earth Defense War of two centuries ago. No words or images are inscribed on the solitary gleaming pyramid that silently refracts the sunlight on the snow foam from above the Earth.

The entire Earth world can be viewed from this vantage point. Surrounding the small dazzling sun are the continents and oceans, as if the sun had drifted there from the Arctic Ocean.

"Can this small sun really shine forever?" Yiyi asks Li Bai.

"At least till the Earth civilization evolves enough to be able to build new suns. It's a mini white hole."

"White hole? The reverse of a black hole?" Big Tooth asks.

"Yes, it's connected to a black hole two million light-years away through a space wormhole. The black hole revolves around a star, absorbing the star's light and releasing it here. You can see the white hole as the output end of an optical fiber that transcends space-time."

The tip of the pyramid is the southernmost point of the Lagrange axis that links the North and South Poles of the hollow Earth. It is named after the zero-gravity Lagrange points that constituted the two ends of a thirteen-thousand-kilometer axis between the Earth and the moon before the war. In the future, humans will surely launch various satellites along the Lagrange axis, and, compared with what had to be done on the prewar Earth, these will be very easy launches: you have only to transport the satellites to the North or South Pole, by a mule cart if you prefer, and then kick them skyward with your foot.

Yiyi and the others are looking at the pyramid when a larger sledge comes up carrying a group of young travelers. As soon as they get off the sledge, these people leap up high along the Lagrange axis, turning themselves into satellites. A great many small black dots, tourists and assorted vehicles, can be seen drifting along the axis at zero gravity, marking its length. In fact, it is possible to fly from here directly to the North Pole. However, since the small sun is located midway along the axis, some of the tourists who flew along the axis in the past and who could not decelerate because of faulty jet-propulsion packs headed straight toward the sun and were evaporated long before they actually reached it.

On the hollow Earth, it is easy to reach space by jumping into one of the five deep wells at the equator (known as land doors), falling a hundred kilometers down (or up?) through the crust and being flung into space by the centrifugal force of the Earth's revolution.

Now, in order to see the Poetry Cloud, Yiyi and the others have to go through the crust, too. But since they are taking the land door at the South Pole, where the centrifugal force from the Earth's revolution is zero, they will be able to reach only the outer surface of the hollow Earth and will not be flung into space. When they finish putting on their light space suits at the control station of the Antarctic land door, they enter the hundred-kilometer-deep well. At zero gravity, it might be more apt to call it a tunnel, since they, in their weightless state, have to rely on the jet-propulsion pack in their space suits to move themselves forward. It takes them half an hour to reach the outer surface, way slower than dropping from the land doors on the equator.

The desolate outer surface of the hollow Earth contains only intersecting neutron matter reinforcement rings, which, like latitude and longitude lines, divide up the surface of the Earth into numerous rectangles. The South Pole is the juncture for all the longitudinal rings. When Yiyi walks out of the land door, he finds himself on a not-very-large plateau. The reinforcement rings are like mountain ridges that originate from the plateau and radiate in every direction.

Looking up, they see the Poetry Cloud.

The Poetry Cloud, located where the solar system used to be, is a spiral nebula one hundred astronomic units in diameter, its shape resembling the Milky Way. The hollow Earth is at the edge of the cloud, as was the sun in the original Milky Way. What is different is that the orbit of the Earth is not on the same plane as the Poetry Cloud, so it is possible to see from the Earth an entire side of the cloud, unlike the Milky Way, which offered a view only of its cross section. However, the distance between the Earth and the Poetry Cloud plane is insufficient to allow the people here to observe the cloud's full shape. In fact, the entire sky of the Southern Hemisphere is covered by the cloud.

The Poetry Cloud emits a silvery radiance that casts shadows on Earth. It is said that the cloud emits no light of its own and the silvery radiance is caused by cosmic rays. Owing to the uneven distribution of cosmic rays in space, large haloes of light often surge through the Poetry Cloud. These multihued haloes course through the sky, like giant glowing whales swimming in the cloud. On the rare occasions when the intensity of the cosmic rays increases dramatically, glimmering sheens of light will appear and the Poetry Cloud will no longer be cloudlike: the whole sky will look like the surface of a moonlit ocean seen from underwater. The asynchronous rotations of the Earth and the Poetry Cloud allows for an occasional glimpse into the night sky and the stars through the gap when the Earth is in between the spiral arms. The most sensational view is the cross section of the Poetry Cloud seen when the Earth is at the edge of a spiral arm. It looks like cumulonimbus clouds in the Earth's atmosphere that transform into majestic shapes capturing one's imagination. These gigantic shapes emerge high above the rotation plane of the Poetry Cloud, giving off a sublime silvery glow, like a never-ending hyperconscious dream.

Yiyi draws his gaze back from the Poetry Cloud. He picks a chip up off the ground. This kind of chip is scattered all around them, glistening on the ground like ice shards in the dead of winter. Yiyi holds the chip up toward a sky densely covered by the Poetry Cloud. The small chip is half the size of his palm, completely transparent if seen from the front, but by tilting it to one side, one will catch on its surface the iridescent reflection of the Poetry Cloud. This is a quantum storage device. All the texts produced in human history would take up only one billionth of a chip's storage capacity. The Poetry Cloud is made of one thousand forty of such chips, which store all the output from the ultimate poetry composition, produced from the matter that used to form the original sun and all the nine planets, and of course the Devourer Empire as well.

"What a great piece of art!" hails Big Tooth sincerely.

"Indeed, its beauty lies in its content: a nebula ten billion kilometers in diameter that comprises all possible poems; it's really amazing!" Yiyi looks up into the nebula and says with passion, "Even I have begun to admire technology."

Li Bai, who has been in low spirit, sighs, "It seems we are moving toward each other. I see the limits of technology when applied to art. I . . ." He sobs, "I am a loser, oh . . ."

"How can you say that?" Yiyi points up to the Poetry Cloud. "That encompasses all possible poems, which of course includes those that surpass Li Bai's."

"Yet I cannot get hold of them," Li Bai says, then stamps his foot, leaps a few meters high, and curls himself into a ball in midair. He buries his face between his knees in a fetal position and descends slowly in the tiny gravity of the Earth's crust. "Since the ultimate poetry composition began, I have been working on the poetry-recognition software. However, technology met again with that unsurpassable obstacle in art, and a program that can appreciate ancient poetry is yet to be written." He points to the Poetry Cloud while still in midair. "I have indeed composed the most supreme pieces of poetry by means of our great technology, but I have been unable to locate them in the Poetry Cloud. Alas . . ."

"Is the essence and nature of intelligent life really unreachable by technology?" Big Tooth looks up and questions the Poetry Cloud. After having been through all these experiences he had become more philosophical.

"Since the Poetry Cloud encompasses all possible poems, some of them naturally describe the entirety of our past and about all possible or impossible futures. Bug Yiyi must be able to find one that describes his thoughts when he clipped his nails on an evening thirty years ago, or the menu of a lunch twelve years from now. Ambassador Big Tooth should also be able to find a poem that depicts the color of a scale on his leg in five years' time . . ." Li Bai has already landed on the surface as he speaks and hands out two chips that glitter under the glow of the Poetry Cloud: "This is a gift for you two before I go. These are the trillions of poems culled from the quantum computer with your names as the keyword. They portray all your possible future lives, which, of course, account for only a tiny portion of all the poems that are about you. I have only read a few dozens of them. My favorite is a heptasyllabic poem about Bug Yiyi that tells his love story with a pretty village girl by the riverside. . . . After I leave, I hope humans and the remaining dinosaurs can coexist with each other; humans should also have good relations among themselves. It will be trouble should the hollow Earth's crust be blown open by a nuclear bomb. . . . The good works in the Poetry Cloud do not yet belong to anyone, and I hope humans can write some of them in the future."

"How did it go with me and the village girl?" Yiyi is curious.

"You live happily together ever after," Li Bai chuckles under the silvery glow of the Poetry Cloud.

7

"SCIENCE FICTION"

A Chapter of *Daughter*

LO YI-CHIN

TRANSLATED BY THOMAS MORAN AND JINGLING CHEN

There were three large elevators, like you might see in a morgue, big enough for a gurney, roomy, but with a cold, metallic feel. We had name tags on, and I was guessing the idea was that when we reached the proper level we were to match the numbers on the tags to numbers on carts, in the carts would be isolation gowns prepared especially for each of us, and at first I was sharing an elevator with two men who talked on and on about some guy (I didn't catch the name) they had met in Japan at a conference on detective fiction who, I gathered, had just divorced his wife, and every morning he ate at the breakfast buffet by himself, just him by himself at a table for four, ignoring everybody, and the odd thing was he seemed to eat nothing but runny poached eggs, he also always had orange juice, and his table was always covered with the little dishes they served the poached eggs in. We stopped and I got out and switched to a different elevator. I did that because I knew we were going to have to take off our clothes and put on high-quality personalized isolation gowns with biologic monitoring devices, and I had no intention of getting naked in front of those two guys who talked too much. When I stopped and got off, I was surprised to find a cart with my name tag on it parked right in front of the elevator. How could they have calculated exactly where I would get off? From what I could see, the whole floor was like a place where construction is over but finishing work hasn't begun, or maybe better to say like a travel agency gone bust and everybody's left. In any event, there was no one around. I gave in to an urge and lit up a cigarette and nobody came out to stop me, no voice came over a loudspeaker saying, "Number 4273, please put out your cigarette."

So I started to change my clothes, but I felt odd. It was like when I used to go to the sauna a lot. You know, a sauna for men. You look perfectly respectable as you walk through the gaudily decorated front doors, but then you walk in past rows and rows of numbered metal lockers, like niches in a columbarium, and you come out from the locker room naked, like a plucked chicken. So everybody walks around stooped over, arms down, penis dangling, some guys have huge guts, other guys are like apes with gray hair all over their chests. I never understood why they didn't put out piles of bath towels or something you could cover yourself with. But they didn't, so you had to make a spectacle of yourself, strolling around dick out and ass bare (or, if you were a mob boss, with your bright Flood Dragon tattoos showing), and so you'd walk over to the steaming main bath feeling awkward as hell. There were always just a few shriveled old guys soaking in the main bath, and in the half dozen or so smaller Jacuzzis spread around the room like so many hot springs it was the same, nothing but naked old guys, each with a white washcloth on his head. Usually I would shower and then put on one of the Japanese-style, narrow-waisted cotton bathrobes with an indigo-dyed pattern that were stacked on one side, and then I would walk past the fitness center and the vending machines, or past the darkened room with the big television monitor and about a hundred recliners where there were always a whole lot of old guys lying there like seals on a rocky beach, rattling the place with their snoring. Then I would turn down a hidden corridor where a guy in a suit would enter a pass code into an electronic lock on a metal door. Inside the door was like an ant nest, there were a lot of dark little rooms and in each room was a narrow massage table, and (still wearing the Japanese bathrobe) I would sit on the edge of the massage table and smoke a couple of cigarettes. Then a woman would knock and come in. Usually she would be carrying a washbasin. You just lie there like a baby and let her massage you (usually she is a bit older, but in the dark she is beautiful, like a flower on a night-blooming cactus) and rub you with oil, getting you a little aroused, then she turns you over, you don't even have to help much, and then gently but expertly, like a prostitute from classic times, she'll give you head or straddle you and fuck you, and usually I cum right away.

In the cart in front of the elevator was an isolation gown, the material light and delicate like the rice paper used on lanterns, and a biologic monitoring device to attach to my chest, like a little microphone, with a coil cord leading to a control box about as a big as my fist that was to go in my pocket, also shoe covers, and a mask and gloves like a surgeon wears.... Obediently, I put it all on, like I was supposed to, and threw my clothes into the cart (when I am ready to leave the sauna I go back to the lockers and change back into my clothes, and I usually give NT$100 as a tip to the attendant, who is always standing off to the side in his embroidered suit vest, his head respectfully bowed). I got back into the elevator and rode down, going deep, deep under the ground. Every time I take this ride, long-forgotten scenes from my childhood come to my consciousness, they stay in my head for just a moment, but they are vivid, like the secret memories of an Alzheimer's sufferer: a garden full of white butterflies; a young mother smelling of milk; a hose spraying water in the sunlight on the big Pomeranian that died when you were three years old; a piece of caramel candy stashed in a desk drawer, melted, crawling with ants, a dozen dead ants stuck to its thin wax paper . . .

I got off at I don't know which floor—by this time you usually lose any practical ability for deductive reasoning. Whatever floor it was, it was busy, like the reception area of a military service office or a tax office, jam-packed and loud, the lights bright. The crowd was divided into long lines that trailed out from doorways separated by screens, everybody waiting, one behind the other. Everybody was wearing an isolation gown the same as me. I cut in line, squeezed my way into a small room, and showed my name tag to a nurse, who said, "Oh, it's you, sir . . . ," and then she rolled up the thin-as-paper fabric of the left sleeve of my isolation gown and injected me with some pale-blue drug (I imagine it was a liquid-crystal antirejection agent or something like that, something cooked up in the nuclear biological chemical labs as part of some meaningless project that did nothing but swindle research funds). I walked out of the room feeling light-headed, and some guy grabbed my arm.

"Never expected to run into you here."

I stared at him blankly. He was old. He took off his surgical mask and surgeon's hat. "You don't remember me, do you son? I'm _____, your father's best friend, I knew you when you were a baby."

It was like what happens every time you are in the headquarters of some big organization and you run into an old acquaintance. He told me all the gossip about the mischief and dirty tricks behind the scenes of the Daughter Project, the scale of which was so large that nobody had the full picture. Money disappeared into it as if into a black hole. Different teams of international contractors either clashed with or were downright antagonistic to one another on basic dynamics theory, so it could turn out that maybe the product's feet operated on two different systems, so the left big toe of German manufacture stuck out like a thumb, while the right big toe had a Japanese-made ball-bearing joint and all five of the right toes flexed in unison, and these were just the design flaws that somebody with his level of security clearance was aware of, but what if the left brain and the right brain and the left atrium and the right ventricle were put together from American, Japanese, German, Korean, and Chinese parts each with its own different standard? Different kinds of CPU, different kinds of interstitial fluids and pumps, different kinds of circuits and shafts, different kinds of heat and light sensors, different kinds of audio and visual components, different titanium alloy skeletons . . . I don't know if it was because I had just had the shot or if the sudden change in elevation had affected my ear canals, but everything went black.

Just then, oddly enough, my cell phone rang (how was that possible? I was several thousand feet underground), and everybody stopped what they were doing and looked at me, so I had no choice but to make a face and answer it.

"Hello? Is this Mr. _____? Excuse me for bothering you, but my name is Zhang, and I am with the credit office at _____ Bank. You submitted an application for a small line of credit at our Hsin-sheng branch, but we've been checking the information on your form, and while you say you work at the _____ Publishing House, when we call them they say there is no one by your name who works there, and we discovered that your health insurance isn't registered with them. May I ask you for the address of your publishing house, please? [I couldn't think of it.] Okay, well, then, can you tell me their phone number, please? [I couldn't remember it.] . . ."

At this moment two men and one woman appeared, all of them in smocks and all wearing those thin, wrinkly surgical caps with an elastic band that make it look like you have a muffin on your head, and they directed me through a door and down a hallway with door after door on both sides, and I knew that locked behind every door was a seven- or eight-year-old or maybe thirteen- or fourteen-year-old girl. They were gynoids—female androids—each made to the design particular to each of several different projects, and obviously during some key test each design was revealed to have a fatal flaw. But because the manufacture and installation of their RAM circuitry had required the painstaking efforts of entire teams of specialists over a long time, like a Suzhou embroidery master in an entire career completing only a single standing screen of a lifelike landscape stitched in silk: mandarin ducks, shadows of ripples on the water, pavilions, peonies on the shore, and a beautiful young woman with a fan enjoying the flowers . . . That's why the gynoids in all these rooms, each with her own number, hadn't been melted down in a furnace like tens of thousands of other failed products were. Project after project was started up only to be closed down, and the people in the teams who worked on the girls disappeared from the organization, leaving behind nothing but file folders full of records organized by project number— "Item. Detailed lab journal covering the uploading of personality profile scenarios, including notes on the reactions of No. 23 during various tests of emotions. At one point our strong, reliable operating system produced a worrisome microgap. It was as if we were dealing with an equational pitfall, which might worsen in the future, and we had to find a different constant or find the segment of code in the operating system where we overlooked something"—filing cabinet after filing cabinet was filled with folders of this stuff. I looked at these endless (No. 6, No. 9, No. 11, No. 15 . . .) records of experiments (you couldn't say they'd failed, it was just that something had happened to run each aground, where it was abandoned), each experiment based on a different theory of multidimensional universes. And who knows what had happened to the personnel (known only by code names) in all those different projects over the years.

All that remained from all these projects was what you could see through the spy holes in each of the many metal doors, inside, sitting upright on the edges of their little metal cots, eyes blank as if their pupils had been gouged out, looking like children forgotten in a detention home, each waiting (forever in vain) for the day her parents would come through the door, hug her, and then plug all kinds of devices into her head, pry open her chest, wonder fretfully how to "save her," all of this enveloping her like the past . . . all these still, silent female androids.

I followed the three people in smocks into the room at the far end of the hallway, where I knew that my "daughter" was waiting for me like a girl in a nunnery. Two men (one English, one Chinese) were talking to her. I knew this was part of her "curriculum," so I tried not to disturb them; I tried to make myself invisible, standing with the three engineers on the far side of the one-way glass, watching everything that was going on in the room.

The only woman among the three of them handed me a stack of manuscript pages covered in characters written in fountain pen in a graceful hand. I leafed through them.

"She wrote this?"

"Yeah. Over the course of the past six months or so."

I picked out a passage at random and read it. It was detailed, evocative prose, and an odd feeling of melancholy came over me.

"She's a genius."

This is what was written on the pages in my hands:

Lute wedged her small stool between Mammy's feet and the railings, afraid to miss a single word. So it was real?—the nether world, that immense organization busily functioning, pulsing underfoot like a factory in the cellar. What crowds, what excitement. The gigantic ferris wheel of re-incarnation that everyone was forced to mount, driven by demons with pitchforks, to fall through the air screaming and land in a midwife's hands.[1]

I looked back up at the woman, her face half obscured by her surgical mask (my guess was she had a PhD in genetic engineering).

"Who's Mammy?"

She turned red. "Me. Also Ms. He and Ms. Qin from the lab, and Director Tong, but of course most of the minor characters are virtual, not real."

I sighed. "Maybe we set the 'micromemory' parameters too high. The poor child is suffering."

I read some more, and it was hard to believe that this involved, detailed, heartfelt, humble honesty could have come from artificial intelligence:

> The tortures in hell had no terror for her, for she would not sin of course. Why should she go out of her way to do bad things? It was just as unlikely that she would be so extraordinarily good she would go to heaven and be out of the re-incarnation system forever. She would not want it for one thing. She would just do well enough to be sentenced to another human existence. To be somebody else! And not once but again and again to infinity. She had never even dared dream of anything like this when she toyed with the notion of being a blonde little girl in a foreigner's house. In re-incarnation one had no choice of what to become but the chanciness was part of the excitement. There was hardly anyone she would really mind being—not forever, but just for a lifetime. The good lives were worth waiting for. The waiting might take unconscionably long. But even her present life meant endless waiting and seemed never to come.[2]

"Wait a second," I said. "Did you let her have contact with any of the gynoids from any of the discontinued projects?"

"No. I don't think so, no."

"There's something odd then. Has Mr. Hu[3] been here lately? Was he ever alone with her?"

"He was here last month. He told us to always do what you say. He said you . . ."

"He said I was what?" Back when things started that old bastard had enormous influence on everything. He had more pull with the project leaders, the investment bankers, and the board of directors than anybody really imagined. And that's despite the fact that there was supposedly a group of people working to undermine him, and he seemed to have no allies, and he was a bit of a libertine so every so often you'd hear gossip about him and a female scientist or a nurse or some other woman. Later new people were brought in to take over the project, and I guess they were very clever in isolating him, and he was shunted to one side, demoted to a sort of spectral consultant. I also heard that there had been a separate project, which started at the same time as the Daughter Project, but no doubt with a different team of engineers in a different secret underground facility, that used him as the model during research and development for an "Adonis Android" that was to be yet another "cosmic singularity" that would set off a new big bang, start nuclear fusion, create star dust, planets, black holes, spiral nebulae, and white dwarf stars. It seems, however, that during supercomputer calculations to test a few of his theories and model a multidimensional universe formed from a matrix of numbers derived from the six mysterious numbers that shaped everything, a systemic corruption occurred, as if there had been an attack by hackers, and the supercomputer entered into "eternal return," to use the term the engineers gave it, or "cybernetic death," in which beautiful star charts multiplied endlessly, obscuring the dark matter parameters.

The woman in the smock said, "Sir, he said you are the 'father' . . ."

"He said that?" It occurred to me that maybe the old bastard had been hitting on this woman; all I could see of her face behind her surgical mask was her eyes, and it was like what Bai Juyi wrote of Yang Guifei, "When she turned and looked at you, her eyes spoke volumes," or you could say, "There was something about her that would make any man feel unworthy." Of course, because I was in the Daughter Project, which was not of high priority among all the projects ongoing in the huge mazelike ant nest where the people in one lab didn't know what was going on down some other corridor under some other code name or what sort of experiments were being rolled out based on somebody's crazy idea, mobilizing who knows which leading experts in who knows what branches of science, and everybody trying to figure out how to right the sinking ship, the hull ripped open by a mine and taking on water, therefore when I heard I'd earned praise from a fabled master trickster who came and went like a ghost, it was hard not to feel pleased with myself, and I blushed.

"When he went in that time, what did he say to her?"

"I'm not sure. He made us turn off the monitors. I . . . we told him that was against regulations . . ." Her ears, which her surgical mask was hooked around, turned red.

I sighed. Who could resist him?

"I think he told her that he had to go on the run because a lot of people were out to capture him and hurt him. They talked for about an hour, and after he left she put her head down on the table and sobbed. We found this note he left . . ."

The girl in the smock handed me the note and I unfolded it. It was his handwriting all right. He had written just one sentence, a paraphrase of Cao Cao: "Disaster approaches, my lips are dry, my mouth is cotton."[4]

I was thinking that everything etched onto her brain lobes, all the precisely engineered and intricately complicated circuitry, and the Bloch Sphere that mapped space-time decoherence, we had controlled for all that, and I sensed there was an error somewhere, and the error hadn't come at the start of the Daughter Project, which had involved hundreds of high-IQ supersmart scientists and many, many all-night sessions of intense discussion, debate, and supposition plus myriad calculations and recalculations . . . the error was like a small tear in the calf of a silk stocking, just a tiny cool spot at first, a premonition lying in the subconscious like a snake.

I looked back down at the manuscript in my hands and turned to the last few pages she had written:

> Laotze had come from the last people of Shang who after the fall of Shang had made a living on their knowledge of old traditions and priestcraft, turning into hereditary priests but careful to keep out of the administration's way. So centuries after the deaths of those two brothers their clansman Laotze taught the clan's wisdom of survival with constant admonitions to be frightened, keep to the wall and walk fast, always beware of trouble. In the eternal struggle between *yin* and *yang* he apparently believed *yin* the female and passive would win most of the time.[5]

This was all certainly well beyond anything I could have ever imagined when we began. It was like looking close-up at some dazzling but terrifying constellation of stars looming overhead, something like the Milky Way, formed over billions of years, its winding, endless, marvelous light flowing slowly but not so slowly you couldn't detect the motion with your naked eye as it was swallowed by a black hole, like a toad, with emotionless eyes, swallowing a whale, which raises its tail and fights, and then silence, not even a burp.

I had to admit that my head was feeling a little fuzzy. Mostly it was exhaustion. I had been using antidepressants of dubious manufacture for a long time and also taking a sleep medicine called Stilnox that was habit-forming, so it was like my limbic system was full of tiny men who were cutting it up into pieces with the blue flames of acetylene torches. I remembered that the night before I'd attended a seminar about the Daughter Project. I remembered that in my remarks I had made reference to Peruvian author Mario Vargas Llosa's novel *The Storyteller*, which is about a tribe of people called the Machiguenga who live in Peru's mountains. They travel among villages that are cut off from one another by high peaks, they aren't shamans or witch doctors, they pick up news as they travel and bring the news to the next village they visit. They are "storytellers." Their stories are about everything: they talk of taboos, incest, murder, villages ruined because of ancient curses, one story was about a man and his wife both with skin as pale as that of angels who came to visit a village, where they were given a warm welcome with wine and dancing, but after dark the villagers were possessed by devils, they hacked the man to death and then the village men gang-raped the woman until she was dead. . . . The storytellers didn't just talk about what they saw and heard, they put themselves into their stories, weaving everything together into a confused tapestry that blended fact and fiction. Their stories took history, myth, and otherwise-to-be-forgotten legend about the horrifying things they had done or their ancestors had done, things you didn't know what to make of and would only whisper about, and the storytellers took all this as if it were dreams in amber or in frozen agar compressed into blocks, which they put on their backs and carried along ridges and through valleys to the next village, where they emptied their baskets full of stories in the middle of the small square where all the tribe's people, all the men and women, all the young and old, would be gathered waiting for them around a bonfire.

Because I was nervous, after I had made reference to the Vargas Llosa novel, I said that in the days when the people on the two sides of the strait were cut off from one another, the authors of the greatest works of mainland Chinese literature were just like Vargas Llosa's storytellers, they "emptied their baskets full of stories" at our feet. But in the moment, I stupidly credited a novel by one important author to a different writer. I realized this only after the seminar, when a woman scholar came over and told me I had made a mistake. Sure enough, at the banquet that night, when I went with the scholars and writers at my table up to the head table

to make toasts, when I raised my glass to the author whose (very important) novel I had screwed up on, he turned away, but in his pretended
distraction he couldn't hide his hurt feelings.

It seemed that half the papers given at the seminar alluded to, appro-
priated, or used as a metaphor the woman writer who was the behind-
the-scenes model for the Daughter Project. Mostly people talked about
her mysterious disappearance. She hid herself for more than fifty years in
some dark place with no news of her whatsoever except for the faintest
threads of clues, as if her life was the most baffling of mystery stories.
About every decade or so there was a new flurry of interest in her. Different
generations of historians became fascinated by her in her absence. They
played crime scene detective and were always able to find some new piece
of evidence that overturned the previous theories about her life that had
long since become the conventional wisdom. It made one wonder: by
choosing to "live as if dead" and endure a lonely existence in an apartment
somewhere in the United States, was she perhaps sacrificing her life for
the sake of making herself a legend? Or was it because the awful experiences she had as a girl destroyed her, leaving her with pain greater than
we can imagine, pain like a black hole that ate away at her ability to live
an ordinary life while she fought not to go mad, fought to go on "living,"
pleading weakly, "Just please leave me alone"?

Most important, her little trick of "let him see you only in profile, smile
but don't speak, lower your head so your neck curves like a dying swan"
wormed its way into the brains of countless generations of girls, taking
possession like a devil, like a leech laying eggs. Without being aware of it
they copied her studied aloofness and her deliberate, affected tone of sarcastic ridicule. A good-for-nothing opium addict father like "a dead baby
pickled in alcohol," trapped in a dark room, pacing, reciting memorials,
calls to arms, briefs for the emperor, and eight-legged essays, nothing
having anything to do with the real world. A mother stubbornly thinking of herself as a maiden, always radiating pheromones but her womb
never conceiving, with bound feet but wearing Western dress and carrying a lace parasol. A mansion full of flickering shadows of ghosts, home
to a grand family, elders, wives and concubines, servants, all of them
together forming a structure that seemed to teeter on slender supports
but was still standing, the connections among them as intricate as cais-
son ceilings or Gothic arches or the bones in a rotting fish head, and all

their hypocrisy, dissembling and backbiting sharp as an executioner's sword, ready to slice and dissect anybody who was not there and did or said anything dubious in the slightest, cutting him into pieces, leaving nothing but "strange shattered bones."

But these imitators, Young Woman No. 5, Young Woman No. 9, Young Woman No. 17, Young Woman No. 23 . . . they made the choice to cast themselves into polar regions, into hell, barren, cold, and deathly silent, leaving us to picture them in some imagined collapsed colorless universe, when in fact they desired lives of splendor, they wanted to go to parties and gossip, they wanted to sit in coffee shops and cheerfully eat colorful macaroons and crèmes brûlées and drink Bellinis. They felt compelled to post to Facebook cute selfies taken looking up at the camera close-up so their eyes looked big. When they were young they had secret affairs with powerful but prudent sugar daddies at least twenty years older who mentored them. He would be emotional and a little distant and from time to time he might talk about how evil people were where he came from, where every anxious step was taken as if on thin ice. But now they were in the middle of a prosperous golden age, and their lips weren't dry, their mouths weren't cotton.

I got to know a few of these "young" women, who were actually around forty, during the time of their upside-down, misdirected, broken-glass-strewn "sentimental education"—take, for example, the plan for Daughter Project Android Queen I, which was as exquisite and delicate as moss in a forest: never fall in love, cut love away like removing dead tissue with laser surgery, love is just the exegetics of lies, disgusting dried semen on your thigh the morning after, nothing but endless annotation to an ancient text—but they all had stories about passionate affairs, love stories so strange and poignant they could only come from a split personality.

Thus when the Stilnox hadn't worn off, all this in my head was like gunk stuck in a drain, and it left me feeling confused, so at conferences, which I always dreaded anyway, my attention would wander and I'd make mistakes.

Many things, of course, were out of my control, including the guiding forces behind the whole enormous project. I knew nothing about the influential old men and their power struggles that went on out of sight like a riptide. One of the old men once gave a series of talks in the main lecture hall of our underground fortress that lasted for a week. I was there with representatives from the other independent working groups that had been put together eons ago. I had never met any of them before. They worked on the X Project, the Angels Project, the Naruto Project, the Androgyny Project, the Desolate Man Project, the Chaos and Confusion Project, the Inscribed Backs Project, the Unwounded Age Project, the Possessed Project, the Life Is Not Worth Living Project, the Last Year at Marienbad Project, the Dream Devourer Project, the Alubar Project, the Demon Killer Project, the Daybook Project, the Devil's Madness Project . . . all of us had been sent a memo requiring that we attend the lectures, which were called "Explaining Mr. Tang Yongtong's *On Wei Jin Metaphysics*."

The program listed the title of each lecture:

1. "Reading *The Study of Human Abilities*"
2. "On the Distinction between Word and Meaning"
3. "An Introduction to Wang Bi's *Summary of the Great Expansion*"
4. "Explaining Wang Bi's Argument That the Sage Has Emotions"
5. "A New Reading of Wang Bi's Commentary on the *Book of Changes* and the *Analects*"
6. "The Zhuangzi and Confucius of the Xiang-Guo Commentary"
7. "The Influence of Xie Lingyun's *On Religious Debate*"

In the seat next to me a woman with a shaved head and wearing a sheath dress sighed and said, "Motherfucker, looks like I'm going to catch up on sleep whether I want to or not."

The old guy stood up there at the podium looking lonely, mumbling, seemingly with tears brimming in his eyes, speaking to maybe a dozen people in an auditorium that held a thousand (and those dozen were sprawled out asleep in sunglasses, or eating instant noodles, or humming along to MP3 music in their earbuds, or checking their Facebook pages), but in fact what he said was, to my surprise, enlightening (even though I have completely forgotten most of it). I do remember a line from Wang Bi's annotated version of the *Book of Changes* that he read in a faltering voice:

Whenever activity ceases, tranquility results, but tranquility is not opposed to activity. Whenever speech ceases, silence results, but silence is not opposed to speech. As this is so, then even though Heaven and Earth are so vast that they possess the myriad things in great abundance, which, activated by thunder and moved by the winds, keep undergoing countless numbers of transformations, yet the original substance of Heaven and Earth consists of perfectly quiescent nonbeing.[6]

Something suddenly became clear to me and I felt like crying, it was like there was some ancient ancestor gently stroking the blue-veined skin of your face. They were talking about the "singularity" in the first 10^{-43} seconds after the big bang, they were talking about a dark, stinking world where dead souls are pushed here and there, shackled in dust-filled light in a wooden hut, you assumed those people lived in a dank world of snot and phlegm, eating ground fetuses, binding girls' feet into gnarled roots, cooking opium, shitting into wooden buckets because they have no plumbing, brother doing sister-in-law and father doing daughter-in-law, and a young widow took a lover so the villagers dragged her out and drowned her, but they came up with a description of their own, like our calculation made with ten thousand supercomputers, "suppose the universe has a nuclear fuel rod with an infinite fuel supply at its center," they have described "nothingness" and the "clarity of the void" in comprehensive, flowing, flickering, graceful, lyrical fashion. For every single dazzling expanding multiverse of folding time they have long since set in place a descriptive model based on an opposition of "activity" and "tranquility." Matter is created and destroyed, *à la recherche du temps perdu*, affect and affectlessness, free-and-easy wandering, a shining eternal spiritual realm.

But why create for the universe the two civilizations of "activity" and "tranquility" and then add "political, economic, and tribal struggle and war between nations, the mobilization of troops, bureaucracies, religious ideology, the servility and madness of the crowd, pestilence, conspiracies and struggles among party factions and crazed monarchs who use lofty language to justify killing their enemies and executing all their enemies' relatives and relations, inventing all manner of torture to violate, lacerate, and break bodies"? Could these complicated formulae in tangled calculations produce something like my Daughter Project, which was like an "ominous black hole" that shuts out all light with a bizarre mortise structure so dense it cannot be penetrated? Like some beautiful magic celestial mussel, incubating for a thousand years before it drops two dark, ugly, wailing black eyes? Could it produce Young Woman No. 1, who was born in "tranquility," stamped and sealed, wings cut off, eardrums punctured, vocal cords scorched, a bolt through her scapula chaining her inside a damp hell after *The Fall of the Pagoda*? Could it produce *The Book of Change* that she wrote in "activity," in "free-and-easy wandering," with its chilling line, "keep to the wall and walk fast, always beware of trouble," her vitality burned away in a jungle of hypocrisy, cheating, and lies, and guarding against the lies of others, the work becoming something to counter a system of loveless, undependable values that is a far-flung network of "counterfeit software," a warning that we could be betrayed and abandoned at any time but still, as Su Shi wrote, "Do not be frightened by the unexpected, do not be angered when insulted without cause"?

After the lecture, I went up to pay my respects to the old man. He looked dejected and exhausted as he put his lecture notes back into his briefcase. I startled him a bit, and he looked up in surprise (he was accustomed to monologue, just him droning on abstrusely for hours on end to an auditorium empty except for a dozen or so people, most of them asleep and snoring).

I said I'd learned a lot from his lecture, and he stared at me over his glasses (with a chilly smile).

He said, "I've heard them mention you."

I don't remember much about our conversation, which didn't last long and was like dharma combat between a Zen master and a monk. But when we parted (to leave the auditorium and go back to our respective departments), he clapped me on the shoulder.

"Boy, don't get lost in fantasies. Keep your shoulder to the wheel." As I recall, the next thing he said was . . .

"Imagine that we have between us two huge axial-flow turbine jet engines. According to the classic *Wikipedia* schematic representation of the principles involved, each engine has an inlet, a compression chamber, a combustion chamber with a turbine, an exhaust opening, and an afterburner. The compressor functions by the meshing of stator blades and rotor blades. These engines operate under conditions of extreme stress, and so all the material and construction must be to the highest standard. We are talking here, of course, about engines for supersonic fighter jets. Intake valves pull in air violently, subject it to high pressure, and expel it under the airfoil, causing a change in pressure gradient. But suppose these two turbine engines were drawing in not air but rather, for argument's sake, time, or drawing in all of humankind's virtue and sin, drawing in the pollutants drifting through the universe, something intangible like that, and suppose it could make a concentrate of it all and hide it in plain sight among the thousands of winged angels of our collective dreams or among the ancestors who flow past us like a river of flowing bubbles, all the terror, violence, sex, miracles, and love contained in stories, all civilizations that are like the gold leaf and colored tiles on temples, all civilizations that are like filth stuck in a drain, corpses, toxins . . . if we had these two 'magic engines' that could take all this microscopic, ephemeral stuff found in the universe, which is like mayflies, like smoke, like a billion jellyfish, if they could draw this all in, and with something like divine fury or divine mercy subject it to high temperature and compression and by a ten-power geometric series of blades make it explode, producing something that our ape brains could never imagine or understand, producing 'hyperdrive,' what would that be?"

"Well, it would be like Picasso's *Guernica* or a Jackson Pollock, something that looks like it's been spit out from a meat grinder, right?"

No, he said, I didn't explain it well. It's not a meat grinder, or a cement mixer, and it's not like some art student who is just screwing around spraying different colors of paint on a naked girl and a boy in a thong as they run back and forth. The important point is, I am speaking of what you may suppose to be a girl whose existence as a god you take as a given, just as we take the presence of the dead as a given when we sacrifice to them, I'm speaking of her pupils, of the two "worm-wheel engines of civilization" in the ventricles of her brain. I am speaking of the "flight of civilization," not of corpses, wreckage and rubble, I am speaking of the androids of old who advanced backward, holding their useless wings, faces full of pain, like Paul Klee's *Angelus Novus* in a typhoon that blows toward the future.

Imagine that in the area of the gynoid's left and right temporal bones, we install the kind of propulsion engines I'm talking about, and they take the dreams of civilization, compress them and inject them so that she feels them all clearly, so they sway before her like curtains of Northern Lights. "In the eyes of the gods" humanity is bacteria grown beyond control in a petri dish; it grew, evolved, escaped from the petri dish, some-how invented machinery, spread out, took over, and eventually destroyed the entire mystical "laboratory of dreams."

But I was too tired. Those days my brain was like a computer you couldn't turn off. You could hear a laptop's fan humming and dispelling the heat when I was in meetings or eating, or in the shower or taking a shit, when I took the long elevator ride down into the project's under-ground offices, digital numbers flashing, and even when I was deep asleep and dreaming, in my head I was always drawing—the Daughter Project was about to enter its second stage, and I had heard that the dis-continued previous generations of androids, their memory chips fried, had all run into their fatal flaw at this stage, at this juncture when careful calculations fell victim to an unexpected variable—a lifelike map for a fictional city like something out of *Dream Reminiscences of Tao'an*, detailed down to the alleys. This of course was according to a model based on the idea of "tranquility" (like *Dream of the Red Chamber*?) and "activ-ity" (like *Journey to the West*?), which forced both into an overlay on each other. Those star physicists lured away from NASA and the Large Had-ron Collider project told me that if we superimpose each of two different models on the other, making a "radical advancement that exceeds what our theories predict" (the scholar from India said, "If we sleep with the devil"), then from nothing we can produce (perhaps only as large as a tea egg in the event) a "universe in miniature," but it would be a vibrating string lying outside a gap through the thin membrane of our universe. It should not occur in "this universe of ours." Perhaps it might swallow up our universe in an instant.

All this sounded like poetry to me. But what I wanted to do—just like when we uploaded compressed memories like "microgods" and stitched them into the very being of the girl in stage one (Daughter No. 1, an AI girl the scope of whose wisdom went beyond what we'd imagined) every single fold in her cerebral cortex and every nerve fiber uploaded with "nanoeconomy" (she said plaintively, "I want to throw up")—was some-thing completely different: I wanted to do something that was like taking a balled-up page from a newspaper and ironing it flat.

In my head I had something like a Google Earth map of city streets, the kind where the focal point keeps changing (I was going to put Daugh-ter No. 1 into it, like in that old computer game Princess Maker, and there she would have a life like a real life), but there was no bathhouse, no "People's Assembly" or any such architectural legacy of colonialism, no library (perhaps because of some limitation of my imagination), even no movie theater or general hospital (I like the specialized clinics squeezed into small rooms behind arcades that run along the street: Zhang's Dermatology, Shining Star Dental Clinic, Taishō Ophthalmology, Li's Obstetrics and Gynecology, Qiu Bizong's Pediatrics, Zhesheng's Ear, Nose, and Throat, a Western pharmacy of the kind you always find in old-style markets), no five-star hotel (what to do if the hotel's shuttle bus needs to leave for the airport?), and nothing like the green-felt-covered gambling tables of Macao with their colorful chips and dice . . . it was all like a fancy casino as tightly sealed as a hospital clean room or a soundproof room, maybe it would have subway stations, department stores, underground shopping centers, or a place like an Eslite Bookstore, just to give her a 3D immersive sensation like stepping into a hollow space in an Impressionist painting, the faces on the people in the crowd indistinct, as if the pixels were bright but blurred. My fictional metropolis was a re-creation of what I liked in a noisy and crowded city (and so I labored over the details as obsessively as a lepidopterist studies tiny distinctions between species), and there were many places that sold lottery tickets (for me, these small places only a single *ping* in area with a yellow cabinet and on top of the cabinet a reclining God of Wealth, a plug-in *maneki-neko* Lucky Cat, a Money Toad, or play money gold ingots, behind the lottery vending machine there is a middle-aged woman, or a man with cerebral palsy, or a woman in a sexy see-through gauze dress, or a pretty young matron in light makeup, or a little girl, no more than third grade, her hair in pigtails, or a crew-cut gang boss, tattoos crawling up his arms, chewing on betel nut . . . but each signifies something completely different); and into the profusion of vegetation swallowing the walls along the streets with a flood of green, wisteria, melaleuca, peepul, royal palm, fringe trees, royal poinciana, banyan, frangipani, Yoshino cherry trees, chinaberry, red maple, common nandina, magnolia, night-blooming cactus, plum, and camellia, I inserted all sorts of little crisscrossing lanes with intricately changing light and shadow. A sixty-year-old church, a little Ma Zu temple at the end of an alley, and at an intersection a mosque, by which there is always a group of Africans and Indonesian girls; and of course, many shops whose names alone were like the flickering lamps in *Dream*

Recollections of Tao'an, beautiful jade pendants that flourished in impossible profusion, coffee shops, secondhand bookstores, imported women's clothing stores, stores selling secondhand name brand handbags from Paris; pashmina, jewelry and hat stores, and arrayed under glass: rose *matcha* blueberry toffee lemon dark chocolate tangerine kiwifruit peppermint . . . colors named after flavors, a shop with macaroons in many colors spread out as on a watercolor palette, shops that roast coffee beans of a hundred kinds from all over the world, Japanese wine bars with blue cloth door curtains and dim lighting, Tibet stores that smell of sandalwood and the strange aroma of butter lamps and sell thankas, turquoise and agate and bone prayer beads, and Tibetan instruments decorated with bone, ivory, and silver, tobacco shops, essential oil shops that make it seem as if all the nouns in the world could each be kept in its own small glass bottle, and all the different types of specialty tea shops where different types of tea are sealed in labeled tins, as if in each ghosts and monsters sleep, waiting for the seal to be broken, waiting for boiling water, so they can spiral up and out, changing into plumed phoenixes and scaled *kirin* or taking the hems of their gowns in one hand and lowering the other to the ground in a bow, like sages of old.

This city, which blurred at its edges, was entirely in my head (including the black cat that walked silently along the moss-covered wall with broken glass embedded in its plastered top; including the postman in his sweat-soaked green uniform, the surveillance camera hidden on the back of a lamppost, the massage parlor where all the masseurs are blind middle-aged men whose eyes look like they have been pulled out with pliers, including the retired army captain who is the doorman at the old apartment building and who still lovingly combs his quiff every day, but it is now so sparse it looks like a bar code, and he still looks intently at all the "ladies" who walk by in high heels, and he is sure to bow and smile, then stare at their asses and legs and think dirty thoughts, and glare with obvious suspicion at the young men in T-shirts, shorts and sneakers . . .). There was rustling in my skull as if millions of cilia of cephalopods were brushing up against every microinch of the hardware, searching, even boring through and infiltrating it. I knew that this was the Daughter Project trying to remove out from my brain, as with an ice cream scoop, everything that was in there frozen solid or half frozen but this was part of the bargain. Of course maybe I was just overworked.

One day I found myself sitting in the dark with my legs tucked under me. (An engineer was projecting a PowerPoint. The auditorium lights were down, and he was speaking in a low, toneless voice, "How will the quantum mechanics of creation get its processing power into the frontal lobes of the brain through quantum decoherence and ensure that the supercomputer that is sequencing the human genome integrates with the similarly randomly generated hundred million dreams of a person's lifetime, with the dreams of an aborted fetus, with dreams that coil like tapeworms, or the momentary, meaningless dreams of spermatozoa?") The faces of the people seated randomly around me were stained with the colors of the projection, like blue light falling on water. I fell asleep. Probably for only a minute or two because when I woke with a confused start and gathered myself, I ascertained that "I'm here in the underground laboratory of the Daughter Project, in one of the meeting rooms." It was still the same slide up on the screen that I had been looking at when I fell asleep (on the slide was a photo taken down at a forty-five-degree angle of the side of a Shang-dynasty bronze vessel and next to it a close-up photograph of the bronze's underside: it looked like a bronze cup with an engraving of a dragon with glaring eyes, its mouth open and clamped around a shaman, but if you flipped the image upside down, you saw the male shaman on the bottom with his penis in the vagina of a female dragon).

I was asleep for only a second, but every frame of my dream was composed and lit exquisitely and vividly.

It was a simple dream and even though it happened within narrow brackets of time, there was no sense of jump cuts or any feeling that it was rushed. Everything unfolded at a leisurely pace, like life would be this way forever, time hanging heavy. I felt at ease but lonely, it was like the feeling in childhood on a summer afternoon, the loud sound of cicadas, the adults are all gone, and you are lying hot and sleepy on a bamboo recliner, shooing flies with a plastic fan, staring blankly out the window at sunlight-dappled leaves.

In the dream, my wife had gone out with our two sons (so I have a wife and two children?) and I was home alone in our little apartment, to which we'd added a wooden second-story loft that extended halfway out over the first floor. Because I was bored (I had nothing to do but wait for them to come home) I reached into the crazy pile of stuff on the youngest boy's desk, a jumble of all kinds of toys, stuffed animals, a Gundam action figure, a Batman mask, hollow plastic triceratops, pterodactyls, brontosauruses, and Tyrannosaurus rex, and a bunch of weirdly funny cloth puppets of beasts that aren't human but not animal either, like from Sesame Street, and I picked up a hot-air balloon, small, one-thousand-to-one scale. In the dream the feel of the little hot-air balloon in my hand was fleetingly real. The hydrogen-fuel tank was so exact it astonished me, so with my other hand I reached into my pocket and took out my plastic cigarette lighter and sparked it next to the tank's nozzle.

But apparently there was a leak in the fuel tank and with a bang the little flame from my lighter bloomed big like a night-blooming cactus flower and enveloped the gondola in fire. Startled, I let go of the thing, and the balloon, so small but so real, slowly floated halfway up to the high ceiling. In the dream, I watched it fly up toward the loft, thinking that that was my wife's bedroom up there, and so in a panic I ran up the spiral staircase two steps at a time. The balloon had floated over into a corner of my wife's bookcase where there was a stack of old books bound in red—I watched the miniature conflagration: blue flames climbed the dozen or so cables from which the gondola was intricately suspended and with a boom the entire balloon caught fire then shrank, listed, and fell—the books immediately caught on fire. In the dream, I was instantly struck with a strangely doubled fear directed at the two different levels of the dream: on one level I thought, "What a disaster, all my wife's books (the secret to the whole dream?) are going to be burned up"; and on the other, "What a disaster, the fire might spread and burn up the entire apartment (the dream's 'space capsule'?)." But I went directly to the sink at one side of the room and got water and put out the flames, which were already reaching as high as my knees.

Oddly, while some of my wife's books had been burned to ashes and the ones that hadn't been burned had been soaked, when my wife came back with the boys later on, none of them noticed that we had just had a small, now-extinguished house fire. Nobody smelled smoke in the air. I was joking around with them as if nothing had happened, but I felt guilty because I was hiding from them the "airborne fire" I alone had caused and that had "almost cast everything into flame."

That's when I woke up. As I have said, I was still in the auditorium, and we were still on the same PowerPoint slide of the Shang-dynasty bronze decorated with "a beast devouring a person" or "sex between man and beast." The speaker was still mumbling something about "Shamans. Hallucinogens. My views on electrical theory and hypertheory."

It was, however, after that day, I think, that my "urban projection drawing" seemed to have been infected by a computer virus, and it started to fill up with vaguely defined dark things.

For example, the little shops along the lanes and alleys would be spreading as fast as invasive vines, and I would suddenly lose my concentration (it was like when you are dreaming and it goes along for a long time with you obeying that vague tacit agreement so you know it's a dream but then all at once you suddenly think, "Hey, I don't think I've ever looked in a mirror during a dream to see what I look like in this particular space-time, have I?" and so a mirror appears before you but this is against the rules, so to speak, or it breaks the mechanism that keeps the boundary between dream and waking in place, and so each time it gets to this point, the dream's computer screen goes into forced quit and abruptly the entire lifelike dreamworld with its light and shadow goes dark) and I would want to take a look at the old Japanese-style houses with their black roof tiles that I slowly and hesitantly had repeatedly built in my brain, along with those mottled, collapsing courtyard walls, and at the doorplates and house numbers on all those "peaceful happy homes,"[7] but I would discover that it was a mistake to worry about "doorplates and house names" because there was never once when the names of the streets or the street numbers on the houses were the same as the previous time.

But it didn't really matter, did it? I consoled myself with this thought.

But how was I going to get my "daughter" into a world that was always slipping away? How was she to live there if its scale kept changing and its dimensions kept shifting? If she wanted to write to a far-away friend what would she use as the return address? (Or would it be best just to exclude the entire concept of "friend" from her world?) Or suddenly the rotted red wooden door of the dependable old Japanese-style house that I passed by last time (which actually looked like a movie set) opened with a bang and a silver-haired old woman, her skin shriveled like an animal's, wearing a cheongsam, her eyes still beautiful (even though she is ninety years old), stared at me with sparkling eyes.

(I almost cried out in alarm, "Where did you come from?")

This became a worry that I could not rid from my brain. It was as if somebody were at a keyboard in there entering keywords. Clack. Clack. Clack clack clack clack clack. Clack clack clack clack clack clack clack clack.

Or I would walk by a used bookstore that once had a black and white cat, the proprietor was middle-aged and wore glasses, and he would have books spread out under the sun in the courtyard (among them a lot of old Japanese books that came from the nearby apartment of a professor who passed away and were brought over in a truck by a refuse collector, and books by Lu Xun, tattered pages of excerpts from Tanizaki Jun'ichirō copied out in a beautiful hand by some Taiwanese intellectual half a century ago, and old, yellowed long out-of-print novels, philosophy books, and manga), or he would be playing vinyl LPs of the high plaintive notes of the Chinese fiddle and the soft, smoky vocals of Fujian folk music.

8

BALIN

CHEN QIUFAN

TRANSLATED BY KEN LIU

I judge of your sight by my sight, of your ear by my ear, of your reason by my reason, of your resentment by my resentment, of your love by my love. I neither have, nor can have, any other way of judging about them.

—ADAM SMITH, *THE THEORY OF MORAL SENTIMENTS*

Balin's dark skin, an adaptation for the tropics, appears as aphotic as the abyss of deep space, all reflected light absorbed by the thick layer of gel smeared over his body and the nanometer-thin translucent membrane wrap. Suspended between bubbles in the gel, microsensors twinkle with a pale blue glow like dying stars, like the miniature images of me in his eyes.

"Don't be afraid," I whisper. "Relax. Soon it'll be better."

As though he understands me, his face softens and wrinkles pile up at the corners of his eyes. Even the scar over his brow is no longer so apparent.

He's old. Though I've never figured out how to tell the age in his kind.

My assistant helps Balin onto the omnidirectional treadmill, securing a harness around his waist. No matter in which direction he runs and how fast, the treadmill will adjust to keep him centered and stable.

The assistant hands the helmet to me, and I put it over Balin's head myself. His eyes, bulging with astonishment like two lightbulbs, disappear into the darkness.

"Everything will be fine," I say, my voice so low that no one can hear me, as though I were comforting myself.

The red light on the helmet flashes, faster and faster. A few seconds later, it turns green.

As though struck by a spell, Balin's body stiffens. He reminds me of a lamb who has heard the grinding of the butcher's knife against the whetstone.

A summer night the year I turned thirteen: the air was hot and sticky; the scent of rust and mold, prelude to a typhoon, filled my nostrils.

I lay on the floor of the main hall of my ancestral compound. I flattened my body against the cool, green mosaic stone tiles like a gecko until the floor under my body had been warmed by my skin; then I rolled to the side, seeking a fresh set of tiles to keep me cool.

From behind came the familiar sound of scuffling leather soles: crisp, quick paced, echoing loudly in the empty hall. I knew who it was, but I didn't bother to move, greeting the owner of those footsteps with the sight of my raised ass.

"Why aren't you in the new house? There's air-conditioning."

My father's tone was uncharacteristically gentle. The new house he referred to was a three-story addition just erected at the back of the ancestral compound, filled with imported furniture and appliances and decorated in the latest fashion. He had even added a spacious study just for me.

"I hate the new house."

"Foolish child!" He raised his voice, but then quickly lowered it to a barely audible mutter.

I knew he was apologizing to our ancestors. I gazed up at the shrine behind the joss sticks and the black-and-white portraits on the wall to see if any of them would react to my father's entreaties.

They did not.

My father heaved a long sigh. "Ah Peng, I haven't forgotten your birthday. I had an accident on the way back from up north with the cargo, which is why I'm two days late."

I shifted and wriggled like a pond loach until I found another cool spot on the tiled floor.

The cigarette stench on my father's breath permeated the air as he whispered at my ear, "I've had your present ready for a long while. You'll like it; it's not something you can buy in a shop."

He clapped twice, and I heard a different set of footsteps approach, the sound of flesh flapping against stone, close together, moist, like some amphibious creature that had just crawled out of the sea.

I sat up and gazed in the direction of the sound. Behind my father, a lively black silhouette, limned by the creamy yellow light of the hallway light, stood over the algae-green mosaic tiles. A disproportionately large bulbous head swayed over a thin and slight figure, like the sheep's head atop the slender stick that served as a sign outside the butcher's shop in town.

The shadow took two steps forward, and I realized that the backlight wasn't the only reason the figure was so dark. The person—if one could call the creature a person—seemed to be covered from head to toe in a layer of black paint that absorbed all light. It was as though a seam had been torn in the world and the person-shaped crack devoured all light— except for two tiny glows: his slightly protruding eyes.

It was indeed a boy, a naked boy who wore a loincloth woven from bark and palm fronds. His head wasn't quite as large as it had seemed in shadow; rather, the illusion had been caused by his hair, worn in two strange buns that resembled the horns of a ram. Agitated, he concentrated on the gaps between the tiles at his feet, his toes wiggling and squirming, sounding like insect feet scrabbling along the floor.

"He's a *paoxiao*," my father said, giving me the name of a creature from ancient myths who was said to possess the body of a goat, the head of a man—though with eyes located below the cheeks, the teeth of a tiger, and the nails of a human, and who cried like a baby and devoured humans without mercy. "We captured him on one of the small islands in the South China Sea. I imagine that he's never set foot on a civilized floor in his life."

I stared at him, stupefied. The boy was about my age, but everything about him made me uneasy—especially the fact that my father gave him to me as a present.

"I don't like him," I said. "I'd rather have a puppy."

A violent fit of coughing seized my father. It took him a few moments to recover.

"Don't be stupid. He's worth a lot more than a dog. If I hadn't seen him with my own eyes, I would never have believed he's real." His voice grew ethereal as he went on.

A susurrating noise grew louder. I shuddered; the typhoon was here.

The wind blew the boy's scent to me, a strong, briny stench that reminded me of a fish, a common, slender, iron-black, cheap fish trawled from the ocean.

That's a good name for him, isn't it? I thought.

———— ∞ ————

My father had long planned out everything about my life up through age forty-five.

At eighteen I would attend a college right here in Guangdong Province and study business—the school couldn't be more than three hours from home by train.

In college, I would not be allowed to date. This was because my father had already picked out a girl for me: the daughter of his business partner Lao Luo. Indeed, he had taken the trouble to go to a fortune-teller to ensure that the eight characters of our birth times were compatible.

After graduation, Lao Luo's daughter and I would get married. By my twenty-fifth year, my father would have his first grandchild. By twenty-eight I would give him another. And depending on the sexes of the first two, he might want a third as well.

Simultaneous with the birth of my first child I would also join the family business. He would take me around to pay my respects to all his partners and suppliers (he had gotten to know most of them in the army).

Since I was expected to work very long hours, who would take care of my child? His mother, of course—see, my father already decided it would be a boy. My wife would stay home; there would be two sets of grandparents; and we could hire nannies.

By age thirty I would take over the Lin Family Tea Company. In the five years prior to this point, I would have to master all aspects of the tea trade, from identification of tea leaves to manufacture and transport, as well as the strengths and weaknesses of all my father's partners and competitors.

For the next fifteen years, with my retired father as my adviser, I would lead the family business to new heights: branching out into other provinces and spreading Lin tea all over China; and if I'm lucky, perhaps even breaking into the overseas trade, a lifelong goal that my father had always wanted—but also hesitated—to pursue.

By the time I was forty-five, my oldest child would be close to graduating from college. At that point, I would follow in my father's footsteps and find a good wife for him.

Everything in my father's universe functioned as an essential component in an intricate piece of well-maintained clockwork: gear meshed with gear, wheel turned upon wheel, motion without end.

Whenever I argued with him over his grand plan for me, he always brought up my grandfather, his grandfather, and then my grandfather's grandfather—he would point at the wall of ancestors' portraits and denounce me for forgetting my roots.

This is the way the Lin family has survived, he would say. *Are you telling me you are no longer a Lin?*

Sometimes I wondered if I was really living in the twenty-first century.

I called him Balin. In our topolect, *balin* meant a fish with scales.

In reality, he looked more like a goat, especially when he lifted his eyes to gaze at the horizon, his two hair buns poking up like horns. My father told me that *paoxiao* have an incredibly strong sense of direction. Even if they were blindfolded, hog-tied, tossed into the dark hold of a ship, hauled across the ocean in a journey lasting weeks, and sold and resold through numerous buyers, they'd still be able to find their way home. Of course, given the geopolitical disputes in the South China Sea, exactly what country was their home was indeterminate.

"Then do we need to leash him like a dog?" I asked my father.

He chuckled unnaturally. "*Paoxiao* are even more accepting of fate than we. They believe everything that happens to them is by the will of the gods and spirits; that's why they'll never run away."

Gradually, Balin grew used to his new environment. My father repurposed our old chicken coop as his home. It took him a long time to figure out that the bedding was meant for him to sleep on, but even after that he preferred to sleep on the rough, sandy floor. He ate just about everything, even crunching the chicken bones leftover after our meals. I and the other children of the village enjoyed crouching outside his hutch to watch him eat. This was also the only time when I could see his teeth clearly: densely packed, sharp triangles like the teeth of a shark; they easily ripped apart whatever he stuffed into his mouth.

As I watched, I couldn't help imagining the feeling of those sharp teeth tearing into me; I would then shudder with a complicated sensation, a mixture of pain and addictive pleasure.

One day, after Balin had eaten enough, he leisurely crawled out of his enclosure. His thin figure sporting a bulging, round tummy resembled a twig with a swelling gall. A couple of other kids and I were playing "monster in the water." Balin, waddling from side to side, stopped not far from us and watched our game with curiosity.

"Shrimp! Shrimp! Watch out if you don't want one to bite off your toes!" Shouting and screaming, we pretended to be fishermen standing onshore (a short brick wall) gingerly sticking our feet into the (nonexistent) river. Dip. Dip. Pull back.

The boy who was the water monster ran back and forth, trying to grab the bare feet of the fishermen as they dipped into the river. Only by pulling a fisherman into the river would the water monster be redeemed to humanity, and his unlucky victim would turn into the new water monster.

No one remembered when Balin joined our game. But then Nana, a neighbor, abruptly stopped and pointed. I looked and saw Balin imitating the movements of the water monster: leaping over here, bounding over there. Except that he wasn't grabbing or snatching at the feet of fishermen but at empty air.

Children often liked to imitate the speech or body language of others, but what Balin was doing was unlike anything I had ever seen. Balin's movements were almost in perfect synchrony with Ah Hui, the boy who was the water monster.

I say "almost" because it was impossible to detect with the naked eye whether there was a delay between Balin's movements and Ah Hui's. Balin was like a shadow that Ah Hui had cast five meters away. Each time Ah Hui turned, each time he extended his hand, even each time he paused dispiritedly because he had missed a fisherman—every gesture was mir-rored by Balin perfectly.

I couldn't understand how Balin was accomplishing this feat, as though he were moving without thinking.

Finally, Ah Hui stopped because everyone was staring.

Ah Hui took a few steps toward Balin; Balin took a few steps toward Ah Hui. Even the way they dragged their heels was exactly the same.

"Why are you copying me?" demanded Ah Hui.

Balin's lips moved in synchrony, though the syllables that emerged from his mouth were mere noise, like the screeching of a broken radio.

Ah Hui pushed Balin, but he stumbled back because Balin also pushed him at the same moment.

The crowd of children grew excited at the farcical scene, far more inter-esting than the water monster game.

"Fight! Fight!"

Ah Hui jumped at Balin, and the two grappled with each other. This was a fascinating fight because their motions mirrored each other exactly. Soon, neither could move since they were locked in a stalemate, staring into each other's eyes.

"That's enough! Go home, all of you!" Massive hands picked both of them off the ground and forcibly separated them as though parting a pair of conjoined twins. It was Father.

Ah Hui angrily spat on the ground. The children scattered.

Balin did not imitate Ah Hui this time. It was as though some switch had been shut off in him.

Smiling, Father glanced at me, as though to say, *Now do you under-stand why this present is so great?*

"We can view the human brain as a machine with just three functions: sensing, thinking, and motor control. If we use a computer as an anal-ogy, sensing is the input, thinking is the computation carried out by the switches, and motor control is the output—the brain's only means of interacting with the external world. Do you see why?"

Before knowing Mr. Lu, I would never have believed that a gym teacher would give this sort of speech.

Mr. Lu was a local legend. He was not that tall, only about 1.72 meters, his hair cropped short. Through the thin shirts he wore in summers we could see his bulging muscles. It was said that he had studied abroad.

Everyone in our class was puzzled why somebody who had left China and seen the world would want to return to our tiny, poor town to be a middle-school teacher. Later, we heard that Mr. Lu was an only child. His father was bedridden with a chronic illness, and his mother had died early. Since there were no other relatives who could care for his father and the old man refused to leave town, saying that he preferred to die where he was born, Mr. Lu had no choice but to move home and find a teaching job. Since his degree was in the neurology of motor control, the principal naturally thought he would be qualified to teach phys ed.

Unlike our other teachers, Mr. Lu never put on any airs around us. He joked about with us as though we were all friends.

Once, I asked him, "Why did you come back to this town?"

"There's an old Confucian saying that as long as your parents are alive, you should not travel too far. I'd been far away from home for more than a decade, and my father won't be with me for much longer. I have to think about him."

I asked him another question: "Will you leave after both your parents are gone, then?"

Mr. Lu frowned, as though he didn't want to think about the question. Then he said, "In my field there was a pioneering researcher named Donald Broadbent. He once said that it was far harder to control the behavior of humans than to control the stimuli influencing humans. That was why in the study of motor control it was difficult to devise simple scientific laws of the form 'A leads to B.'"

"So?" I asked, knowing that he had no intention of answering my question.

"So no one knows what will happen in the future." He nodded and took a long drag on his cigarette.

"Bullshit," I said, accepting the cigarette from him and taking a puff.

No one thought he would stick around our town for long.

In the end he was my gym teacher from eighth grade through twelfth grade, married a local woman, and had kids.

Just the way he predicted.

At first we used a pushpin, and then we switched to the electric igniter for a cigarette lighter. *Snap!* There it was: a pale blue electric arc.

Father thought this was more civilized.

The people who had sold Balin to him had also taught him a trick. If he wanted Balin to imitate someone, he should have Balin face the target and lock gazes. Then he should "stimulate" Balin in some way. Once Balin's eyes glazed over then the "connection" was established. They explained to my father that this was a unique custom of Balin's kind.

Balin brought us endless entertainment.

As long as I could remember, I'd always enjoyed street puppetry, whether shadow puppets, glove puppets, or marionettes. Curious, I would sneak behind the stage and watch the performers give life to the inanimate and enact moving scenes of love and revenge. In my childhood, such transformations had seemed magical, and now with Balin I finally had the chance to practice my own brand of magic.

I danced, and so did he. I boxed, and so did he. I had been shy about putting on a performance in front of my relatives, but now, through Balin's body, I became the family entertainer.

I had Balin imitate Father when he was drunk. I had him imitate anyone in town who was different: the madman, the cripple, the idiot, the beggar who had broken legs and arms and who had to crawl along the ground like a worm, the epileptic . . . my friends and I would laugh so hard that we would roll on the ground—until the relatives of our victims came after us, wielding bamboo laundry rods.

Balin was also good at imitating animals: he was best at cats, dogs, oxen, goats, pigs; not so good with ducks and chickens; and completely useless when it came to fish.

Sometimes, I found him crouched outside the door to the main house in the ancestral compound spying on our TV. He was especially fascinated by animal documentaries. When he saw prey being hunted down and killed by predators, Balin's body twitched and spasmed uncontrollably, as though he were the one whose belly was being ripped open, his entrails spilling forth.

There were times when Balin grew tired. While imitating a target, his movements would slow and diverge from the target's, like a windup figurine running down or a toy car with almost-exhausted batteries. After a while, he would fall to the ground and stop moving, and no matter how hard we kicked him, he refused to budge. The only solution was to make him eat, stuff him to the gills.

Other than exhaustion, he never resisted or showed any signs of unhappiness. In my childish eyes, Balin was no different from the puppets constructed from hide, cellophane, fabric, or wood. He was nothing more than an object faithfully carrying out the controller's will, but he himself was devoid of emotion. His imitation was nothing more than an unthinking reflex.

Eventually, we tired of controlling Balin one-on-one, and we invented more complex and also crueler multiplayer games.

First, we decided the order through rock-paper-scissors. The winner got to control Balin to fight against the loser. The winner of the contest then got to fight against the next kid in line. I was the first.

The experience was cool beyond measure. Like a general sitting safe far from the front lines, I commanded my soldier on the battlefield to press, punch, dodge, kick, roundhouse . . . because I was at a distance from the fight, I could discern my opponent's intentions and movements with more clarity and devise better attacks and responses. Moreover, since Balin was the one who endured all the pain, I had no fear and could attack ruthlessly.

I thought my victory was certain.

But for some reason, all my carefully planned moves, as they were carried out by Balin, seemed to lack strength. Even punches and kicks that landed squarely against my opponent did little to shock the opponent, much less to injure him. Soon, Balin was on the ground, enduring a hailstorm of punches.

"Bite him! Bite!" I snapped my jaw in the air, knowing the power of Balin's sharp teeth.

But Balin was like a marionette whose strings had been cut. My opponent's fists did not relent, and soon Balin's cheeks were swollen.

"Dammit!" I spat on the ground, conceding the fight.

Now it was my turn to face Balin, controlled by the victor of the last round. I stared at him as ferociously as I could manage. His face was bloody, the skin around his eyes bruised and puffy, but his irises still held their habitual tranquility. I was enraged.

Glancing out of the corner of my eye, I observed the movements of Ah Hui, Balin's controller. I was familiar with how Ah Hui fought. He always stepped forward with his left foot and punched with his right fist. I was going to surprise him with a low spinning sweep kick to knock him off his feet. Once he was on the ground, the fight would basically be over.

Ah Hui stepped forward with his left foot. *Here it comes.* I was about to crouch down and begin my sweep, but Balin's foot moved and kicked up the dirt at his feet, blinding me in an instant. Next, his leg swept low along the ground, and I was the one knocked off my feet. My eyes squeezed shut, I wrapped my arms about my head, preparing to endure a fusillade of punches.

However, the fight did not proceed the way I imagined. The punches did land against my body, but there was no force behind them at all. At first, I thought Balin was probably tired but soon realized that was not the case. Ah Hui's own punches against the air were forceful and precise, but Balin apparently was holding back on purpose so that his punches landed on my body like caresses.

Without warning, the punching stopped. Something warm and smelly pressed itself against my face.

Laughter erupted around me. When I finally understood what had happened, a wave of heat suffused my face.

Balin had sat on me with his nude and dirty bottom.

Ah Hui knew that Balin's punches were useless, which was why he had come up with such a dirty trick.

I pushed Balin away and leaped up off the ground. In one quick motion, I pressed Balin to the ground and held him down. Tears poured out of my eyes, stung by the kicked-up sand as well as humiliation and rage. Balin looked up at me, his swollen eyes also filled with tears, as though he knew exactly how I felt at that moment.

Then it hit me. *He's just imitating.* I raised my fist.

"Why didn't you punch with real force, like I wanted you to?"

My fist pounded against Balin's thin body, thumping as though I were punching a hollow shell made of fragile plywood.

"Why don't you hit me back?"

My fingers felt the teeth beneath his lips rattling.

"Tell me why!"

A crisp *snap* of bone. A wound opened over Balin's right brow, the torn skin extended to the tip of his eye. Pink and white fascia and fat spilled out from under the dark skin, and bright red blood flowed freely, soon pooling on the sandy earth under him.

A heavy, fishlike scent wafted from his body.

Terrified, I got off him and stepped back. The other children were stunned as well.

The dust settled, and Balin lay still, curled up like a slaughtered lamb. He glanced at me with his left eye, the one not covered in blood. The tranquil orb still betrayed no emotion. In that moment, for the first time, I felt that he was like me: he was made of flesh and blood; he was a person with a soul.

The moment lasted only seconds. Almost instinctively, I realized that if I had not been treating Balin as a human being until this moment, then it was impossible for me to do so in the future either.

I brushed off the dirt on my pants and shoved my way through the crowd of children, never looking back.

I enter "Ghost" mode, experiencing everything experienced by Balin, trapped in his VR suit.

I—Balin—we are standing on some beautiful tropical island. Based on my suggestion, the environment artist has combined the sights and vegetation from multiple South China Sea islands to create this reality. Even the angle and temperature of light are calculated to be accurate for the latitude.

My intent is to give Balin the sensation of being back home—his real home. But the environment doesn't seem to have reduced his terror.

The view whirls violently: sky, sand, the ocean nearby, scattered vines, and from time to time even rough gray polygonal structures whose textures have yet to be applied.

I feel dizzy. This is the result of visual signals and bodily motion being out of sync. The eyes tell my brain that I'm moving, but the vestibular system tells my brain that I'm not. The conflict between the two sets of signals gives rise to a feeling of sickness.

For Balin, we have deployed the most advanced techniques to shrink the signal delay to within five milliseconds. In addition, we are using motion capture technology to synchronize the movements between his virtual body and his physical body. He could move freely on the omnidirectional treadmill, but his position wouldn't shift half a millimeter.

We're treating him like a guest in first class, anticipating all his needs.

Balin stands rooted to his spot. He can't understand how the world in his eyes is related to the bright, sterile lab he was in just a few minutes ago.

"This is useless," I bark at the technicians through my microphone. "We've got to get him to move!"

Balin's head whips around. The surround sound system in his helmet warns him of movements behind his body. A quaking wave ripples through the dense jungle, and a flock of birds erupts into the air. Something gigantic is shoving its way through the vegetation, making its way toward Balin. Motionless, Balin stares at the bush.

A massive herd of prehistoric creatures bursts from the jungle. Even I, no expert on evolutionary biology, can tell that they don't belong to the same geologic epoch. The technicians have used whatever models they can find in the database to try to get Balin to move.

Still, he stands there like a tree stump, enduring waves of Tyrannosaurus rex, saber-toothed tigers, monstrous dragonflies, crocodilian-shaped ancestors of dinosaurs, and strange arthropods as they rush at him and then, howling and screaming, sweep through him like wisps of mist. This is a bug in the physics engine, but if we were to fix the bug and fully simulate the physical experience, the VR user would not be able to endure the impact.

It isn't over yet.

The ground under Balin begins to quake and split. Trees lean over and topple. Volcanoes erupt and crimson molten lava spills out of the earth, coalescing into bloody rivers. Massive waves more than ten meters tall charge at our position from the sea.

"I think you might be overdoing this a bit," I say into the mic. I hear faint giggles.

Imagine how a primitive human tossed into the middle of such an apocalyptic scene would feel. Would he consider himself a savior who is suffering for the sins of the entire human race? Or would he be on the cusp of madness, his senses on the verge of collapse?

Or would he behave like Balin: no reaction at all?

Suddenly, I understand the truth.

I back out of Ghost mode and remove Balin's helmet. Sensors are studded like pearls all over his skull. His eyes are squeezed tightly shut, the wrinkles around them so deep that they resemble insect antennae.

"Let's stop here today." I sigh helplessly, recalling that afternoon long ago when I had punched him until he bled.

—— ✹ ——

As the time approached for all the high school students to declare our intended subjects of study before the college entrance examination, the war between my father and me heated up.

According to his grand plan, I was supposed to major in political science or history in college, but I had zero interest in those subjects, which I viewed as painted whores at the whim of those in power. I wanted to major in a hard science like physics, or at the minimum biology—something that according to Mr. Lu involved "fundamental questions."

My father was contemptuous of my reasons. He pointed to the houses in our ancestral compound, and the tea leaves drying over the racks in the yard, glistening like gold dust in the bright sunlight.

"Do you think there are any questions more fundamental than making a living and feeding your family?"

It was like discussing music theory with a cud-chewing cow.

I gave up trying to convince Father. I had my own plan. With Mr. Lu's help, I obtained permission from the teachers to cram for common subjects like math, Chinese, and English with students who intended to declare for the humanities, but then I would sneak away to study physics, chemistry, and biology with the science students. If class schedules conflicted, I would make my own choices and then make up the missed work later.

My teachers were willing to let me get away with it because they had their own selfish hopes. Rather than forcing someone who had no interest to study politics and history, they thought they might as well let me follow my heart. If they got lucky, it was possible that I would do extraordinarily well on the college entrance examination as a science student and bring honor to them all.

I thought my plan would fool my busy father, who was away from home more often than not. I was going to surprise him at the last minute, when I had to fill out the desired majors and top-choice schools right before the examination. Even if he blew up at me then, it would be too late.

I was so naive.

On the day we were supposed to fill out the forms, all my friends received a copy of the blank form except me. I thought the head teacher had made a mistake.

"Uh . . . your father already filled it out for you." The teacher dared not meet my eyes.

I don't remember how I made it home that day. Like a lost, homeless dog, I wandered the streets and alleyways of the town aimlessly until I found myself in front of the ancestral compound.

Father was entertaining himself by playing with Balin. He had dug up an old army uniform and put it on Balin. The loose folds and wide pant legs hung on Balin like a tent, making him resemble a monkey who had stolen some human clothing. Father had Balin follow orders he had learned during the time he was in the army: stand at attention, stand at ease, right dress, left dress, march in place, and so on. When I was in elementary school, Father had enjoyed ordering me around like a drill sergeant at the parade ground, and I had hated those "games" more than anything else.

It had been years since he had tried anything like that with me, but now he had found a new recruit.

A soldier who would obey every one of his commands without question.

"One-two-one! One-two-one! Forwaaaaard-march!" As he barked out the commands and demonstrated the moves, Balin goose-stepped around the yard, his pant legs muddy as they dragged on the ground.

I stepped between them and faced my father. "You have no intention of letting me go to college, is that it?"

"Riiiiight-dress!" My father whipped his head to the right and shuffled his feet. I heard the sound of feet scrabbling against the ground in synchrony behind me.

"You knew about my plan a long time ago, didn't you?" I demanded. "But you said nothing before you played your trick so I wouldn't have a chance to stop you."

"Maaaaarch in place!"

Enraged, I turned around and held Balin still, not allowing him to proceed any longer like a mindless drone. But he seemed unable to stop. The pant legs slapped against the ground, whipping up wisps of dust.

I grabbed his head and forced him to lock gazes with me. I pulled out the electric lighter from my pocket and flicked it; a pale blue arc burst into life next to his temple. Balin screamed like a baby.

I looked into his eyes; now he belonged to me.

"You have no right to control me! All you care about is your business. Have you ever thought about what I want for my future?"

As I screamed at my father, Balin marched around us, his finger also pointing at Father, his mouth also screaming. The circle he made around the two of us tightened on each loop.

"I'm going to college whether you want me to go or not. And I'm going to study whatever I want!" I clenched my jaw. Balin's finger was almost touching my father. "Let me tell you something, Father: I *never* want to become like you."

The militaristic arrogance melted from my father. He stood there, his face fallen and back hunched, like crops that had been bitten by frost. I expected him to hit back, hard, as was his wont, but he did not.

"I knew. I've always known that you don't want to walk the path others have paved for you," my father's voice faded until it was barely a whisper. "You remind me so much of myself when I was your age. But I have no choice—"

"So you want me to repeat your life?"

My father's knees buckled. I thought he was going to fall, but he knelt on the ground and embraced Balin.

"You can't leave!" he shouted. "I know what's going to happen if you go away to college. No one who leaves this town ever returns."

I struggled against the empty air so that Balin, moving in sync with me, could free himself from my father's grasp. As long as I could remember, my father had never hugged me.

"Don't be so childish! Open your eyes! See the world for what it is."

Balin was like a windup toy that had malfunctioned. His limbs whipped about in a frenzy; the military uniform he wore was torn in multiple places, revealing the dark, unreflective skin.

"The way you spoke just now is just like your mother." Another pale blue spark came to life over Balin's temple. Abruptly, he ceased struggling and held my father tightly like a long-lost lover. "Are you going to abandon me just like she did?"

I was stunned.

I had never thought about this matter from my father's perspective. I had always thought that he wanted to keep me close at hand because he was selfish, narrow-minded, but I had never seen it as a reaction to the fear of being abandoned. My mother had left us when I was too young to view it as trauma, but it cast a shadow over the rest of his life.

Wordless, I approached my father, who held on to Balin tightly. I bent down and caressed his spine, no longer as straight as in my memory. Maybe this was as close as the two of us would ever be.

I saw the tears spilling from the corners of Balin's eyes. For a moment, I doubted myself.

Maybe it isn't just about control and power, but also love.

There are many things I wish I had known before I turned seventeen.

For example, the fact that most of the structures in the human brain have something to do with motor functions, including the cerebellum, the basal ganglia, the brain stem, the motor region of the cerebral cortex and the direct projection of the somatosensory cortex to the primary motor cortex, and so on.

For example, the cerebellum contains more neurons than any other part of the brain. As humans evolved, the cerebellar cortex grew in step with the rapidly increasing volume of the frontal lobe.

For example, any interaction with the outside world, whether informational or physical, including moving limbs, manipulating tools, gesticulating, speaking, glancing, making faces—each ultimately requires activating a series of muscles to realize.

For example, an arm contains twenty-six separate muscles, and each muscle on average contains a hundred motor units, each made up by a motor neuron and its associated skeletal muscle fibers. Thus, the motion of a single arm is governed by a possibility space at least 2^{2600} in size, a number far greater than the total number of atoms in the universe.

Human motion is so complex and subtle, and each casual movement represents the result of so much computation, analysis, and planning that even the most advanced robots are incapable of moving as well as a three-year-old.

And we haven't even discussed all the information, emotion, and culture embodied in human motion.

On the way to the high-speed-rail station, my father maintained his silence, only clutching my suitcase tightly. The northbound train finally appeared before us, shiny, new, smooth in outline, like something that was going to slide into the unknowable future the moment the brakes were released.

In the end, my father and I failed to reach a compromise. If I was going to college in Beijing, he would not pay for any of my expenses.

"Unless you promise to return," he said.

I gazed through him, as though I were already seeing the future, a future that belonged to me. For that, I was willing to be the black sheep from a white flock, the sheep in perpetual exile.

"Dad, take care of yourself."

I grabbed my suitcase to board the train, but my father refused to let go of the handle, and the suitcase awkwardly hung between us. A moment later, both of us let go, and the suitcase fell to the ground.

I was about to erupt when my father slapped his heels together to stand at attention, giving me a crisp military salute. Without a word, he turned and left. He had once told me that it was bad luck to say good-bye before going to war. Better to leave each other with other memories.

I watched his diminishing figure, raised my hand, and returned his salute gently.

I did not truly understand the meaning in my gesture.

⎯⎯ ∝∝∝ ⎯⎯

"I never thought we'd fail because of a wild man," says my thesis adviser, Ouyang, who is also the project leader. He claps me on the shoulder, his smile disguising the sharp edges of his words. "It's no big deal. Let's keep on working at this. We still have time."

But I know him too well. What he really means is, *We are running out of time.*

Or, to put it another way, *This is your idea, your project. Whether you can get your degree in time will depend on what you do next.*

Of course he will never mention how much of our time he has taken up in the past to handle the random projects he promised business investors.

Frustrated, I massage my scalp. My eyes fall on Balin, now shut in his pink-hued pet enclosure. Eyes glazed, he stares at the floor, as though still not recovered from his ordeal in the VR environment. The contrast between the pink pet enclosure and his appearance is comical, but I can't make myself laugh.

What would Mr. Lu do?

Everything began with that idle conversation with him years ago concerning "A leads to B."

Traditional theorists believe that motor control is the result of stored programs. When a person wants to move a certain way, the motor cortex picks out a certain program from its stored repertoire and carries it out much the same way a player piano follows the roll of perforated paper. The program's instructions determine the activation patterns in the motor regions of the cortex and the spinal cord, which then, in turn, activate the muscles to complete the motion.

This naturally raises the question, if the same motion can be carried out in infinite ways, how does the brain store an infinite number of motor programs?

Remember that arm whose potential possible number of movements exceeds the number of atoms in the universe?

In 2002, the mathematician Emanuel Todorov came up with a theory in an attempt to answer this question. Basically, he argued that motor control is really an optimization problem for the brain. Optimality is defined by high-level performance criteria such as maximizing precision, minimizing energy consumption, minimizing control effort, and so on.

In the optimization process, the brain relies on the processing powers of the cerebellum. Before the commands for movement reach muscles, the cerebellum predicts the results of anticipated motion and then, combined with real-time sensory feedback, helps the brain evaluate and coordinate the motor commands.

A simple example: when ascending or descending a set of stairs, we will often stumble because of miscounting the number of steps. If feedback-based adjustments are made in time, we can recover and not fall. Feedback, of course, is often noisy and involves a delay.

Todorov's mathematical model is compatible with all known evidence concerning the neural mechanisms of motor control and can be used to explain all kinds of behavior phenomena. Given some physical parameters, it's even possible to predict the resulting motion using his model: for instance, how an eight-legged creature would jump in Pluto's gravity.

Physics engines based on his models are used by Hollywood to produce naturalistic movements for avatars in virtual environments.

By the time I was in college, the Todorov model was already treated as textbook authority. Experiment after experiment provided more evidence that it was correct.

And then one day, Mr. Lu and I discussed Balin.

After I left home for college, he and I had kept in touch via email. He was like an oracular AI from whom I could get answers for everything: academics, awkward social situations, even relationship advice. We wrote long emails back and forth discussing questions that must have seemed ridiculous to anyone else, such as, would an out-of-body experience engineered by technology violate religion's claim on spirituality?

By an unspoken agreement, both of us avoided talking about my father.

Mr. Lu told me that Balin had been sold to another family in town, a nouveau riche household that was often mocked for conspicuous acts of consumption that appeared ridiculous in the townspeople's eyes.

I had known that Father's business had run into a rough patch, but I hadn't imagined that he would be so short on cash as to consider selling Balin.

I shifted the topic to the Todorov mathematical model, and a new thought struck me. Balin was capable of imitating movements with perfect precision. Suppose we had him perform two sets of identical movements: one through subconscious imitation and the other by his own will; do these two sets of movements go through the same process of motor control?

Mathematically, there was only a single optimal solution, but was there a difference in the way the optimal solution was arrived at?

It took Mr. Lu three days to get back to me. Unlike his usual free-flowing, loquacious style, this time he wrote only a few lines: *I think you're asking a very important question, one whose importance perhaps you don't even realize. If we can't distinguish between mechanical imitation and conscious, willed movement at the level of neural activity, then the question is, does free will truly exist?*

I couldn't sleep that night. I spent two weeks designing the prototype experiment and even more time studying the feasibility of my proposed study, soliciting feedback from my mentors and other professors. Then I submitted my project for approval.

It wasn't until everything was ready that I realized that this experiment, one seeking to address a "fundamental question," lacked a fundamental, required component.

I had no choice but to break my promise to myself and go home.

I'm going just to get Balin, I reminded myself again and again. *Just for Balin.*

Just like how A leads to B. Simple, right?

I once read a science fiction novel called *The Orphans,* which was about aliens who had come to earth. They could imitate the appearance of specific humans and pass as human in society, but they couldn't perfectly capture the characteristic ways their targets moved or the subtleties of their facial expressions. Many aliens, exposed as frauds, were hunted down by humans.

In order to survive, the aliens had to study how humans communicated via body language. They pretended to be abandoned orphans and, once taken in by kindhearted families, proceeded to use the opportunity of living together to imitate the mannerisms and expressions of their adoptive parents.

To the parents' surprise, their children became more and more like them. And once the alien orphans decided that they had learned enough, they killed their father or mother, took on their appearance, and took their place. The scene where an alien killed his father and took his mother as his wife was unforgettable.

Though it became harder to tell aliens apart from humans, people finally discovered the fundamental difference between the extraterrestrials and humans.

Although the aliens were able to imitate human movements with perfect fidelity, they lacked the mirror neurons unique to human brains and thus were unable to intuit the emotional shifts occurring behind human faces or to experience similar neural activation patterns in their own minds. In other words, they lacked the capacity for empathy.

And so humans devised an effective means to detect aliens: bring harm to those closest to the disguised aliens and observe the aliens for signs of pain, fear, or rage. The test was called the stabbing-needle test.

The story's lesson seems to be that humanity isn't the only species in the universe that has difficulty relating to their parents.

Mr. Lu knew everything about Balin. He thought of *paoxiao* as an example of overdevelopment in the mirror-neuron system. He was fascinated by Balin, but he disapproved of the way we treated him.

"But he's never resisted or even wanted to run away," I used to counter.

"Overactive mirror neurons lead to a pathological excess of empathy," he said. "Maybe he just couldn't tolerate the look of abandonment in his tormentors'—your—eyes."

"I guess that could be true," I said. "I must be an example of underdevelopment of mirror neurons."

"Cold-blooded, one might say."

But when Mr. Lu took me to find Balin on my return, I realized that I wasn't the most cold-blooded, not by far.

Balin was naked, his body full of bruises and lacerations. Thick, rusty chains were locked about his neck and shackled his arms and legs. He was shut inside a tiny brick-and-mud enclosure, about five *chi* on each side. The interior was dim and the stale air saturated with the gag-inducing stench of excrement and rotting food. He was thinner than I remembered. Flies buzzed about his wounds, and the outlines of his skeleton poked from under his skin. He was like an animal about to be sent to the butcher's.

He looked at me, and there was no reaction in his eyes at all. It was just like the first time we had met, that summer night when I was thirteen.

"They had him mirror the movements of animals . . . mating—" Mr. Lu was unable to continue.

Memories of the past flood into my mind in a flash.

I have no recollection of what happened next. It was as though I had been possessed by some spirit, and I moved without remembering wanting to move.

According to Mr. Lu, I rushed into the house of Balin's new owners and grabbed the Pomeranian beloved by the family patriarch's daughter-in-law. I opened my jaw and held the neck of the whimpering creature between my teeth.

"You said, 'If you don't let Balin go, I'm going to bite all the way through,'" Mr. Lu said.

I spat on the ground. Though I didn't remember any of it, this did sound like something I would do.

Mr. Lu and I rushed Balin to the hospital. As we were preparing to leave, Mr. Lu stopped me. "Do you want to see your father?"

That was how I found out that my father had been hospitalized. Once in college, I had had almost no contact with him, and gradually I had stopped even thinking about him.

He looked about ten years older. Tubing was stuck into his nostrils and arms. His hair was sparse and his gaze unsteady. A few years ago, when Pu'er tea was all the rage, he had gambled with all his chips and ended up as the last fool to buy in at the height of the mania. He was stuck with warehouses full of tea leaves as the price collapsed and ended up losing just about everything.

As he looked at me, I noted that his expression reminded me of Balin, as though he were saying, *I knew you'd be back.*

"I . . . I'm here for Balin," I said.

My father saw through my facade and cracked a smile, revealing a mouthful of teeth stained yellow by years of smoking.

"That little gremlin? He's much smarter than you think. We all thought we were controlling him, but sometimes I wonder if he was controlling all of us."

I didn't know what to say.

"It's the same way with you. I always thought I was the one in charge. But after you left, I realized that you had always held a thread whose other end is looped around my heart. No matter how far away you are, as soon as you twitch your fingers, I suffer pangs of heartache." My father closed his eyes and put his hand over his chest.

Something was stuck in my throat.

I walked up to his bed and wanted to lean down to embrace him. But halfway through the motion, my body refused to obey. Awkwardly, I clapped him on the shoulder, straightened up, and walked away.

"I'm glad you're back," my father said from behind me, his voice hoarse. I didn't turn around.

Mr. Lu was waiting for me at the door. I pretended to scratch my eyes to disguise the emotional turmoil.

"Do you think fate likes to play jokes on us?" he asked.

"What do you mean?"

"You wanted to escape the route your father had paved for you, but in the end you ended up in the same place as me."

"I think I'm coming around to your way of thinking."

"What's that?" he asked.

"No one knows what will happen in the future."

We've failed again.

The original premise is very simple: Balin's hypertrophic mirror-neuron system makes him the ideal experimental subject because his imitation is a kind of instinct. Thus, his movements during imitation ought to be free from much of the noise and interference found in human motor control because of conscious cognition.

We use noninvasive electrodes to capture the neural activity in Balin's motor cortex as he's imitating a sequence of movements. Then we have him repeat the sequence under his own will and use motion capture to ensure that we get a perfect match between the two sets of movements. Mathematically, that means that the two sequences are indistinguishable; they are the same motion.

Then, by comparing the two sets of neural patterns captured during the process, we can find out if the same neural signals were activating the same regions of the motor cortex in the same sequence and with the same strength.

If there are differences, then the Todorov model, accepted as gospel, will have been revealed to be seriously lacking.

But if there are no differences, the consequences will be even more severe. Maybe human beings are doing nothing but imitating the behaviors of other individuals and are operating only under the illusion of free will.

No matter what, the result of the experiment ought to be earth-shattering.

Yet the experiment was a failure from the very beginning. Balin has refused to look into anyone's eyes and has refused to imitate anyone's movements, including me.

I can guess the reason, but I have no solution. My team has vowed to solve the secret of human cognition, yet we can't even heal the psychic trauma inflicted on a mere "primitive."

I thought of the idea of using virtual reality. Situating Balin in an environment completely disconnected from the reality around him may help him recover his normal habits.

And so we went through a series of virtual environments: islands, glaciers, deserts, even space; we manufactured incredible catastrophes; we even devoted enormous effort to construct avatars of *paoxiao*, hoping that the sight of others of his kind would awaken his dormant mirror neurons.

Without exception, all these tricks have failed.

Now, at midnight, only I and the zombielike Balin remain in the lab. Everyone else has left. I know what they're thinking: this experiment is a joke, and I'm the man who has finished telling the joke and looks around confused, unsure why everyone else is laughing.

Balin is curled up into a ball in the pet house made from pink foam boards. I remember Mr. Lu's words. He was right. I've never treated Balin as a person, not even now.

A colleague once implanted a wireless receiver into a rat's brain. By electrically stimulating the rat's somatosensory cortex and the medial forebrain bundle, my colleague was able to induce sensations of pleasure and pain in the rat, thereby controlling where the rat moved.

There's no qualitative difference between that and what I'm doing to Balin.

I am indeed a bastard whose mirror neurons are atrophied.

Unbidden, the memory of a children's game resurfaces, the game in which Balin first showed us his fantastic ability.

"Shrimp! Shrimp! Watch out if you don't want one to bite off your toes!"

I chant in a low voice, embarrassed. I pretend to be a fisherman, dipping my foot into the imaginary river from the shore and quickly pulling back.

Balin glances at me.

"Shrimp! Shrimp! Watch out if you don't want one to bite off your toes!" My chant grows louder.

Balin stares at my clumsy movements. Gently, slowly, he crawls out of the pet house, stopping a few steps away from me.

"Shrimp! Shrimp! Watch out if you don't want one to bite off your toes!" My legs are jerking wildly like some caricature of a pole dancer in a club.

Abruptly, Balin jumps at me with incredible speed, moving the exact way Ah Hui used to.

He remembers; he remembers everything.

Balin leaps and bounds, grabbing at my dipping leg. A babylike gurgle emerges from his throat. He's laughing. This is the first time I've ever heard him laugh in all the years I've known him.

He is now reenacting the movements of everyone in town who had been a bit different. All their movements seem to have been engraved in Balin's brain, so vivid and precise that I can recognize whom he's replaying at a glance. In turn, he becomes the madman, the cripple, the idiot, the beggar who had broken legs and arms, and the epileptic; he is a cat, a dog, an ox, a goat, a pig, and a crude chicken; he is my drunk father and me, dancing about in joy.

In a moment, I've traveled through thousands of kilometers and returned to the hometown of my childhood.

Without warning, Balin begins to play two roles simultaneously, reenacting the day of the rupture between me and my father.

Watching the argument between me and my father as an observer is eerie: the movements before me are so familiar, yet my memories have grown indistinct, unreal. I was so angry then, so stubborn, like a wild horse that refused to accept the bit. My father, on the other hand, was so pitiful and meek. Again and again he backed off; he suffered. It is nothing like how I remember the scene.

Balin quickly switches between roles, gesturing and posturing like a skilled mime.

Though I know what happens next, when it does happen I'm not prepared.

Balin wraps his arms about me, just the way my father back then wrapped his arms about him. He hugs me tightly, his head buried in the crook of my neck. I smell that familiar fishlike scent, like the sea, and a warm liquid flows down my collar like a river that has absorbed the heat of the sun.

I stay still, thinking about how to react.

Then I give up thinking, allowing my body to react and open up, hugging him back the way I would hug an old friend, the way I would hug my father.

I know that I have owed this hug for far too long, to him and to my father.

I think I finally understand how to solve the problem.

At the end of *The Orphans*, the team that had come up with the stabbing-needle test found, to their horror, that even when they harmed the aliens passing as human, their dear ones, the real humans, also failed to react. Their mirror-neuron systems would not activate.

Humanity is a species that was never designed to truly empathize with another species.

Just like those aliens.

Good thing that's just a bad piece of science fiction, isn't it?

"We need to think about this from his perspective," I say to Ouyang.

"His?" It takes a full three seconds for my adviser to figure out what I mean. "Who? The primitive?"

"His name is Balin. We should make him the focus and construct an environment that will put him at ease rather than cheap tourist scenes we imagine he'll enjoy."

"What are you talking about? You should be concerned about how you're going to finish your project and get your degree instead of worrying about the feelings of some primitive. Don't waste my time."

Mr. Lu once said that the progress of a civilization should be measured by its degree of empathy—whether members of the civilization are capable of thinking from the values and perspectives of others—and not by some other objectified scale.

Silently, I stare at Ouyang's face, trying to discern some trace of civilization.

The face, so carefully maintained to be wrinkle-free, is a wasteland.

I decide to work on the problem myself. Several younger students join me on their own initiative, restoring some of my faith in humanity. To be sure, most of them are motivated by their hatred of Ouyang, and it's not a bad way to earn a few credits.

There's a virtual reality program called iDealism, which claims to be capable of generating an environment based on brain-wave patterns. In reality, all it does is select preexisting models from a database whose brain-wave signatures match the user's—at most it adds some high-resolution transitions. We hacked it for our own use, and since our lab's sensors are several orders of magnitude more sensitive than consumer-grade sensors, we add a lot of new measurement axes to the software and connect it to the largest open-source database, which contains demo data from virtual reality labs from around the world.

And now, Balin is going to be the Prime Mover of this virtual universe.

He will have plenty of time to explore the linkage between this world and every thought in his mind. I will record every move and gesture Balin makes. Then, when he returns to the real world, I will reconnect with him. I will imitate to the best of my ability each of his gestures. The two of us will be as two parallel mirrors, reflecting each other endlessly.

I put the helmet on Balin's head. His gaze is as placid as water.

The red light flashes, speeds up, turns green.

I enter Ghost mode and bring up a third-person POV window in the upper-right-hand corner. In it, I see a tiny avatar of Balin trembling in place.

Balin's world is primordial chaos. There is no earth, no heaven, no east, west, north, or south. I struggle against the vertigo.

Finally, he stops shaking. A flash of lightning slowly divides the chaos, determining the location of the sky.

The lightning extends, limning a massive eye in the cloud cover. A web of fine lightning feelers spreads from the eye in every direction.

The light fades. Balin lifts his head and raises his hands. Rain falls.

He begins to dance.

Drops of rain fall with laughter, giving substance to the outline of wind. The wind lifts Balin until he is floating in the air, twirling about.

It is impossible to describe his dance with words. It is as if he had become a part of all Creation, and the heavens and the earth both respond to his movements and change.

My heart speeds up; my throat is dry; my hands and feet are icy cold. I'm witnessing an unsought miracle.

He lifts his hand and flowers bloom. He lifts his foot and birds flutter forth.

Balin dances between unnamed peaks, above unmapped lakes. Everywhere he sets foot, joyful mandalas bloom and spread, and he falls into their swirling, colorful centers.

One moment he is smaller than an atom, the next he encompasses the universe. All scales have lost meaning in his dance.

Every nameless life sings to him. He opens his mouth, and all the gods of the *paoxiao* emerge from his lips.

The spirits meld into his black skin like dark waves that rage and erupt, sweeping him up, up into the air. Behind him, the waves coalesce into an endless web on which all the fruits of creation can be found, each playing its own rhythm. A hundred million billion species are in search of their common origin.

I understand now.

In Balin's eyes, the soul is immanent in all Creation, and there is no difference between a dragonfly and a man. His nervous system is constructed in such a way as to allow him to empathize with the universe. It is impossible to imagine how much effort he must put into calming the tsunamis that rage constantly in his heart.

Even someone as unenlightened as me cannot be unmoved when faced with this grand spectacle produced by all Life. My eyes swim in hot tears, and threads of ecstasy inside my heart are woven with the dizzying sights in my vision. I stand atop a peak but a step away from transcendence.

As for the answer I was seeking? I don't think it's so important anymore.

Balin absorbs everything into his body. His avatar expands rapidly and then deflates.

He falls.

The world dims, grows indistinct, lifeless.

Balin is like a thin film stretched against the tumbling, twirling spacetime. The physics engine's algorithms undulate the edge of his body as though blown by a wind, and fragments rise into the air like a flock of birds.

His shape is disintegrating, dissolving.

I disconnect Balin from the VR system and take off his helmet.

He lies facedown on the soft, dark-gray floor, his limbs spread out, unmoving.

"Balin?" I don't dare move him.

"Balin?" Everyone in the lab is waiting. Will this joke of an experiment turn into a tragedy?

Slowly, he shifts in place. Then he wriggles to the side like a pond loach until he is once again flattened against the floor, adopting the posture of a gecko.

I laugh. Like my father years ago, I clap my hands twice.

Balin turns, sits up, stares at me.

It is just like that hot and sticky summer night the year I turned thirteen, when we first met.

9

THE RADIO WAVES THAT NEVER DIE

LA LA

TRANSLATED BY PETULA PARRIS-HUANG

*P*ioneer One ... buzz ... in front of you ... buzz ... over ..."
"... buzz ... we recommend that you change your orbit ...
your current orbit looks very unstable ... buzz ..."

"Changing course to 77–1045–37– ... buzz ... zzzzz ..."

The Background Sound Generator let out one last groan before packing it in altogether. Suddenly, as the last trickle of energy drained away from the connector plugs, the room was invaded by a thick cloak of darkness. A few seconds later, the emergency lights lit up, casting feeble green rays around the room.

Nikuulla reached forward and waved his hand up and down in vain. There was no response at all. The main fuse must have blown.

After a few more seconds, a quiet humming could be heard as the power slowly crept back into the room. Sighing, Nikuulla straightened himself in his chair. The mechanical smart arms connected to his shoulders detached themselves simultaneously, sprayed out a shot of lubricating gas, then disappeared back into the wall. Nikuulla stood up and, stark naked, waited for his left and right arms to float out of the storage locker and reattach themselves to his shoulders.

Nikuulla let out a short cough. The sound thundered around the room, startling him and reminding him that he had forgotten to disconnect his speaking system from the room's shared communication channel. It seemed he wouldn't be able to trace the signals back any further with this old time-space pod, on which the basic time unit was a rather bulky ten million seconds. In any case, even if he'd wanted to try, there was a certain someone who wasn't going to let him.

Nikuulla walked out of the recreation room in a sulk. Kager, who was at the other end of the center tending to the repair, spotted him straight-away. He opened a floating portal just behind Nikuulla and hurried angrily after him.

"Hey! You! Why don't you just sod off, you little imp!" Kager greeted Nikuulla enthusiastically. As a rule, hosts of entertainment centers liked nothing better than to have a client holed up in a room somewhere, constantly pumping money in the direction of the till. Nikuulla, how-ever, was the exception to that rule for Kager. At around three hundred thousand seconds earlier, Kager had announced that if the power supply at the Scoundrel Bar overloaded just one more time, he would be throw-ing Nikuulla out on his ear. It looked as though his pledge was about to be fulfilled.

"Don't worry," Nikuulla retorted on his way out. "I'm leaving."

"Well you shouldn't have bothered coming in the first place! Look what you've done—you've managed to use up a whole sixty thousand kryptons just by yourself! What on earth were you doing in there anyway? Did you just stick the plug into your mouth and suck the energy straight out of it?"

"I was using the time-space pod. It is part of your equipment, isn't it?"

"We never actually use that thing! It's just there to fool the electricity inspectors!"

"Well, I'll just have to go somewhere else then, won't I?" Nikuulla mumbled as he hurried down the narrow corridor that led out of the Scoundrel Bar. The rest of his body parts were struggling to keep up with him and return themselves to their rightful places. His Auditory System was the last to reposition itself back inside his head. As it did so, he heard Kager shouting after him. "Well, why don't you go to the Honest Sailor Bar, then? They've got one hundred time-space pods there, and they mea-sure by every hundred thousand seconds! That will be accurate enough for you to retrace the moment your godforsaken ass entered the world, won't it?"

Nikuulla paused and spent a few seconds to consider Kager's sugges-tion. He actually felt quite moved. The Honest Sailor Bar was another recreation center nearby and was much larger than the Scoundrel Bar. Unsurprisingly, the owner of the Honest Sailor Bar was Kager's sworn enemy, yet Kager had impetuously yelled this out. He was bound to regret it later. In fact, he'd probably want to send his Logical Assessment Unit to the factory for a checkup.

"Fine, I'm going."

"And may the Almighty curse you on your way!" Kager barked, bid-ding him farewell. The Honest Sailor Bar was, in truth, a great deal classier than the Scoundrel Bar. On entering the front lobby, one could bump into almost anyone from the city—except, of course, for the few individuals who frequented the Scoundrel Bar. Everyone appeared to be in a hurry as they rushed toward their chosen worlds to unwind. They first removed their lower limbs, torsos, and propellers, and then dumped them in the storage room, which was full to the point of bursting. There were enough parts stashed inside it to fit out an entire spaceship. The sales assistants at the counter were no doubt very pleased with the situa-tion, which served as a constant reminder of just how many clients were in the recreation rooms swiping away happily with their credit cards.

Nikuulla stuffed his hands into his trouser pockets and plodded slowly over to the counter. The assistant on duty rarely came across such "clean" organic bodies. He cast a glance over to the storage room. He was prob-ably grumbling to himself how this guy wouldn't be paying for any parking.

"I'd like to use one of your time-space pods," Nikuulla announced in a youthful, nonchalant voice.

"Which model?" the assistant asked with an instant smile.

"Any model is fine," Nikuulla replied. "I just need to be in a completely uncontaminated space with no interruptions so that I can time-space travel and search for background signals in space."

The assistant's smile froze for a few seconds.

"Great . . . and will you be requiring any of our special discounted services?"

"No."

"You know, using the pod isn't cheap," the assistant said a little causti-cally. "If you don't need any other services, I'll have to set a minimum charge . . ."

"That's fine." The assistant dropped a card onto the counter. "Go inside, 3,775th floor, room 1190," he said curtly, dispensing with any further nice-ties. "It will be a thousand dollars for every six hundred seconds. Drinks not included."

The room was pitch-black, meaning that Nikuulla had to feel around for a while before he was able to locate the chair. It was made from Lla-sidragon leather and was hard and cool. Nikuulla sank back into the seat. He felt something crawl into the skin at the back of his neck, after which a cool gust of wind blew deep into the inner reaches of his mind.

Nikuulla's consciousness had connected with the control panel in the room. He then carefully examined each of the various switches on the panel.

Suddenly, a beam of light running from floor to ceiling appeared a short distance in front of him. As it began to widen, Nikuulla realized that it was the curtains opening in front of a full-length window.

The brightness in the room soon reached dazzling proportions. Located on the 3,775th floor, the room sat above the thin atmospheric layer of the planet Lathmu. On the right-hand side of the skyline, the twin stars Ploaedes and Lagaol shone unhindered, projecting their brilliant rays directly into the room. Although a protective black membrane quickly generated itself over the outer layer of Nikuulla's eyes, it still took him a while to get used to the intensity of the light.

Nikuulla stood up and walked over to the window. The gloomy arc of the planet Lathmu lay far below him, emitting weak orange rays. Few celestial bodies could be seen in this remote corner of the Milky Way. Not so many millilight seconds ahead of him was the lonely image of the Gol-moddon Space City, while further away to the left he could even make out the spectacular Tasha dust cloud. Far away in the distance, at a spot less than five hundred light seconds from the United Systems of Ploaedes and Lagaol, the dust cloud's colossal body whirled away as it went about forming a new planet. Attracted by its pull, much of the star dust on the outskirts of the United Systems was sucked into the vortex of the cloud, forming a waterfall of light that stretched across the sky for several hun-dred light seconds.

"What an incredible place," Nikuulla grinned to himself. In fact, this was probably the most amazing place on the entire planet.

Nikuulla sat down again in the chair and detached his arms. He then connected the arms supplied in the room for controlling the time-space pod. The new arms were heavy and his body seemed to be rejecting them. As a result, it took a while for him to open up each of the control windows and turn on the pod's various switches.

The room vibrated slightly before breaking away from the building and drifting off into space. Before it had traveled very far, the room was enveloped and then dissolved by indescribable purplish rays. Towed by the gravitational transmission line, the pod began to slide slowly into the corridor of time.

On first glance, the universe looked the same as always. However, on closer inspection, Nikuulla noticed that the faraway Tasha dust cloud was turning in a very peculiar manner. Sometimes it would rotate clockwise, and at other times counterclockwise. The vast curtain of light that was being sucked into the dust cloud became so blurred that it looked as if the star dust were flowing both in and out of the cloud at the same time. All these changes were controlled by Nikuulla's right hand. With the slightest movement of his fingers, the pod sped to and fro through time on the scale of approximately thirty billion seconds[1] (this was the maximum range for the machines on Games Street). The main problem was energy. The room was charging a thousand dollars for every six hundred seconds traveled, which was mostly to pay for the outrageous energy use.

Nikuulla positioned himself about a hundred billion seconds after the last signal he had received and then dropped his gravity anchor. The pod shook a little in the time-warp gap. Nikuulla swapped his control arms for a pair of receiving arms that he had assembled in the Wireless Interest Group. Immediately, his mind filled with a jumble of confused signals originating from the background depths of the universe. Nikuulla searched patiently through each of the signals. He was looking for a very specific bandwidth. It was not long before the voices he was after floated out from within the din.

"Da Gama Ten . . . buzz buzz . . . this is *Pioneer One* . . . buzz . . . our position is . . . approximately eleven thousand light seconds away—the path set by the guiding rocket is very clear. . . . The stellar rings are at position 6–2 and are approximately three thousand light seconds away . . ."

"*Pioneer One*, please reconfirm your orbit. Your plane of orbit is approximately 1.5 percent off course."

"*Da Gama Ten*, we can see the path very clearly. We can pass through the rings."

"*Pioneer One* . . . the signal is . . ."

" . . ."

"*Pioneer One*! Why did the communication link just cut out? *Pioneer One*, please respond!"

"This is *Da Gama Ten* . . . *Pioneer One*, please respond!"

Here, the signal cut off completely. Nikuulla smiled in satisfaction. He had finally managed to track down the origin of the signal. And by the sound of things, "they" were still on the road a hundred billion seconds later.

I suppose that now might be a good time to explain things a little more clearly—starting with the fact that Nikuulla was a member of the Hermits, a division of the Organization of Listeners.

There were all sorts of organizations and societies across the United Star Systems of Ploaedes and Lagaol. However, the Listeners was one of the more prestigious of these for the simple reason that, in the past, the prosperity and advancement of Lathmu depended on the group.

In reality, the people of Lathmu were not natives of the planet on which they were now residing. The people native to the planet had all ended up on the Lathmu people's dinner plates long, long ago. At approximately one hundred eighty billion seconds in the past (starting from the current time on Lathmu and not that in Nikuulla's time-space pod), the forefathers of the people of Lathmu had traveled from an unknown location all the way across the great expanse of the Milky Way and had entered the United Star Systems of Ploaedes and Lagaol. Subsequently (and as is true of most stories of this kind), their spaceship broke down just as it was landing on Lathmu (that is if you can call a dilapidated spaceship that has traversed billions of light-years through space and then smashes straight into a planet "landing"). The Lathmu people lost all they possessed, including the knowledge and technological expertise that had brought them to Lathmu in the first place. The survivors spent the next several hundred years devouring—and trying not to be devoured by—the aborigines of their new planet. Had they continued thus, they would have had to evolve from the Stone Age all over again.

As luck would have it, however, the survivors from the spaceship managed to salvage a small number of ancient technologies, including the all-important deep-space electromagnetic wave receiver. The United Star Systems of Ploaedes and Lagaol lay far beyond the core region of civilization in the Milky Way. Therefore, before they were able to recover their technological culture and join the Milky Way Civilization Network, a handful of the survivors spent considerable lengths of time listening carefully to signals from outer space. Bit by bit, they received and decoded electromagnetic waves that were intermingled with the microwaves of the universe. Even after several billion years—even after having traveled from all corners of the Milky Way—these radio waves endured. The signals brought with them the knowledge and culture that enabled the desperate people of Lathmu to piece the remnants of their civilization back together again.

It was at a moment around six billion seconds in the past that the people of Lathmu finally returned to the circle of civilization in the Milky Way. From that moment on, the Milky Way Civilization Network became a bridge that connected them to the rest of the universe, and listening to radio waves became a way of reminiscing about the past. It gradually became something of a refined hobby, a way of whiling away boredom, with members of the listening group being monklike—at least so people thought. The listeners eavesdropped on sounds from across the universe and were constantly working to improve the capabilities of their receiving devices. The Organization of Listeners was made up of a number of different divisions or sects, with each attempting to receive and decode different sounds. These sounds included the groaning of the Milky Way; the clear bell-like tolls of the Great Cygnus; the constant rattling of the β-4 system; the whizzing of the planet Solus as it crossed the skies; the whispering of dust particles in the Ox Nebula; and the endless drumbeats of a strange people in the Bachakean Galaxy, who never seemed to tire of beating them but eventually seem to have beaten their civilization out of existence—for in the past three hundred years, all sound had ceased. By far the most exciting sound, however, came from the raging rivers of the Clecous cloud as they cascaded into the Tasha dust cloud and produced a rumbling that was as deafening as the big bang itself. The listeners who enjoyed this sound belonged mostly to the Mortification Society. Members of this group often needed their Auditory Systems replaced at least once every two months, and some even required counseling.

Aside from bringing them endless pleasure, listening to the universe was what had helped the people of Lathmu develop as far as they had. The only sound completely unknown to them was that of their own mother planet. At some point during the course of their remarkable interstellar journey, they had forgotten who they were and where they were from. This is why they chose to call themselves the people of Lathmu. For, as far as they were concerned, Lathmu was the planet on which they had been born and raised.

As has already been mentioned, Nikuulla was a member of the Hermits, the most conservative and traditional of all the listening groups. He may have looked like an unruly, ill-mannered adolescent; he may have dressed in a way that drove his mother crazy; he may have spent all his days hidden away in recreation centers; and he may have been a user of drugs . . . However, fate is a funny thing, and you never quite know where it might take you. During his university years, at a particularly wild party, Nikuulla accidentally overdosed. Wholly oblivious to what he was doing, he shut himself away in a laboratory and managed to invent a completely new kind of wireless receiving device.

This was a device for listening to the past. It could receive only waves under one hundred ten megahertz, at the lower end of the electromagnetic spectrum. At this end of the spectrum, electromagnetic waves traveled properly through space under the First Speed of Light.[2] It was not a bandwidth used in the Milky Way Civilization Network. For the more backward peoples living in the remotest parts of the Milky Way who might use this bandwidth, it would take several thousands of years for their radio waves to travel across even a small patch of the galaxy, and it was therefore sheer luck that the waves were picked up by a device like this. It was the more advanced civilizations, however—not the backward—that had saved the people of Lathmu from the dark ages. So who could be bothered to waste their time listening to snippets of communications left-over from ancient civilizations that were probably already extinct? It was for this reason that receiving these ancient frequencies was considered very—to use a phrase popular among university students—"off-the-wall." In fact, no one else had ever researched this area. Therefore, as well as having the honor of becoming the very first person to research this subject, Nikuulla was also granted enough funds to enable him to spend the rest of his life doing as he pleased.

Nikuulla's first "rebellious phase" in life helped him unlock his passion for looking back into the past. He loved studying history, and so it was rather unfortunate that the people of Lathmu didn't really have any. Neither did they have any traditions or culture of their own, nor even a single museum. If anyone logging onto the Milky Way Web tried Goooooooooooling the words "history and culture," he or she would be met with around one trillion pages of results. If, on the other hand, that person searched for "Lathmu history," the results would come in at less than a thousand pages—eight hundred of which were concerned with Lathmu's peculiar culinary culture.

This crazy receiving device must have somehow found its way out of Nikuulla's subconscious. It supplied remnants of history but little else. From the countless background noises that floated around the universe, Nikuulla's receiving device picked out the faint, primitive signals. Each signal represented a piece in the puzzle of forgotten history. The signals came from peoples and cultures that might have been long extinct. All these years later, these static noises were all that was left to tell of the stories of love and hate among people who had met their demise over the course of history. Nikuulla set about recording and filing each and every signal. Who knew what historical secrets of the Lathmu people might be hidden within?

It was at around two hundred thousand seconds in the past that Nikuulla discovered the special bandwidth that contained these primitive audiovisual signals that had already burned up most of their energy trudging across the vast cold space of the Milky Way for thousands of years. Picking up these signals at all thus often depended on little more than sheer luck.

At first, Nikuulla paid little attention to this particular chain of signals. The Milky Way was full of signals telling the same old story. It was as if every people that had ever existed were desperate to make itself known to the rest of the universe. After listening to these communications a few times, however, Nikuulla was surprised to discover that the signals on this bandwidth showed distinct characteristics of belonging to speakers of the Latin-based family of languages.

The Milky Way's circle of civilization was home to billions of different civilization groups, all of which communicated with one another via one of two key language systems. The first language system—Lachiwei—was made up of 34,564 semantic and 47,125 phonetic lexes. This incredibly complex language system could be used to describe almost all the dreadful phenomena in the Milky Way and was thus adopted as its lingua franca. The second key language system was the Cakcark family of languages, made up of a series of sounds (yes, a series—no one could ever calculate exactly how many), such as "enn," "ooo," "uuhh," and "aah." Although the individual sounds did not carry any precise meanings in themselves, speakers used them to convey the essence of what they were trying to say, thus forming a real language in the mind of both speaker and listener. This language family was most common among the peoples around the core star groups in the Milky Way, who had superhigh IQs and did not even bother to communicate with peoples that still relied purely on their mouths to speak.

In contrast, the native language of the people of Lathmu was derived from the Latin-based language system, which contained fewer than sixty phonic symbols. During the dark ages, the people of Lathmu had pretty much forgotten their mother tongue altogether. As soon as they evolved far enough to join the Milky Way's circle of civilization, they adopted the Lachiwei language system. The reason for doing so was very simple. With fewer than sixty phonic symbols, the Latin-based languages were just too monotonous. There were hardly enough words even to swear at people in the vast Milky Way circle! Although there were certain benefits of using such a simple language system (less time was lost on speaking, for example), only a handful of backward civilizations living around the edge of the Milky Way still cared to use such archaic languages. In worlds where the speed of light was the limit, transmitting complex linguistic signals was simply a nuisance.

Nikuulla had spent some time studying the Latin languages—it was, in fact, one of his hobbies. This came in very useful when trying to decipher the linguistic shards picked up by his receiving device. Even so, listening to these backward languages could still be very frustrating. Even after the signals had been triple filtered via the Language Machine, there were all sorts of colloquialisms, swear words, and pleasantries (such as asking after someone's eighteenth generation of ancestors) that could not be gotten rid of. Inferior peoples used the Latin-based languages, which represented a very specific stage in the evolutionary process. It was often the case that, before crossing the threshold into the circle of civilization in the Milky Way, inferior peoples would have stretched their languages to the absolute limit. After that, all they could do was to pray to God for help in using their barren languages to express their thoughts more accurately.

The first signal that Nikuulla had ever received on this special bandwidth was as below: "*Voyager Six* . . . buzz . . . this is Port Putian . . . The deep-space laser navigation signal has already been transmitted."

"Roger. The signal is very clear. *Voyager Six* requests permission to leave port."

"*Voyager Six*, the port is open. You can leave in one hundred seconds' time."

"Roger. Commence countdown to main engine ignition!"

". . . buzz . . . buzz . . ."

"*Voyager Six* . . . you must start the turbo engine in one thousand one hundred seconds . . . buzz . . ."

"Port Putian . . . buzz . . . we have taken off . . . we have taken off!"

"*Voyager Six*. In two thousand seconds, you will need to open your solar sails to a width of five thousand kilometers, at an angle of thirty-seven degrees, and to receive seventy millijoules of solar radiation . . . the solar wind will supply you with the propulsion you need to travel through the universe . . . In twenty thousand seconds' time, you will enter into a deep sleep; the sun will already be far behind you . . . In three billion seconds' time, your speed will reach four-fifths of the speed of light . . . buzz . . . Before losing the gusts provided by the solar wind, you will need to find a new source of propulsion. . . . Your target is . . . the Great Memphis Rift. . . . You . . . buzz . . . In five hundred years' time, you will leave the spiral arm in which we are currently located; at that point, you will no longer be able to count in days or years . . . seconds will be your only measure of time as you travel through the endless fields of space. . . . You are leaving your home planet behind forever; you will never be able to return . . . buzz . . . buzz . . . *Voyager Six*, so long!"

"So long . . . Dirt!"[3]

——— ∞ ———

Relatively speaking, this signal contained little meaningful data. After much effort, however, Nikuulla managed to identify five different vowels and twenty-one different consonants from the muddled utterances. In total, twenty-four base letters were used, from which, according to his translation machine, about two hundred thousand different words could be created—a Latin language that could hardly be more pure. Nikuulla traced the signal back to the far end of the чш–4700 spiral arm of the Milky Way, which was located less than a hundred billion light seconds away from Lathmu. This told him that the signal's sender would have still been alive a hundred billion light seconds earlier.

Nikuulla could tell just from a linguistic perspective that this people obviously still had a long way to go before reaching the level of the Milky Way civilizations. Their language was unable even to literally translate phrases such as "multilevel convection Kairadees gravitational logic ring," having to use instead the crude term "time tunnel." Indeed, the language they were using was so archaic that they had to add "tenses" to elucidate the meaning of each sentence. Nikuulla had already identified six different tenses in this short signal but estimated that the speakers would normally use no fewer than fifteen.

For a wireless wave to cross the universe was akin to taking part in a great lottery. The signals needed to traverse vast stretches of space and cross through invisible electromagnetic fields, gravity traps, and high-radiation neutron stars . . . For such weak energy to be received all these thousands of years later was nothing short of a miracle. Therefore, no matter how hard Nikuulla worked on improving his receiving device, the amount of information that could be collated for this time spectrum was still very limited.

All that Nikuulla could do was to trawl through time for the few surviving signals. After traveling forward on the time axis for approximately three billion seconds from his first signal, Nikuulla found a second:

"*Voyager Six* . . . this is Port Putian . . . buzz . . . the signal has met with interference . . . we don't know if you will be able to hear this message. . . . We are sorry to inform you that the solar wind has stopped blowing sooner than expected . . . buzz . . . the sun has ceased to function. . . . We don't know what has happened . . . we have witnessed some very strange changes in Neptune's outer orbit . . . Pluto has already . . . *Voyager Six* . . . we are sending you an early wake-up signal. . . . As soon as you awake, you will need to choose an alternative destination. . . ."

At this point, the signal cut off.

Then, just one hundred million seconds later, the situation had become very serious. Even after having crossed the cold and empty vastness of space, the speaker's voice revealed to Nikuulla a sense of urgency and anxiety (or at least this is what his Emotion Translation System told him). This section of signal was extremely weak, as if the transmitting equipment used to send it were running out of power.

"*Voyager Six* . . . *Voyager Nine* . . . *Advance Fleet* . . . where are you? . . . buzz . . . we are unable to locate your position . . . we don't have much time . . . the Oort cloud may have already disappeared. . . . Space is warping so badly that we can no longer accurately monitor the skies. . . . Something is flying toward the solar system (?). (A noun. Nikuulla's Translation Machine suggests that the system is named after their star.) Hello? Is anyone there? We are calling you. . . . Where are you? Please do everything in your power to send us your star chart immediately. We are unable to leave, unable to leave! The Great Catastrophe is already . . . buzz . . . Who else will be able to continue our civilization if our life here is destroyed? Please . . . please . . ."

The remainder of this chilling piece of information was lost forever in the immensity of time-space. Nikuulla searched back and forth along the time axis but was unable to pick up any more signals coming from that specific arm of the galaxy. The civilization he had been listening to must have withered just as it was making itself known for the first time.

Nikuulla called a friend he knew at that end of the galaxy and asked him what had happened to the tiny star system that had once been located in that spiral arm. "Huh? Oh, that. A supernova exploded and sent a neutron star hurtling like a ping-pong ball twenty thousand Telaz,[4] and then . . . Well, what would you expect a neutron star to do? It swallowed up everything in its path and then exploded again to form a nova. Why are you even asking me this, anyway?"

"I was just wondering . . ."

"Just wondering?"

". . . there was this small people . . ."

"You're telling me that the neutron star finished off some measly hornets' nest?" His friend laughed uncontrollably at the other end of the phone.

"Anyway. Thanks, Turner. Good-bye."

"Okay. You owe me lunch. See ya."

As far as Turner from Great Cygnus β was concerned, a backward people living on some marginal planet was indeed about as important as a hornets' nest in his backyard. Turner belonged to the Alahen, who had huge bodies, repulsive big-toothed jaws, and liked to eat lesser peoples for fun. Nikuulla simply couldn't' convince himself to feel the same. In fact, listening to this last signal had sent shivers straight to his soul. He couldn't help thinking about the mother planet from which the Lathmu people had originated. Perhaps his forefathers had been gobbled up by a more powerful race long ago. . . . Nikuulla was desperate to know the fate of the remnants of this people—the passengers sent into space just before the Great Catastrophe struck.

Nikuulla pointed his receiving device in the direction of the ecliptic plane of the Milky Way and searched back and forth. He widened his search range from ten billion seconds to one hundred billion. For people that were still in the process of evolving, this was an incredibly long period. Finally, at a point some forty billion seconds after the previous signal, a chain of broken signals ended the silence.

"Putian Two . . . this is *Transporter Seventy-Seven* . . . we request permission to enter port."

"*Transporter Seventy-Seven*, your bearing ratio is too low."

"We know. The planetoid Anmuu has already dried up. We were unable to find any more mineral resources. . . . We need to replenish our energy reserves in order to proceed to the next . . . I just hope that . . ."

"*Transporter Seventy-Seven*, may the Lord protect us all . . ."

From the newly found signal, Nikuulla could calculate that "they" had already been living in space for a very long time by their standards—perhaps even far longer than their life spans. They were still a long way from developing the technology that would enable them to travel freely across the multiple dimensions of the Milky Way, so they must have used cryogenic technology to prolong their life spans. It was this method that had originally enabled Nikuulla's forefathers to travel to the planet Lathmu (although the Lathmu people had long since suffered from collective amnesia).

Of that primitive people, only the passengers of *Voyager Six* had survived.[5] At a point around two hundred billion seconds earlier, they had settled in a tiny star system located on the edge of the spiral arm nearest to the spiral arm in which they used to reside. Unfortunately, this meant that they were even further away from the core region of the Milky Way than before.

In the tens of billions of seconds that had followed, the passengers of *Voyager Six* did all they could to keep their civilization going. However, the situation kept getting worse.

"The public . . . buzz . . . reactor will be closing in two thousand kiloseconds . . ."

". . . Colony HQ expresses its deep regret at this closure . . ."

". . . buzz . . . Colony HQ . . . the energy reserves for *Colonial Satellite Number Seven* are stretched to the absolute limit . . . we request immediate . . ."

"Colony HQ . . . the mineral factory is about to close . . ."

"We cannot find the appropriate people . . ."

". . . the Public Affairs Committee requests that you reduce the number of projects . . . going to the space factory . . ."

". . . we don' have enough raw materials to keep supplying the space projects . . . Colony HQ, we request that you reduce the number of projects . . ."

In this tiny star system, there were only two planets that could sustain the life of the colonists. But their energy sources were already running dry. The planets were without sufficient resources and were thus unsustainable. The colonists had not yet evolved far enough to develop interstellar travel technologies and had already used up most of their resources. Had they been lucky, they might have been able to keep their civilization alive in the form of a backward, self-sufficient society. But if they were unlucky . . .

Nikuulla waited for them to perish.

Several hundreds of millions of seconds later, it seemed as though they had reached the moment that would decide their ultimate fate. Some of the signals coming through were clear enough, while others were jumbled. This tiny world was being torn in two—between those who would advance and those who would not.

"*Da Gama Ten*, Colony HQ has already issued instructions . . . buzz . . . to make immediate preparations to leave port."

"Putian Two . . . we are trying to start the engines. . . ."

Prepare for launch; two-thousand-second countdown commencing."

"But Putian Two! That doesn't give you enough time to reach the fleet . . . buzz . . . we need to wait . . ."

"We don't have time . . . buzz . . . Colony HQ has ordered that we be retrieved . . . *Colonial Two* must launch immediately . . . buzz . . . all contact with the planet must be cut . . . buzz . . . else you will lose your launch window . . ."

"Roger. This is Da Gama Ten. All launch preparations are complete . . ."

Something huge had happened. Nikuulla sat up with a jolt and brought the pod to a standstill. He waited in silence. The signal cut out for twenty-eight hundred seconds before resuming again.

"*Da Gama Ten* . . . your speed on leaving the dock is already one hundred thousand kilometers per second . . . your destination star chart has been sent to the main processor . . . buzz . . ."

"Roger. Colonial Two, we have set our path through the Great Rift. Our current course is 6–71–51. We are headed for the Sipulition star system. We will reach the speed of light in twenty-two thousand seconds."

"*Da Gama Ten*, are you sure that you need to pass through the Great Rift? The star chart is not very precise . . . buzz . . . the distance may be further than estimated . . . buzz . . ."

"*Colonial Two* . . . we don't have any choice . . . buzz . . . we have limited time and fuel. . . . We will have to run the risk, otherwise . . . Once we have passed through the Great Rift, we will transmit a beyond-visual-range positioning signal toward the sixth latitude. You should follow us closely . . . buzz . . ."

"Roger. *Da Gama Ten*, you will be spending thirty thousand years alone in the vastness of space. We wish you a safe voyage! God bless us all! Good-bye!"

"*Colonial Two* . . . buzz . . . good-bye. Till we meet again!"

". . . buzz . . . we have cut all contact with the ground . . . our energy and resource supplies have both been cut . . ."

"As they retreat into caves, we advance into space!"

"That's right. *Da Gama Ten* . . . we pray that you will be able to . . . we will be waiting in orbit until . . . We will wait in a deep sleep until you send the signal to wake us up . . ."

"Good-bye . . . Dark Planet . . . Good-bye . . . human race."

What followed next was several tens of billions of seconds of silence. Although the background radiation for this frequency remained throughout, no more signals were sent. Evidently, the passengers of *Da Gama Ten* and *Colonial Two* had fallen into a deep sleep. As for the humans left on Dark Planet, they never turned their attention to the skies again.

Since *Da Gama Ten* traveled at a speed faster than low frequency electromagnetic waves, its own signals lagged far behind as it traversed the universe. Therefore, while carefully calculating the relation between space and time, Nikuulla kept pushing back little by little in an attempt to capture those elusive waves.

Suddenly, seventy-seven billion seconds later, the passengers of *Da Gama Ten* woke up with a start. The situation sounded tense. For some reason, the crew had turned on the public address system so that their conversations could be revealed directly to recipients unknown.

"Based on our current time, we have already deviated twenty thousand—no, thirty-two thousand—light seconds off course. . . ."

"That's impossible . . . the recalibrated gyroscope is normal. . . . The gyroscope has been firmly pointed at Proxima Centauri for the past seventy-seven billion seconds!"

Some nervous rustling could be heard.

"Here is the latest star chart as recorded by the flight computer for the past twenty billion seconds. And here is the predicted voyage chart from before we left Dark Planet . . . the gap between the two has already widened to . . ."

". . . I should remind you that we're aiming for the Red Giant . . . and it's right in front of us!"

There was a frightening silence.

From his previous research, Nikuulla estimated that there would be around two hundred or two hundred fifty passengers onboard *Da Gama*

Ten, but only three to six of them would be in key leadership roles. The other crew members usually called one of these people captain and another navigator (coincidentally, the pronunciation of the word "navigator" was very similar to the word for "governor" used on Lathmu).

The conversation recorded above took place between the captain and the navigator. While the navigator had concluded that the spaceship was off course, the captain was certain that the spaceship was proceeding in an almost perfectly straight line toward its target. Nikuulla could understand why they would have been worried. Although he had been born in the Milky Way's circle of civilization, he had researched many ancient peoples and their various attempts at crossing the universe. When they were traveling through the universe, if one wasn't aiming for "somewhere," then one would be going "nowhere." Most ordinary spaceships took very few supplies on their journeys—in general only just enough to reach their destination. By the time a spaceship realized that it had veered away from its flight path, it could require several hundreds of billions of seconds to correct the mistake—or of course they could choose to take a much longer road to an alternative destination. The doors to hell were always open!

Many peoples had gone extinct by deviating from their intended flight paths. Indeed, there was a popular saying that "few ants ever returned to the nest."

"But our constant positioning on the star chart shows that the H-η1117 star system, which is our second reference point, and the Unihorn Star, our third reference point, have both remained in their exact locations on the flight map throughout our journey . . . that can only mean that there must be a problem with the main reference point . . ."

"But based on the Three-to-One Principle . . . the flight computer should be able to tell which direction is accurate . . . which means that . . ."

"Why would the flight computer wake us up early then?"

"I don't know . . . buzz . . . but if the flight computer judges this to be the correct flight path . . ."

". . . Grove . . . behind us . . . *Colonial Two* has already been launched . . . they have even fewer supplies than we do . . . and they are carrying ten times as many people! If we were to guide them toward the wrong path . . . buzz . . ."

Next came a stream of electromagnetic interference, which blocked out a lot of the details. The signal did not recover until a thousand seconds later, and Nikuulla had, by that time, already blown the main fuse at the Scoundrel Bar. He had little choice but to wander over to the Honest Sailor Bar, a place he detested.

Now, Nikuulla managed to relocate the correct frequency, but the signal was very unclear. What had happened to *Da Gama Ten* as it drifted alone through space during the seventy-seven billion seconds since the signal had been cut off? What had happened to the *Colonial Two* spaceship and Putian Two dock after they ceased all contact with the planet and started their patient waiting in Dark Planet's orbit? Nikuulla studied his star chart carefully. The Great Rift that the speakers mentioned was in fact a spatial divide between the spiral arm чш–4971 and the secondary spiral arm чфю1277. Dark Planet was located at the outer edge of spiral arm чш–4971. If the desperate colonists had wanted to return to the resource-rich interior of the Milky Way, the shortest—but also the most desolate—route was to cut straight across the Great Rift.

The planet Lathmu was located on the east end at a right angle across the Great Rift. It was thus, perhaps, no coincidence that Nikuulla had been able to pick up this series of signals.

Nikuulla brought his time-space pod back to the present and went to the main desk to order a cup of coffee. He sat mutely in his seat holding his cup. Most of the peoples in the Milky Way consumed fluids directly into their bodies through a siphon, just like the Tasha dust cloud sucked in the water clouds around the twin stars Ploaedes and Lagaol. The Lathmu people were the only people to have retained the peculiar habit of filling a vessel with fluid and then drinking it through a mouth that was not at all suited to the purpose.

From now on, picking up the signals was going to be more of a gamble, a gamble with time. Based on the Time-Space Return Principle, the pod could not keep on traveling back and forth along the same time-space orbit. In other words, if he jumped to the wrong time-space point and then kept on going back and forth through the same section of time-space, at some point the space in between would, relative to him, contract. This would create a closed loop, which would prevent him from ever returning to that section of time-space again. For Nikuulla, this would mean losing the chance of ever finding out what had happened to the survivors.

In the last signal that Nikuulla had picked up, the speakers mentioned some "stellar rings":

"*Da Gama Ten* . . . buzz buzz . . . our position is . . . approximately eleven thousand light seconds away—the path set by the guiding rocket is very clear. . . . The stellar rings are at position 6–2 and are approximately three thousand light seconds away . . ."

"*Da Gama Ten*, we can see the path very clearly. We can pass through the rings."

"*Pioneer One* . . . *Pioneer One* . . . The signal is . . . *Pioneer One*! What has happened to the communication link? *Pioneer One*, please respond!"

Sighing, Nikuulla logged on to the Milky Way Wide Web and searched for the "Great Rift."

The Great Rift was a vast and lonely wilderness that was almost completely devoid of any sorts of star systems. All there were were some odd starlike objects or dark stars. The question as to how this impermanent star matter had ever managed to get into the wilderness was something that stumped even the most advanced Milky Way civilizations. It was possible that they were rogue bodies that had been cast out of their own systems for some reason and then got trapped in the absolute darkness of the Great Rift, but this was only conjecture. The "absolute darkness" had long been a hotly debated topic. At this point, all that was known for sure was that (1) there was something there, (2) this "something" could not be detected by monitoring devices, and (3) the only way of detecting it was to risk subwarp jumping into the Great Rift—and become, in the eyes of others, a flash of light that vanishes as soon as it appears.

This absolute darkness, however, posed great risks only for objects that were in the business of subwarp jumping. It was as if there were a huge traffic warning sign hanging in front of the Great Rift saying, "No Jumping Allowed." The Milky Way civilizations took this warning in stride. Seeing that the Great Rift was such a worthless space, no one could be bothered to spend two hundred billion seconds of real time crossing it just to see what might happen.

But "they" were on their way, crossing the Great Rift. What would happen to them? Nikuulla decided that he needed to create a planning sheet. Taking the Time-Space Return Principle into account, he estimated that he had only three or four more chances to jump within this spectrum.

Nikuulla finished off his coffee and came to a decision. Rather than searching aimlessly through space, he decided to follow "their" path as closely as possible. In the Great Rift, there were only three celestial bodies that had rings. These were the red giant Sislan (the remains of a dead fixed star, which had probably been banished to the Great Rift by a supernova); the blue giant Erlen'rad (a star that hardly emitted any light itself but that was wrapped in a strong luminous blue electromagnetic field generated by the violent churning of the planet's dual-layered surface); and the planet Balard (a stone). These three celestial bodies were located in three different corners of the Great Rift, with substantial distances between them. The difference in time required for radio signals to reach Lathmu from these corners of the Great Rift was several tens of billions of seconds.

Would "they" be heading for a star or a planet?

Nikuulla pointed his receiving device at the planet Balard and traveled forward one hundred ten billion seconds from the previous signal. He brought the time-space pod to a stop and waited in silence. After a good deal of time had passed, however, he realized that even the microenergy leakage radiation background noise that was usually generated on this channel was completely absent. Nikuulla's heart sank. Could they really have tried passing through the rings of one of the stars?

One jump had already been wasted. As Nikuulla adjusted the pod, he felt so nervous that his brain was shaking. At some 100.7 billion seconds later, the electromagnetic waves transmitted from the red giant Sislan were just about to reach planet Lathmu. After a period of silence, a weak electromagnetic wave could finally be heard.

"...buzz...buzz..."

"...buzz...*Da Gama Ten*...we have already...passed through the rings to...the Red Giant..."

"*Pioneer*...buzz..."

"*Da*...buzz...I just don't know how to describe this...you won't believe it..."

"*Pioneer One*...what has happened? Your curvilinear flight path is extremely dangerous....You are about to collide with the Red Giant...Pioneer One..."

"No! Our flight path is correct . . . , at least I think it is . . . *Da Gama Ten* . . . We are about to reach the Red Giant . . ."

"*Pioneer One!* You're crazy!"

"*Da Gama Ten* . . . the red giant Sislan has no gravitational offset. I repeat: it has no gravitational offset . . ."

"But that doesn't necessarily mean that . . . buzz . . . the Red Giant's gravity distortion field may lie on a different latitude . . . we aren't living in the twentieth century anymore . . . we know better than to trust our intuition . . . buzz . . ."

"*Da Gama Ten* . . . we are now speeding toward the Red Giant . . . we need to give this a try, otherwise *Colonial Two* behind us will never make it . . . we would rather . . . buzz . . . we are making our descent . . . descending . . . two light seconds away from the Red Giant!"

"No, Alex! No!"

Nikuulla shut his eyes. He waited for the desperate voice of the captain to return. Pioneer One was the scout ship for *Da Gama Ten*, while *Da Gama Ten* was the scout ship for *Colonial Two*, which had escaped from Dark Planet before its fall. If they failed to reach their goal now, all would be lost.

Several thousand seconds later, the bridge of *Da Gama* had already become a frenzied inferno of hysteria. A voice rang out once again.

"*Da Gama Ten* . . . *Da Gama* . . . this is *Pioneer One* . . . please respond if you can hear this message . . . we are speaking to you from a complete void . . ."

" . . . "

"*Da Gama Ten* . . . Are you there? We may no longer be in the same universe . . . we don't know where we are . . . *Da Gama Ten* . . . our coordinates show that we are at the core of the red giant Sislan . . ."

" . . . "

"*Da Gama Ten* . . . we will be transmitting an electromagnetic pulse into space in thirty seconds . . . if you receive it, it means that we are still in the same dimension . . . Counting down from 13, 12, . . . 1 . . ."

Nikuulla lit a cigarette. The flame created a tiny light in the dark pod. It was one of the few customs leftover from pre-Lathmu civilization, to put a lighted stick into one's mouth when one felt anxious, which would tell the processing chip in one's frontal lobe to relax one's cells.

At this moment—at a point several hundred million light seconds away from him and several hundreds of billions of seconds in the past—there must have been people in *Da Gama Ten* sucking away at something similar. It was always such torture to await the revelation of one's fate.

"*Pioneer One!* We have received your return signal! It is very clear . . . buzz . . . we have already verified your location! You . . . you . . . you are on course. . . . Where is the Red Giant?!"

"*Da Gama Ten*, there is no Red Giant here. I repeat, there is no Red Giant . . . buzz . . . we are surrounded by images . . . it's unbelievable . . . the redness is so dazzling . . . space is no longer visible . . . everything has been engulfed by the Red Giant . . ."

"*Pioneer One!* Are you saying that the Red Giant is . . . hollow?"

". . . no . . . there is simply no Red Giant here."

"What?!"

"It's hard to explain . . . *Da Gama Ten* . . . but we assume that we must be in some kind of a projection of a real universe. . . . We have entered into the Red Giant, but no matter where we fly, all we see around us are distorted images of the Red Giant's surface. . . . It's all around us. . . . We are transmitting the images back to you now. . . . Can you see them?"

"*Pioneer One* . . . the images are very clear . . . I . . . we can't believe that . . ."

"*Da Gama Ten* . . . we are lost . . ."

Nikuulla leaped up from his chair and dialed the number of the university observatory. Because he was making a call to the "past," it took a while for the signal to be sent through. The person who eventually picked up the phone was Nikuulla's classmate. It sounded like the observatory was holding a cosmic celebration party, so Nikuulla had to turn the volume down to a point where he could only just hear.

"The Red Giant?"

"Yes, Sislan."

"The navigator?"

"Navigator?!"

"Sorry, that's just what we astronomers usually call it. What's the matter with it?"

That was a very good question. Nikuulla didn't really know what the matter was. He chose his words very carefully. "It's . . . it's empty."

"It's empty! My God! You've called me across time to tell me that Sislan in the Terksasi Galaxy is empty! I love it! Are you going to let me take the credit for this discovery?"

"Listen, mate. I'm being serious. You know very well that I'm talking about the Red Giant Sislan in the Great Rift."

"So, you're interested in star projections?"

"I don't understand." Nikuulla's head was buzzing.

"Buddy, Sislan in the Great Rift is a spatial projection of Sislan in the Terksasi Galaxy."

Nikuulla was in prison, a prison of time. He had no jumps left and would be kicked out of this time-space spectrum at any moment. The only solution was to wait patiently in the time-space pod until the story came to a close—or at least until the signal broke off. It could have been a lot worse. There were some supplies in the pod and there was electricity, so it wasn't like he was going to die. Having been shuttling back and forth so many times, he had lost track of the current time. The only thing he knew for sure was that the number at the bottom of his bill at the Honest Sailor Bar was going to be higher than the total sum of all the time constants he had ever traveled.

So the red giant Sislan was just a projection. Even if his friend at the observatory wasn't willing to give him a proper explanation, Nikuulla could guess most of the details for himself. The problem was that, all those hundreds of billions of seconds earlier, this group of people knew nothing of this phenomenon, one that even Nikuulla himself had never heard of before. Their signals continued to arrive in dribs and drabs. Maintaining a considerable distance from each other, *Da Gama Ten* and *Pioneer One* drifted in unison toward the opposite end of the Milky Way. They had to make a decision, but they lacked the energy needed to stop or change the direction in which they were traveling. Their decision would decide the fate of thousands of people, as well as whether an entire civilization had any hope of surviving.

The seconds continued to tick by. Nikuulla knew that the central brain chips in all the passengers onboard were likely to have overloaded.[6] It hadn't taken them long to work out that the problem lay in the route they had selected. For a people with limited time and resources, and anxious to cross a vast expanse of space, their options were limited, so they had sought the shortest possible route to their destination—crossing the Great

Rift to reach the outskirts of the minor spiral arm чфю1277. In order to navigate their way through this vast, empty space, they had had to choose a fixed celestial body with a calculable orbit to serve as their navigation point. In this great region of nothingness, only the weak rays emitted by the red giant Sislan were bright enough to be seen several hundreds of billions of light seconds away.

They had now discovered, however, that the Red Giant was not really there. Not only was it not there, but it also, incredibly, shifted its position in space depending on the location of the viewer.

The crew concluded after a few thousand seconds that there was an enormous mass of matter in the Great Rift—so much that it perhaps even exceeded a civilized person's imagination. Because the matter was so heavy, it sank and distorted the space around it. It might have ended up completely "wrapped up" in the distorted space and so was unable to be detected by any sensor. The distorted space must have formed a lenslike gravitational field that magnified part of another, far-away star system and projected it onto the Great Rift. The Red Giant was such a virtual, mirrored image, and a multidimensional virtual image on the scale of the universe was nothing like the candlelight in a laboratory. Therefore, although they had "entered" into the heart of the Red Giant, they were still seeing its exterior. During the latest seventy-seven billion seconds of their voyage, their distance from this gravitational lens—and thus the focal length—had been constantly changing. Their course had been readjusted accordingly, which led them to the point of no return.

Okay. The universe was playing a joke—and anyone who didn't find it funny was always welcome to leave.

For some strange reason, Nikuulla couldn't help but feel that he was partly to blame, as though he had been the one to put the red giant Sislan there to confuse the passengers onboard the spaceships. Having followed these people for so many billions of seconds, he felt as though he was already getting to know a good number of them. Port Putian, Putian Two, *Voyager Six, Colonial Two, Da Gama Ten, Pioneer One*, the captain, the navigator . . . They had crossed the Milky Way for years on their own, struggling all the way. Now, however, it looked as though their time was finally up.

After *Pioneer One* reunited with *Da Gama Ten*, the radio went silent for a very long time. Maybe it would be silent forever. In comparison with the boundless universe, the two spaceships were smaller than comets. They had no supplies, no landing ports, no homeland, no destination . . . There was nothing around them for several hundreds of millions of light seconds—except for the projected image of the Red Giant that was burning wildly away and laughing at their ignorance. So? This wasn't a big deal. Innumerable peoples had gone extinct. Countless planets had fallen. Hadn't the fellow citizens of these people back home chosen to sink from sight as well? But then again, even though they would never be able to explore the universe again, perhaps they were still alive and content . . .

Various possibilities rushed into Nikuulla's central brain chip like a flurry of tiny insects. His Logical Assessment Unit concluded, however, that the crew onboard *Pioneer One* and *Da Gama Ten* had already perished. Although this annoying chip had come up with the same conclusion several hundreds of millions of seconds earlier, this time Nikuulla knew that it was right.

Nikuulla straightened himself, disconnected the control arms, and prepared to close the pod down. But just at that very moment, a sound came floating through his receiving device.

"*Pioneer One*, your speed on leaving the dock is 3,371; your direction is 17–37 . . . buzz . . ."

"*Da Gama Ten* . . . everything on the ship seems normal . . . they are already sleeping . . . In four hundred seconds, we will also enter into a deep sleep, the course is already . . ."

Nikuulla leaped up from his seat. They were still moving! But where could they be going? Where?!

"*Pioneer One* . . . buzz . . . the star chart has already been sent to your central computer . . . we are not certain . . . but this is our only chance . . . there is a dust cloud there that is forming a new planet . . . if there are any other planets in this system, then . . . anyway . . . we don't have . . . buzz . . ."

"We will await our destiny as we sleep."

"We will be able to light your way . . . buzz . . . our reactor is going to explode in 1,776 seconds' time . . . Please send our position to *Colonial Two* . . . We will burn in space for 6,000 seconds . . . it isn't very long . . . but it should be enough time for their navigation equipment to realign their positioning . . ."

"So long, *Da Gama!*"

"So long . . ."

A short pause followed.

"Alex, are you still there?"

". . . buzz . . . I'm still here . . ."

"If . . . please don't forget us . . ."

"To forget would be to betray, *Da Gama Ten.*"

Four hundred seconds later, the entire crew of *Pioneer One* entered into a deep sleep. This was their last chance, so as to save every single second of supplies. One thousand seven hundred seventy-six seconds later, *Da Gama Ten* morphed into a burst of light that sparkled a moment in the cold universe before vanishing forever.

There could be no doubt that there would be no more signals for a long, long time. *Colonial Two* and *Pioneer One* had both changed course and were drifting through the darkness. Based on past experience, the odds that the living things sleeping onboard would ever wake up again were stacked at 99.999 percent against.

The air-conditioning inside the time-space pod droned on monotonously. Nikuulla decided that he couldn't wait any longer. Before returning to the present, he sighed and stretched in his chair. Far in the distance, the Tasha dust cloud rumbled loudly as it sucked in water vapor from all around. Many, many billions of seconds later, a planet would be formed. Compared with the infinite life span of the universe, any organic life was so insignificant as to be laughable.

But, then again, perhaps it wasn't quite so laughable . . .

Perhaps it wasn't funny at all . . .

Perhaps . . .

Perhaps the dust cloud they had been talking about was Tasha?!

Nikuulla was shaking as he restarted the engine in the pod. The figure flashing in front of him labored from "2" to "1." His time-space return function was up. After one more jump, this time-space spectrum would be closed to him forever and he would never again be able to experience this section of history and search for the signals that were alternately suffused with hope or completely lacking it. Even if he were to enter this "period" using the pod again, the time-space would be silent and devoid of excitement for him.

The operating system in the pod waited patiently for Nikuulla to enter the time coordinates to his next destination. It was a long wait. Finally, he entered "the present" in the "Start" column. Then, after another long while, he input one hundred eighty billion seconds in the past into the "Destination" column.

Tasha's heavy body began to turn, going faster and faster. The universe turned around on its side and then upside down. A dazzling array of stars swept into the skies around Lathmu before slowly fading away again. The starscape of one hundred eighty billion seconds in the past gazed back at Nikuulla, who released his control arms, stood up, and walked over to the window.

Lathmu lay a long way below him. At this point, it was still in a state of barbaric ignorance. There were no buildings, no lights, no time-space travel fleets shuttling to and fro. The time-space pod floated spectrally thousands of kilometers above the ground.

The receiver crackled with the electrostatic sound drifting through space.

Nikuulla had already lost track of the time when, suddenly—

"... buzz ... this is *Colonial Two* ... buzz ... *Da Gama Ten* ... buzz ... *Pioneer One* ... buzz ... zzzzzz ..."

The hairs on Nikuulla's back stood up on end.

"... *Da Gama Ten* ... we are unable to receive your signal ... buzz ... we are unable to position accurately ... we can see ... the destination planet is very clear ... *Pioneer One* ... Where are you ...? Have you already landed ...? Can you see us ...? Calling *Da Gama Ten* ..."

Without the help of any instrument, Nikuulla could see a spot of light near the lower left-hand corner of Tasha. It was very bright, like the flame generated by a low-grade space thruster leaving the speed of light.

After completing a treacherous journey of hundreds of billions of light seconds, *Colonial Two* had reached the destination that *Da Gama Ten* had used the last few seconds of its existence to guide it toward. The *Colonial Two* spaceship had been so pummeled by time and space that it was now swaying and shaking as it approached its destination. Although it was almost there, the impact of leaving the speed of light meant that it was becoming increasingly fragile.

A few hundred seconds later, a long stream of light erupted from the *Colonial Two* spaceship.

"... buzz ... *Da Gama Ten* ... we are experiencing some mechanical failures ... I am not exactly sure ... I can see some of the cabins breaking away from the ship ... *Da Gama Ten*! *Pioneer One*! We are in trouble ... the ship is shaking violently ... we don't know ..."

The spot of light left a trail of smoke and glittering debris. Then it plunged straight into the orbit of Lathmu. Standing at sixty thousand meters above ground, Nikuulla almost felt the spaceship sweep right under his feet. He could see the battered cabins and the dented bridge. The better part of the spaceship was wrapped in a thick cloud of smoke.

"Is anyone there? Please help us! Help! Most of the passengers are still asleep ... *Da Gama Ten* ... if you are there ... please help!"

Nikuulla rushed wildly between the windows in the pod. Behind the thick walls of both glass and time, all he could do was stand by and watch helplessly as the spaceship shot over to the far end of the horizon. The cries coming through the receiving device were getting louder.

"Warning! Warning! The main engine has died! We are losing power ... we are losing power!"

"Deceleration has failed! Deceleration has failed!"

"We are speeding up. . . . We are going to crash!"

"Stabilize the ship!"

"The fire in Cabin Number Four cannot be contained. . . . It's spreading. It's spreading!"

"Captain! This is Cabin Number Four! Please abandon us immediately! Abandon us!"

"... Cabin Number Four has been detached ... Cabin Number Four has crashed ..."

"The fire cannot be contained!"

"Captain! The fire has spread through the central cabin!"

"We've lost eight hundred seventy people!"

"Captain! Unless we take immediate action, we will crash in one hundred fifty seconds!"

The spaceship bolted out from the other end of the horizon, engulfed in flames. Nikuulla covered his mouth with his hands as, for the first time, history played itself out before his very eyes. The cast was a group of lonely, desperate people who had worked relentlessly for generations and had trudged for hundreds of billions of seconds across the universe to be suddenly awoken from a deep sleep. The universe looked away as these tragic scenes etched themselves onto the face of history.

"This is the captain speaking . . . To the entire crew onboard *Colonial Two* . . . we have only one choice left . . . only one opportunity . . . we have only enough power to launch one cabin and allow it to land safely . . . Crew, we do not have much time . . . You must decide immediately which cabin to launch . . ."

"Cabin Number Seven, Captain!" someone suggested.

Faint, crackling voices could be heard coming from the various corners of the disintegrating spaceship.

"Yes. Cabin Number Seven is women and children."

"But . . . there are no technicians among them . . . if we crash . . . how will they survive?"

"As long as they can propagate, there is a way."

The crew in each of the remaining cabins expressed their agreement, though the number of cabins was dropping fast. In the space of a few tens of seconds, many had already been replaced by silence.

"Prepare for launch!"

"Cabin closed!"

"Good-bye, Alina!"

"Launch complete!"

A ball of light escaped the spaceship and hurtled straight down toward Lathmu. The spaceship flew around and around the tiny planet. Although it had now been completely engulfed by roaring flames, the voices within lingered on. "The cabin has entered the atmosphere!"

"Their flight altitude looks normal!"

"The deceleration parachute has opened. . . . Their speed is dropping . . ." "Hurrah! The cabin will land safely!" Few people cheered at the last sentence. Most had already succumbed to the great fire.

". . . this is *Colonial Two* calling . . . *Da Gama Ten* . . . *Pioneer One* . . . Are you there? We have, according to plan, already sowed our seed on an unknown planet . . . thank you . . . we do not know where you are now . . .

it does not matter . . . Alex . . . once, we lost everything. . . . Once, we wandered the skies. . . . Once, we almost gave up. . . ."

"But now we have finally found our home."

From the perspective of the universe, this great fire had hardly existed. Even so, these radio waves continued to pierce through the cosmos and proceeded with determination toward a far-away future.

10

1923: A FANTASY

ZHAO HAIHONG

TRANSLATED BY NICKY HARMAN AND PANG ZHAOXIA

Everyone needs ideals in life, don't they?

Jia Su's ideal was to create a machine.

Bubbles's ideal was to make revolution.

Meiying's ideal was to make an honest woman of herself.

This was the 1920s in Shanghai. Everywhere you went, you heard the ravishingly honeyed, husky tones of popular singers like Zhou Xuan and Bai Guang floating in the air. People who breathed this in drifted through life day by day looking slightly tipsy, blithely ignoring the fact that their country was on its knees.

I can already hear angry protests as I write these words. After all, was not Shanghai in the twenties a hotbed of revolution? Sure, some parts of the city were awash with money and a playground for comprador foreigners, but that was only the demonic flip side of the coin. Take Bubbles for example. She is an unusual personage, because she belongs to the other side of Shanghai life, yet here she is, veering off course and into a gaudily lit nightclub by the name of Flowers of Shanghai.

No doubt I have been too influenced by how Brigitte Lin looked in the Hong Kong film *Peking Opera Blues*, but I imagine Bubbles as having a rather strange hairstyle. For no very good reason, I see her with her hair cut short like a man's. This would not raise an eyebrow nowadays but at that time was considered far too "advanced." Her thick black eyebrows were set low over a pair of lively dark eyes, and these features dominated a face that was more sharp than pretty.

At the door of the Flowers of Shanghai nightclub, Bubbles was greeted by the hostess, who patted her coquettishly on the chest, pushing a white rose into the breast pocket of her Sun Yat-sen jacket as she did so. "Good evening, sir . . ."

The hostess's words were no sooner out of her mouth than she flinched, her fingers fluttering from Bubbles's chest like a startled bird. The corners of Bubbles's mouth twitched in a smile, which allayed the hostess's surprise.

"I'm looking for someone," Bubbles announced calmly and slipped into the brightly colored world of the club's interior, crowded with customers cruising in the glittering, nighttime waves of light like brilliant tropical fish. Bubbles melted into the pool of colors, with a flick of her tail as it were, almost giving my imagination the slip. Just at that moment, Jia Su appeared.

As Bubbles approached him, it seemed to her that his face emerged like a solid and sharply contoured rock from the water. It was a rock that many women would want to lean on.

But Bubbles was not a woman, she was a revolutionary.

If only I could conjure up the first meeting of Bubbles and Jia Su in my mind's eye and hear the words spoken between them. Perhaps he said, "Hello, I'm the one you're looking for," or, "I'm Jia Su, are you looking for me?" It has become almost an obsession with me to write their lines for them. Am I slighting the third protagonist in this story, Meiying, with my extraordinary enthusiasm for Bubbles and Jia Su? I do not think so.

Meiying was my great-grandmother. I lived with her and my maternal grandparents until I was ten years old, and she first told me my great-grandfather's story when I was nine. A ninety-year-old's memory and a nine-year-old's powers of understanding are an unpromising combination, certainly not enough to compel me to write the story down. Yet nearly twenty years after my great-grandmother died, I suddenly found myself wanting to record it, fragmentary and timeworn though it was. The trigger was a family genealogy and a box.

A month before, I had arrived back in China on holiday. The air quality was worse than in any number of other countries where I had lived, and very soon I had a persistent, hacking cough and was unable to go out. While I was at home with nothing to do, it occurred to me to go through some family bits and pieces that had lain untouched for many years and sort them out.

There was a cupboard containing a number of things that my parents had brought with them from their old home, things that I had never paid any attention to in the past but that I now inspected with care. There was a rusty iron box with a brass padlock hanging from it that looked quite old. Out of curiosity, I wiggled the padlock. It held firm—and unfortunately there was no key.

"What's inside it?" I asked my mother at dinner that evening.

"I have no idea. I think it belonged to your great-grandmother, and she buried it in their yard during the Cultural Revolution, for safekeeping."

"That's interesting."

"Apparently it contains the family's genealogical records, but I've never seen inside."

Were family records really as heavy as that? I wondered. "And what about the key? Where is it?"

"If there was one, I'd have opened the box ages ago. We only got it when my grandmother passed away. I've no idea where the key is."

I picked up the box carefully and weighed it in my hands. "I don't believe that! A padlock like this isn't hard to force, yet you've waited all this time!"

"If you wish to amuse yourself with it, take it with you," my mother said with a dismissive wave of her hand. "There can't be anything valuable in it, or she wouldn't have lived in such penury all those years."

Very interesting. I coughed again.

———— ∞∞∞ ————

Jia Su, courtesy name Tingtao, style name Ningjiang, was born in Ke Town, Shaoxing Prefecture, Zhejiang Province in 1894, and died in 1945 at the age of fifty-one. He came from a long line of scholars dating back to the Qian-long period, many of whom achieved the supreme grade of jinshi *in the imperial examinations. From childhood, Tingtao was bright and hardworking and excelled in classical poetry and prose . . . at the age of eighteen, he won a Boxer Indemnity Scholarship to attend Cambridge University, where*

he gained a master's degree in physics and a doctorate in chemistry.
Having completed his studies, he returned home in 1923. . . .

These snippets, expressed in semiclassical style, tugged at threads of memory lurking in the deepest recesses of my mind. They were not family records but merely brief biographical notes written by my great-grandfather's friends after his death. They were written in a fine and elegant "regular script," and the small characters ran from top to bottom of the page, and from right to left. The brittle paper was yellowed with age. Alongside the notes were two very heavy, dark bottles. I shook them. They appeared to contain liquid.

In August 1923, he arrived in Shanghai onboard the British ship HMS
Tyndareus.[1]

In 1925, the aqua-dream machine he was developing failed. He married
Xu Meiying, and they left Shanghai for Beijing. There he took up a teaching post at Yenching University.

My great-grandfather's image seemed to leap from the photograph I found inside the notebook, slowly growing bigger and bigger, his mouth even widening into a smile.

My great-grandmother first met my great-grandfather when she was working as a dance hostess in the Flowers of Shanghai. At the time, her father was a rickshaw puller, her mother was suffering from TB, and her elder brother had been shot dead while on strike and participating in a demonstration. The family was in dire straits, so she had little option but to become a dance hostess.

Jia Su had just returned to China. Friends overseas had entrusted him with some papers that he was to pass on to the revolutionaries. He was to go to the Flowers of Shanghai, where his contact would be a young woman with short-cropped hair in a black Sun Yat-sen suit. That was Bubbles, the woman who so fired my imagination.

———— ✺ ————

"There's nothing special about this stuff," Jia Su said to Bubbles. "What possible use could you have for it?"

"What counts as ordinary abroad is hard to get hold of here," Bubbles said with a faint smile. "Besides, you can't judge a book by its cover." The vagueness of her reply seemed to hint at something portentous.

The cryptic exchange between the two of them was swallowed up by the songs and chatter from the dance floor.

Meiying was fated to choose this moment to make her appearance. Her mother's TB was getting worse and her father had to pull his rickshaw even at night. With her family in disarray, she had to do her bit to help. She had arrived breathless in the club's makeup room, getting a vicious pinch on her neck from the boss as she passed. The woman continued to yell at her as Meiying put on her makeup and powdered over the shameful pinch marks.

She pinned up her glossy black hair in two stylish rolls. Her eyebrows were finely arched and her almond-shaped eyes most alluring. Her lips curved in what seemed a natural smile—I have seen an old photo of her from that time. The woman in the picture looks just like the classical beauties on cigarette packets that were sometimes unearthed from old trunks when the retro trend was on. So sweet, so gentle. I could not reconcile this beauty with the old lady with rough scaly skin and gray hair that I remembered. The beautiful Meiying was long gone; she had belonged only to that epoch.

—————⧉—————

Jia Su first heard the song and then noticed the singer. Her singing was filled with melancholy, but it carried a peculiar force hinting at a struggle to survive.

He turned his head and saw Meiying. She was not stunningly beautiful, but she conveyed the impression of being immersed in the song, body and soul. Everything she had was being drawn along by that song to a place—she did not know where—that she desperately needed to find.

It was one of Bai Guang's songs. She did not have Bai Guang's husky, sexy voice, but even Bai Guang could not sing it the way she did . . .

> Without you
> What will I do?
> My heart is broken, there's nothing I can do
> I don't care how high the sky
> I don't care how deep the earth

As long as you're by my side
You're the meaning of my life . . .

Jia Su fell under the spell of that voice. He stood rooted to the spot looking in her direction. Meiying was singing with half-closed eyes. Suddenly she opened them wide and saw that rocklike face.

~~~

I opened the hi-fi cabinet and found an old CD, *Songs of Yesterday*. I pressed the button and listened to Bai Guang singing, "Without you . . ." How I wanted to turn back the clock and listen to Meiying singing that night eighty years ago.

My great-grandmother's opinion of her husband was succinct. She said that to see a person like Jia Su in that kind of place astounded her. She said you could tell at first glance that he was "someone you could rely on," and faces like that were hardly ever seen in nightclubs. Her poverty and need for someone to rely on understandably made her do everything in her power to get close to him.

The same story may be written quite differently by different writers just as the same incident may be seen differently by different people. In Bubbles, Jia Su's discomposure aroused a hint of contempt. This Western-educated person was no more than a playboy, she thought. My initial fantasies therefore came to an abrupt halt here. Bubbles gave a graceful wave of the hand and walked away. Jia Su's astonishment as he watched her can be readily imagined: this woman walked like no one he had seen before, slicing her way through the swirling colors of the dance floor like a knife. Sharp. Clean.

But Jia Su let Bubbles go. On this first encounter, my great-grandmother gained a slight upper hand. I think this was because the striking impression Bubbles made concealed her femininity. She was an enigma, sharp as a dagger and cold as ice, and she completely mystified him. Meiying, on the other hand, was like a glass of fine wine, fragrant and inviting. She attracted him as a woman attracts a man.

~~~

Tonight, I carefully opened the long-sealed iron box. Inside, I saw two opaque, sealed containers. My left eyelid started to twitch. The containers were shaped like bottles and were very heavy. I held one up and gave it a shake. It seemed to me that there was liquid inside.

What could it be? I wondered.

In old stories, long-sealed liquids could only be wine. I felt a bit disappointed at the thought. But these two containers were not like wine bottles or wine jars. Besides, I simply could not imagine Jia Su as an avid wine drinker.

I heard the *glug-glug* of liquids again. It seemed to have come through a long time tunnel, revealing to me its long-buried secrets.

"Mr. Jia, someone to see you."

Jia Su frowned when he heard the school caretaker's message. He thought it must be Meiying. At this time of night, few people in the school would trouble him.

In those days, it was considered shameful for a gentleman, even one who had been to the West, to be visited at the school by a nightclub dancer, and Jia Su had to play by the rules just like anyone else. But it was Bubbles who had arrived at the school gate, carrying a suitcase.

"What . . . ?" Jia Su asked, looking puzzled.

"Mr. Jia, can we talk somewhere else, please?" Behind Bubbles's calm exterior there was a hint of anxiety. You did not have to be very clever to tell that she was in trouble.

Jia Su ushered her from the porter's lodge into his laboratory, thus violating one of his own rules.

"Whatever are you doing in here?" asked Bubbles, in astonishment at the sight that greeted her.

In the middle of the lab stood a gigantic figure made of brass, its many arms outstretched like a thousand-armed Buddhist guardian god. In each hand, there were glass containers of different colors and sizes. The liquids they held were of colors seen only in dreams. They oscillated and sang. Around the edge of each hand, there were adjustable temperature gauges. "Veins" in rainbow hues crawled from the palms and up the arms. The glittering liquid in the veins converged in the giant's belly, a semitransparent glass jar, bubbling up in a rainbow of colors. Steam rose from the belly jar, through pipes the size of a man's arm, into the giant's head, a round vessel in which more water was being heated. About one-third of the way up the vessel was a protruding pipe, apparently the mouth of the giant. At that moment, the mouth was closed tight with two stop valves. The giant also had nostrils, two airholes in the middle of the water vessel. Thin wisps of vapor erupted from the nostrils, leaving strangely shaped trails in the air.

The combination of noises—the bubbling of the boiling liquid, the scalding steam erupting from the mouth of the bottles, the chuntering of the internal heater, the hissing of chemicals heating up—produced an extraordinary effect. If it took you unawares, it could make you hallucinate or even send you to sleep.

Bubbles's face was covered in a sheen of sweat. Her thin lips were noticeably reddened in the moist atmosphere. "This is fantastic!" she breathed.

"You are safe here," Jia Su said. "Hurry up and tell me what the matter is."

"I'm wanted by the authorities. Could I hide with you for a couple of days?" said Bubbles.

"In here?" Jia Su looked around. His gaze lingered on the brass giant as if he could see that hiding someone wanted by the authorities might destroy everything he had achieved.

The corner of Bubbles's mouth twitched. "I am truly sorry. We barely know each other, after all."

"No, it's not that," Jia Su said, with a hasty shake of his head. "It's just so sudden. Wait a moment," and he left the room.

Bubbles lifted a corner of the heavy dark-blue curtain and saw Jia Su in the distance, talking to the caretaker and waving his hands in the air. You can tell when honest people are lying: they make meaningless gestures, blush, look nervous, and so on. Jia Su displayed none of these signs. He looked completely genuine, as if he were just explaining that he had a moral obligation to put a friend up for a few days.

As Bubbles watched, she started to have doubts about whether she could trust him—a man who had been to the West and whom she barely knew. But she had no choice. Everyone she could rely on was under surveillance. She had to take a gamble and put her life in Jia Su's hands.

She turned back to the room, which was stacked from floor to ceiling with glass bottles of every size and color, both clear and opaque. Her anxious gaze was reflected in the bottles, her dark pupils appearing to rise and fall along with the gurgling liquids inside. All of a sudden, the mouth of the giant opened—or rather, the stop valves in the brass tube were released—and a whoosh of colorful steam erupted from it. At the same time a long-drawn-out moan was emitted from the depths of the giant's belly. The cry, "Ai . . . ya," came from all the containers in unison and was like a sigh from far away and long, long ago.

Bubbles was filled with confusion but found herself giving an accompanying sigh. The tense muscles of her back and shoulders relaxed and she put her black suitcase down.

She looked around again. The lab was not big. There were altogether four rooms, of which two were for the storage of chemicals and instruments, and one was a cubicle where someone working late could sleep. The main room held a variety of chemicals laid out for experiments and the thousand-armed warrior, which stood in the center and took up more than half the space.

The air in the room had a smell that was slightly acidic while also giving hints of new grass. The steam from different liquids merged into twisting, tangled, ever-changing shapes and colors. As Bubbles breathed in the atmosphere and the strange chorus of sounds reached her ears, the tension in her body eased. She had been leaning against the windowsill and now she slid to the floor. She saw red and blue smoke whirling in the air and forming itself into the shape of a woman who danced bewitchingly, the dark blue hem of her dress floating over Bubbles's head. Bubbles stared, then froze in shock: she recognized this sinuously swirling figure. Even though its beauty and sexuality had been exaggerated by the transformation, it was clear that the figure in the mist was none other than Meiying—my great-grandmother, Meiying.

———— ∝∞∾ ————

What on earth was an "aqua-dream machine"? I assumed it had something to do with the power of water to retain memory. The only time I had read about something like this was an article about a Frenchman who had been awarded the Ig Nobel Prize for his theories on the subject. Jia

Su's research into an aqua-dream machine had failed because there is no such thing as water that can retain memory. Nevertheless, these colored vapors came flooding over me from the time of those old photos, brusquely taking possession of my imagination. The vapors began to dance to the scratchy old recording of Bai Guang's husky voice. A voluptuous Meiying opened her arms toward me in an extraordinarily realistic way. The song seemed to come out of "her" opened mouth, a hole behind the misty dancing figure.

> Without you
> What will I do?
> My heart is broken, there's nothing I can do

That evening, Jia Su went to meet Meiying as usual. But he was distracted by worries about his aqua-dream machine, left in the lab with Bubbles.

Meiying immediately sensed Jia Su's uneasiness.

"Mr. Jia, what's troubling you?" Her words were soft and coaxing, but they hung in the air as if she were determined to draw the words from him little by little.

"I'm a bit worried about my lab," he said. There was some truth in this. "It's time for you to go to work, and I have to get back to keep an eye on things. I won't come to the nightclub tonight."

"Mr. Jia . . ." A sense of crisis engulfed Meiying. In five short months, from the chance meeting in the nightclub to occasional meetings outside and then regular evenings at Jia Su's place, where she cooked dinner for him before leaving for work, she had forged the relationship between them into a bond. But she still worried. If she could not make Jia Su accept her soon, her desire to make an honest woman of herself would remain a dream, like flowers in the mirror, like the moon on water. She bit her lip and said resolutely, "In that case, I won't go to work either."

"Don't be silly . . . just think of your family." Jia Su was obviously taken aback at her response.

She sighed, tears welling in her eyes.

Jia Su looked down, his face reddening. They were effectively lovers—he was aware that they were in that kind of relationship. But he doubted he had the courage to put his hand on his heart and say that he was going to marry a woman who was a nightclub dance hostess.

"Am I pressing him too hard?" wondered Meiying, her thoughts in a whirl. She was not sure if she should advance or retreat. But she kept the sweet smile on her face nevertheless.

It was getting dark and the first rays of moonlight told her that she should leave. Never before had she found it so hard to drag herself away. She was in an agony of indecision. A woman's oversensitive intuition sometimes spirals out of control and causes her misery.

I found a set of tools capable of opening any bottle in the world and prepared to deal with those left by my great-grandmother. It was probably the train of thought inspired by the three words "aqua-dream machine" that had me imagining that what filled the bottles was an ancient dream more evocative and aromatic than an old wine. If it were possible, I wanted more than anything to see Bubbles.

When I was little, my mother said to me rather mysteriously that my great-grandfather had once sheltered a woman in Shanghai who was a revolutionary wanted by the authorities. "She was really something special, a member of the Chinese Revolutionary Alliance, the Tongmenghui." My mother's words all those years ago planted a seed in my mind that now took root and sprouted exuberantly. That 1920s revolutionary seemed to me like a tree that had of its own accord burst into foliage and flower and imbued the history of my family with a subtle and lasting fragrance.

My hands on the bottle openers were damp with sweat and my heart was pounding. Out the window, there was a bright moon and a gentle breeze. A night just like that night more than eighty years ago.

Night had fallen. On one side the moon shone bright, on the other side was the Big Dipper. The gentle breeze carried a pleasant coolness that calmed her spirits. However, Bubbles dared not draw attention to herself by staying outside too long. She sat in the campus grounds for a short while and went back to the room where she was hiding. She could not fall asleep. The air in the cubicle was laden with the smell of chemicals. The bedding carried the odor of a man, which she found unsettling. Between sleep and wakefulness, she felt as if she were floating at sea, tossed on the waves of the roaring machines nearby.

As she drowsed, a sound suddenly startled her. She felt under the pillow for the pistol, opened the door, walked through the lab, which somehow made her shiver, and stopped at the entrance door.

"Rat-a-tat-tat . . . ," someone was knocking at the door. She heard Jia Su's voice. "Are you in bed?" he asked. Since he had his own key, it was gentlemanly on his part to knock.

She opened the door, nodded to him, and, without further ado, went back to her room.

Jia Su toiled away in the lab till late that night, then left without saying good-bye to Bubbles. He may have come because he was worried that she would meddle with his equipment but must have been relieved to see that she was behaving herself with decorum. As he sweated amid the clouds of steam that rose from the bubbling mixtures, he had a sudden image of Bubbles's face when she answered the door. In the pale moonlight, she had looked wan. Like a magnolia flower, her face made him feel for the first time that inside this mysterious and dispassionate revolutionary there was, after all, a woman.

Sometime after Jia Su left, Bubbles awoke. She rubbed her eyes and got up to push open the door to the lab. The extraordinary atmosphere inside, together with a sudden rise in the noise from the machinery, made her head swim, and, still half asleep, she swayed on her feet.

The liquids in dozens, perhaps hundreds, of bottles were singing.

Their cadence sounded faintly familiar. Her senses were engulfed in the sweet-smelling mist, and the water droplets seemed to be dancing around her head. Suddenly she recognized a song from her childhood, one her mother used to sing when it was too hot to do anything and they sat together in the shade.

> One little girl, walking on the bridge;
> Two black pigtails, swinging round her head;
> Meeting a boy, she bows with a giggle . . .

Bubbles waved her arms as if by pushing away the steam she could banish the melody from her ears. But the tune seemed alive, like the whip for an old-fashioned top, spinning her around and around. The song grew louder and louder in her head and shadows emerged dimly from the steam. Fragments of a golden past swirled past her. They twinkled only briefly before they were extinguished, but the impressions they left were crystal clear: her mother singing under the glittering stars that carpeted the summer night sky . . . the crickets and other autumnal insects hopping around the courtyard of a private school. . . . Her mother had died in middle age, a sad figure worn down by the trials of her life. But now Bubbles felt the last touch of her gnarled hand on her head . . . smelled the reek of printing ink in the little workshop where they printed revolutionary magazines and leaflets . . . relived her terror as, heart pounding, she hid from the authorities . . . breathed the stuffy heat of the rainy season in Canton . . . saw Sun Yat-sen's impassioned expression as he rallied his troops . . .

What's happening?

What's happening?

She was in a panic. It was a long time since she had been afraid, but now she was really frightened.

As she threw herself to the ground, she heard her own voice coming from hundreds of bottles: I am a revolutionary, I am not a woman, I am a revolutionary, I am not a woman!

There was an infinitesimal time lapse between each echo, and she had the impression that the entirety of space had been precisely measured out so that each sentence had its allotted place and was just waiting its turn to enter her consciousness.

I am a revolutionary, I am not a woman; I am a revolutionary, I am not a woman!

"Stop, stop!" she cried hysterically.

Then she saw her face.

To be exact, she saw her face in the mirror. How many times had she looked into the mirror, muttering as if trying to hypnotize herself: "I am a revolutionary, I am not a woman!"

This was a scar she hid deep in her heart. In 1923 and even earlier, a woman who wanted to join a revolutionary party had to be prepared to make enormous sacrifices. She had to make a choice and had made it without regrets. But she did not enjoy hearing her secrets echoing repeatedly from hundreds of bottles.

"Stop, I beg you, please stop," Bubbles found herself addressing them as if they were alive. "I want to be a woman as well." The bottles emitted startled whisperings at that and the earlier echoes scattered and began to fade away. "I want to be a woman as well," Bubbles said to herself and, seemingly, to the brass giant. "But if I have to make a choice, I will choose revolution."

This is how I imagine the aqua-dream machine. It was a machine that could endow liquids with the power to communicate, remember, and play back. Though no one knows the truth of the matter—that is, no one knows what really happened to Bubbles during her stay in Jia Su's lab.

What we do have on record is that Jia Su gave up his work on the aqua-dream machine in 1925 and married my great-grandmother. They encountered fierce resistance from Jia Su's family, and a permanent rift nearly resulted. However, Jia Su and my great-grandmother had a happy marriage from which five children were born. The third child was my grandfather.

Then what happened to Bubbles? My great-grandmother could not answer that question. She said only that they lost touch with her and had never heard of her again.

Was Jia Su as ignorant as Meiying as to Bubbles's fate? Is it possible that he knew something but never told anyone, taking the secret to his grave?

They spent such a short time together, but her influence on him must have cast a long shadow. What message did the giant transmit to him as, day after day, Jia Su worked amid those dream-filled clouds of steam? Is it possible that everything in Bubbles's past—her childhood memories, her inner struggles, her desire to be a woman, her revolutionary ideals—were carried by the mist through his pores into his body and transformed into his memories? Just as the image of Meiying emerged from his memory to dance sinuously in front of Bubbles, is it possible that Bubbles's frailties and passion lingered with him forever after she had left?

I was pushing hard on the bottle opener as I was thinking about all this, and the metal bottle top popped off.

Zhou Xuan used to sing a song called "Peach Blossoms at Longhua." I vaguely remember the last line went, ". . . Longhua peach blossoms can never go home."

Longhua was the name of an execution ground.

So when the word "Longhua" came to me from the mass of bubbles that burst from the bottle, you can imagine my grief and shock.

"Longhua peach blossoms can never go home."

———— ✿ ————

I carefully tilted the bottle sideways. A viscous, silver-blue liquid rose above the rim but did not overflow. As it made contact with the air, its heavy viscosity suddenly seemed to lighten.

Just like words that rush to our lips, like the words of the Buddha that remain unspoken and instead unfold into the lotus flower, "the words of the bottle" expanded suddenly into a semiliquid silver-blue flower that inflated and grew transparent like a balloon over the mouth of the bottle until it finally popped, scattering countless silver-blue stars into the air and filling the room. Each star hissed gently as it floated and blossomed into more translucent bubbles.

The bubbles brought with them the scent of lingering memories. They were multicolored: silver-blue at the base but glittering, in the thinnest, most transparent parts, in a fantastic array. There were images in the bubbles, too, flashing by in vivid glimpses the way pictures are seen in a film trailer. Some were linked, others not. The bubbles popped with a gentle "phut" as they collided with one another, taking with them faint scraps of conversation and a few melancholy notes.

I looked around me. I was surrounded by hundreds and thousands of bubbles making puttering sounds as if bidding one another farewell. All kinds of delicate images passed between them and then vanished. I could vaguely make out the Flowers of Shanghai at night, Jia Su's lab with his brass giant, and the back of a woman dressed in a *qipao* lifting a soft hand to her head and coiling up her jet-black hair. And there was more, and more . . .

———— ✿ ————

That day, in the warm afternoon sunshine, Jia Su hurried to a farm on the outskirts of Shanghai.

Bubbles had asked him to meet her. She was going to Canton to join the next uprising to be led by Sun Yat-sen.

As Jia Su jolted along in the horse-drawn cart, he was tight-lipped and silent. He seemed deeply worried by something.

Jia Su was nearly at the farm when he caught sight of Bubbles in the distance. In the farmyard, thatching grass was spread out to dry. Bubbles was wearing a man's shirt casually unbuttoned at the neck and was lying on the roof of a low farm building also covered with drying grass that shone golden in the sunlight. The sun's rays rimmed Bubbles in gold, too. The whole tableau had the intimate air of a nineteenth-century rustic oil painting.

Jia Su was transfixed at the sight. His mouth opened but it was a long moment before he shouted her name.

Bubbles stood up when she heard his voice and hopped down. When Jia Su came nearer, he saw she had a wheat straw in her mouth and a small bottle of liquid in her hand. The smell of soap hung in the air from the bubbles that had burst.

"You've come," Bubbles smiled. Like a man lighting his cigarette, she dipped the straw into the soapy liquid, placed it between her lips, and blew.

A string of shining, bright bubbles dispersed in the breeze.

Then she gave a boyish smile.

"When are you leaving?" asked Jia Su.

"This evening," she replied. "I just wanted to say thank you again before I leave. But it's too dangerous for me to go to town, so I had to put you to the trouble of coming here."

"Will you be coming back?"

"Uh-huh. But by then we'll be the ones in power."

"Are you going to fight?"

She gave a smile.

He then said something.

Her expression changed. First there was shock, then her face flushed as if a pair of pink butterflies had alighted on her cheeks. Her skin shone translucent in the sunlight, and you could almost see the butterflies' wings trembling.

After a while, the flush receded and Bubbles regained her composure. She said something back.

He stiffened and his eyebrows drew together as if in pain.

She smiled, a smile of understanding and of sadness.

Then he gave a smile, desolate but still warm.

I so wanted to hear what they said to each other but it was inaudible. A host of bubbles brushed momentarily against my fingertips, were instantly turned into mist, and vanished. Those moments when the bubbles burst were like electric shocks, the information they transmitted far too complex for me to grasp or even to feel.

And so Jia Su and Bubbles's brief exchange that day among the golden grass faded away. I tried so hard to catch the sounds, and once I almost succeeded, but they seemed to slip through my fingers like an eel.

Then I heard five syllables spoken with crystal clarity. As cleanly and smoothly as the popping of bubbles, the sounds burst in the air: "It's not the right time."

As they parted that day, Bubbles said to Jia Su, "I like your machine, but if you'll forgive me for being blunt, it's really not the right time for research like that."

China in the twenties did not need an aqua-dream machine, nor did it need Jia Su.

I do not know to what extent Bubbles's blunt advice influenced Jia Su, but in the end he gave up his plans for an aqua-dream machine. Soon after, he got married and had children and became just an ordinary physics and chemistry professor.

But had the aqua-dream machine really failed, as the biographical notes said? If so, then how could I explain my discoveries today, how could I explain that roomful of memory bubbles, the flashing images, the smells given off, the pulsing sounds?

. . . I am giving frantic chase to the bubbles, my fingertips making contact with the distant memories of former generations. Faster and faster I go, because those bubbles might vanish away at any minute, as absolutely as that whole period of history has vanished.

The nerve endings at my fingertips have never been as sensitive as they are today. They listen, touch, absorb, and their knowledge accumulates.

My fingertips begin to burn, redden, and go numb. They seem to have a life of their own—they dance, they sing.

The bubbles have all dissolved in the air, but the room still feels shrouded in silver-blue gauze, the smell of disappointment mixed with the settling dust of olden days.

I feel a stream of anguish and a peculiar sweetness, which flows and throbs in my chest, numbing it.

I clutch the other bottle and promise myself I will never release the genies of memory from it. I should let the Jia Su, Meiying, and Bubbles, whom I have come to love so much, live on in the dark bygone days of that bottle.

I find that I am humming to myself: "Without you, what will I do . . . ?"

I hear not Bai Guang or Meiying but rather the strange low tones of Bubbles as she looks at herself in the mirror one night. The bubble had vanished in an instant, yet it allowed me to see her moist, slightly upturned lips and the fine down on them.

I cannot hear Jia Su's call to her in the pale-blue bubbles, but at this moment I decide to name this remarkable woman Bubbles.

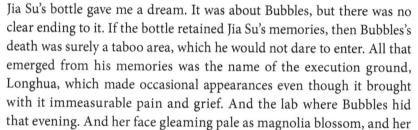

Jia Su's bottle gave me a dream. It was about Bubbles, but there was no clear ending to it. If the bottle retained Jia Su's memories, then Bubbles's death was surely a taboo area, which he would not dare to enter. All that emerged from his memories was the name of the execution ground, Longhua, which made occasional appearances even though it brought with it immeasurable pain and grief. And the lab where Bubbles hid that evening. And her face gleaming pale as magnolia blossom, and her extraordinary eyes—innocent, determined, reflecting the melancholy rays of the moon.[2]

PART III

OTHER FUTURES

11

THE PASSENGERS AND THE CREATOR

HAN SONG

TRANSLATED BY NATHANIEL ISAACSON

1. THE PASSENGER CABIN

A tremor under my rear end.

"Ladies and gentlemen, your attention please. We are experiencing some turbulence, and there may be some bumpiness in the cabin. Please remain in your seats and secure your safety belts. The restrooms will be closed." A hoarse female voice emanating from the speaker overhead is broadcast throughout the cabin.

I quickly fasten my safety belt and turn my head sideways to the window, looking out in trepidation. A shroud of darkness. Legendary turbulences come and go but you never see them in reality. The turbulences last a while, the nauseating jostling finally stops, and precious stability and tranquility are restored. The air-conditioning system releases a thin stream of warm air, unknotting the apprehension that has gathered in the pit of everyone's stomach.

My seat is 31A. I stretch out my legs and watch them stick out akimbo like a crooked index and middle finger.

Beside me, passenger 31B has fallen asleep. There are three hundred and some people in the whole World and the majority of them are already under the spell of deep sleep. Throughout the journey, sleep, like a dog, has been mankind's faithful companion.

Whisks of pale yellow light flow down from the overhead lights, and I begin to get drowsy. Before I fall asleep, I force myself to stand up and straddle my way over the unmoving 31B, following the aisle to the back as if I were setting foot upon one of those rugged mountain paths I see only in my dreams.

I walk alone—the cabin is filled with people, but it seems as if no one were here. Trembling, I pull my gaze away from the procession of faces that bloom out of the rocklike seats, looking instead at the unending rows of silvery, oval cabin windows.

—Darkness, nothing but darkness surrounds us.

A small cluster of lonely and wary human shapes stand by the door of the restroom. They're waiting. Maybe the guy inside is defecating, or maybe having a shower (the restroom doubles as a shower stall).

After a long, long time the door opens and a pair of gaunt middle-aged men emerge, their flushed faces covered in sweat. The people in the doorway hang their heads in embarrassment: they're a gay couple. No wonder it took so long. Not an ounce of public decency.

Eventually, it's my turn. I piss noisily, then flush. Seeing water gives me a bitter taste in my mouth. In this metallic World, it's impossible for human beings to know where water really comes from. This is the kind of thing that makes you wonder, but then again it does not matter.

As I piss, I stare at the sign on the wall:

No Smoking

The rest is mostly graffiti, but as far as I can tell, it's the same old stuff:

I like you, 35G
22A has been here
18C is a son of a bitch

After that, I drag my feet back down the aisle to my seat, row upon row of motionless black heads arrayed before me.

Seat—aisle—bathroom—aisle—seat, this is the only path in life. This is how we live our lives.

Darkness, always darkness. A boy firmly tied down by his safety belt cries out, but the sleepers keep on sleeping.

2. PASSENGERS

31B's sleeping posture is a bit odd.

I give him a nudge. His breathing is shallow and thick; white, pungent foam burbles from the corners of his mouth. Heart disease or brain embolism? A skinny cockroach is perching vigilantly on the fatty folds at the back of his neck.

I press the button to summon the stewardess, and a slender figure glides over. The Flight Attendants are on a rotating basis, selected from among the female Economy Class passengers. She gives 31B an indifferent look and calls another attendant over. They exchange a quiet glance, then carry 31B off.

The cockroach loses his footing and falls to the floor. He seems desolate, crawling away down the aisle all alone. Gaze fixed on this creature, I watch it make its way silently under the many dull leather shoes and disappear through the winding path formed by them before I breathe a sigh of relief.

The Flight Attendants strain to support the sick man, the three of them cobbled together like a makeshift toy, headed straight to the back of the cabin. A few passengers glance up briefly but most pay them no notice. As for what would be done with 31B, no one is interested.

A fetid odor wafts up from the recently vacated seat. It will soon be filled by a new person, which means that some woman from the Economy Class will soon have the good fortune of being given the right to bear a child.

But the person chosen to sit in 31B will not necessarily be that unborn infant. Seats have to be reassigned. This is a rule—passengers are not allowed to sit next to another for too long; if they were to become too familiar and begin to interact, problems could arise.

Who gets to sit where will be discussed in the Business Class cabin and then decided in First Class. Those flying First Class have a passenger manifest that lists all human beings. A maroon velvet curtain always hangs between the First, Business, and Economy Class cabins—though it's soft, it's as impenetrable as iron. Economy Class passengers such as myself have no chance of crossing over and no way of seeing what's on the other side.

The grating sound of the woman on the loudspeaker blares out again. The passengers called to their seats stand up like languid marionettes, on their faces the seemingly comprehensible smile of one for whom a heavy burden has been lifted. As if practicing tai chi, bit by bit they open the ashen-gray overhead compartments, remove the valises and suitcases that they never have and never will use, and carry them off to their new seats in a somnambulatory torpor, and the moment their bottoms hit the seats, they are asleep again.

I have been assigned to 18G. Next to me, the man in 18H is already seated comfortably. "Hi," he says to me. In this World, no one would introduce himself of his own accord. My heart leaps like a frog in my chest. My new neighbor looks like he's twenty-six or twenty-seven years old; his face shines clearly like a starry night, suffused with a jadeite glow. My jaw nearly drops. It has been a long time, so all the passengers in the Economy cabin know one another's faces, but this man looks to be a complete stranger.

But it doesn't matter; in this World nothing matters.

3. THE SYSTEM

Some nuanced but noticeable changes take place in the space outside the cabin windows. The darkness is not an even mass; some clear cracks exist out there that we have no way of understanding. Sometimes, stars display themselves. Sometimes lightning flashes and thunder roars. Sometimes a golden orb emerges, and washed in its gentle glow, indistinct rows of serrated black clouds billow forth, like a chorus of demons performing on an empty stage.

All these wondrous transformations occur out there just beyond our World, just like that. But passengers are separated from it by a thin membrane and can see it only through their windows. In reality, they are partitioned off and completely unfamiliar with one another.

Sometimes, out there, in those very dark recesses down below, tiny sparks like clusters of stars form into a structure, silhouetting the shapes of chessboards and mazes; still others resemble spurs jutting forth, inside of which one can discern loops of differing lengths, glimmering in the depths of the darkness.

But they are no more than temporary splotches and patches whose time in our field of vision is short-lived, drifting lazily away behind, their size rapidly diminishing as they are absorbed by the infinite darkness and can be seen no more. Could they be like us, bouncing along on the turbulence?

Clearly, outside our World there is some macrosystem. And maybe out there in its midst are other different and independent worlds. But what are they really like? There are explanations. But there is always a sense of doubt, a murky plasma that sometimes churns forth, coursing back to the cacophony of the heart.

4. 7 X 7

The children born in Economy Class will gradually grow up. During this time, the monitors in the backs of the dilapidated seats flicker on at irregular intervals. Their specialized education has begun.

I vaguely recall having received such an education myself while growing up, but I can't be wholly certain.

Basic education includes fastening safety belts and changing seats. Politics is mostly the prohibition of smoking and admonitions against graffiti.

Natural sciences are a bit more important. When the holographic instructor on the 3D monitor is done lecturing, homework is given. These are standard questions presented by a voice simulator that has seen so many years of use that it has become a clamor of crackles and skips: "What—is—this—World—ca-ca-ca-ca-ca-ca-called?" The correct answer is "7X7."

7X7, that's what our World is called. Some of the children get it wrong, saying "seven," "seven one," "seven six," or "seven eight." Then, like spiteful housewives, the Flight Attendants will slap them on the palm with a little steel spoon.

Yes, this is our World. The spacious cabin always seems to be immersed in an undulating cloud of light-purple fog; on the two dark foot-worn aisles with ragged carbon-fiber compound flooring, the tightly packed

and regularly spaced old seats are fixed, their covers worn through revealing the rotten foam padding; and then, outside the window and in the
midst of the infinite darkness, the indistinct rise and fall of two long
wings jutting forth from the center of the World. X is just a symbol; it is
used to represent uncertainty.

The holographic instructor is an expressionless, wizened woman wearing traditional folk dress. I can't tell how old she is, but she also serves as
the voice of the announcer on the loudspeaker. She says the World was
created $7X7$ years ago and then time stopped. That's the essence of the
story.

Then there's us, put here in this sealed system by the Creator, a system that floats in the midst of what is said to be a vast atmospheric bubble that revolves around $7X7$. We spend most of our time sitting still like
potted plants, our countenances facing the same direction, expressionless as if carved from wood. The bright objects we occasionally see
outside, those faint stars, are nothing more than evidence of small bubbles wriggling along the walls of the air cell, or what is referred to as a
mirage.

$7X7$ is the only thing that stays constantly still, a self-sustaining ecosystem full of lives, supporting what seems to be the only meaningful
thing in this bubble of a universe.

5. MEALS

We sleep at the appointed time, and after that we take our regular meals.
All the Cabin Attendants wear a blank, unsmiling expression as the four-
wheeled metal cart swishes along through the aisle and they dole out our
meals. Steam wafts up from the chicken or beef and rice wrapped in foil
packaging, but the portion is too small, so we never get to eat our fill.
Along with the main course, there's orange juice, coffee, or green tea.
Sometimes, we are offered a bowl of watered-down, stale broth. This costs
extra.

Before eating, the passengers intone a prayer: "Boeing bless us.
Amitābha."

As we speak, we trace the outline of a five-pointed star on our chest using our left index finger. Boeing is the honorific name of the unseen Creator, and Amitābha is a modifier of respect.

Food and drink are produced as if by magic, in an endless stream. Of course, when it comes to the source, they are provided by the Creator, Boeing.

His existence can be verified empirically. Sometimes, in the abyss of darkness outside the cabin windows, a long slender shadow like a specter reflected on the water will suddenly appear. Just like our World, two delicate wings protrude from its sides. It hums softly as it comes closer to us, extends a long, flexible hose from its front end, and docks with our World.

We commonly refer to it as 7X7 the Provider. Of course it is dispatched to us by the Creator—"dispatched" is jargon used to refer to the meaning of existence. However, if the Creator made only one actual 7X7, then we might surmise that the Provider was merely our doppelgänger. It supplies us with sustenance and energy—but there is no communication, and then, as elegantly as all parallel universes, it disappears into the dark vastness like a dancing ballerina, returning to the side of the unseen Creator.

The existence of the Provider 7X7 is affirmation of the precision and logic of Creation.

When the carbohydrates in your stomach begin their intense chemical reaction, you gaze intently upon the metallic shimmer of the unfoldable fine silverware laid out upon the seat-back table, and that glass that is almost unimaginably transparent, you can't help but marvel that the World is itself a miracle.

O, Boeing.

Amitābha.

6. SKEPTICISM

Everything is quite normal except my new neighbor, who is a bit strange.

When everyone else is asleep, he is always awake; when everyone is taking their meal, he is talking to himself. The time he takes going to the bathroom is longer than others, and sometimes I suspect he is the graffiti artist who no one has ever caught in the act.

"And why did the Creator banish us?" he says once, sitting calmly in his seat but also mumbling to himself, almost startling me into leaping out of my own.

But I quickly regain my composure, think for a moment, and determine myself to classify this as a minor issue. This helps me gather the courage to say, "Because we have done wrong."

"But, what sort of wrong have we done?" He seems excited to hear my unexpected response.

"It is Original Sin. But even if we know this, what can be done? It doesn't matter." My heart beats wildly. Exchange. Is this the dangerous exchange? How could I have done this?

"Have you ever wondered where we were before we were banished?"

I feel a pathetic urge to laugh and just shake my head with a sophisticated air. Then, a wave of caution that felt like measles or a blister fills my chest. I have lived this long and received all this education, and yet I have never known that among the three hundred and some members of the human race there could be a person who talked like this. This fellow is too weird, and a little bit dangerous. I trembled as I answer, "Another pointless question."

"Have you ever wondered what those twinkling lights outside the windows are?"

"Wondered? About those mirages?"

"What if they aren't mirages but are other very real worlds with life on them?" Inconceivable. I hold my breath, turning my head to look at the stars outside the window. The stars overhead are so small and faint, they don't seem to move at all, so you can't really make much of them. But the chessboards and mazes of stars slipping slowly by below aren't the same. The spaces between them and the paths they trace are fairly distinct. They look like glistening cubes of gelatin on a food tray, and looking closer you can almost make out traces of human artifice in their formation. Could there be humans dwellings down there? What is their relationship to the Creator? Unsettled, I turn my gaze away.

"Have you ever wondered if they have been absolved?" says 18H.

Worried and yet curious, I glance at him again. In comparison with the rest of the passengers in Economy Class, there is nothing noteworthy about his clothing and grooming; but an aura of indescribable strangeness radiates from someplace on his person.

I decide to close my mouth and say nothing, closing my eyes like a dead fish, but the blood only courses through my veins more violently.

Before long, under the influence of 18H's suggestion, it dawns upon me that the stars sweeping slowly by below always appear at regular intervals. That is to say, that which we have seen in the past will eventually return as before, floating by once again before our eyes and flashing out again before casting themselves back into the darkness. Counting your heartbeats you could prove beyond a doubt that this is a regular cycle.

Why are there cycles outside the closed World? The 3D instructor's explanation is that the bubble surrounding us is constantly rotating. But why would a bubble rotate? Why do the stars overhead remain unmoving? What is outside the bubble? Could there be an even bigger bubble? Trying to figure out questions like these leads only to more questions, and it'll give you a headache. To be honest, I'd never wondered about this sort of thing before.

The other question 18H asks is, "Why are our surroundings always dark?" That's right, he asks about our surroundings.

7. FLIGHT

There's too much food and water in my stomach, so I go to the restroom again. I run into some of my old seatmates, and we nod indifferently to one another.

We don't chat, but it's not because loose lips sink ships. Generally speaking, in life, at least in Economy Class, passengers don't develop close relationships, since there's really no need for mutual assistance.

When it comes to women, of course no one has any improper thoughts. The Code has been clear for a long time: the young ones among them will be summoned at set intervals to Business Class, while the young and beautiful will be summoned to First Class. A while after they have returned, the bellies of some of them will begin to grow like ugly tumors until eventually they can't even fasten their safety belts.

The Economy Class women all sit properly together, maintaining a stipulated distance from the men. Aside from the Cabin Attendants who bring food, it's very hard for men to get near them. If you get the urge, you just do it with the man next to you—reach out your hand to rub and tug underneath his zipper, or go to the bathroom and have a poke, that's okay. But the women are strictly off limits—that's forbidden in Economy Class.

There was one person who violated the taboo. When everyone was sleeping, he seduced a Cabin Attendant, and they did it in the bathroom at the back of Economy Class (he must have thought he was a Business or a First Class passenger, but how could they use that sordid bathroom?). Such a situation, if discovered, is generally disastrous for the man. According to customs of our World, he is castrated; one of the senior Cabin Attendants wields the knife, and they are never the least bit gentle.

When a woman gets pregnant, and there is no extra seat available at the time—that is to say, there hasn't been anyone recently disposed of because of illness or some similar matter—that also becomes a problem. The baby will have to be aborted. That is a custom as well.

All in all, because of the general reverence for custom in Economy Class, serious incidents rarely occur. For the most part, the men abide by the rules, and no one thinks to go out of their way to break them.

But how could it be this way?

This time, there is new graffiti in the bathroom.

—When will we stop flying?

What does "fly" mean? It is without doubt quite special, since the 3D instructor never taught us this term. I stare blankly at it for a while, my heart feels as if someone had poured a cup of scalding coffee over it, and hot blood courses through my whole being. Suddenly, I feel that rare hardening sensation down between my legs.

8. CRUISING

"Seen something?"

18H watches me as I return. He seems to know everything but asks as if he had no knowledge of what's going on, flashing me a gentle, blue lotus–like, grin, dusted with cynicism.

It feels as if something inside me has awakened. Unfortunately, I can't seem to soften up down there, and my cheeks sear as if they were covered in gunpowder, burning and erupting across the surface of my epidermal cells. I can't help stuttering as I tell 18H about the graffiti. Half covering his mouth, he snorts out a laugh, as if choking on some food. That's it, just one chuckle, as his gaze drifts toward the bizarre protuberance in my lap, and says, "You ever wondered what would happen if we flew faster?"

"What do you mean?" I hasten to take my seat.

"What if it's 7X7 that's moving, and not the bubble?"

"Hush, please."

Fear crawls up the length of my spinal cord, creeping like a snake into the dark, chaotic morass of my thalamus. Preposterous—what's flying? What's flying faster? Right now, I'm really hoping there will be another reorganization of our seating so I can get away from the frightening 18H; but I feel conflicted: I'd actually hate to leave 18H—I want to hear more of his novel cosmological theories.

And 18H is also one of those pretty good-looking young men.

I do my best to cover up what's going on down there, as beads of sweat roll down from my forehead, soaking my pants. Slimy . . . I can't take it. Maybe I've caught some kind of disease. Am I going to die? That would be a relief.

9. THE LUGGAGE COMPARTMENT

Off in some corner, another passenger has died, and so another rearrangement of seats is under way. Finally I can get away from 18H, I think, a sigh whistling from my mouth. But little did I imagine, as I take my new seat, there he is again like a specter who has followed me over, plopping down next to me. This is really odd—unless has he gotten some sort of special authorization from First Class? Nothing could be more alarming than that. The strange thing is this secretly pleases me.

Then I realize that 18H—no, now I should call him 25E—has begun to follow me to the bathroom.

Is he after me as well?

Every time I come out of the bathroom, I see 25E leaning against the dingy doorway, mouth half-covered, giving me a furtive smile. My legs are like jelly.

"You . . . need something?" my heart races as I ask; thinking about my own age, I feel a sense of inferiority. I look worriedly at the other passengers, but no one has noticed us. Having sat there so long, human beings have lost the desire to keep tabs on their own kind.

"Got some stuff I'd like to show you, you in?" 25E asks me in hushed tones, infused with male affection.

I feel overwhelmed by his offer, nodding assiduously, feeling as if I'd become young again. At this, 25E takes me by the hand and leads me to the back of the World. His hand is cool and soft, brisk and stimulating like early spring. My heart is dancing in my throat. I've never been to the back of the World before, since usually only Cabin Attendants are allowed here. This is the galley and storage station, and the women also use it to organize the supplies that are sent over from 7X7's doppelgänger.

Two girls are immersed in their work, and when they catch sight of 25E, they exchange a knowing grin as if they are familiar with each other. My face must be flushed. I feel both suspicious and envious, letting go of 25E's hand in shock, but feel bad about it afterward. The Attendants leave as soon as they've finished up their work, at which point 25E reaches down, and with practiced ease pulls open a trapdoor in the floor. Below, I see a capacious space.

In a hushed whisper 25E says mysteriously, "The Luggage Compartment."

I hadn't imagined that he was merely taking me to see this. I'm somewhat taken aback, and my boiling blood suddenly cools off a few degrees. But the Luggage Compartment has sucked me in anyway—it exists only in myth, you know, and now it appears right in front of me, and inside I can make out a cluster of bobbling green lights. Upon further inspection, I realize that these glowing pinpricks are a cluster of human eyes. Never before had I known that there were people actually living in the Luggage Compartment.

Someone looks up and greets 25E, "Hi!"

"Hi!" 25E laughs back.

For the sake of politeness 25E has me greet him as well. I stare blankly at him, then utter timidly, "Hi."

Thirty or forty people are crowded in the Luggage Compartment, but there is no assigned seating. Customs here are clearly different from up in Economy Class. There are elderly people and children. The children are playing with cockroaches and mice. A naked man is pressing a naked woman to the floor beneath him (this is the first time that I have ever seen sexual intercourse with my own eyes in this World). Two men are hard at work operating a small plastic grinder, beneath which a crimson liquid is oozing out, flowing down an aluminum spout and into the mouth of a Coca-Cola bottle. An ugly, middle-aged woman standing to one side heaps scoop after scoop of a viscous, chunky, yellow, congeelike substance into the grinder.

This congeelike substance is being taken from the body of a stinking corpse lying on the floor. A few husky young men carve up the body enthusiastically. I count five or six corpses, and among them I recognize 31B, who has been reduced to little more than a glistening carapace of skeleton. His head still rests untouched atop his neck, making him look like a hydrocephalic infant.

10. CABIN ATTENDANTS

I don't know when it began, but trade between the Luggage Compartment, Economy, Business, and First Class has been quietly taking place all along, but this is a secret shared by only a few.

The Attendants sell the corpses of the dead or soon-to-be dead to the passengers in the Luggage Compartment, who process them, then give the finished product back to the Cabin Attendants, who sell it in First Class. And thus, short-rib soup (the only locally produced, gourmet nutritional product in the World) came to be sold in great quantity in the First Class cabin—who knows why, but the passengers in First Class had endless streams of money. Then the Cabin Attendants would split the earnings with the people in the Luggage Compartment, usually seventy:thirty, with the latter taking the larger share. However, when they are buying corpses from Economy Class, the guys in the Luggage Compartment have to pay up as well. In the end, the Cabin Attendants can get about forty to fifty percent of the total profits from this chain of exchange, and as a result they have become the wealthy of Economy Class.

All of this has been hidden from us.

In Economy Class, every woman has the chance to become a Cabin Attendant. For this reason, the economic status of women is much higher than that of men, which is perhaps why we simply and meekly play by the rules and make no fuss.

Sometimes the supply of corpses exceeds the demand, and First Class has eaten their fill, so the surplus goes on sale in Business Class at a discount. If more becomes available, Economy Class might eventually get to share.

Have I ever drunk the soup? I can recall the taste of watered-down short-rib broth.

The Luggage Compartment is the first hidden world that 25E took me to see. That 7X7 is a World of multiple layers has already been established. But, what I wonder now is . . . is what I see before me actually real? And if not, then has everything I have seen before been an illusion?

11. THE LANDING GEAR

As the trust between 25E and me gradually grew stronger, he came to reveal his true origins to me. He came from the Wheel Well World—yet another unknown level of 7X7.

In order to get to the World of the Wheel Well, we first have to pass through the Luggage Compartment. Only by following 25E's lead do I dare pass through that maggoty, fetid congregation of men and corpses, but I am stricken with terror nonetheless. Then we have to worm our way through the hydraulics compartment, whose spiderweb of pipes and assemblage of scarred spare parts lining the walls is truly an eye-opening spectacle. The World is such a complex assembly, a gigantic and precise machine, and had I not seen it with my own eyes how could I have known about it?

We have arrived. With a clank, 25E opens a metal door beneath which the locus of his life before he ventured out is revealed.

A cold gust of wind buffets my face. The lonely hermits residing in the cramped confines of the Wheel Well are bundled up in thickly padded clothing against the cold. There are very few of them, but they are the elites of this multilayered World. They call themselves the Seekers. They don't want to be bothered by anyone, so they've hidden themselves away in the Wheel Well to conduct their secret work. But I have a sense that, at the very beginning of Creation, they had already made the decision to live here in the Wheel Well. They were never normal passengers in our World.

But what's a *landing gear*? Such a terrifying question. Suddenly, the feeling of coming to begins to well up again, and my whole being is awash in a wave of desire to remember something. But I can't do it, nothing comes to mind. 25E cocks his head to one side, gazing at me with keen interest. But why has he brought me here to see this? Who am I?

The people in the Wheel Well don't say hi to me. They are all hard at work reading, and no one has time to pay heed to visitors. The reading materials all came from the Luggage Compartment. There used to be a huge pile of baggage there, but eventually the baggage was cracked open by the residents of the Wheel Well. Inside, they found some valuable texts contradicting the teachings on the television in Economy Class.

Based upon what was gleaned from these texts, the Seekers carried out a series of experiments. They stole the necessary materials from various corners of the World—things like fuel and oxygen tanks—and cobbled together what they call a rocket pack. Strapped tightly to one's back, and then ignited, it allows one to leave the 7X7 World and explore the vast bubble of gas out there.

Is this where the notion of "flight" comes from? If the entirety of 7X7 is indeed in flight, and the bubble of gas is not moving, then this notion is a true challenge to the human capacity for reason.

A passenger like myself can't help but feel envious of the passengers in the Luggage Compartment or the Wheel Well.

"Do the First Class passengers know about your existence?" I ask cautiously.

"If they did find out, they'd pretend they hadn't," 25E answers paradoxically.

25E is one of the agents dispatched by the secret Wheel Well World. He entered into Economy Class life, but he can change seats according to his own free will. This in and of itself is most puzzling, since there are strict population controls in 7X7, among them the passenger manifest system, which makes it an act most people would not even dare to think of.

I ask how he does this, and he says, "It's easy. I bribe the Business and First Class passengers."

That's how I learned for the first time that there is in this world a thing called bribery.

When the jet pack is ignited, it evokes a very subtle feeling. A Seeker, bundled in a puffy jacket, covers his face with an oxygen mask stolen from the passenger cabin. A pair of short, thin, awl-shaped nozzles protrude from the half-meter-long metal tanks strapped to his back, like some extraneous extension of his backbone that emits two piss-yellow bursts of flame. His body drops through the opening in the floor of the Wheel Well and falls away from the immense body of 7X7. With a *whoosh*, he disappears into the thick blanket of darkness, as if he were embarking on a rendezvous with the fading stars. At this point, all my internal organs feel as if they had seized up in a malarial torpor.

Upon his return, the adventurer says he has seen "the Light."

12. THE THREE-DIMENSIONAL DIAGRAM

"The Light is a difficult perception to put into words, but I'll do my best to explain it to you," 25E says. "If you were to turn around and fly backward, or if you increase your speed and fly forward, you would be able to see some traces of it. By then, the Seekers are already far, far away from 7X7. A part of the apparently limitless blackness begins to become uneven and fade away, bit by bit. The edges of the universe grudgingly begin to allow a sliver of red flame to emerge. It is as capricious as a woman's face, varying from rosy to reddish black. Then the world becomes differentiated by a riot of colors, the tones shifting constantly as they fatten out. It's as if your eyes had been wasted on you before. Then, you get scared and you want to return to the darkness."

It's hard for me to believe any of this. The holographic teacher never mentioned the Light. The reason is simple: if the Creator put us here in infinite darkness, what need would there be for him to call attention to light? How are we to know that what the Seekers have described to us isn't just an even greater mirage?

25E says that since the jet packs can travel only so far, none of the Seekers have managed to fly all the way into the Light, so no one can know for certain how far away from us the Light really is. All you can do is observe it from far, far away.

"So, aside from going backward and forward, has anyone ever tried going down? Have you ever tried descending into those drifting chessboards and mazes of stars down there? . . . you said they aren't mirages."

I feel as if I've scared myself with my own question, and 25E's expression has shifted subtly as well. His countenance elicits tender feelings like those toward a sick child. He does his best to explain: "Those are two different questions. Going down involves greater levels of complexity and technique. Most crashes happen during takeoff and landing. Among the Seekers, a clear solution to this question has still not been worked out."

He stops and sighs, eyes misted over in sadness as he gazes at me, speaking more slowly: "We did, we had people go down, but it's not like flying horizontally, and they didn't make it back. Clearly, the Creator made a vertically acting force whose effects are imbalanced. We've been calling it gravity."

An oppressive silence settles over us. We gaze at each other for a long, long time until gradually breaking away. In the depths of his eyes, I see a spark of reverence and despair. "Ugh," I sigh quietly to myself.

"No matter what the difficulties are, once you have been out, you will gain the objective frame of mind and perspective to see the true nature of our World."

25E quickly regains his composure, forging bravely ahead: "It floats like a great suitcase in the indescribable vastness of space. Lights that shine dimly as if through an orange peel wink faintly through the windows. It roars with an unending stream of thunder and spits out roiling tongues of heat that can shred all inorganic matter. It has a vigorous and terrific sensation of motion, so we say it is flying, and while the flickering lights on the surface of the bubble of gas are immobile, they are the authentic background. How long are we actually going to keep flying? Where are we flying to? What kind of Creator could design such a perfect and unending journey? Who, after all, is Boeing?"

And this is not the most amazing discovery. According to the observations of the Seekers, in the darkness of space there are an infinite number of 7X7s, each of them a floating agglomerated mass, their geometrical shape just like our World, differing only in size. They fly steadfastly and silently along with us. When the Seekers put on their jet packs and wander about, they eventually come to see this vast array. It is a soul-stirring sight.

"We have calculated it: within the range of jet-pack flight, we have observed at least five thousand 7X7 Worlds. Their never-ending roar echoes across the gas-bubble universe. Starlight pours over their silver-gray bodies like water; they are like a pod of migrating whales seen only in dreams."

The Seekers have tried to establish contact with those worlds and were eventually successful in gaining access to their Wheel Wells and Luggage Compartments. In the end, they discovered that only the passengers aboard our 7X7 World had managed to invent jet packs. The other worlds all remain mired in the age of prehistoric ignorance.

"This made us feel a sense of obligation—a mission to enlighten. And most important, we have finally proven that we are not alone. If we have been cast off by the Creator, then perhaps we are a whole race of outcasts," 25E says. "It is hard to believe that it could just be a coincidence: the passengers of different Worlds are all separated from one another, but everyone speaks the same language, even the graffiti in the restrooms is written in the same script."

13. THE CAPTAIN

For the first time, I realize our 7X7 is not the entire World, and the three hundred and some passengers are not the whole of humanity.

Little by little 25E is making me smell danger. Truth is, the danger has always been there; it comes from his having consciously approached me and his deep interest in me. Perhaps he has some motive I cannot fathom, but it is not the kind of innocent feeling that I had yearned for. Is it a conspiracy or a trap?

All this time, I've been feeling at turns depressed and excited, ashamed one day and hopeful the next. I want to ask 25E if I can use their jet packs to try flying outside myself and confirm what he has told me (what I really want is to satisfy my own curiosity). But I'm so afraid of an embarrassing rejection that I swallow my request.

Gradually, I am struck by a premonition that something very important is about to happen to me.

Finally, one day right after I enter the bathroom, 25E pushes his way in behind me. He locks the bathroom door and patiently watches me finish peeing, then says to me solemnly, "Based upon our extended investigations, we've confirmed that you are the one we have been looking for. I can officially announce that to you now."

"You've been looking for me all along? Who . . . am I?"

I feel a sharp, wet shadow surge toward me, as if a hole were being drilled in the top of my fossil-like cranium, penetrating into my brain, whipping it around and stirring up something very old. In the mirror above the sink, I see my face has gone ashen. Tense and anxious, I lick my lips like a black bear, my hands pausing in the act of fastening my belt.

25E calmly utters the strange word "Captain."

These syllables stir in me a cyclone of fear and excitement, as if they were both familiar and completely foreign. I try to turn it over in my mind for a moment, but it slips from my grasp as quick as a loach in the mud.

"The Creator created you so that you might control this World. You aren't a common passenger. Only you can guide 7X7 into the Light. I came to the Economy cabin to look for you."

25E encourages me, "Zip up your pants, wash your hands, and come with me."

14. THE FIRST CLASS CABIN

At the entrance to the Business Class I instinctively come to a halt. This is a restricted area. But 25E is calm and collected as he leads me by the hand into territory familiar to him. For the first time, I am seeing a special group of passengers who have lived in the same World but whom I have never before set eyes upon. They all have the countenances of hypocrites, wearing fine clothing and maintaining a collective silence as if engaged in solemn contemplation.

25E greets them, and they smile and give 25E a nod. I wonder, what did 25E use to bribe them?

Later I learn it was cigarettes—a prohibited article in the World of 7X7. Passing through the Business Cabin, we begin to approach First Class— "approach" is another piece of jargon used to describe the particular characteristics of the World. First Class is not nearly as intimidating and luxurious as I had imagined; only the seats are a bit more spacious. The passengers look the same as us—no extra noses or ears, but their average age is a bit higher. They are more sanctimonious, their clothes are finer, and their deportment more dignified—and they are all men.

One other difference with Economy Class is there is a stronger odor here. To be specific, it's the smell of death. I notice that some of the passengers have their safety belts fastened tightly about them, and their bodies are in an advanced state of decay with a mess of white bones protruding from their half-empty chest cavities.

But here, no one takes the bodies away to be made into broth. I suppose this is the custom in First Class. The seats are coffins, and people won't leave them even after they have died.

I can't help thinking that if we keep on "flying" like this, the prospects are pretty grim. If the last person in First Class dies, and they don't make room for someone else, does that mean their spirits determine the birth rate in Economy Class? Chaos will surely follow.

This makes me realize the importance of 25E—and the role that I may have to take on. I feel distressed rather than excited. The fact is, if not for 25E how could I have found out these frightful secrets? And our lives would have just gone on as they had before, as utterly perilous as that would be. But is there anything I can do about it?

Yes, I'm totally ignorant. Business and First Class are cordoned off from Economy Class, and aside from the secret sexual services and trade in human flesh, there is no other communication between them. The lips of the women who come out from there are all sealed—they must have been paid off.

But 25E doesn't stay in First Class for long but quickly leads me instead to approach the front of the cabin and, out of nowhere, produces a key that he uses to open another door.

15. THE COCKPIT

Behind the door, there is another cabin. Again, I am seized with wonder—the apparently seamless World is actually divided into so many subsections, each possessing its own wonders. What hidden plan was there in the Creator's design?

The cabin before me is completely unoccupied. 25E calls it the Cockpit. Laid out in front and on both sides, the usual oval windows are replaced by irregular rectangular ones, providing an unequaled field of vision. Beneath the windows are two leather seats, in front of which six LCD monitors are arrayed with green numerals and lines flashing on the screens. Top to bottom and left to right, hundreds of dials, switches, and lights cover every surface. This orderly arrangement of objects smoothly comes into view, but in my heart it stirs up a turbulent sense of déjà vu. I still don't remember who I really am, however, and that pressing question bubbles to the surface: what is the job of the "Captain"?

25E points to the seat on the left and says solemnly, "That is your seat." His face suddenly reveals a look that seems like respect. This saddens me.

25E digs around in the pocket of his jacket for some time and pulls out a yellowed ID (a pilot's license) to show me. My picture is on it, and on my head is a strange-looking peaked cap, printed on the bottom are the words NAME: Wang Ming, POSITION: Captain.

In 7X7, we had always referred to one another by our seat numbers. Having just learned that I have a first and last name, I am dumbstruck with shame. After a while, I ask 25E hesitantly, "Do you have a name, too?"

"You can call me *Something.*"

Now, this young man named *Something*, who comes from the Wheel Well, pulls out some more IDs, labeled Copilot, Navigator, Flight Engineer, Communications Officer, and Flight Attendant. I know the people in all the photos—they are all passengers in Economy Class. It turns out they also all have names, like Guohang, Quniao, V₁, or Daigan, What is this all about?

"The Flight Crew," says *Something*. The ID cards have been recently found in a suitcase. This is the latest breakthrough, and it acts as an important piece of evidence. The Seekers are hard at work establishing contact with the other members of the Flight Crew.

"Flight Crew?"

"We infer that this World used to be operated by a group of people, and you were their leader, so you had control over everyone."

Everyone? Control? All three hundred and some passengers? I look again at the chair, the dials and switches. A vague sense of familiarity begins to well up in me, then just as quickly evaporates. Does this separate space really belong to me? For a long time, I have sat benighted with everyone else, cramped into Economy Class, changing seats every so often. But suddenly, here is this empty cabin, and it is said that I used to control it; all this seems to spark an insecurity in me. Furthermore, our names sound awkward and harsh; it feels as if they couldn't possibly have been given to us by the Creator. One can't help but feel uneasy with all of this. A wave of fear passes over me, and I ask, "Is this the head of the World?"

"Yes. Right now it's unoccupied, which is a problem."

"The World—you mean to say it's not automatic?"

"Technically speaking, the Creator may have made the World completely automatic, but we don't want it to continue this way."

"Why not?"

"It doesn't feel natural."

"Is it because of the Light?"

"Yes, perhaps . . ."

Something's face suddenly turns deathly pale, radiating brilliance in the darkness, suffused with an ingratiating delicacy. I gather my courage, then put my arm around his waist, hugging him tightly. It doesn't matter—even if it's dangerous, I like the tranquility of the Cockpit.

After that, we sit down. The darkness suffused with the light of scattered stars pours in through the windshield before us. *Something* and I sit there silently for a long time. His face is like an ivory carving, with a scarlet translucence emanating from deep within. I thrust my hand into his palm and feel an icy coldness beginning to melt there as it shakes like a typewriter.

16. AIRSPEED AND DIRECTION

"The reason why we can't fly out of the darkness is because of our speed and direction," *Something* says, looking at me seriously, his eyes radiating a deep-blue wisdom. The first thing that attracted the attention of the Seekers was that all 7X7 Worlds were flying in the same direction at the same speed. 7X7 is a bilaterally symmetrical physical system on either side, but this is not so from front to back; this bears a clear relation to the direction of flight. With our frequent encounters with turbulence, this layout makes sense in terms of the principles of "aerodynamics" (but what is that?).

Something says, "Based upon our study of the cycles, we have been able to deduce that 7X7 is constantly revolving around a large, ball-like object beneath us, never ceasing. This is the only explanation why passengers could have observed the recurring disappearance and reappearance of specific patterns down in the depths."

But why do we never arrive at the realm of Light glimpsed by the Seekers? Theoretically speaking, this is because the ball-shaped object is rotating at the same time, and therefore we were either flying too fast or too slow. Which is to say, the angular velocity of 7X7 is the same as the angular velocity of the ball-shaped object's rotation; this seems to be the result of a meticulously calculated arrangement.

Continuing on like this, the Creator ensured that 7X7 would always be mired on the side of darkness. In other words, our flight is always chasing after the darkness and we will never catch up with the constantly shifting line that divides darkness and daylight.

But another question presented itself: why must he exile us into darkness? Trying to find out what the passengers' Original Sin was is no longer a meaningless question.

"No matter what, the only way to find the ultimate answer is to guide 7X7 out of the darkness," *Something* says poignantly. "After all, the Seekers have already caught a glimpse of the Light, and based upon what we can glean, only you, Captain, know how to break away from the constant speed of the World. Perhaps in the end we will learn how to make a jet pack that flies farther and faster, but we cannot ignore the fact that our 7X7 alone is home to more than three hundred passengers, and all around us there are so many other 7X7s. Only when all these Worlds fly together into the Light will it be meaningful. Wang Ming, you must take control; things start with you."

"But won't this violate the will of the Creator?"

"Why don't we apply reverse thinking here; what if this was exactly what the Creator was hoping for? Maybe we weren't driven into exile by Him, and this exile has been self-inflicted all along—do you understand? But no one has self-knowledge. Now is the time to press forth on the path to our true destination."

Suddenly, as if awakening from a dream, I feel as if I have realized the purpose of the landing gear.

17. THE FLIGHT CREW

Then, with the help of *Something*, I quickly make contact with the rest of the Flight Crew. Including me, there are fourteen people—four men and ten women.

That's right, four men and ten women, and together we become a unit. Of course, this sort of unusual relationship between men and women could take place only in unusual circumstances. Its formation and structure are admittedly a bit awkward, but there is also a certain sense of secret excitement about it. It will be necessary for us to overcome our psychological discomfort. This World has never before had the concept of a "collective," and for me, the most urgent need is to recover a sense of what's known as leadership.

And so, the real work begins. From what we have been able to glean from the main monitor on the flight deck and the flight checklist, we all dedicate ourselves to remembering our fabled "flight skills." According to *Something*, this includes how to make 7X7 accelerate or decelerate, make a turn and change the direction of flight, and descend from a higher point in order to approach the chessboards and mazes of stars that lie below.

But very soon we realize that all attempts from the Cockpit to regain control of the resources at hand are in vain. Without a doubt, some sort of brainwashing had occurred. After that, the Flight Crew was made into regular passengers, and we were all banished to Economy Class, where we received our education in politics, general knowledge, and natural science. And at the same time, the Omnipotent Creator succeeded in switching over to autopilot, or perhaps I should say He took over the Cockpit, hidden away somewhere in command by remote controls. Maybe 7X7 was facing some grave threat at the time? Maybe if this had not taken place, it would have disintegrated. The Creator had lost faith in us.

—This is *Something's* explanation. What he and his mates want to do is restore the Creator's faith in reestablishing the dialogue between man and machine so that 7X7 can be controlled by the "liveware" that had been bred inside it.

But what if these things *Something* is saying aren't true? There is no third party to make a final determination. This could all be just a drama put on by the Creator. Its title would be "The Farce of the Light" or something like that. *Something* and his mates would be the props, without being aware of it themselves. Because of their own selfish needs, the heretical, uncultured Wheel Well had shamelessly counterfeited both us and our flying licenses. Maybe there was no such thing as the Captain and the Flight Crew.

—Among the Flight Crew, there are those who suspect this to be the case.

"Our world has always been a stable place, and everything is provided for. There is no need for us to fret; isn't that our aim in following the Creator's purpose all our lives? And what's wrong with staying in the dark? I don't see any harm in it," the young male Copilot, whose name was Guohang, said. "But now that we've made a mess out of something originally quite simple, we may as well follow it through."

There seems to be something profound in what he is saying. I give him an anxious glance. Meanwhile, the putrid scent emanating from First Class keeps growing thicker in the air.

18. THE MONITOR

The rebellion against the First Class cabin breaks out during a particularly strong episode of turbulence.

The instigator is Guohang. He secretly drew in all the members of the Flight Crew except for myself, and using the sharp-edged cutlery as weapons, they carry out a surprise attack on First Class.

A struggle ensues. The First Class cabin has grown old and senile and naturally lost out, resulting in their being driven into Economy Class. Guohang takes a seat in First Class, and the passengers in Business Class express their unanimous assent.

Guohang had not invited me to participate in the uprising, calling our relationship into question. This is of course related to my position as Captain. What had we done together before? Thus, our recently formed team has been transformed.

After that, *Something* and I no longer have the opportunity to enter the Cockpit, which has become a crypt filled with the rotting corpses of those cleaned out of the First Class cabin. A seal is placed over the door by Guohang, and it has become a truly restricted area.

The Copilot assumes his true role in the World: the Monitor.

And *Something* catches wind of an even graver danger. During this time, he leads me about, surreptitiously collecting the "life jackets." As it turns out, these strange objects had been stuffed underneath everyone's seats, as if their purpose were predetermined. Then he gives the life jackets to the residents of the Wheel Well. The Seekers tear them to pieces, then begin reassembling them as "parachutes."

In no time at all, they produced ten parachutes. *Something* forcibly encases my body in the vest containing the parachute. He then goes and picks out nine more passengers and gives each of them a parachute. There are more than three hundred people in this World, but only these few are given parachutes. I am seized with an unshakable apprehension: have the Seekers given up on their plan to bring everyone to the Light?

Ashamedly, *Something* explains, "This is the last resort for escaping the darkness if everything else fails. You haven't had any professional training so can't yet operate the jet packs."

The critical moment is drawing nigh. This seems to have been apparent ever since Guohang started the insurrection. *Something*'s eyes look bloodshot, for the first time, as if this were a final farewell. He continues, "Since we can't recover control of the World and successfully fly it into the Light, then we'll make it fall." My heart sinks at the despairing tone in *Something*'s voice. "Come what may, if it keeps on flying like this, it eventually has to fall. We have already found out that this creation of the Creator has a limited life span. The insulation for 7X7's cables, electrical outlets, and circuits has already begun to deteriorate. The fire alarm has already signaled three false alarms, and components of the propulsion system are beginning to wear out. If one of the bearings fails, we won't be able to restore it. According to our analysis, the end will be upon us any day now. There is no more time. If we can't save everyone, we'll just have to pick some representatives for an escape."

Two fine streams of tears roll down my cheeks.

"When the time comes, you ten will use the parachutes to drop down to the constellations below and tell them what has happened here." He struggles to smile as he issues this earnest exhortation, lifting his hand up to gently brush away my tears.

"And what about you?" I look at him, touched.

"I have to take care of the passengers first, and you will bear witness to the disaster. There is a limited number of jet packs, and not even all the Seekers will be able to escape."

19. CHANGE OF COMMAND

Very quickly, Guohang institutes a new order. He dismisses the Flight Crew and selects a group of boys to act as Flight Attendants, charged with instituting strict monitoring. The children proved to be apt for the job, and as a result the graffiti in the bathroom—which left one in palpitations, between tears and laughter—is soon eradicated.

After that, the cleansing begins. The boys plunged, screaming, into the Luggage Compartment and the Wheel Well, arresting the residents of the lower strata. The majority of them have no time to grab a jet pack and make their escape, and they are dragged up to the main cabin. The Flight

Attendants execute them by strangling them with safety belts. Their crime: "disruption of World balance by a stowaway."

Illegal commerce is uprooted, so the basis for the bribery is removed; the female passengers reassume their rightful places. It seems as if a great new world is about to be born.

Passengers in Business Class "volunteer" to carry out the task of processing the new corpses, and a spoonful of the resulting soup is given out equally for the common enjoyment of the Business, First, and Economy Classes. It is to be like this from now on; no one has special privileges, and equality and fairness are the ultimate standards championed by Guohang.

The jet packs are seized as contraband, and the boys hoist them up for display in the common area. These were the tools of subversion, and they had almost shaken the foundations of Boeing's legitimacy.

20. EVASIVE ACTION

After the death of *Something*, I stop getting hard-ons.

I have not been killed but am put on lockdown, and when I go to the bathroom a Flight Attendant accompanies me. I have no way of making contact with those nine passengers who have secretly gotten parachutes. Luckily, Guohang is not aware of the parachutes' existence.

More and more, I meditate on the question of "falling."

"You will use the parachutes to drop down to the constellations below and tell them what has happened here."

Something's last testament echoes in my ears. Who is "them"? I've never looked forward as much as I do right now to finally meeting those strangers who don't live here in 7X7.

The Flight Attendant monitoring me also has a name. He is called Wake, he's twelve or thirteen, and he has sat by me once a long time ago.

"Wang Ming, what did you do wrong? Did you do it with one of their women?"

"Is that what you think, Wake?"

"Mmmhmm, were they good?"

"Well, if that's what you mean, then yes, they weren't bad. Very different from the women in Economy Class. Unfortunately, you guys killed all of them."

"Made them into broth? That is too bad."

Wake chuckles, and I am suddenly struck with the realization that a profound change is taking place in the World—the ordinary folk in Economy Class have begun to get interested in the opposite sex.

He constantly pesters me for stories about the women down below. I tell him about the erotic scenes I witnessed in the Luggage Compartment, carefully choosing the tidbits I recount. He listens so raptly as to stop breathing, purple arteries bulging out on his sinewy neck. Eventually, he pulls down his pants in front of me.

"Do it," he says.

"It's not like that . . ."

This is a great disappointment. The precocious boy spins around, rearing up spitefully as if he is about to strike me. But he doesn't actually hit me; instead he turns back around and, tittering as he leans over the sink, he sticks his stringy little ass into the air in front of my nose.

This is an old habit of our generation, and it has finally been passed on to the children. Wake had the chance to escape it, to break free of us, and to go in search of his other half that really did belong to him, but now it's gone. This is a World filled with regret.

I take a stainless steel fork and shove it up his rectum. Blood dark as ink gushes out, soaking my face.

I try my best to imagine that this is revenge for *Something*.

21. RUINATION

I take a look at the sign that says No Smoking and begin to waver.

This was, after all, the only World that had reared me. I had never imagined that I would tear its order asunder. And the new generation—so different from us with their first and last names and their interest in the opposite sex—has already begun to come into their own.

Is the world outside really worth the venturing out into?

But *Something's* face appears in the mirror. Actually, the face is a hovering instrument panel, inching its way out of a crevice in the autopilot relay.

"Who are you?" *Something* inquires mournfully.

"Who am I?" I respond in a firm voice to the blood-drenched face in the mirror, standing my ground. Pitiful as a fading mist, he disappears.

I make up my mind to stop vacillating. Trembling, I withdraw three objects from my pocket. These were given to me by *Something*: cigarettes, a lighter, and a bottle of alcohol. I take out a cigarette, light it with the lighter, take a drag, and then nestle it in the hair of the dead boy, then I pour the alcohol over his head and body. After that, I carefully scrub my face clean, slowly exit the washroom, and return to my seat.

A short while later, the alarm begins to howl and a cloud of thick black smoke wells up in the aft of the cabin. A group of Flight Attendants, armed with fire extinguishers, charges down the walkway all aclamor. Since the creation of 7X7, this is the very first fire in the World. The boys don't show any fear—they are enjoying themselves as if playing a game.

Amid all the chaos, I shout out the seat numbers of those nine passengers. Five of them come running over to me, their anemic faces tinted with a soft white sheen of hope. I lead them quickly into the galley, where I assign them their duties. Some are to go into the main cabin, locate those special spots marked in red, and pry open the emergency doors; some are to sneak into the hydraulics compartment and destroy the cylinders that maintain stability; others are to make their way into the wings and puncture holes in the fuel tanks.

Alone, I stride off toward the Cockpit. I can't say exactly what I am going to do, but it feels as if I must do this. Just then, I notice a flaming cockroach struggling to move in the same direction. Immediately, my face is covered in tears.

The cabin is filled with the popping and banging of explosions. Fire, smoke, and debris rain down all around. The passengers scream incessantly. No one has ever experienced anything like this before. I shove my trembling hands into my pants pockets and begin whistling tunelessly. Suddenly, I remember the tune of that song "Waiting for the Condors" and march forward following that brave and unwavering cockroach. The outer layers of the World peel back with a howl, revealing never-before-seen cracks; shimmering beams of starlight clatter as they spill in. *Pa-clack, pa-clack*, the oxygen masks clatter as they drop out of the compartments overhead. A cyclone of chilled wind, sparks, and smoke swirls wildly about. I can't breathe. I don't know what is about to happen.

At this point, 7X7 begins to nosedive, shaking violently.

22. RESOLUTION

It's true, our precious stability and balance have been lost.

The "fall" prophesied by *Something* has begun.

In the suffocating, bitter-cold, low-pressure air, I scream to myself, "DON'T PASS OUT!"

Then, amid the smoke and shock waves I see the indistinct figure of Guohang stumbling toward me, looking bewildered and exhausted.

"You're trying to get to the Cockpit now?" he asks, apparently concerned.

"I . . ."

"You have done the worst thing you could possibly do," he says, dejectedly. "You're the Captain, but you've neglected your duty to keep the World safe," he says listlessly as he smashes the cockroach, crawling indefatigably forward, under his foot. It emanates a loud cry of despair as a burst of black liquid squirts from its body.

In that same instant, I feel as if a foul handful of my own brains had been squeezed out, polluting the World. I do a double take, as if awakening from a long dream. What have I done indeed? Is this really what I should do? I start to feel guilty, losing my resolve to approach the Cockpit. I glance to one side at the gaping hole, hesitate, then make my way over to it. Guohang makes a flustered swipe at me.

We are rapidly losing altitude.

The moment of resolution has arrived. I leap out.

But I don't begin to fly; instead, I immediately begin falling. I have the vague sense that behind me, someone else has jumped as well. Is it the other five passengers, or is it Guohang?

Darkness, unending darkness. The immaterial, untouchable outside world seems like a lie. Overhead, I hear a thundering roar, an unrestrained, unfiltered rumbling that sounds as if the universe were about to be turned on its head. Five thousand, ten thousand, maybe a hundred thousand 7X7 Worlds are flying in formation above me. I turn my head up and suddenly see millions of shimmering windows, like pearls scattered in a dazzling array across the vault of heaven.

I can't help but feel a profound pity for them.

Those 7X7s keep steadily on their courses in the darkness, while I, the "Captain," have abandoned myself to plummet from mine.

This has been a long time coming and has never happened before. I catch sight of the stars below and dream of the far-away Light.

I don't know how much time has passed, until suddenly my body becomes light as if I had been seized by a great hand and am lifted up.

23. TOUCHDOWN

When I awaken, I find myself hanging from some object, my body still wrapped in the parachute made of life jackets.

I am hanging from some soft, green, branchy thing, and roughly ten meters below me I can vaguely discern a vast expanse of some hard, ocher substance. It is nothing like the double walkways in 7X7 that I am accustomed to seeing, and there are no rows of seats placed one next to the other.

Is this the starry world of chessboards and mazes that I saw through the windows?

But it's not round, as they predicted it would be.

For the very first time, the darkness that has been with me my entire life suddenly begins to fade away. In the distance, a faint glow gently floats up. The memory comes back to me in a flash and I conclude it must be the "horizon." I am startled. This alien landscape is exactly as *Something* described.

Delicate tendrils of crimson light seep through the thick mists, scattering all about me. This really is another world. It is unusually steady, without the slightest jostle of turbulence, fraught with an abundant life force.

Beginning in front of me and extending back, the world grows more and more brilliant, but it isn't the man-made lamplight of 7X7.

. . . Is this the Light?

A red orb, shimmering all over, emerges unsteadily from the depths of what must be the Light, and soon it has become so bright that I can no longer look directly at it. In that instant, I hear the arrow of time shoot past my ear with a whirr.

Ashamed, I lower my head and see a pile of broken human bodies emerging from the water-stained shimmer. The passengers who jumped with me are still wearing their orange parachutes, which they could not open.

A bit further off, a great pile of twisted metal is spread about, and there is a raging conflagration that pops and bangs as it burns. Broken limbs and severed body parts are scattered all around. On one of the larger, trapezoidal pieces of wreckage, I can make out a letter X. Now I remember— that was the world I used to live in, and X represents uncertainty—actually, I finally realize that in reference to the passage of time, it in fact represents the future.

In the next instant, every cell in my body is overcome with the sorrow of having destroyed the World. A new World that was still unborn has been torn asunder by me.

And *Something*—did he ever really exist, or will he ever exist?

And once we had broken free of the fetters of speed and course, only our World would descend and fall to the ground. What about the tens of millions other Worlds? And what about my fellow men who go on flying through the darkness?

24. BOEING

The next step is the clarification of some essential questions:

Just who was it who had banished us to flying through the darkness? Had we actually done this to ourselves? And who was the Creator, Boeing?

I am anxious to liberate myself and begin to try to release myself from the parachute, preparing to drop down on that solid and expansive ocher surface.

At that very moment, the sound of an ear-piercing whistle rings out all around. Soon after, I spy a group of black metal carapaces like cockroaches riding on four spinning wheels speeding toward me. They stop and surround me, forming a skirmish line. From inside the metal carapaces, a number of golden-haired, tin white-skinned men leap out, speaking in a garbled tongue I cannot understand.

Is it "them"?

They raise some sort of metal sticks, aiming the ends at me.

Bless and protect me, Boeing.

Amitābha.

12

THE REINCARNATED GIANT

WANG JINKANG

TRANSLATED BY CARLOS ROJAS

1. THREE NEWS RELEASES

This year, 2012, J-nation's media broadcast three heatedly debated news items, all of which had to do with Imagai Nashihiko, the head of the Western Steel Group. Of course, anything concerning someone of Mr. Imagai's stature would inevitably become a hot news item. Mr. Imagai was seventy-two years old and was the richest man in J-nation. Before the country's economic bubble burst, he had even been at the top of the Forbes 500 list for many years. He personally owned more than one-sixth of the land in the entire country, making him an embodiment of wealth itself, and I suspect that even the legendarily wealthy King Solomon might well have been his inferior. Mr. Imagai was ruthless and decisive, with a gaze like a knife and a penetrating understanding of people and events, and was revered throughout the country—and particularly within business circles—as the spiritual father of J-nation's financial world. Another famous tycoon, Harita Akio, worshipped the ground he walked on, calling him a great man who comes along only once every few centuries, like Tang-dynasty China's Taizong emperor. Then, Harita would sigh and add, "Why should he be born, now that there is me?"[1]

The first of the three news items concerned Mr. Imagai's personal lawyer, Kiminao Ninzen, who was asked to petition the court for an "uncontested, preemptive guarantee of rights" on Mr. Imagai's behalf. This petition was truly bizarre and may very well have been unprecedented in all the world's legal systems, because according to existing legal practices the right to sue presupposes that there be a counterpart who is alleged to have transgressed on the rights of the litigant. It was, therefore, already a significant victory for Imagai's resourceful lawyer, Kiminao, to have convinced the court to acknowledge Imagai's petition:

. . .

MR. KIMINAO: On behalf of my client, I am petitioning the court for an "uncontested, preemptive guarantee of rights." My client has developed a cancerous tumor in his right arm and will have to have the arm amputated immediately, and he is considering having a new arm attached in its place. But after his arm is amputated, he will no longer be able to sign checks in his original handwriting and, furthermore, will lose an important symbol of his identity—which is to say his fingerprints. In order to secure my client's rights, I therefore request that the court preemptively guarantee that he will retain all his original rights even when he loses his arm and has the new one attached.

JUDGE: First of all, I'd like to express my condolences to your client for his illness. In a strict legal sense, however, a "person" is understood as a holistic entity, and although the concept of "personhood" lacks clear statutory provision, someone who loses an arm would clearly retain all his original rights. On this point, it is simply not necessary to request a preemptive guarantee of rights. With respect to the issue of not being able to sign his checks in his original handwriting, a few simple technical adjustments will suffice.

MR. KIMINAO (laughing): No, it is not so simple. My client truly shows great foresight. From this seemingly inconsequential matter he has observed an enormous loophole in the contemporary legal system, which is precisely what Your Honor has just referred to—namely, the fact that the law is currently not able to provide a precise definition for the term "person." Suppose, for instance, that my client were not only to lose his right arm but also—and please forgive me for raising this unfortunate possibility—to have a car accident in which he would lose both arms, his eyesight, and which would furthermore leave him disfigured, with damaged vocal cords and in need of an artificial heart. In other words, suppose that he were to lose all the external characteristics that currently define him, to the point that even a genetic analysis might prove inconclusive, since his new limbs and organs would contain foreign DNA. It is possible, in fact, that only his magnificent brain would remain intact. Would you agree that, under these circumstances, he could still be regarded as the same respected Mr. Imagai? Would he retain all the rights that Mr. Imagai currently enjoys?

JUDGE: Of course. That goes without saying.

MR. KIMINAO: Good! That is precisely my client's wish. He doesn't wish to change the nation's laws overnight but instead simply wants to make a modest arrangement with respect to his own personal rights. In other words, my client simply asks the court to preemptively recognize that, with respect to his body, his brain is the only determinant of his identity. This sort of arrangement may, in the end, prove to have been excessively prudent, but there is never any harm in being prudent.

. . .

In the end, Kiminao Ninzen won the case and received from the court a formal certification of rights for his client. Although this "uncontested, preemptive guarantee of rights" was, indeed, unprecedented, there was no disputing the analysis he had presented. Who wouldn't agree that a person's brain is his or her most fundamental organ? Furthermore, J-nation, after a contentious multiyear debate, had just passed a new law that made brain death, rather than cardiac death, the new standard for determining an individual's death.

Though there was much conjecture concerning Mr. Imagai's motivations at the time, no one suspected that he was actually laying the legal groundwork for a historically unprecedented operation. I was the lead surgeon for the operation, but it was far from a simple amputation or arm transplant.

———— ∞ ————

The second of the three news items concerned Mr. Imagai's lawyer's advance purchase of an anencephalic fetus for his client. The reporter who reported this story remarked with consternation, "This must be in preparation for Mr. Imagai's arm transplant, but how can he, who is 1.67 meters tall, possibly be given an infant's arm?"

At the time, Mrs. Yamaguchi was already twenty weeks pregnant, and ultrasounds and alpha-fetoprotein tests had confirmed that the fetus was anencephalic. Mr. Kiminao had placed informers at several dozen hospitals, and the day he received news of Mrs. Yamaguchi's diagnosis he took me with him to see her. My job was to examine the fetus and confirm that, apart from lacking a forebrain, all its other organs were healthy. The results of my examination were very reassuring. The Yamaguchis were fisherfolk in financial straits, which is the reason why Kiminao had picked them. Meeting with the couple when they had not yet recovered from the shock of the diagnosis and were depressed and disconsolate, Mr. Kiminao said to them earnestly, "Please accept my condolences for your tragedy. I represent a good-hearted old gentleman, who would like to do something for you. You need not worry about your medical expenses, since the gentleman is willing to cover them for you."

The couple thanked us politely, although they were clearly suspicious of this unsolicited generosity.

Mr. Kiminao asked, "Do you plan to have the fetus induced?"

Mr. Yamaguchi replied sadly, "That is our only option. The doctor says that this sort of congenital disease is untreatable."

"That is correct. Current medical technology has no cure. However, I have a suggestion that I would like you to consider. Would you perhaps be willing to allow this unfortunate child to live in someone else's body? Yes, I am speaking of organ transplant. The fetus's eyes, heart, liver, gallbladder, kidneys, pancreas, spleen, hands, and feet—in fact, its entire body could live healthily in someone else's. I believe that this might be of some comfort to you. Also, please rest assured, when conducting the organ transplants we will use only the most humane methods. We'll hire the best doctors and nurses to look after Mrs. Yamaguchi until she safely delivers, and after delivery we'll use a heart-lung machine to keep the infant alive for at least half a year until we can confirm that there is no possibility of a cure, and only then will we begin the transplant procedure. In addition," the lawyer added softly, "you will receive considerable nutritional subsidies. You and I both know that organ selling is illegal, but the law does not forbid the family of a deceased patient from voluntarily donating the corpse, nor does it forbid a charitable individual from giving some nutritional subsidies to an unfortunate couple."

A gleam of greed shone through Mr. Yamaguchi's eyes: "How much?" Mr. Kiminao replied, "It depends on your needs."

Mrs. Yamaguchi tugged at her husband's sleeve, and he said hesitantly, "Can I talk this over with my wife?"

"Of course. That goes without saying."

After we stepped out of the hospital room, we could see through the half-open door Mr. Yamaguchi and his wife conversing quietly. She seemed to be resisting, while her husband was trying to persuade her. We heard him say, "The child will not survive anyway, so it is not a question of our callousness." While they were talking, Kiminao simply gazed off into the distance with his hands clasped behind his back. In the end, Mrs. Yamaguchi gave in, and when Mr. Yamaguchi invited us back in he announced resolutely, "Twenty million J dollars. Nothing less."

I knew that the starting price for these negotiations had originally been pegged at eighty million J dollars, and therefore Mr. Yamaguchi's asking price was much too low. Mr. Kiminao, however, replied calmly, "That is too much. For a nutritional subsidy, this price is much too high. Mr. Yamaguchi, you put me in a very awkward position." Mr. Yamaguchi opened his mouth to speak, but Kiminao cut him off with a wave of his hand and said, "However, since I've already given my word, I will find a way to deal with this problem myself. I'll do my best to convince my client, and I believe he will ultimately agree. As I've already mentioned, he is a very generous man. However, I must emphasize one point: you may subsequently learn who has received the infant's organs, but you must not, under any circumstances, disturb that person. There is a clause in your contract that spells this out very clearly, and if this clause is breached you will have to pay a penalty of double the amount. Please remember, my client is very benevolent but also very principled, and there is nothing he likes less than incessant demands from greedy people."

This calm threat clearly left a deep impression on the couple, and Mr. Yamaguchi quickly nodded his assent: "We definitely won't break our word. We will maintain absolute silence. You can rest assured of that."

The fetus was delivered by Cesarean section at seven months (on account of the fact that anencephalic fetuses often die before they reach full term). As promised, the parents did indeed disappear after receiving their money. Regardless of how hot the news subsequently became, they apparently kept their word, since there was no further sign of them. We used a heart-lung machine to keep the infant alive for six months. You could say that this was to abide by the terms of the contract, but in reality this clause of the contract was nonsensical. Who, after all, has ever heard of an anencephalic infant being cured? There was not the least possibility of this. To tell the truth, we had planned from the beginning to carry out the organ transplant operation after six months, as the chance of success would be greater then.

At the end of the year, Mr. Kiminao held a press conference in which he announced that Mr. Imagai would undergo organ transplant surgery. This was the third piece of groundbreaking news. This announcement did not comport with the discretion with which this godfather of the financial world normally conducted his business. However, people would subsequently come to realize that he had his reasons for proceeding in this manner.

The reporters rushed forward, desperate for inside information, each hoping their coverage would make the front page. They were all very bewildered, however: what organ is Mr. Imagai going to receive? The previous report of Mr. Imagai's developing a malignant bone tumor in his right arm was clearly a misdiagnosis since, for nearly a year after these initial reports, he has remained perfectly healthy, continuing to use his distinctive florid handwriting to sign one enormous check after another. Some of the more astute reporters had already guessed that this was not even a misdiagnosis but rather that the earlier announcement had simply been a smoke screen put up by Western Steel. What organ, therefore, was the great Mr. Imagai going to receive from the anencephalic infant?

Mr. Imagai did not appear at the press conference because, at the time, he was actually in an operating room in the Neurological Surgery Clinic in Yamadai prefecture. I myself was in the disinfection area washing my hands and was about to put on my green surgical scrubs and begin the operation. Apart from Mr. Kiminao, Western Steel's director of general affairs, Nakasane Ichū, was also at the press conference. Nakasane was one of Mr. Imagai's most competent assistants, and for a month after the operation (which is the amount of time it takes for accelerated nerve regeneration) he would oversee the company's daily operations. Mr. Imagai's personal assistant, Komatsu Yoshiko, also attended. The pretty Ms. Komatsu Yoshiko was often referred to as Mr. Imagai's sleep-in secretary, because everyone knew that the great Mr. Imagai was also very well endowed sexually, and even at seventy-two he was still in full possession of his sexual prowess. His semipublic girlfriends numbered in the dozens, including movie stars, Olympic athletes, bar girls, college co-eds, and female politicians. Komatsu Yoshiko, however, was the most highly favored of them all and received sixty million J dollars a month (and remember that Mr. Imagai paid only twenty million to purchase the anencephalic infant!). It was impossible for outsiders to know with certainty the exact reason why she was so highly favored, but it was rumored that she could use a very you-know-what technique to satisfy this old man's peculiar sexual appetites.

The media had never criticized Mr. Imagai's promiscuity, which was probably owing to the widespread attitude that it was perfectly natural for this alpha male, who owned one-sixth of the nation's land, to have more than one woman. In fact, some people even complimented him on his egalitarian style, given that when it came to potential lovers he didn't limit himself to high society.

As I watched Komatsu Yoshiko's showy demeanor onscreen, however, I couldn't help suspecting that her sixty-million-a-month salary was no longer secure, given that following this operation and for many years to come, Mr. Imagai certainly won't be requiring her services.

None of Mr. Imagai's family was present at the press conference. His wife had already passed away, and neither of his two sons made an appearance. I, of course, knew the reason for this: if this operation proved successful, the two unfortunate sons could no longer look forward to inheriting the Western Steel empire. They must have been very unhappy with their father's decision, if not actually hating him for it. Mr. Imagai, however, had already arranged to give each son a portion of his fortune, and they had already left the company to set up their own businesses, following different paths from their father.

. . .

CAPITAL DAILY REPORTER: Could you tell us precisely which organ Mr. Imagai will be receiving today? We already know that he didn't really have a tumor on his right arm.

MR. KIMINAO (*smiling*): This is precisely why I have convened today's press conference. I am officially announcing that Mr. Imagai will receive a full-body transplant, including both legs, both arms, heart, liver, gallbladder, kidneys, pancreas, spleen, eyes, ears, tongue, nose, and torso. All organs but one—his brain.

KHN REPORTER (*looking dumbstruck*): You're saying . . . that Mr. Imagai is not actually having an organ transplant, but rather he is transplanting his own brain into the body of the anencephalic infant?

MR. KIMINAO (*solemnly*): That is incorrect; you have mixed up subject and object. As everyone knows, an anencephalic infant cannot be viewed as an actual person. It doesn't have an identity, and in Christian nations priests don't perform mass for them when they die. My client's brain, on the other hand, is his only effective representative, the rights of which we had already preemptively requested the court to guarantee. For example, people often say that the sun rises in the east, but that is merely a figure of speech, and if you were to use rigorously scientific language you would have to say that the earth revolves toward the east, toward the sun. Similarly, if we use rigorously legal language, we can only say that my client is receiving a new body today.

JIJI PRESS REPORTER: This sort of brain transplant is unprecedented. What is its likelihood of success?

MR. KIMINAO (*offering another correction*): No, this is not a brain transplant, it is a body transplant. We are confident that the operation will be a success and have been preparing for it for twenty years.

KHN REPORTER: I assume that when you filed for a preemptive certification of rights six months ago, it was in preparation for today's operation?

MR. KIMINAO: You could certainly see it that way. Now, the operation is about to begin, and all our honored guests will observe the entire process. The operation, however, will not be displayed on a monitor, since that sort of observation has no legal standing. Instead, you will watch it live through the observation windows of the operating room. What you are about to witness is the brain belonging to my client, and to no one else, being transplanted into the cranium of the anencephalic infant. I will be obliged for your assistance in one thing, which is that after the operation everyone present sign a document of witness. Now, everyone please follow me to the observation room.

Mr. Kiminao led the twenty-five reporters into the observation room, from which they could clearly observe the operating room through a large glass window. More than ten nurses had already completed the pre-op procedures, and the anencephalic infant was lying on an operating table, covered by a white sheet with only its deformed skull exposed. The heart-lung machine was still operating. Mr. Imagai Nashihiko was sitting on another operating table, and today his normally stern face was smiling broadly as he waved to the reporters through the window. The KHN reporter was allowed to enter the operating room, representing the reporter pool. He put on surgical scrubs and, holding up a microphone, asked Mr. Imagai to say a few words. Imagai serenely observed: "Today is a life-and-death gamble for me, so please pray for me. If I am able to leave this operating room with a new body and a new face, I hope no one will fail to recognize their old friend. As they say, you shouldn't judge a book by its cover, or a person by his face."

His humor did not elicit any laughter. This is not because the reporters' responses were slow but because they were so in awe of him that they hardly dared even to smile in his presence. Imagai, using the microphone, answered some questions from the reporters waiting outside, and I, as the chief surgeon, also answered a few.

Then the operation began. The infant's heart-lung machine was removed, and the remnant of its cranium was opened up. After Mr. Imagai was given general anesthesia, his own skull was also opened up. His brain was then carefully removed and transferred to the infant's cranium, where we used biocompatible polyprole tubes to bridge the brain to the infant's optic nerve, spinal cord, and other extracranial nerves. This sort of bridge would help the nerves to regenerate faster, enabling them to establish permanent connections in less than a month, at which point Mr. Imagai would "awaken" in his new body.

Carrying out this extremely complicated procedure under the gaze of dozens of pairs of eyes, I couldn't help but be somewhat nervous. I had, however, carefully planned everything out. In fact, you could even say that I had been waiting for this operation my entire life. I had already spent twenty years preparing for it and had carried out hundreds of successful experimental trials on animals. Failure was simply not an option. Apart from my professional honor and responsibilities as a world-renowned surgeon that rested on the success of the surgery, I, Dr. Motose Zekū, would also stand to gain something more substantial— namely, a twenty percent stake in Western Steel.

2. HUMAN GRAFTING

After graduating from the renowned Capital Medical School twenty-two years earlier, I completed my residency at the not-so-famous Neurological Surgery Clinic in Yamadai prefecture. Not long before the completion of my residency, I was presented with a very difficult case. The patient was a four-year-old girl who was suffering from a congenital deformity wherein a portion of her meningeal membrane, including her pituitary gland and hypothalamus, protruded into her mouth through a fissure in her cranium, such that if the membrane were to accidentally tear while she was eating, it would immediately precipitate a life-threatening emergency. After the joint consultation by the residential specialists it was determined that she should be operated on immediately. The operation, however, would be extremely risky, and our hospital didn't have enough experience, so several senior doctors suggested that the patient be transferred to another hospital. But I insisted that we accept the patient and even offered to serve as the lead surgeon. The operation was a success, and overnight I, the twenty-five-year-old Motose Zekū, became a celebrity within J-nation's medical community.

Shortly thereafter, Mr. Imagai Nashihiko, through the agency of his lawyer, expressed his desire to meet me. I was immensely flattered by this invitation, because to be favored by the nation's richest tycoon surely meant that wealth and status awaited me. Furthermore, I had a particularly strong sense of curiosity about this tycoon who owned a sixth of the nation's land and therefore wanted to observe firsthand what he was really like. As for why he had wanted to meet me, I didn't really understand at the time. His empire was built on the leisure industry, steel, and railways rather than on medicine or biotechnology. Furthermore, he couldn't possibly want me to be his personal physician, since my specialty as a neurosurgeon was much too narrow for me to serve as a personal physician. I had mixed feelings; while I hoped that this would be an opportunity for advancement, I couldn't help but feel hesitant. Everyone knew Imagai's famous motto, "Don't use talent, use mediocrity." He ruled his business as an emperor would his empire, and like all emperors, he did not appreciate maverick underlings. Imagai followed the dictum of the Chinese philosopher Xunzi, who viewed human nature as inherently evil. Accordingly, he viewed all new employees with a skeptical eye until their loyalty had been proven through performance. This kind of master was not easy to get along with.

Mr. Imagai was of average height and dressed very simply. Even his leather shoes were worn out. But he had a very sharp gaze, an imposing mien, and a naturally imperious air. His assistants, including his second in command, General Affairs Head Nakasane Ichū, all showed him the greatest respect. He invited me to sit down and immediately got to the point: "Mr. Motose, I know you are an extraordinarily talented doctor. I am now fifty-two years old and should begin planning for my old age. Please tell me your views on aging and mortality. Can they be avoided?"

I replied cautiously, "There are many different schools of thought on this. One reliable view is the 'programmatic' model, which holds that an organism's aging process and subsequent death are determined by its genes. For instance, a human cell will die after dividing fifty times, which in turn brings on the death of the body itself. But reproductive and cancer cells are able to extend their lives by 'resetting' their internal clocks, hence they do not die. If one could only find a way to alter this natural programming, death would not necessarily be unavoidable."

"How, then, could one reset all one's cells? I know fruit trees can accomplish this through grafting. For instance, if a black-plum tree is grafted onto a wild peach tree, the young peach would reset the plum's internal clock to zero, so if the plum were to be repeatedly grafted generation after generation, it would effectively become immortal. Can humans be grafted?"

For a moment, I didn't understand: "What do you mean by human grafting? How could it be done?"

"I mean grafting a brain. If a brain is accepted by a new body, and if the brain accepts the body's genetic commands, then the brain's internal clock will be reset to zero while retaining its original consciousness." He saw my startled expression and said calmly, "Don't reject this out of hand. Please give it some careful consideration before you decide."

This was a very bold idea. I considered it very carefully and eventually replied, "Your suggestion is ahead of its time, but in theory it is feasible. The transplanted brain cells could very possibly be reset to zero by the new host body. The actual surgery, however, would be extraordinarily difficult. There have been successful cases of head transplants in primates, but it would be much more difficult to transplant a brain only. The transplanted brain would have to be grafted onto the host body's myriad extracranial nerves and connective tissues, including the spinal column, the optic nerves, auditory nerves, lingual nerves, and facial nerves. Moreover, the difficulties of regenerating the central nervous system would remain."

"I am aware of these difficulties. I just want you to say whether or not there is any hope of success? And within the next twenty or thirty years? Money is no object."

I hesitated for a long time: "I wouldn't say it's not possible."

Mr. Imagai replied decisively, "Then we should definitely try. I would like to hire you to supervise this venture. What do you think? I am aware of your talent and your courage, and beyond that you would enjoy the world's most generous financial support. Take hold of this opportunity and try to achieve this breakthrough while I'm still alive. As for your remuneration"—he looked at me intently—"there are two arrangements that you can choose from. You can take a fixed salary at five times what you are currently receiving, irrespective of whether or not your research is successful. Alternatively, you can continue receiving the relatively low salary that you have now, but after you succeed you will receive a twenty percent stake in Western Steel." He added, "As for determining whether or not the operation is successful, we could agree that as long as I can survive for at least a year following the surgery, the operation will be deemed a success."

A twenty-percent stake in Western Steel! This would make me one of the richest men in the world overnight. I'm not a very greedy person, but it would be absurd to claim that the prospect of billions of J dollars did not have considerable appeal. I gazed at him in astonishment, not daring to believe my ears. He said impassively, "It would not bother me at all to give you a twenty percent stake in the company. If I am able to live forever, I wouldn't need to pay the government the seventy-percent estate tax that would be owed upon my death, so I would still be saving approximately fifty percent of my overall net worth. As you know, the law here is that if someone's personal worth exceeds two billion J dollars, everything above that amount is taxed at a rate of seventy percent." Mr. Imagai said coldly, "This is a typical robber-baron law—it's even more shameless than outright theft."

He asked me, "What do you think of my proposals? I personally hope that you accept the second one, because"—he looked at me again with a piercing gaze, as though he could see right through me—"there are perhaps some people who are not greedy for money but who will exert their maximum effort only when the reward matches the result."

He dangled this juicy bait in front of me, callously appealing to my innermost greed, not leaving me even a trace of a fig leaf to hide behind. For an instant, the awe that I normally felt toward him was tinged with hatred. I hesitated for a moment, then swallowed hard and said, "Okay, I accept your offer, and I wish to take the second arrangement."

He looked as though he had known all along that I would respond the way I did. He nodded calmly and said, "Very good. I like your attitude and am confident we will work very well together."

3. A PREMATURELY WISE INFANT

In the autumn of 2012, a seventy-two-year-old infant was born. His first cry announced the success of my twenty years of labor (as well as the efforts of more than ten thousand researchers who worked under me). Upon hearing the cry, I thought happily that my twenty percent stake in Western Steel was almost in hand.

Strictly speaking, however, this cry did not belong to Mr. Imagai, but rather it was an instinctive response on the part of his "host" (which is to say the anencephalic infant). As Mr. Imagai's brain gradually connected to the nervous system of his host, he gained more and more control over his new body, and within a month he had already completely "emerged" from the infant's body. I found myself confronted, therefore, with a bizarre beast with the body of a seven-month-old infant (if we include the six months he had lived prior to the operation) with delicate limbs that waved about, very tender and sensitive skin, a fat little bottom . . . and an enormous head. Although Mr. Imagai's seventy-two-year-old brain had already shrunk somewhat, the infant's original skull was still too small to hold it, and therefore I had to surgically create a larger one.

A large head with the facial features clustered in the lower portion of the face is precisely the typical appearance of an infant. This enormous cranium, therefore, made Mr. Imagai look even more infantlike, and people couldn't help feeling affectionate toward him. But anyone who looked into his eyes wouldn't feel that way. His gaze was still that of an old devil, sharp as a knife and capable of figuratively stripping one bare and leaving one shivering in naked terror.

Now, he looked at me with this ice-cold gaze and uttered his first words: "Motose, it looks as though you already have your twenty percent stake in hand."

His voice sounded infantile, but his tone was mature and sarcastic. I found this stark contrast very disconcerting. I couldn't help being shamed into anger, because this "infant" who had just learned to speak had instantly unveiled the greed buried deep within me. I replied sarcastically, "Thank you for remembering your promise. I was originally going to run tests on your consciousness, but now it looks as though that won't be necessary. From your tone of voice, it is clear that it is indeed Mr. Imagai in front of me. This much cannot be doubted."

Having been employed by Mr. Imagai for the past twenty years, I was already intimately acquainted with him, and I knew him to be dictatorial, harsh, and mean. Everyone who worked for him was completely subservient, and even if he were to spit in their faces they would only smile then wait until he had left before wiping themselves off. Even the highly positioned Mr. Nakasane was like this, though it is possible that Kiminao may have been slightly different. My position, however, was somewhat special—I had control over Mr. Imagai's mortality and therefore didn't need to be so servile. I remained respectful, but now this respect was tinged with hatred. When he addressed me too caustically (and he rarely failed to use such a tone), I would respond with sarcasm. Later, I discovered that he actually liked this—he liked having someone who was willing to stab back at him. Perhaps he had heard too much flattery and had eventually gotten sick of it. Therefore, when he heard my sarcasm, he laughed out loud, screeching like an owl. He announced imperiously, "I'm hungry! I want milk!"

During the month prior to Mr. Imagai's awakening, we used an intravenous drip to keep him alive, but a wet nurse had long been ready and waiting. In fact, we had arranged to have three. Of course, an infant doesn't need that many wet nurses, but I was very cautious and figured that there was nothing wrong with being overly prepared, particularly when money was not an object. I quickly realized how wise this decision had been. The three wet nurses had all been hired from remote rural areas. This was not done to save money but rather because urban mothers nowadays often find that they don't have enough milk. When the first wet nurse entered, she was clearly startled by the sight of the infant's enormous head. But she didn't say a word and instead proceeded to hold Mr. Imagai up to her chest while lifting her blouse. She had very full breasts, and they were already leaking milk that gave off a sweet aroma. Imagai sized up these breasts, then nodded to me with satisfaction as he grabbed one and greedily started to nurse. I could clearly hear him eagerly swallowing. He quickly finished both breasts and started to cry angrily (this was another instinctive reaction of the host body). Then the crying abruptly broke off and was replaced by a harsh command: "I want more. Bring me another!"

The wet nurse did not know that the infant in her arms could already speak, much less did she expect that he would speak in such a tone. She stared at him in shock, but I quickly waved her out and called in the second nurse, and after her, the third. Mr. Imagai actually made his way through six separate breasts before he was finally satiated. Then, Nurse Kurihara held him and patted him on the back till he let out a contented burp and said, "I want to get back to work. Tell Nakasane Ichū to come see me."

Mr. Nakasane immediately came over with five underlings, and they proceeded to brief Mr. Imagai on Western Steel's developments over the preceding month. Mr. Imagai sat in the nurse's arms continually issuing instructions in a decisive manner as he listened to the reports. The sight of six grown men standing respectfully in front of a large-headed infant was truly a remarkable sight.

However, I didn't have time to appreciate the scene. I ordered my underlings to immediately go find several more wet nurses. Based on the appetite Mr. Imagai had shown just now, I estimated that three nurses would soon fail to suffice. Confirmation of my decision was not long in coming as Mr. Imagai's appetite quickly soared, vastly exceeding everyone's expectations. By the seventh day he needed ten wet nurses, two weeks later he needed twenty-five, and a month later the number grew to a hundred. His growth was even more astonishing, and if you stood next to him as he nursed, you could almost see his body's inexorable growth.

The nurses' remuneration had also been arranged by Mr. Imagai prior to his "reincarnation." The terms of their employment were similar to my own, in that they were allowed to choose between two payment options. One option involved a high fixed salary, while the other offered instead a low salary with a bonus of twenty million J dollars a year later. Most of the nurses chose the second option, since for these poor women the lure of twenty million J dollars was virtually irresistible. However, most of them were ultimately unable to collect their bonuses, since they typically ended up fleeing after only a month or two. There were two reasons for this. First, this large infant (by this point he was already as big as a ten-year-old boy) was simply too greedy and would often continue nursing until he started drawing blood, thereby causing the nurses excruciating pain. The second reason is harder to explain. When Mr. Imagai grabbed the nurses' breasts as he was nursing, his eyes too were busy at work. There was a trace of evil in his gaze, which was definitely unlike the way a normal infant would view its mother's "nursies" (breasts). I had actually noticed this look early on but hadn't told anyone. I knew that in this infant's body, Imagai's well-developed male instincts were already awakened, and that he probably regarded the wet nurses as the full-breasted Ms. Komatsu Yoshiko.

All I could do was strive to increase our supply of wet nurses. Originally, Mr. Imagai had insisted that I recruit only domestically, since he wanted to guarantee that he would be consuming only "pure milk from the people of the rising sun." But by this point we already needed a thousand wet nurses, and it proved impossible to assemble that large a corps of nurses drawing solely from domestic sources. After my repeated entreaties, Imagai finally agreed to loosen his criteria and permitted me to recruit from the third world.

I quickly found the requisite number of wet nurses and told Mr. Imagai that most of the new recruits had opted for the first compensation option. I explained that these unenlightened women were all rather shortsighted, and that they regarded as real money only that which they could pocket immediately. I claimed to have no choice but to abide by their requests, though in reality I had secretly persuaded them to take this option, since I couldn't bear to see them fleeing empty-handed.

Of course, there were always some nurses who didn't believe my good intentions and insisted on receiving the second compensation option. When I found myself secretly pitying them, I couldn't help wondering whether I was any smarter? Perhaps there was no basis for comparison, since I had, after all, basically already succeeded, and my twenty percent stake in Western Steel was virtually in hand. However, I couldn't be sure that Kiminao was not secretly pitying me, just as I was secretly pitying the wet nurses. He, after all, was working for a fixed salary.

We left the hospital and moved into the Prince Hotel owned by the Imagai dynasty. The hotel was closed to outside business, because the need to provide room and board for a thousand wet nurses had exhausted its capacity. Every day, a continuous procession of nurses marched in and out of Mr. Imagai's room, like images on a revolving lantern. This chain of nurses seemed interminable, and the daily consumption of a thousand nurses' two thousand breasts was a truly enormous undertaking. Imagai continued to grow at an amazing rate, and within three months he was already 1.7 meters tall. His growth could no longer be described with terms like "felt like" and "was like," and now, if you stood next to him while he nursed, you could actually see his body inflating like a balloon. I was awed by this sight and wondered what other being could have such exceptional vitality combined with such a strong desire for possession? Without a doubt, the directives for this growth came from Imagai's brain and not from his corporeal host. To think that the anencephalic infant's body could, upon receiving instructions from Imagai's brain, become so powerful was something absolutely incredible. No one else in the world could have accomplished this, and therefore you cannot but bow down before this exceptional man.

Today, Mr. Kiminao and Mr. Nakasane hurried over with some bad news. Kiminao reported that domestic public opinion had gradually become antagonistic, and many people had come to believe that it is unconscionable for a tycoon to avoid his obligations to pay estate tax by abusing science and repeatedly replacing his body so as to maintain his position in the world. The public therefore was urging relevant governmental departments to take appropriate actions, but legal experts reported that the law had no authority over this matter since it could not strip Mr. Imagai of his rights, given that his brain was in fact still alive, not to mention the fact that he had filed a petition preemptively guaranteeing his right to be represented by his brain. As Kiminao and Nakasane discussed these matters, Mr. Imagai did not stop nursing. He merely watched them out of the corner of his eye, and then said coldly, "As long as the law has no authority over me, public opinion is not worth squat!"

Kiminao looked at Nakasane, who said anxiously, "Public opinion should not be underestimated. There are some powerful figures with considerable political influence already severing their ties to Western Steel, including even . . . the prime minister, who has always had a special relationship with us."

Imagai didn't stop nursing but after a while said calmly, "Then we should turn public opinion around. This is very easy. Find several of our reporters and have them write stories around the 'infant' in order to stir up society's maternal instincts."

Kiminao at once began to nod repeatedly, appearing to recognize the brilliance of this suggestion right away. He and Nakasane briefly discussed the details of how to carry this out, then stood up and prepared to leave. At this point I took the opportunity to offer a suggestion: "Mr. Imagai, the expense of a thousand wet nurses is too great. You already have the body of a fifteen-year-old and a mouth full of teeth. Why don't you try eating solid food?"

Before Kiminao and Nakasane had a chance to express an opinion on this matter, Imagai responded furiously, "You want to deprive me of my right to breast milk? Don't forget, no matter how big my body might be, I am still only two months old, and it is my sacred right to feed on breast milk. I want to nurse for at least a year before weaning." He added coldly, "Don't worry about your shares— the cost of a thousand wet nurses won't make a dent in my fortune."

I was left speechless. How I wanted to spit in this monster's face and stalk off. However, I couldn't help thinking about the shares that were soon to be mine. I was annoyed to discover that after Mr. Imagai's transfer to his new body, his temper had deteriorated, to the point that he now acted like a spoiled child. Mr. Kiminao turned to me and smoothly changed the subject: "I'm sure Mr. Imagai realizes that your suggestion was well meant, and I hope you will not take offense. But the topic of weaning need not be raised again. Mr. Imagai's health remains our foremost consideration."

Mr. Kiminao is very talented, and he effortlessly turned public opinion around. His solution was very simple—namely, to strategically release a dozen photographs of Mr. Imagai's new existence, photos that we had previously kept in strict confidence. They were labeled,
—A large-headed infant is born
—He nurses sweetly
—The wet nurses watch him tenderly
And so forth.
All these photographs concealed Imagai's icy glare and gave the impression that he was nothing more than a weak and helpless infant, an ingratiating little fellow. Who, on seeing these images, could possibly bear Imagai any ill will? Who could continue to regard him as a financial predator intent on devouring billions in tax revenues?
Seeing the positive response to these photographs, Mr. Kiminao continued releasing similar images, in chronological order:
—Today, little Imagai grew eleven millimeters!
—Look at the 1.2-meter-tall two-month-old (excluding the six months that the anencephalic infant had been alive)!
—The nursing infant is already taller than his wet nurse!
—Observe little Imagai's appetite: one thousand wet nurses take turns nursing him!
These photographs were hilarious, and after they had been released they naturally influenced Mr. Imagai's "awe-inspiring" reputation. I thought that no one would ever again fear him like a god. In fact, it was precisely this hilariousness that effectively neutralized the public enmity

toward him. When the public saw these photographs, after laughing uproariously they couldn't help but regard him as their own child.

⸙

I, however, committed an inexcusable technical mistake. As the little Imagai was eating ravenously and growing by leaps and bounds, I was so amazed at his extraordinary vitality and desire for possession that it didn't even occur to me to consider whether he might exceed his growth limit. I thought that even though he was growing at an astounding rate, he was merely advancing on and compressing the growth a normal person would experience, and I assumed that once he reached a certain height, such as around two meters, he would stop. I thought at most he would not exceed two and a half meters, which is humanity's height limit. All living things have their own growth limit, a secret code inscribed by God into their genes, and in the millions of years of its operation, this limit has never failed. But I hadn't anticipated that Mr. Imagai would be even more powerful than God.

When Mr. Imagai's height began to approach two meters, I belatedly tested his pituitary gland and skeletal growth. When the results came in, I anxiously came to the nursing room and asked the wet nurses to step out for a moment. Then I reported guiltily, "Mr. Imagai, I think we have a problem."

Mr. Imagai looked very annoyed at having been interrupted from his nursing and replied with a frown, "Out with it! And, remember, I don't want to hear useless excuses."

I forced a smile: "First, the good news. Your neurological exam reveals that everything is excellent—exceeding even my most optimistic expectations. The original cranial cavity has already been filled with regenerated nerve tissue, and the 'brown' tissue (as a brain ages, it accumulates waste) has been greatly reduced, almost all reabsorbed by the body. I can state with certainty that your seventy-two-year-old brain has already accepted the infant's body's commands, thereby effectively 'resetting' your internal clock."

Imagai nodded, "Good, as I expected. The money I paid you has not been wasted."

"However, I also have some bad news. The results of another test reveal that your body has forgotten its command to stop growing once it reaches a certain size, and as a result you may very well continue growing without limit." I explained how the commands normally control a body's growth, such as how the epiphyseal plates of the spine and bones ordinarily shut down once someone reaches a certain age, meaning that the person's height will also stop increasing. And also how a body's cells are normally controlled by a certain "restrain on contact" command, such that when the surrounding cells start crowding one another, they will automatically stop dividing—the only exception being cancer cells. But now, Mr. Imagai's body had forgotten all these self-regulating commands and was continuing to grow unchecked. I concluded, "It is very strange, but somehow your brain has managed to alter God's commands. I'm afraid I had never anticipated this possibility."

Imagai replied casually, "What's wrong with that? I think I own land enough to hold my body, regardless of whether I am two meters tall or a hundred. No matter how tall I grow, I will never go hungry." Over the past few days he had already become quite overweight and consequently kept gasping for air when he spoke. Panting, he continued, "Perhaps a hundred-meter-tall body would be justly suited to my vast wealth. I'm not afraid of becoming a living Bamiyan Buddha."

I laughed bitterly. "No, it is not that simple. You should know that the strength of any animal's skeletal structure is proportional to the square of its height, while its weight is proportional to the cube of its height. That is to say, your weight will eventually outstrip the strength of your skeletal structure, which is why there are inherent limits to how large animals can grow. The largest terrestrial animal, for instance, is currently the African elephant, which can weigh up to six or seven tonnes. African elephants, however, never lie down until they topple over after dying—because if they did, their internal organs would be crushed by their weight. The largest terrestrial animals that ever lived, meanwhile, were the sauropods, which could weigh up to a hundred tonnes. This is also the weight limit for terrestrial animals." I added in concern, "Mr. Imagai, from your current growth trajectory, it is entirely possible that you may grow to be larger than a sauropod, in which case your own weight will eventually cause your body to collapse."

Once he realized the seriousness of the matter, he was silent for a moment. Then he said coldly, "It's your responsibility to figure out what to do. I'm not paying you this much money to have you simply come and show me a grim face."

I had no defense and merely retorted softly, "But all my trials on animals were successful. You yourself know that in all the trials, the transplanted brains were reset and rejuvenated, while the growth rate of the host body remained normal and within its normal growth limit. I suspect that your condition is a result of your particular character. Perhaps your desire for possession is simply too strong—so strong as to have exceeded God's commands. I have already tried using drugs to control this, but with no apparent effect."

Imagai was furious. "I won't change my nature simply because of your ineptitude. Stop telling me nonsense about gods and go figure out a solution." He added caustically, "I know you will work hard on this, since you still want your twenty percent stake in Western Steel."

On this particular day I didn't dare talk back to him, because I truly was in the wrong. I said guiltily, "I will do my best. But if it turns out that there really is no solution, you will have no choice but to live temporarily in water. The maximum weight limit on animals can increase substantially if they are in water, since its buoyancy can help support their weight. Whales, for instance, are among the biggest animals that have ever lived, and the weight of blue whales can reach 180 tonnes, which is more than even the sauropods. Once we have transferred you to water, I will find a solution as quickly as possible."

4. SUDDEN GREATNESS

Four months later, I still had not come up with a means of controlling his growth process, but by this point Imagai had reached six meters. I had workers convert a three-story-high hall into a bedroom, since he was already too large to cram into conventional rooms. This solution, however, was only temporary, and I needed to quickly come up with another, given that within a few days he would be so large that there would be no way of getting him out the front door. Imagai's appetite and growth rate had shown no signs of diminishing. A thousand wet nurses came and went through the passage on the third floor that led to the hall, where they leaned against the railing to nurse Mr. Imagai, who stood on the first floor—the scene rather like a giraffe eating leaves from trees.

I hesitated for a few days before finally making the hard decision to move him to water. Of course, the most convenient thing would have been to move him to a lake, but, unfortunately, although Mr. Imagai owned one-sixth of the country's land, that vast territory—indeed, the whole country—didn't contain a lake large enough to hold him (because we also had to take into consideration his future growth). At that point I truly regretted that our ancestors had not had the foresight to lay claim to Lake Baikal or the Great Lakes. In the end, we decided to take him to the ocean, and more specifically the area around Australia's Norfolk Islands. It was fairly warm there, and the water quality was excellent. Australia was also a close ally, and therefore everything could be managed.

We leased a ten-thousand-tonne freighter and transformed it into an enormous richly decorated bedroom, the ceiling of which could be pulled away for loading purposes. I exhorted the workers to work around the clock, because Mr. Imagai's growth was bearing down on me and we didn't have a second to spare. After seven days, all the preparations were complete. We leased the country's biggest, fifty-six-wheel, nine-hundred-tonne flatbed freight truck to transport him to the harbor, and then used an eight-hundred-tonne crane to lower him into the freighter. We then closed the roof and transported him to his destination, where we used another, five-hundred-tonne ship-mounted crane to lift him back out. After seeing him safely lowered into the ocean, I finally let out a long sigh of relief.

His body-fat percentage was quite high and, together with the fact that the relative density of the salty ocean water was also quite high, he didn't even need to swim but simply floated effortlessly in the water. He immediately liked his new environment, because after he entered the water his breathing at once became more relaxed as the pressure on his internal organs was eliminated. This mountain-sized creature floated comfortably in the calm ocean water, shifting his position periodically, sometimes on his back, and sometimes on his side, all very relaxed.

A J-nation destroyer cruised around nearby, and a team of twenty frogmen in black wet suits patrolled the surrounding waters to protect him. The destroyer and frogmen were leased by the day from J-nation's military at enormous expense. Although Imagai had a very close relationship with the prime minister and the head of defense, they didn't dare let him use the military for free. I circled around him several times in a motorboat, and seeing his enormous body, I couldn't help thinking that he was, without a doubt, the largest and greatest person that had ever lived— and there was no end in sight to the process of his becoming even greater.

It had been ten months since Mr. Imagai was "transplanted" into his new body, but if you counted the six months that the anencephalic infant had been alive before the transplant, he was now already sixteen months old. Yet he still insisted on nursing and was determined to maintain his sacred right as an infant and drink breast milk for at least one year. But by this point his appetite had already exceeded the capacity of a thousand wet nurses, and besides, it would have been too much trouble to have had all these nurses follow him into the ocean. In selecting this particular region, however, I had already come up with an excellent solution to the problem—namely, to have him drink whale milk. A mother whale can produce four hundred fifty liters of nutritious milk a day, and furthermore it was completely free. I wouldn't even need to worry about the number of wet nurses. As the southern Pacific alone had several thousand blue whales, there would be more than enough wet nurses.

I happened to know that in Australia there was a "whale professor" who had just retired. This old fellow treated the whales like old pals and could summon an entire pod using an artificial whale whistle. Kiminao managed to track him down and, deploying all his formidable negotiating skills, managed to convince him to cooperate with us, on the condition that we would donate a large sum of money to global whale conservation efforts. But we came out even, given that this amounted to the equivalent of what we were already spending on our one thousand wet nurses.

What was more of a challenge, however, was convincing Imagai to accept whale milk instead of human breast milk. Before setting out, I discussed this with Kiminao. The latter was worried, but I already had a plan. I knew that although Mr. Imagai could be extremely stubborn, when confronted with matters of life and death he tended to be quite realistic. For example, when it turned out that there were not enough wet nurses to be found in our own country, he gave up his insistence on ethnic purity and agreed to use women from the third world. This time was no different. I patiently explained why we had to use whale milk and noted that whale milk is so nutritious that a whale calf can gain up to ninety kilograms a day. Having already grown accustomed to drinking breast milk, Mr. Imagai was naturally not very happy about this arrangement, and he glared at me darkly for a long time before finally assenting.

A motorboat came toward us, with the gray-haired whale professor standing proudly in it, using whale songs to summon the pod behind him. We could barely hear his songs, which, at twenty hertz are near the limit of the range of human hearing. Behind him were more than twenty plumes of water shooting into the sky, one after the other. They rose almost ten meters high and were accompanied by enormous roars. As the whales approached, it became evident that it was a pod of blue whales, around forty in all, with light-colored speckles on their navy or gray-colored bodies. About seventeen to eighteen females were in lactation, each followed by several calves. The professor sent out another call, and a mother whale obediently swam over to Mr. Imagai's side and curiously gazed at this huge nursling with her small eyes. Blue whales are astonishingly large, and it is said that fifty men can stand on one's tongue. A blue whale's heart is as large as a car, and its arteries so large that a human infant could crawl through them. But today the human race had no reason to feel inferior before them; we now had an outstanding representative who could match them in size.

The professor waved his hand, and one of the frogmen swam over and affixed a sucker to one of the whale's teats. I don't know how the whale professor managed to convince the whale to go nurse a surrogate offspring belonging to another species, but somehow the whale waited patiently. The sucker was connected to a tube as thick as a fireman's hose, which in turn was connected to a rubber nipple that Imagai grabbed and began to suck ravenously. We hadn't brought the thousand wet nurses along on this journey, and he had had only bottled cow's milk to drink, so he was famished. The tubing was transparent, and you could see the white milk rushing through it and into his huge, dark mouth. This female whale's teats were soon sucked dry but Imagai, who was still hungry for milk was reluctant to relinquish the nipple and instead continued to suck ravenously. The flow of white milk in the tubing slowed, even as it started to carry traces of blood. The whale twisted its body in pain, kicking up furious waves with its tail. The whale professor and I both noticed this and quickly sent the frogman to disconnect the sucker. The whale quickly escaped, as though it had just been granted a reprieve.

The whale professor was beside himself with rage and began cursing furiously, adamantly refusing to let the frogmen touch any of the other whales. He had been convinced to cooperate with us in part because of the massive sum we had promised to donate to global whale conservation, and in part because of his adventurous personality—he said that it would certainly be very interesting to see a whale nurse a human surrogate offspring. But he had never expected that the human would be so greedy that he would injure his whale "sisters." The professor continued to curse and, ignoring my pleadings, insisted on leading his whales away. I was at a loss as to what to do. I smiled bitterly at Mr. Imagai, but since his authority had no purchase over this "whale blood brother," he wisely quieted down and didn't say a word. At this crucial moment, it was again his lawyer, Kiminao, who came up with a solution. He approached in a skiff, pulled up alongside the professor's motorboat, and proceeded to angrily upbraid him: "Professor, how can you be so cruel to a child? Yes, it is true that he sucked too greedily, but he was simply hungry. He hadn't had any decent milk the entire trip out here and therefore was absolutely famished. Regardless of his size, he's still only ten months old. He's just a child, he doesn't understand anything. How could he know that he should be so restrained in drinking his milk? Can you in good conscience just leave and let him starve to death?"

The professor was placated by this stern chastising. Although he was still furious, he nevertheless halted his efforts to depart. The lawyer immediately adopted a more pleasant tone and said, "Professor, don't be childish about this. As long as we explain the situation to him, he definitely won't be as greedy next time. Let's try again, okay?"

I was also on the boat with Kiminao as he talked and was very worried that Imagai would say or do something that would let the professor know that he wasn't actually a naive nursling. Even if Imagai didn't speak or do anything at all, if the professor were to catch a glimpse of his cold and calculating eyes, he would immediately see right through the lawyer's false claims. Fortunately, however, we were in the open ocean, and Imagai was several dozen meters away, and consequently the professor couldn't see the expression in his eyes. He hesitated for a long time but finally acceded. He, however, asked us to first guarantee that no further harm would come to his whales, to which we at once agreed.

The skiff then went alongside Imagai, and Kiminao, stern faced and angry, said in a low voice, "Why did you have to be so greedy? There are seventeen or eighteen female whales here—you think you'll go hungry? Next time you need to have more restraint, or even I won't be able to fix things!"

Imagai had never heard the lawyer speak to him in such a tone of disrespect. He glared back angrily, making Kiminao reflexively look away. But, as I said, when it came to matters of life and death, Mr. Imagai was very realistic. He knew that although what Kiminao said was unpleasant to hear, it nevertheless needed to be obeyed. Therefore, he silently acceded, whereupon another whale wet nurse was sent over, and Imagai once again started sucking greedily, but without making the same mistake as before.

A month passed, and the whales gradually came to love this big surrogate offspring. Every day more than a dozen whales would punctually come over and nurse him until he was sated, and it got to the point where they would come even if the professor wasn't present. After the whales finished nursing, they would often hang out around him for a long time, calling in low voices as though they were trying to converse with him. The whale calves grew quite accustomed to their surrogate brother and would use their snouts to play with him. However, Imagai did not have any interest in this sort of thing, and when he wasn't nursing he would hasten to take care of the many reports from home. It occurred to me that these calves were really very generous, since whenever it was one of the mother whales' turn to nurse Imagai, her own calf had to go hungry. Despite this, they seemed to bear no resentment toward this enormous milk-snatching little brother.

With the help of these wet nurses with such strong maternal instincts, together with their nutritious milk, Mr. Imagai achieved greatness even more rapidly. By now he was already twice as big as the mother whales themselves—and you mustn't forget that these were blue whales that were more than thirty meters in length—making him the biggest creature that the world had ever seen. According to my calculations, by this point he was already sixty meters tall and weighed more than three hundred tonnes. His head was like a mountain, his nostrils like the caves of Ali Baba, and each of his body hairs was thicker than a rat's tail. I decided to wait a little longer, until I had some free time, before submitting this as a new Guinness world record for the biggest and most massive animal that had ever lived.

When first deciding to transfer Imagai to the open ocean, there remained the very difficult problem of safety. There were sharks and killer whales in these waters, and they would undoubtedly be very interested in this big chunk of flesh. Therefore, we hired a warship and a team of frogmen to patrol the waters around the clock. Eventually, however, we discovered that this was not necessary. Sharks and killer whales did indeed approach, but they merely circled around Imagai at a safe distance and then quietly slunk away, not daring to have any designs on him. Were they intimidated by his great size? I suspect not. When the first killer whale paid a visit, Imagai was not yet as large as the blue whales, and the fierce killer whale has no qualms about attacking even blue whales and giant squid. It was only afterward that I realized that Mr. Imagai had unwittingly set up a system of self-defense. Having such an insatiable appetite, he naturally also produced enormous amounts of excreta, to the point that the sea water surrounding him had become quite noxious, driving off all sea creatures. Eventually, there was not a single living creature within a radius of ten nautical miles, giving him a defensive perimeter that was even more effective than the imperial army's Sankō Sakusen, or Three Alls Policy.[2] We remained on the ship, while a nauseatingly intense smell of ammonia assaulted our noses. Only the mother whales continued to approach and nurse him, not disgusted by him at all, solid proof of the fact that motherly love conquers all.

5. JOYS AND SORROWS OF A FIRST BIRTHDAY

Another twelve days, and it would be Imagai's first birthday (not including the six months that the anencephalic infant had lived before the transplant). This was a day worth celebrating—for both Mr. Imagai and myself. On this day, I would become a twenty percent stakeholder in

Western Steel, which would immediately put me at the top of the Forbes 500 list. I would become a god of the neurosurgical world, and history would commemorate the brain transplant technique I had developed.

We began preparing for the celebration. Needless to say, we couldn't publicly announce this as a first birthday. Imagai's legal age was seventy-three, and if we were to openly acknowledge that he was only a year old, he would no longer be able to avoid paying estate taxes. We had already spent several hundreds of billions on this endeavor and weren't about to commit that sort of stupid mistake. On the other hand, it's true that Imagai's new body was in fact only a year old, and we therefore devoted considerable attention to deciding what precisely to call this celebration. Nakasane came up with a name that he thought sounded pleasing—First Spirit-Transference Year. Kiminao, however, pointed out that it is only after people die and are buried that you can speak of their spirit's being transferred. After further discussion, we decided that we had no choice but to call it something along the lines of a first anniversary of the operation. This didn't sound at all impressive, and Imagai was very displeased with it, but since no one was able to come up with anything better he ultimately had to agree.

Given that it was not easy for Imagai to travel because of his enormous body, we had little choice but to hold the celebration right here in the middle of the ocean. Many important political figures were expected. The prime minister would certainly attend, since Mr. Imagai had long had a close relationship with him and had donated massive sums dozens at times to his political campaigns, and when the prime minister convened meetings of his party faction, he always held them in the Prince Hotel owned by Imagai's empire. Because recent public opinion had not been very favorable, the prime minister had been trying to distance himself from Imagai. By now, however, the controversy had already begun to pass and the prime minister didn't need to continue maintaining his distance. He would, furthermore, be accompanied by a large group of representatives from the government and both houses of parliament. Imagai's two sons naturally couldn't come, because if they did and were faced with their one-year-old father, it would be extremely awkward. I wish to note, however, that Ms. Komatsu Yoshiko, whom I had theretofore looked down upon, was actually quite gracious. During this past year, Mr. Imagai had not needed her special services and had therefore cut her sixty million J dollars monthly salary to the point that she had no choice but to find another sugar daddy to help cover her living expenses. She nevertheless still missed Mr. Imagai such that she was willing to come attend this celebration at her own expense. I wondered, however, how she might react when she saw this gargantuan one-year-old.

Imagai had remained naked ever since we transferred him to the ocean. The reason for this was very simple: if he were to wear clothes, they would need to be larger than theater curtains, and it would have been simply too difficult to put them on and take them off. Besides, the water wasn't cold, and Imagai was able to do perfectly well without clothes. But this time was different, since he couldn't very well have his penis hanging out when he hugged the prime minister on such a dignified occasion. We discussed the matter and eventually decided to make him a special bib that would cover his chest and genitals. His rear would still be exposed, but since he had grown accustomed to floating faceup in the water, the bib would be just sufficient to provide him with some modicum of respectability if he retained the same posture during the ceremony—though, needless to say, even to provide this minimal amount of coverage the bib would need to be astonishingly large.

The stench from Mr. Imagai was becoming increasingly unbearable. We ourselves had been there for so long that we had gotten used to it, but visiting dignitaries definitely would not be able to handle it. We also came up with a solution wherein we would relocate Mr. Imagai to a different area of the ocean for the day of the ceremony, then use helicopters to help disperse the smell by sprinkling perfume in the area. There was yet one major concern: Imagai had finally agreed to wean himself as of the following day. After the ceremony, the whale wet nurses would bid him farewell and a specially outfitted culinary ship built under the supervision of Mr. Nakasane would anchor nearby. The ship would be equipped with fifty cooks and automated cooking equipment, and every day they would be able to produce thirty tonnes of sushi or other food, which would be sufficient to satisfy Mr. Imagai's appetite.

All preparations having been made, all we had to do was wait for the day of the ceremony.

———∞———

It had already been three months since Mr. Imagai had been transferred to the ocean, and we were very fortunate that, during this period, the weather had remained generally calm. Kiminao laughed and said that this was because Mr. Imagai was blessed with good fortune. No one expected, therefore, that a storm would suddenly develop two days before the anniversary celebration. Actually, it was two storms: a political storm followed by a meteorological one.

To begin with, we received the tragic news unexpectedly from home that the police had discovered Mr. Nakasane dead in his apartment, having committed suicide. It turned out that the police had long been secretly investigating Western Steel's financial irregularities, including its concealment of the true proportion of shares held, its release of falsified financial statements, as well as its secret manipulation of its stock price. Two days earlier, the police had summoned Nakasane and confronted him with evidence that was so damning that he had no choice but to confess to everything. Undoubtedly feeling too humiliated to face his master, he proceeded to take his own life that same night.

Just as the news of Nakasane's suicide arrived, our patch of the ocean experienced its first storm since our arrival. Heavy clouds hovered over us, the sky grew dark, and the wind blew up enormous waves four to five meters high. The destroyer rocked violently in the waves, and the frogmen who should have been patrolling the waters had to retreat temporarily to the safety of the ship. Mr. Imagai, however, was not affected by the storm and remained perfectly at ease floating in the ocean. His enormous body flattened out the waves, and the wind merely rocked him gently back and forth. During those days, we had gotten into the habit of calling his body Imagai Island, and he even became our safe harbor; the little skiff that I was riding on now was tied to his little toe.

Thunder echoed through the sky, but the sound was vastly inferior to Imagai's own roaring. With his enormous mouth, his enormous vocal cords, and with the resonance provided by his even more enormous chest, his angry curses stirred up distinctively shaped waves that were even fiercer than the ones produced by the storm itself. "Good-for-nothings! Incompetent jackasses! You can't even resolve minor matters like these? Western Steel has been handling things this way for decades, and it's no different from how most other consortiums handle them. It was only during the short time when he was serving as acting director that problems occurred!"

In my view, his fury was not unreasonable. If Imagai had maintained his position at the helm of the company, I'm confident that he could have easily dealt with this situation using his finesse and his prestige, but Mr. Nakasane's ability and prestige were both significantly inferior to Imagai's. Imagai's fury, meanwhile, compromised my respect for him, since, as everyone knows, anger is generally an expression of ineptitude. I thought regretfully that it looked as though the body of the anencephalic infant was beginning to have a negative influence on Imagai, making him act increasingly juvenile.

Imagai roared at me, telling me to send for Kiminao immediately. The lawyer had returned home a couple of days earlier to receive the prime minister and other distinguished guests and then to escort them back to see Imagai. I was sure, however, that once Kiminao arrived home he would have heard the bad news, and he therefore should have notified Imagai at the first opportunity. Why, then, was there still no news from him? I used a maritime telephone to contact Kiminao, and a young woman who identified herself as a nurse answered the phone. It turned out that when Kiminao heard the news, he suffered a stroke and fell into a coma from which he had still not awakened. I piloted my skiff up to Imagai's ear and, shouting over the storm, notified him of this development. He became even more furious: "That old fox! He merely wants to escape a sinking ship!"

I was initially very displeased with his slander of Kiminao. Just think of Kiminao, who was so anxious and upset about Western Steel that he had a sudden stroke, and it is not clear even now whether or not he will survive. But now that I think about it with a cooler head, it was also possible that Imagai might have been right. Kiminao, back home, had a better grasp of the current crisis than we did and simply wasn't willing to wade into those troubled waters. As a lawyer, however, it would have been far too unprofessional of him to have simply run away from the crisis, which would have led him to lose all professional credibility. With this stroke, however, people would become sympathetic and stop criticizing him. Yes, perhaps this is what had happened. Imagai and Kiminao had been working together for the past forty years, so he must have understood his lawyer better than I.

The storm raged all night, but by the next morning the wind and waves had died down a little. A seaplane flew over and circled a couple of times around Imagai's head before landing, with difficulty, in the ocean nearby. I wondered whether it was Kiminao coming to rejoin us despite his illness? I quickly went over in my skiff, but it turned out that it was the J-nation imperial police, coming to arrest Imagai. It seemed to me that these police must have been real bumpkins and never watched the news, since they appeared to have no idea how great the criminal whom they were coming to arrest was. They piloted a skiff up to Imagai Island and, dumbfounded, craned their necks to gaze up at the mountainous body. Needless to say, their seaplane would never hold the gargantuan creature in front of them, not even one of his feet. All they could do, therefore, was to read the arrest warrant aloud, ordering Mr. Imagai to remain in the area and wait until the police returned with a freighter. Then they awkwardly reboarded the plane and flew away.

I immediately used the maritime phone to call up my family. It turned out that the current actions against Western Steel were not so simple: crippled by a disastrous domestic economy, the government could no longer afford to ignore the rampant corruption that ran through the financial sector and therefore decided to make an example of Western Steel. The prime minister's spokesman had already announced that the prime minister had no connection whatsoever with Western Steel, explaining that the prime minister used to hold his political faction meetings in Western Steel's Prince Hotel simply on account of the hotel's high-quality service and not because of any personal connections.

When I remembered that this same prime minister had almost attended the anniversary celebrations, I came to truly appreciate the meaning of the phrase "political animal."

But I didn't have time to worry about these trivia, since I was confronted with an even more immediate problem. We had originally planned to have Mr. Imagai wean the next day, but for some reason the culinary ship never arrived, even though the whales had stopped coming a day early. Given that the whales don't read the paper, watch television, or listen to the radio, there was obviously no way they could have known about Imagai's political difficulties, so their unannounced departure could not have been because of any snobbishness on their part. Perhaps this was the doing of the whale professor? Perhaps he didn't want his whales to continue nourishing someone whose misdeeds had been exposed and therefore secretly told them to depart? I didn't know, and at this point I didn't have the energy to investigate. At any rate, the immediate result of these developments was that Imagai didn't have anything to eat. He was at first so furious that he momentarily forgot about his hunger, but it was soon so great that it even surpassed his anger at his political difficulties, and by noon he was in a towering rage. He cursed furiously, "Bastards! Derelicts! Quick, go fix me something to eat! If I don't get enough for lunch, I'm going to take it out of your remuneration."

His threats were needless since I was already frantic. I repeatedly called the culinary ship and the whale professor, but neither of them answered. I therefore had no choice but to ask Mr. Imagai to forsake his "sacred right to mother's milk" a day early and immediately switch over to normal food. As I've mentioned before, Imagai was realistic in regard to such major events, and, after cursing me some more, he agreed. I quickly returned to the destroyer and asked them for all the food they had onboard. I then used the skiff to ferry the food over to Imagai Island and asked a sailor by the name of Sakagawa to unload the food right into Imagai's cavernous mouth. After ferrying three boatfuls of food, I finally managed to blunt Imagai's hunger. By that point Sakagawa and I were so exhausted that we had lost our own appetites. From receiving the news of Nakasane's suicide the previous morning until now, I hadn't slept for one second. I was therefore exhausted and promptly fell asleep curled up on the deck of the boat.

I slept till dinner, until Mr. Imagai's roars and the seaman's shaking woke me up. Sakagawa asked in horror, "Mr. Motose, why has the warship that was protecting us left?" I forced my eyes open and looked off into the distance. Under the vast skies, there remained only the turbid waves rising and falling against the horizon. There was no trace of the ship. It suddenly occurred to me that the contract between Western Steel and the navy ended today, and beyond that, I had already ransacked all the food from the ship. From both legal and logical points of view, therefore, it was perfectly understandable that it had left. But from our perspective it was exceedingly callous for it to have departed like this without notice. Perhaps the navy, too, had had enough of Imagai's surliness and couldn't wait to get away.

Imagai continued to bellow, demanding his dinner. This was a con-tractual obligation from which I couldn't extricate myself, and it was also his sacred right as a one-year-old child, so he paid no attention to the world's collapsing around him. But I was already at my wits' end. Sak-agawa was the only other crew member on the skiff with me, and we scarcely had any food or fresh water left. Neither did we have any fishing equipment, and even if we had, it still wouldn't have done any good, because even if we were to catch a few fish, they wouldn't be enough to fill the cracks between Imagai's teeth. I pondered this for a while and then told my loyal Sakagawa, "You should pilot the boat as fast as you can to the nearest of the Norfolk Islands and do whatever is necessary to find some food and fresh water for tomorrow. I will contact home again and make follow-up arrangements. You should go alone and return as soon as you can. I must remain here; this is my responsibility, and I cannot forsake it."

I left the skiff and climbed up Mr. Imagai's leg onto Imagai Island. Sak-agawa threw me our last two bags of compressed biscuit and a few bottles of water and then set off, the sound of his motor gradually fading away in the night. The food and fresh water were enough to last me one day, but I couldn't consume them myself and instead had to go to feed that insa-tiable mouth—even though, to him, such a tiny amount of food amounted to virtually nothing.

There were no trees or boulders to support me on the human island, but there were body hairs everywhere, each as thick as a rat's tail, and consequently it was not hard to clamber up. I grabbed a few of his hairs and carefully proceeded forward, all the time worrying that I would tum-ble off the convex surface of his rotund body. From his calf, I proceeded to his thigh and then on to his torso and chest, until finally I was stand-ing near his Adam's apple. I stood up and raised the food high, barely managing to get it into his mouth. I said guiltily, "Mr. Imagai, we have only this tiny bit of food and water today. But if you can bear it just for one night, we'll bring more tomorrow."

Imagai was already so famished that he didn't have the energy to be angry. In fact, he didn't even have energy enough to speak. After swal-lowing the food, he closed his eyes and lay there limply without moving, like a corpse. I didn't bother him anymore and instead lay down in the depression under his clavicle, closed my eyes, and dozed off. I felt bad for him. Over the past year I had come to a deep understanding of his appetite, so I profoundly sympathized with him. For him, to miss a meal is truly the most barbarous punishment imaginable. I was terrified by the thought of this gargantuan eating machine's surviving for at least another seventy or eighty years (and this is assuming that he didn't have another reincarnation). How many natural resources would need to be shoveled into this enormous mouth over the next seventy or eighty years, only to be transformed into excrement? Needless to say, however, though his wealth had been significantly diminished as a result of the current scandal, he would still have more than enough to satisfy his enormous appetite.

At this point I couldn't help but think of my twenty percent stake in Western Steel. The assets of the Western Steel Group had shrunk, and the shares would probably no longer be enough to place me on the Forbes 500 list, but they would certainly still be sufficient to make me a very rich man. I would be able to send my son to an expensive private university, buy my wife name-brand clothes and cosmetics, and provide my entire family with top-quality medical care. I had dedicated myself to working for Imagai for the past couple of decades and consequently had spent very little time with my wife and son. I felt I truly owed them, and if I could offer them even this shrunken fortune, I would be satisfied. This perspective, however, was merely what I created to comfort myself in my despair.

I glanced down at my waterproof watch and saw that it was already 12:05 A.M. The "survive for one year" condition in my contract had finally been satisfied. That is to say, even if Mr. Imagai were to starve to death right now, the shares would still be rightfully mine. Of course, it was somewhat immoral to think this way, and I certainly had no intention of letting him starve to death. The contract had finally come to term, and I certainly wouldn't agree to extend it. I had already had enough of this job and of Mr. Imagai. Before leaving, however, I would certainly make all appropriate arrangements. This was part of my conscience as a doctor.

I had already spent an entire day without food or water. I was feeling sharp hunger pangs, and my throat was now so dry that it felt like it was burning up. I couldn't sleep, and by the time the sun was about to come up I found myself in a daze and felt my body slowly levitating. I struggled to open my eyes and found myself suspended several dozen meters in the air. Terrified, I looked around and discovered that I was in the palm of

Mr. Imagai's right hand. The creases in his skin were as deep as mountain ridges, and in the distance several thick fingers were bent upward, like columns holding up the sky. Looking further, I saw I was being held level with his nose, so that we were essentially looking at each other eye to eye. I asked him, "Mr. Imagai, why did you call me? Don't worry, the ship bearing provisions will surely arrive tomorrow—no, I mean today. It will surely arrive today."

Imagai didn't say a word, but as my body continued to slowly approach his mouth I finally realized with horror what he intended to do. I was terrified, even though I couldn't quite believe what was happening. Was it possible that he intended to have me—his creator, who had worked for him for twenty years, Doctor Motose Zekū—as his breakfast? I cried out in terror, "Mr. Imagai, Mr. Imagai, what are you doing? Have you gone mad?"

He didn't answer, but his two enormous eyes shone brightly like those of an invalid running a high fever. He continued bringing me closer and closer to his dark and cavernous mouth. I no longer had any doubts as to his intentions. Yes, he wanted to eat me. He had already gone mad—this guy had the biggest appetite in the world, and missing two meals was enough to make him delirious. It was not Imagai who was trying to devour me but rather his instinctive greed.

Regardless of which Imagai it was who was trying to eat me, however, my fate would still be the same. I certainly did not want to be deposited into that stomach and digested into excrement. I hollered and struggled with all my might. Fortunately, he was not holding me very tightly, and as his body was so enormous, his reflexes were rather slow. Impulses travel along unmyelinated nerves at a speed of only a few dozen meters a second, and it would take at least a full second for his brain to send a signal to the fingers at the end of his thirty- to forty-meter-long arm, which made him much slower than me. Just as I was about to be deposited into that enormous mouth, I nimbly struggled free and leaped out of his palm. Unfortunately, in my confusion, I started running in the wrong direction, and, as I dashed forward, I stepped on something soft (only later did I realize that this was his tongue), whereupon my foot suddenly slipped and I fell into a dark hole (his throat). Above me there was a hanging bell (his uvula). It was extremely slippery here and I couldn't keep my footing, so I slid all the way down a narrow tunnel (his esophagus). This sliding process unfolded very slowly—so slowly that I regained my senses and realized my tragic circumstances. I was paralyzed by fear, and my mind froze. Finally, I landed at the bottom of the hole and found myself standing in a pool of viscous liquid, enveloped by an acrid stench. I knew that this was his stomach, and that here I would be slowly decomposed by gastric acids into amino acids and fructose, ultimately becoming a part of this giant's body and participating in his ravenous consumption of the earth's resources. For some reason, this prospect left me very dissatisfied, and I would have preferred being eaten by a shark. I called out in despair, struggling to knock into and kick the stomach that surrounded me. But he gave no response.

I began to go into shock as a result of the acidic environment of the stomach, but my survival instinct allowed me to remain conscious. I resolved to climb out. Fortunately, his body was lying down so the dark and narrow esophagus was not oriented at a very sharp angle. Without hesitation, I dug into the flesh wall with my fingers and started struggling forward. I climbed and climbed. My limbs were trembling and my mind was numbed; I felt like giving up and then going to sleep forever in the darkness. But my survival instinct was still dimly active, like a single lamp glimmering in the distance as dusk envelops. When I think back to this moment, I even feel very proud of myself—although Imagai Nashihiko's desire for possession was unparalleled, my instincts nevertheless refused to succumb to him.

I crawled into his throat, which was more sharply inclined. Here the air was fresher, which allowed me to recover my spirits somewhat. I grasped his uvula and climbed back into his mouth. Now, through the gaps between his teeth I could glimpse the morning sky and see the possibility of escape. I was afraid that he would suddenly realize what was happening and would chomp down just as I was crawling out between his teeth, biting me in half. Perhaps the reason he had been lying there without moving was because he had been waiting for that very moment? But I didn't have the energy to crawl out through his nostril, since that path was too steep and treacherous. I had no option but to steel myself and follow his tongue past his bottom row of teeth. Thankfully, he did not move. I stood on his bottom lip and jumped, landing with a bang onto his chest, and then immediately began frantically to run away. I intended to jump into the ocean, to prevent him from grabbing me again. There-fore, I—

Wait a second—why hadn't he responded at all? Actually, when I was knocking around in his stomach or climbing up his esophagus, he should have at least made some response. In the Chinese novel *Journey to the West*, when the Monkey King torments Princess Iron Fan from inside her stomach, the princess is left in such agony that she kneels on the ground begging for mercy. I paused and observed him carefully. Sure enough, he was not moving at all. I went back down to the edge of his chest and boldly climbed onto the area above his heart. I lay on the ground (which is to say on the surface of his chest) and listened carefully but couldn't make out a heartbeat, whereas previously his heart had always pounded like a ten-thousand-horsepower two-stroke marine engine.

It turned out Imagai was already dead. He probably died the instant I fell down his throat, so no wonder he had not responded to my irritations. I don't know how he died. Could it be that I had accidentally choked him to death? But whatever the reason for his death, I am at least free from care. As the morning gradually grew brighter, I examined his corpse, this mountainous pile of flesh, and couldn't help feeling melancholy. This great life was my own creation, the product of my sweat and tears over the past twenty years. My twenty years of labor amounted to this?!

I spent the entire morning sitting on his chest, feeling his body tem-perature gradually drop. The sea was calm, the sky perfectly blue, and Imagai Island gently rocked back and forth in the waves. Shortly before noon a ship appeared on the horizon. It was not, however, the provisions ship I was expecting but rather a freighter brought by the police, who had come to complete the arrest proceedings they had initiated the previous evening. After assessing the situation, however, they realized that there was no need to make an arrest, and their task instead became that of investigating the circumstances of Imagai's death. As the only witness, I was questioned meticulously for a long time. This was routine procedure, insofar as the only on-the-spot witness must first be eliminated as a potential suspect.

Next, they summoned a forensic pathologist, who was flown in on an airplane. The pathologist quickly determined the cause of death, asphyxiation—it turned out that as Imagai was lifting his head to swallow me, the too-rapid motion caused him to break his neck (which is to say his spine). So the fundamental reason for his death was his weight. Even in water, his sixty-meter and three-hundred-tonne body was simply too heavy, and in the end he had simply collapsed under his own weight.

The pathologist easily eliminated me as a suspect, and for this I was extremely grateful. However, my gratitude was quickly transformed into fury. Because . . . because this muddle-headed, arrogant bastard put down an incorrect time of death: between 10:00 and 11:00 P.M., on November 15, 2013. I objected, arguing strenuously that Imagai had actually died after midnight, because he tried to eat me before he died, and before that I had looked at my watch and noticed that it was already five minutes after midnight. That is to say, Imagai clearly died *after* the one-year anniversary of his operation. I begged the pathologist to reexamine the corpse and said, "His body being as enormous as this will cause his body temperature to decrease more slowly. Therefore if you had estimated his death to have taken place *later* than it actually did, I would be able to understand the mistake. But how could you possibly come up with a time of death that is *earlier* than it should have been?"

The pathologist looked at me with pity but ignored my request. He simply couldn't understand why I was making such a fuss. He probably assumed that under these unusual conditions I had gone somewhat mad. The police shouldered me aside and began discussing what to do with the corpse. Given that he was already dead, they didn't want to tow him back to his home country. Since there wasn't a crematorium there that was large enough to hold him, if they hauled the corpse back it would be difficult to dispose of, and they certainly couldn't cut him up into eight hundred pieces and cremate each of them separately. It would have been even more impossible to follow the traditional practice of burying him in an urn, since there wasn't an urn in the world that would be large enough to hold him. Eventually, they decided to leave him here for the time being while they asked his next of kin to see if the family would agree to a burial at sea. I assumed that the family would agree, because otherwise they would need to pay a fortune for funeral expenses. The family did agree to a sea burial, but even that became a source of trouble because carnivorous sea creatures had no interest in the corpse. But that is another story.

The police ship returned home, and I went with it. There was no point in my remaining by Imagai's side. As we were about to leave, I stood on the ship's bow and bid farewell to the greatest animal that ever lived. I no longer had any stomach for debating the time of death with the pathologist, despite the fact that his two-hour error had cost me the prospect of collecting my twenty percent stake in Western Steel. I had no choice but to accept it. Such is fate.

What I am concerned about now is where I should go tomorrow to find work to support my family. For the past twenty years I have been earning a low salary, and haven't had a chance to save much. Now, I've even lost my career as a neurosurgeon. Of course, I am the only physician in the world who can perform a brain transplant, but I don't know if this extraordinary skill will ever be of any use. Perhaps, perhaps I could find a new client—a rich old man who wants to avoid paying estate tax when he dies? Hopefully I will be able to find one soon, and hopefully he will not be as disagreeable as Mr. Imagai. Hopefully. But no matter what, I have at least learned enough from this experience to know not to accept payment in stock options. Instead, whoever hires me will need to pay me in cold, hard cash.

13

THE RAIN FOREST

CHI HUI

TRANSLATED BY JIE LI

When Ye Qi woke up, the rain forest that had first made landfall on the East Coast had already engulfed Pusen City.

She threw back her blanket, grabbed her clothes, and hastily got dressed, then packed her belongings swiftly in a backpack. The water in the cup was cold and the hotel had long been abandoned, but after hesitating for a moment, she nevertheless took out a few bills and laid them on the wooden reception desk, where gray moss had already begun to grow.

"You always do such pointless things," Haer commented. "Nobody's coming back here anymore, at least not before your money turns into pulp."

"Since we're going deeper into the rain forest, money won't do us any good anyway, don't you think?" She replied indifferently and replenished her food sack with some instant noodles and biscuits that she rummaged out from one of the hotel's cupboards. "Find me some batteries," croaked Haer. "And meat. Let's see, what else . . ."

Ye Qi turned around to stare at the fist-sized, grayish-green toad on the couch, its body emanating the grayish-silver gleam unique to nanostructures.

"Haer, you'd better tell me what you want right now and then shut up."

"Batteries, meat, clean water—lots of water. Ye Qi, we need these, croak!" Haer jumped off the couch and leaped around the hotel. "Here's food, Ye Qi, and some food-storage bags, croak!"

"I know, I know. I have to find a pair of boots." Ye Qi furrowed her brow as she sized up the fine drizzle and sodden ground outside the window. Corroded by the gray tide of algae, the asphalt highway was full of bumps and hollows and puddles filled with foul water. If they were to go deeper into the forest, the sneakers she was wearing would not work at all.

"We'd better get going, croak. No more humans ahead, Ye Qi, take whatever you can. Croak." Ye Qi stripped off her sneakers, thrust her feet into the boots, and stuffed whatever she found in the hotel cupboard and fridge into her enormous backpack, which was half man-size to begin with. She grabbed Haer: "Don't you think you're being a bit long-winded?"

"A big mouth is a toad's virtue." Haer bulged its cheeks.

Ye Qi, bursting with rage, threw Haer into her backpack and zipped it up. Shouldering the heavy load, she kicked open the hotel's front entrance. The toad kept kicking and thrashing about in her backpack: "Let me out, you savage woman! Croak . . . let me out!"

Ye Qi did not even hear Haer's complaint. Lost in thought, she looked at the familiar yet strange city before her eyes, now changed beyond recognition. A gray drizzle covered the Pusen sky. Bluish-green mosses climbed the glass curtain walls. The skyscrapers melted gradually like chocolate under the erosion of the gray tide, while the rain forest with its metallic hue grew from every corner of the city, slowly blotting out the sun and the sky. She reached out and touched a small blue tree beside the hotel entrance, its branches coarse and as cold as iron. She snapped off a steel flower, and from the break trickled out a gray, sticky liquid that contained billions of nanostructures, pulsing with a rhythm between the organic and nonorganic, flowing over her fingertips.

"Better not touch those nanostructures." Haer finally found a comfortable position in her backpack and stuck out its flat head. "Beware of corrosion."

"I am of no interest to them," Ye Qi observed. "They're not carnivores like you."

Haer croaked unhappily: "How can these nanostructures be compared with us? They evolve automatically, they haven't been modified—that's why they're even more dangerous."

"Nevertheless . . ." Ye Qi wiped away the gray stains from her fingers: "Let's just be on our way."

They walked for an entire morning in the rain forest. As though in slow motion in a film, a skyscraper in the distance wilted slowly, turning into a pile of sludge under the corrosion of a mass of nanostructural moss. In a blink, large numbers of nanostructural plants sprouted from the sludge. Between the grayish-green leaves, dark black steel flowers bloomed in profusion. The GPS was useless under the heavy interference, and the map of Pusen in Ye Qi's hand became increasingly illegible as architectural markers disappeared. "Are you sure this is the right direction?" Haer grasped Ye Qi's arm with three legs and used a front paw to scratch at the map. "Can't even prepare a good map before going into battle. Humans really are irredeemably stupid."

"This is not my war, Haer." Ye Qi cast away the compass that was utterly useless in this metal forest and struck out on her own.

"Am I wrong in saying so?" Haer jumped onto her shoulder. "Is this not a war between humans and plants?"

"No, Haer, this is a war between *us*," answered Ye Qi.

The toad suddenly fell silent, the suckers on its feet tightening their grip on Ye Qi's shoulder. After a while it spoke: "No, Ye Qi, hardly any of my kind is left."

"Even if only three households remain in Chu, it will still defeat Qin," Ye Qi answered. "Haer, you must know what this saying means."

"It's about your human kind of resilience, croak." Haer jumped back inside the backpack, its weight knocking Ye Qi briefly off-balance. Its muffled voice sounded from the backpack: "Back in the day when we had forced humans into the southern corners of the East Asian mainland, you actually took back the whole of Asia within twelve years."

"Aren't you trying to learn as much as possible from humans?"

"Ye Qi, you don't understand." Haer stuck half its head out of the backpack. "No matter how much we learn from humans, nanostructures still cannot exist independently. Take me as an example: my body is forty-seven percent nanostructure, including my brain, voice organs, eyes, and central nervous system, but the other fifty-three percent is that of an actual frog. When humans created us, this is the way they did it. While we've kept trying to improve ourselves these twenty years after we gained our independence, we still haven't been able to make any progress with our organic bodies."

"And so you experimented with plants," inferred Ye Qi.

"Idiotic experiments." Haer's voice rose and fell with Ye Qi's uneven footsteps. "When the corrosion first began, some nanostructures still had enough presence of mind to send back some information. The merging of plants and nanostructures prompted an explosive mutation. They acquired intelligence, but of an altogether different kind from ours and humans'. They are extremely powerful, smart, and . . . they need living space."

"Are you sure you can tell me this?" Ye Qi snickered. "Humans and nanostructures are still at war."

"Damn this war! Croak," Haer spoke as if cursing. "Our entire network on the American continent fell into enemy hands within a week. Nearly the entirety of our species that remained in America was corroded, assimilated, or swallowed up. To this day, there may be no more than ten thousand nanostructural animals still surviving. Now the war is between humans and nanostructural plants—you call them the gray tide—not between you and us."

"From a structural point of view, you and they are more or less of the same sort." Ye Qi shook the water off her raincoat and tried to make out the bumpy road.

"Not the same." Haer's tone had a hint of terror. "According to the information I received, it was as if the plants had swallowed up the nano-structures, rather than the latter driving the merger. Their difference from us is as great as that between us and humans."

"It's actually not so great," Ye Qi muttered.

"What?"

"Nothing." Ye Qi found a relatively dry area and sat down, leaning against a bronze-colored tree. "I need to rest a little."

The year White Forest fell, Ye Qi was nineteen years old.

She did not remember the heavy artillery fire flying overhead nor the clouds of gunpowder smoke filling the air. She was sitting in a truck, holding a bundle her mother had stuffed into her hand and watching as the poplars of her village receded from sight. Trucks headed for the battlefield carrying odd-colored jars that contained chemical weapons designed to counter various specific types of nanostructure. Through the goggles on her gas mask, she watched the plants by the roadside wilt in the thick blue fog. An intense bitter smell saturated the air; it seemed as if all the vegetation were weeping.

Nanostructural animals have biological components and must still eat, drink, and excrete, something all humans knew. The war quickly escalated from merely destroying the nanostructures to destroying their sources of food, including all animals and plants in territories occupied by them, so that the nanostructural animals had no choice but to retreat. This, however, left behind stretches of desert where no humans could survive either. This wasteland lay across the Eurasian continent—beginning in the Korean Peninsula and stretching through northwestern China all the way to the Taklimakan Desert—effectively segregating humankind and nanostructural animals to its southern and northern sides, respectively.

Ye Qi was only one insignificant refugee out of the sixty million who couldn't go home because of this quarantine zone.

After the war to win back Siberia, the twenty-four-year-old Ye Qi returned to her hometown. She still remembered how every spring, when the snow on the hilltops began to melt, the moist black earth would be faintly covered with a veil of soft green. Those young buds, while no more than rice-grain-sized green dots to begin with, would grow overnight into new patches of thick green without flinching in the slightest from the early spring chill.

Yet before her eyes now were nothing but black sand, rocks, and a muddy country road. The remnant snow had long melted away, yet the earth remained lifeless. It was said that the poison that sank into the soil would not dissipate for a hundred years, and until then this would remain an infertile wasteland.

She walked aimlessly, on and on, and suddenly a splotch of green flashed past her peripheral vision. She hurried forward and pushed aside the desiccated thicket, only to discover the remains of a green poison gas shell hanging over a skeletal branch.

We regained White Forest, regained the Northeast and Mongolia, regained Siberia. But, did we really win the war?

She didn't know to whom she should ask the question, nor who would know the answer.

The road became even harder to navigate in the afternoon. There were gray puddles everywhere with the glutinous mud covering Ye Qi's boots and pouring into them, so that they emitted an odd squeak with every step she took. Gradually turning pale, she took out a bar of chocolate, stuffed three quarters of it into her own mouth, and threw the rest to Haer.

"Hey, how much longer is it going to be?" With the chocolate in its mouth, Haer burrowed into the backpack. "Are you really planning to spend the night in a place like this?"

Ye Qi sized up the ruins around her, their original shapes already beyond recognition: "It should be nearby. We'll arrive before dark. Let me take a short break."

Though she said a short break, Ye Qi fell sound asleep as soon as she sat down, her head bobbing up and down. Haer grumbled, jumped out of the backpack onto a giant uranium fruit, and vigilantly surveyed the surroundings.

Ye Qi first met Haer outside the Pusen airport, on the edges of the gray tide of rain forest. At the time, the "gray tide" was already overwhelming the land, and she was the only passenger on the flight to Pusen. Everyone else wanted to leave; only she wanted to return.

Moving against the turbulent human tide, she crossed the airport lobby, and when she walked into the rain forest, Ye Qi suddenly discovered Haer, entangled by a vine, as if being dragged into the forest's depths. For some reason, she unraveled the vine and released the toad. She knew it was a nanostructure, but the look in its eye at that instant was impossible for her to ignore.

Many years ago, she had seen this look on the battlefield, although it didn't come from a nanostructure. It was from a poisoned sparrow that had flown into the quarantine zone by mistake. The light in its small, brown eyes slowly faded. It wanted to live, simply to live.

She had originally wanted to let Haer go, to let it get far away from the rain forest, but the stubborn toad got into her backpack and claimed to know a pretty good hotel.

And so, without rhyme or reason, they became companions.

"Ye Qi! Get up, hurry, Ye Qi!"

Ye Qi was still half asleep when a cold, sticky thing smashed against her face with a loud squishy sound. She jumped up instinctively, only to realize that it was Haer's belly.

"Ye Qi, quick, look at your foot!" Shouting, Haer climbed onto her backpack. She swallowed the curses she was about to utter as an iron vine as thick as a finger had twined itself around her ankles. She pulled out her dagger and slashed at the vine but managed to cut through only half of it when several other vines reached out at her from behind.

She kicked with all her might, breaking the vine around her ankles by force. Not stopping to rid herself of the remnants of the vine, she grabbed her backpack and Haer, leaped to avoid the other vines, and dashed into the depths of the forest. The gray rain forest now tore off its temperate mask. The vines and branches appeared to come to life, meandering, reaching out to halt her steps. Above her head came loud, clacking sounds. She leaped violently as a bronze tree, so thick one could barely wrap one's arms around it, crashed down behind her.

"Heavens! What are they doing?" Haer croaked. "What on earth are you doing? You've scared them into a frenzy!"

"You should say 'it,'" Ye Qi corrected: "The rain forest is a single intelligence. Haer, it hadn't discovered me before, but now it knows what I am."

"Ye Qi, Ye Qi, what else do you know that I don't? Croak . . . ," Haer mumbled and pushed aside a vine that was reaching for the nape of Ye Qi's neck.

"Hold on tight, Haer!" Ye Qi leaped onto a small mound of earth, dodging the branches and leaves, but tripped over a tree root that sprang from the earth. Crying with surprise, she lost her balance and rolled a considerable distance forward, falling into a quagmire.

"That's it, we're doomed," Haer mumbled, only to discover that not even grass grew on this strange empty patch in the middle of the rain forest. Only a few large fungi poked their heads out of the mud.

"We're here, Haer," Ye Qi whispered. "My destination."

She took out several test tubes from her backpack and stuffed them full of mud and fungi. Then she quickly placed them in a small rocket that disappeared into the sky with a swoosh.

"I'm done, Haer." She flashed an exhausted smile: "You really shouldn't have come here, because when I came, I didn't plan to leave."

Haer swallowed a mouthful of fungus: "Same here," he mumbled indistinctly.

"So you also came here for the virus against nanostructural plants."

Ye Qi's eyes widened and she suddenly began laughing. "So you, too, discovered the bald spots in the rain forest—but how did you plan to bring it back?"

"No need," answered Haer. "I'm only a guidepost. Soon my companions will arrive and spread the virus elsewhere."

"Even if Chu has only three households left, it will still destroy Qin."

"We understand nanostructures better than you, croak."

A tender smile flashed across Ye Qi's pale face. "No, maybe you understand them better than humans do, but not better than I." She took off her gloves. The metallic sheen particular to nanostructures shone on her skin: "When we were together, you kept in touch with your companions the whole time, didn't you?"

Haer stared dumbly at Ye Qi's nonhuman skin and answered woodenly, ". . . yes . . . croak."

"I once told you that this whole rain forest is a single intelligence." Ye Qi moved her finger ever so slightly, and a few grayish-green leaves grew out of her fingertips. "I used to be a soldier. I fought against both you and the nanostructural plants. When they began spreading out, I was among the first group of soldiers to be airlifted to the gray tide zone. But they caught me, modified me, took everything from me. Except for my brain, I am composed entirely of nanostructural plants." She smiled bleakly. "In fact, they may have been better off had they emptied my brain. After a billion years of scheming, they still don't understand animal psychology."

"A billion years?" Haer's mouth widened like that of a typical toad.

"Plants did not acquire intelligence only after they merged with nano-structures, Haer, they were intelligent from the start. They share a single memory, the most ancient intelligent life-form on earth. But later, animals became more powerful. Plant intelligence loses a bit of memory with every tree it loses. This death is not a quick death like ours but rather a gradual process of forgetting. As trees fall, as grasses wither, and before new plants can become carriers of memory, it begins to forget. It waited and waited, till the appearance of nanostructures. Plants have endured patiently for a billion years in exchange for roots that can walk. Wolves eat sheep, sheep eat grass, but now the grass wants to eat wolves."

Haer stared at Ye Qi's grayish-white countenance: "I don't understand, Ye Qi—you are a nanostructure, so you should fight for the plants, croak."

"Right." Ye Qi took out the dagger from her boot and slashed at the plant vines that were franticly attacking them. "Physically, I may be a nanostructural plant, but I still carry memories from my human past. I'll never forget the horrible scenes of my comrades being dismembered and gobbled up by nanostructural plants. When plant intelligence modified me, it also shared its memories with me. That's how I learned about the bald spots in the rain forest and of the existence of this virus, so I decided to come here and find the virus that would kill it. Haer, plant intelligence knows no mercy. Like nature itself, it follows its own will, without pity and without weakness, much less compassion. I don't know when it will take away my entire will, but before then I hope to do something more for humankind."

Perhaps because they noticed that simply attacking Ye Qi was useless, the vines and tree roots began to envelop her in thick layers and pierce her body. She tried to struggle, but roots began to grow from within her body, climbing out of her shoes and digging deep into the ground. She opened her mouth to curse but could only spit out a green branch. Struggling, she used her last shred of strength to grab Haer and fling it as far away as she could with arms that were already sprouting leaves and the buds of flowers.

After quite a while, the empty piece of ground finally quieted down. Haer climbed out of the forest and saw that Ye Qi had already turned into an iron tree—branches, leaves, and all. Only her gray face remained on the tree trunk, wearing a serene smile.

The forest rustled as one toad after another, looking just like Haer, jumped out to pick the viral fungi. They would take these fungi all over the world to destroy all nanostructural plants, bringing the last hope of survival to a struggling humankind and nanostructural animals.

It's just that, when the dust settles after the war, what creature could survive on a planet without plants? From its inception, this was to be a war without victors. Humankind, nanostructural animals, nanostructural plants—none had much of a future.

Haer took a profound look at the tree that Ye Qi had become and, with a leap and a bound, disappeared into the depths of the gray rain forest.

14

THE DEMON'S HEAD

FEI DAO

TRANSLATED BY DAVID HULL

eneral Xin Man—they called him Demon Xin Man—had been accused of crimes against humanity and was being held in a little box that was placed in the dock while he awaited trial at the international court.

Throughout history there have been many who have tried to alter the course of war by eliminating a single person, but most have ended in failure. Those desperadoes with lofty moral sentiments left behind nothing but a corpse symbolizing their failure, along with a folktale mixing terrorism with impassioned patriotism. But there are always exceptions. General Xin Man's luck came to an end after he was in power for many decades, having committed all manner of appalling crimes and surviving a number of legendary assassination attempts. Several determined nihilists who were willing to lay down their lives put together a meticulous plan and successfully blew up General Xin Man's secret train in a suicide raid. The general's entire corps of fanatically loyal bodyguards followed him to the netherworld. The scene of the explosion was too horrific for words. Everyone had been blown to pieces, the righteous and the wicked intermingled, although rather unevenly.

The course of the war changed markedly. In truth, before scholars had time to produce an argument on an individual's place in history, most people were more worried whether or not the demon himself had actually been blown up. The general enjoyed going out in public, so people very quickly recognized Xin Man's epaulet on a portion of a shoulder, and, thanks to the extraordinary measures he took to protect himself, the general had luckily preserved most of his body. The only regret was that his head had gone missing. Later, we learned from the *Global Times* that the site of the explosion just happened to be—ah! history will drive you crazy—situated near the International Neurological Research Institute where Professor Ryan worked. The professor had just left the operating room and was getting ready to go outside to breathe in the acidic and putrefied air of war when a deafening sound was heard. The ground beneath him and the old-fashioned glass windows of the hospital both shook. Ryan looked up and saw a semiautomatic rifle fly toward him along with several Imperial Service Medals, a bloody military cap, and a not entirely perfect head. Out of professional habit, the professor dodged the symbolism-laden objects but caught the head in his hand and ran into his laboratory without further thought.

The professor later said that at the time he didn't notice that the thing he had acquired was the head that once ordered the massacre of tens of thousands of dissenters. Without even cleaning the bloodstains off the face, Ryan immediately began open cranium surgery and carried out a specialized examination. The professor's movements were precise and efficient, and the result came quickly: although those lifeless eyes refused to close even in death, the brain inside the skull was still alive. The professor carefully lifted out the shocked and temporarily comatose brain tissue and placed it in a culture solution he had prepared.

Professor Ryan found out what had happened in the evening paper. All the papers covered the assassination at great length. Demon Xin Man's death heartened persecuted people in all corners of the world. Even though there was another "General Xin Man" who immediately appeared to repudiate the rumor, the Allied Forces sent out an official communiqué confirming that the man who was killed was indeed none other than General Xin Man. The professor put the paper down and returned to his laboratory to examine the now-empty skull. He concluded that only twenty-four hours previously, this organ now fated for decomposition had given a tirade inciting a nationalist frenzy.

"Oh, god." The professor crossed himself.

Ryan sat down and thought deeply. In the end, he concluded that there was nothing improper in the rhetoric of the media reports of Xin Man's death. As a scientist, although committed to the truth of things, he also had to take into account the matter of peace for the human race. Based on the complexities of the situation as well as considering his authority in this arena, it would be improper to just rashly hand over this bomb to anyone else or to the public before making some useful progress. He trusted that the Allied Forces would agree with his decision.

The professor's specialty was brain research on humans and all sorts of animals. He had done quite a bit of work on brain physiology, encephelomechanics, and electrical engineering and mechanics. As he studied each day's war bulletins, Ryan busied himself arranging the necessary installations for the comatose brain. General Xin Man was still appearing at various important places, putting out a line of nonsense that no one believed anymore. But people could easily make out an air of apprehension and unease in his face. Everyone had long been passing rumors that the demon Xin Man had secretly prepared clones and set down guidelines on important issues so that after he died another self could stand in and fulfill his grand dream of an all-prevailing empire. But reality is always too complicated: countermeasures for changes in the war situation weren't something a puppet could just look up in a few memoranda or manuals. In the end, the demon wasn't so easy to impersonate.

To pull together a set of sensory organs during the most difficult time of war was no easy task, so now there was a microcomputer connected to the black box, for all kinds of signal-translation processes. Ryan had found an old pair of headphones in a storehouse, but the thought of having the demon speak directly to his eardrums in stereo made him choose a set of low-fidelity speakers instead. A microphone would serve as ears. Because there wasn't a device with good smell recognition, the general would temporarily have to suffer not having a nose. One way or another, the professor was able to complete his secret work, and he decided to awaken this demon who had been floating in the culture solution. He had slept long enough. The monitor showed that the demon in the box had revived. After a bit of thought, the professor chose his first words: "Can you hear me, General?"

Ryan waited uneasily. There was only a hissing sound from the speaker. Ryan thought to turn up the volume, then, worried that he might alert others, he just spoke carefully again into the mouthpiece: "Can you hear me, General?"

After a brief silence, a deep metallic voice came from the speaker: "Who are you? Where am I?"

The professor explained the general's condition to him with extraordinary care. It was clear that General Xin Man was not happy with the new situation, but throughout he maintained an admirable military composure. After the professor had things basically explained, the general said in a rather bored voice, "Ah, I see. A plot." The professor didn't argue with him.

When the general expressed concern about his body, the professor regretfully said that it must have already decomposed. On this, Xin Man in the box gave a long and meaningful silence. The professor was very interested in the general's own sensations. The general demonstrated an impressive insight, cutting to the quick: "It's mainly vision. I feel like I need bifocals, and I can't move my eyes."

The professor expressed profound apology and said that because of wartime scarcity he could find only a low-resolution camera. The general's understanding surprised the professor: "Oh? The people have indeed made huge sacrifices for the fatherland." He followed up with a question about the professor's views on the war. After a brief hesitation, Professor Ryan decided to reply truthfully: "It's a catastrophe, General."

Xin Man was very interested in this, but the sound from the speaker couldn't fully express it. "Surely a member of the elite such as yourself can understand the great significance of the war?" Ryan finally had the opportunity to sit down and calmly discuss this disaster with someone involved in it. The professor said he couldn't see how massacring tens of thousands of innocents and eliminating those who hold a different belief could compensate for the flawed consciences of those who survived. General Xin Man played the same old tune, insisting that the flower of patriotism must be watered by fresh blood and that men of vision have never pandered to the morality of the masses, and so on. When the professor didn't argue with him, the general asked a more substantive question: "What do you plan to do with me?"

The professor thought that it would be best to keep him there until the end of the war. Demon Xin Man quickly objected and tried to invoke the professor's patriotism: "The people need me. I should be put back in a body as soon as possible. You should also think of the glory of the empire."

The professor said calmly but firmly, "You have probably forgotten—I am a scientist. I don't take that sort of glory into consideration."

"You are not one of those who naively think that by eliminating me you can end the war, are you?"

"Of course," the professor said flatly.

"Slaughter doesn't end with war. Hatred always exists."

"But that's certainly no reason to let you go back."

"I still have successors. They even have my genes," Demon Xin Man threatened finally.

"Unfortunately your vile soul remains here."

It was true: those cloned bodies with Demon Xin Man's DNA lacked a powerful brain. Those dregs put up a desperate fight, but the borders of the empire contracted, prices rocketed, and the currency devalued. The long-suffering people became restless, and in the same way that they needed a war in the beginning, they now wearied of it. A psychic epidemic was spreading. The signs were clear: the empire was beginning to collapse on all fronts.

Professor Ryan told all of this to the general. Even though he remained firmly opposed to freeing the general's soul from its imprisonment, he did agree to read the daily news to him to let him witness the empire that he built with his own hands disintegrating piece by piece. "See?" the professor said, taking off his glasses after reading the day's news. "No empire can survive forever."

The general was perhaps heartbroken (if we can say that) at the shattering of his lifelong dream. So in the following few days, the two men (let's put it this way for the time being) entered into a very, very awkward silence. The incompetence of his replacements and his own situation of residing impotently in a box no doubt had a significant impact on the general's self-respect. He therefore did not speak and used silence to express his fierce condemnation of the professor and show his extraordinary fury. In that insufferable environment, the professor felt he had to add some pleasant music from a phonograph. These dreamlike songs of the sweetness and sorrows of the ordinary people instilled a sense of the commonplace and made the professor so happy that over and over again he used these saccharine folk songs to mediate the silence. It got to the point that one day the general in the box finally couldn't take any more of the vulgarity that ran so counter to the sacred, the solemn, and the elegant. He was forced to speak: "Would you play some Mozart for me?" From this point on, the two were on speaking terms again.

The amazing thing was that from that point on, the general did not ask about the empire and instead spoke with the professor only on issues of history and philosophy. The two often had rather interesting discussions on Napoléon and Descartes, which surprised the professor. One day, he told the general that the Allied Forces had taken the capital of the empire, but the general seemed indifferent. The professor could not contain his curiosity. "It seems as though you're no longer concerned at all about the fate of the empire."

The box was silent for a moment before speaking: "Ah, let me tell you a secret. I am not concerned at all. Everything is quite good now. I finally understand what it means to be completely at ease. You have no way of experiencing the joy of having cast aside the body. I think I understand a very important thing: the source of all evil is in our bodies. Hunger, greed, lust, selfishness . . . all these vile desires come from that body of flesh and blood. Sin appeared when Adam and Eve became aware of their corporeality. The implications of this story clearly need a new interpretation. When I found out I was still alive, my first thought was to return to a body and continue to live my fantasy. Looking at it now, I see that was nothing but the inertia of desire. And now it would be hard for anything to entice me, since I swear by God I have no desires anymore."

"Are you telling me that since you were relieved of your body you have lost all your earlier passions?"

"I think this would be a subject very worthy of your research."

The professor was very surprised at this. He sighed after pondering for a long time with his medically trained mind and said, "It would appear that throughout history, all of humanity's heroes and villains, honor and depravity, great dreams and base conspiracies were the product of nothing but bodily hormones."

The war ended. Although there were still guerrillas carrying out acts of destruction and terrorism, the allies had begun to reestablish order. General Xin Man was not interested in this at all. Infatuated with Paganini's violin performances, he even suggested that the doctor supplement his "Evils of the Flesh" theory, because now if he went a full day without hearing excellent music he would lose all strength (This was how he put it. The professor couldn't understand the true meaning.), becoming listless and depressed. The doctor realized that under particular circumstances, music could induce a form of spiritual addiction similar to that of amphetamines.

Professor Ryan was not good at disguising his emotions, particularly since the low-resolution image from his camera did nothing to diminish the general's keen powers of observation. One day, after the two had finished discussing the problems of collusion between men and gods in Homer's epics, the general noticed the professor seemed discomfited, and he asked him to speak his mind. The professor hesitated before finally choosing his words tactfully. "Now that everything is over, I don't think I have the right to continue keeping you here."

The general was indifferent. "If that's the case, do what you feel best."

It seemed as if the professor felt a bit guilty. "I hope you understand . . ."

"I understand perfectly." It was difficult to imagine the butcher who had incited such hatred was now so evenhanded and considerate, speaking words that were so moving. "You don't have to feel bad. You should know that I'm already dead. Only my soul is left. I desire nothing, fear nothing."

The news that Demon Xin Man was still alive shook the entire world. After going through a process of unassailable scientific verification, it was officially announced that the brain of the war criminal Xin Man was still alive. Some people were frightened, but most were enraged. Those who had thought he had died too easily and that he hadn't suffered or been punished agreed that they wouldn't let him off so easily this time. General Xin Man was accused of Sabotaging Democracy, Waging War, Massacring Innocents, and the like, ten crimes all told. So now, the one-cubic-meter box that held all the apparatus had been placed in the dock, and sitting next to it was special assistant Dr. Ryan.

General Xin Man declined to speak in his own defense, admitting every crime without reservation. The court upheld each of the accusations, but there was a dispute on how to carry out punishment. Because the issue was so important, the people were asked to express their opinion. Some radicals demanded the death penalty, but the majority figured that since the body of the accused had already died once, to sentence his soul to a second death would be an inhumane atrocity. Some even said that the accused committed the crimes as a complete human, and so even if his body was obeying orders from his mind, his brain was at most only an instigator. The other conspirators had been punished with death and decay, so, taking that into account, the punishment of the brain should be lenient.

As an important eyewitness, Professor Ryan's testimony was taken quite seriously. The professor had no intention of any sort to defend him, but his statement, presented in an unadorned manner, especially his theory about the body's hormonal drive in the construction of history, caused an uproar. Some people thought that the professor was covertly trying to exonerate the demon of guilt because this would prove that the actual lead conspirator was in fact the body and the brain was simply taking orders and wasn't in control when committing the crimes. The professor didn't argue with them; he simply dispassionately presented all that he knew. He wouldn't worry himself about the rest.

While everyone was arguing noisily away, in the holding room awaiting the verdict General Xin Man expressed his apologies to Professor Ryan. "I'm sorry. It's not fair to drag you into this, too."

"Ah, it's nothing." The professor had always taken such arguing and condemnation calmly.

"Have you heard anything?"

"Well, I hear that the jury wants to be lenient. It might be life imprisonment."

"Contemptible!" The general raised his voice through the speaker. "Are they waiting for me to repent and build it into a villain-turned-saint story? There's no need to let me out for exercise, no need for guards. There's not even a need for a prison cell—half a desk would be enough! Dammit, I demand the death penalty!"

The professor didn't know how to comfort the general. He could imagine how unpleasant it would be to spend his life locked in a box unable to move until he died. The most anyone could do for him would be to give him a rotatable camera, but even if he could see the entire world in free three-hundred-sixty-degree movement, there wouldn't be a shred of joy to mitigate the misfortune.

"You could help me." The general began to put in motion a workable plan.

"I don't understand." The professor looked in puzzlement at the box he had made with his own hands.

"As I see it, the environmental demands of a soul are very stringent. It needs a very delicate balance, and even one drop of slightly concentrated hydrochloric acid could change that balance. For you it would be only the effort of lifting your hand, but for me it would be a liberation."

"My God," Ryan immediately refused. "General, I am a doctor. My duty is to save people, not to kill."

"Surely you wouldn't agree that I should suffer this eternal torment? You can't deny that my plight today is partially your doing. Or perhaps being in league with a demon would be unbearable for you?" The general knew very well how to use the weaknesses of others, but that last remark was unfair. The doctor was silent. For the entire afternoon, he thought of the misfortune he had created, thought about what exactly the duty of a doctor was. The conflict between an abstract justice and the warm contingent humanism that has emerged throughout human history pressed down on his shoulders. As dusk came, Ryan knew what his decision was going to be. The doctor explained his views on conscience and morality, and the general approved. They talked amiably just as before, and the two very quickly reconciled.

The judgment came. Xin Man was sentenced to life imprisonment, to be ended only when the brain died. The one in the box didn't utter a sound. The doctor next to him explained that the general was most likely very unsatisfied; it seemed as if on hearing the verdict he would never again ask about the mortal realm. The judge shrugged.

Professor Ryan explained some technical points to the specially assigned physicians and explicitly stressed that because of the fragility of the brain they were never to open the box on their own initiative. After making this clear, the professor returned home, protected by a large group of bodyguards—because the guerrillas had declared that they would punish the professor for his actions. When Ryan entered his room he did not go to bed; he instead went straight to the package he had packed up the day before. The doctor disguised himself, putting on an overcoat that had in it a false passport and some money. A friend waited at a secret place to pick him up. Right then a sudden burst of gunfire threw his plans for escape into confusion. It seemed as if there had been an attack, but it was quickly put down by the bodyguards. Soon after, the doctor was asked to go to the temporary command center. It turned out the guerrillas were using a diversion: at the same time they attacked the professor they sent a unit of fanatics to storm the secret prison and steal the brain of Demon Xin Man.

"We were going to trick them with an empty box, but it turned out we outsmarted ourselves. The one they took was the real brain of Xin Man. It's clear they have someone here on the inside." The supreme commanding general Hanmo's face was severe. "Of course we have people in their organization as well, and we've received information that the guerrillas are preparing to put Xin Man's brain into a cloned body to bring the demon back to life." The atmosphere was tenser than ever.

"It goes without saying that we must find and destroy them before then," said a high-ranking staff officer.

"The government has made a special dispensation: Xin Man's brain and cloned body may be shot on sight," General Hanmo explained.

The room was grave as respected experts set to drafting several different plans. Then General Hanmo remembered the doctor's presence.

"Do you perhaps have any ideas?"

"I think they should be annihilated immediately," the doctor said decisively. General Hanmo nodded with cold courtesy.

Everyone has heard what happened afterward: the allies moved immediately and resolutely. They found and surrounded the guerrillas' base area with lightning speed, and in one stroke they utterly eradicated the remnants. There was only a brief exchange of fire, since the military had learned its lesson and wouldn't allow anything to go wrong. A guided missile blew up the entirety of the threat in the area, including the wretched brain of General Xin Man.

As all this was going on, Doctor Ryan walked home under the starlight. Taking off his coat, the doctor walked into a secret room and carefully took out his luggage. He lifted out an iron box and gently placed it on the desk, then put on the headphones attached to the box. A deep voice came through the headphones.

"How did things go, Ryan?"

Ryan smiled and spoke into the microphone. "More smoothly than could have been expected. The fanatics helped us out. The demon Xin Man died in a furious allied bombardment. There's no need to worry now. After a while, I will resign my position. I think we can go to the Americas or to Asia. I have friends there."

"I'm very pleased. Maybe we can continue our discussion on Handel and Proust."

"It has been very interesting." The professor smiled. "But it hardly seems all that violence was necessary for nothing more than a pig's brain."

15

SONGS OF ANCIENT EARTH

BAO SHU

TRANSLATED BY ADRIAN THIERET

I

Six hundred and fifty light-years from Earth, our Sun had vanished into the multitude of stars and a huge new star appeared in front of the *Blizzard*.

Long before humans had begun to travel through space, this star had already appeared on ancient astronomical charts. Alexander's soldiers had seen it wink in the Indian night and Columbus's sailors had seen it rise above the waves of the Atlantic. But now was the first time humanity had ever reached this system and set their eyes on this celebrated star up close.

And what a star it was! Even from fifteen AU away, it was an immense red monster that all but dominated our field of vision. It was unimaginably vast, almost incomprehensible to human senses. Were it located in our solar system, its circumference would swallow up the entire orbit of Jupiter. Earth would be, by comparison, a speck of dust invisible to the naked eye. Even our Sun would seem no more than a large grain of sand.

It was Alpha Orionis, the bright right shoulder of Orion. With a luminosity more than one hundred fifty thousand times that of the Sun and a circumference equal to eleven hundred times that of the Sun, it was extraordinarily bright even at a distance of more than six hundred light-years. When we approached, it no longer seemed a star nor even a sun, but rather a fiery red roiling, roaring, boundless sea of fury. Any of the plasma clouds erupting from this sea of fire could be larger than the Sun.

We had come for precisely this reason, to investigate the activity of Alpha Orionis. Four years ago, scientists on Earth had discovered unusual activity from Alpha Orionis: large changes in luminosity, which seemed like the unstable flickers of a dying red lamp. People suspected it might soon erupt into a supernova—or even that it perhaps already had done so several hundred years ago. Consequently, after three years of urgent preparations, we were dispatched on the *Blizzard*, the spaceship prepared for this mission. After nearly a year of hyperspace travel, we arrived here.

But Alpha Orionis was perfectly normal. Although the ferocity of its surface activity greatly surpassed that of the Sun, the unusual flickering that had been observed from the Earth four years ago—which had actually taken place more than six hundred and fifty years ago—had disappeared. The maniacal red beast was peacefully sleeping, at least for now. Our survey proceeded smoothly. This was, however, just the beginning of a projected five-year scientific mission.

At the beginning we made a huge discovery: the mass of Alpha Orionis greatly exceeded our predictions. Scientists on Earth had used spectroscopy to estimate the mass of the star as about twenty times that of the Sun. But when we arrived in the *Blizzard*, we discovered a problem. The gravity acting on our ship put the mass of Alpha Orionis at more than five times greater than previously calculated: it was at least equivalent to one hundred Suns! This mass meant it was a supergiant, yet its luminosity was far less than that of other supergiants. For the time being we did not have a clue as to why this was the case.

We began to survey the star's surroundings. Observations from the Earth had revealed no large planets around the star, but after we arrived we were surprised to discover that the red beast was not a lonely ball of fire after all. It had a small companion, a single terrestrial planet slightly smaller than Earth that circled it at a distance of about three AU. Yet despite being much further from its star than Earth was from the Sun, the extreme size of Alpha Orionis meant that the planet still seemed to be right under the nose of the red monster. We were intrigued by the planet, because it might offer a scientific record of this solar system's history and might also contain the energy and mineral resources needed by our ship. We changed direction and headed toward it.

We circled the planet once to survey it. Its surface was pockmarked similar to the surfaces of Mercury and the Moon. Like them, it lacked an atmosphere and liquid water and was undoubtedly unsuitable for any life-form that we knew. Like the Moon, it was tidally locked: one side forever turned toward Alpha Orionis and the other side forever turned away. The side facing Alpha Orionis was nothing but a searing desert. Soon the *Blizzard* came around to the back side, where we no longer had to face the blazing, explosive surface of the star and could see only the frozen Milky Way, a view that could be had from any corner of the universe, which greatly relaxed the crew.

Yet we immediately made an unexpected discovery. As the *Blizzard*'s cameras swept across the back of the planet, they caught an image of a seemingly fabricated object nestled in a ring of mountains. It was at least fifty meters long and twenty meters wide, had a complex structure, and glimmered with a strange metallic luster. This could indicate that the planet might have intelligent life, which would mean this could be humanity's first encounter with extraterrestrial beings. Nervous and excited, we sent friendly messages toward it and anxiously waited for a reply.

Twenty hours passed. We listened attentively to every frequency, but there was only silence from the direction of the metallic object; there was no reply. We examined the pictures of the mysterious object over and over and discovered that half of it was buried under the rocky surface of the planet. Parts of it were clearly damaged, and there were no similar objects anywhere else on the entire planet, nor were there any signs of life or civilization elsewhere. If the object had belonged to the planet, it was almost certain there would have been other traces of civilization.

The conclusion was obvious: the object had, like us, come from space, from some faraway stars. It was probably a damaged spaceship that no longer contained any life.

The *Blizzard* landed near the ring of mountains, and we began to approach the distant metallic object. When we sent a remotely operated vehicle followed by some crew members to survey the area around it, we discovered one thing after another. Up close, the surface of the metallic object was strange yet seemingly familiar. Not only was it a spaceship; it had some characteristics of Old Earth and reminded the crew of the traces of the pre-Collapse civilization that were frequently seen in museums.

Crew members bravely approached the object and were able to discern many of the characteristics and constituent parts of ancient flying machines. Under the light of the Milky Way, we even discovered ancient characters that recorded its name and model number.

The spaceship's name was ancient English: *Starsong*, which, translated into modern language, means *Xīnggē*. This removed all doubt from our minds: it was a human spaceship that had come from Old Earth.

Earth before the Great Collapse!

II

Checking the complete three-dimensional scan of the spaceship against our database quickly revealed its origins.

It was a sub-light-speed spaceship produced by humanity near the end of the twenty-first century. Able to reach a speed of about two hundred fifty thousand kilometers per second, it had been one of the first human spaceships to approach light speed. At the time, this had been a huge technological advance. Ever since the *Apollo* Moon landing, humans had yearned for interstellar exploration. In the space race of the late twenty-first and early twenty-second centuries, the world powers had produced more than a hundred of these spaceships and launched them to explore the vast space beyond the solar system. That had been the first wave of human interstellar exploration.

But the Great Collapse followed soon thereafter. Earth suffered complete environmental and economic collapse, population overload, and was then engulfed by the fires of the fourth world war. Nuclear conflict between the powerful nations destroyed most of the planet. Past prosperity was forgotten and civilization languished for a thousand years, science and culture both on the brink of extinction, until five hundred years ago, when the renaissance began. It was not until three hundred years ago that humanity, now tempered by experience, again started along the road of space exploration and began to colonize other solar systems. Fifty years ago, humans invented the technique for hyperspace travel, which allowed us to travel thousands of light-years in a relatively short amount of time. That is what enabled us to travel to this system in less than a year.

Despite the short travel time, we were nonetheless six hundred and fifty light-years from Earth, meaning that even light required six and a half centuries to make the journey. In that first wave of interstellar exploration fifteen hundred years ago, most spaceships had headed toward nearby solar systems only a few, or at most a few dozen, light-years from Earth. The most distant known journey had reached the Hyades star cluster, just one hundred and fifty light-years from Earth and reachable in seventy years of ship time. Even so, those explorers could not have lived long enough to make it back to Earth.

Ancient humans had had the ambition to explore the wider universe but had been stymied by several obstacles. The vacuum of space is not entirely empty, for one: every square meter of space contains a few stray hydrogen atoms and other microscopic particles. Spaceships flying through the vacuum at near light speed collided with these atoms at high speed, causing considerable damage to the their hulls. As impact damage accumulated over years of travel, significant problems would arise. The risk factor increased with space dust or meteoroid impacts.

The larger problem was with the astronauts, since humans are a terrestrial species and have difficulty adapting to the vastness and loneliness of space. Many explorers could not endure the loneliness of decades of floating among the stars far from Earth and either grew depressed and committed suicide or went mad and grew delusional. Trying to explore star systems hundreds of light-years from Earth in these primitive sub-light-speed ships was similar to how even more ancient humans attempted to cross the Pacific Ocean in canoes: something nearly impossible. Only with the invention of hyperspace travel did humanity gain the ability to travel far from their home solar system and enter the depths of the Milky Way.

Yet somehow this ancient spaceship had traversed six hundred and fifty light-years to arrive in the neighborhood of Alpha Orionis and had even managed to land on the surface of its only planet. It was impossible, inconceivable. How had they done it? The database revealed that this type of spaceship could reach at most ninety percent of light speed, meaning that the ancients had taken seven hundred years to reach here. They would of course have experienced what we call time dilation, but even accounting for that, the journey would have taken three hundred years of subjective time for the spaceship's passengers.

Three hundred years! At least ten generations. Back then, no one could have lived that long, since the average life span had been only about one hundred years, and they hadn't had a viable hibernation technology. Had it been a generation ship? The database showed that this type of ship could carry only up to six astronauts, so no matter the pairings they could have reproduced for only three or four generations before genetic interbreeding would begin to cause physical and intellectual defects.

The *Blizzard*'s database did not have specific data on this particular ship. After all, one thousand and seven hundred years had passed, and during that time civilization had nearly gone extinct and subsequently endured many cycles of prosperity and chaos. The surviving historical records from that era are pathetically few. But the information we sought must be within the spaceship itself.

Our crew entered the spaceship. The atmosphere within it had dissipated to nearly nothing, leaving it a vacuum. But precisely because of this, the objects inside remained well preserved. When we understood the specifics of the ship's structure, we were astonished at how some of the ancients' technology rivaled our own. But the coarseness of the main structure and the primitiveness of the technology startled us even more: we wondered at how humanity had crossed six hundred and fifty years of space to reach this distant star system using such crude tools.

The corridors, cockpit, and labs of the ship all contained the traces of long-term human habitation, yet we found no bodies. Finally, when members of our crew entered the living quarters at the base of the ship, they found the thousand-year-old desiccated corpse of a middle-aged white male. He must have been the final captain of the spaceship, but we didn't know his name. Or perhaps he had spent his entire life alone and never needed a name.

Soon thereafter other crew members discovered some strange instruments in the ship's rear compartment. Some of them were engraved with ancient scientific terms, and through database searches we confirmed our guesses that these instruments had been used to create, preserve, and cultivate fertilized eggs. The final several generations of people on the spaceship had been unable to procreate in the natural way and had been forced to make use of previously fertilized eggs to continue their space odyssey.

By thus passing the torch ceaselessly from generation to generation, humanity had achieved a miracle, traversing the vast distance of six hundred and fifty light-years in the early days of the space age to arrive at this distant, unfamiliar, and bizarre world, where, for the first time, they gazed with their own eyes upon the breathtakingly vast fiery sea of Alpha Orionis.

But what had they gained from it? Nothing at all. The spaceship had successfully landed on this planet, to be sure, but the single remaining astronaut had no way of living in this dead world, nor any way of returning home. It may not have been long at all before he died. A journey of more than seven hundred years in exchange for a single striking glimpse of Alpha Orionis. The last human on the spaceship had been forever stuck here in this distant system, so far away from his dim home star, the Sun, that it wasn't even visible in the depths of space.

Perhaps he may have attempted to send information back to Earth and tell humanity of his crew's accomplishment, but it would have taken six hundred and fifty years for the information to reach Earth, if it even arrived at all. The Earth would still have been in the age of barbarism that followed the Great Collapse, and weak electronic impulses from space would certainly not have been noticed by the human society of a thousand years ago.

Yet what a magnificent epic the ship and its crew had created among the stars! How heroic and yet how tragic! The experience of the *Starsong* had demonstrated to the universe how much the miniscule human race could accomplish even with limited technology and resources. Like the Phoenician sailors who first circumnavigated Africa or the Greeks who first crossed the Arctic Circle, or the Vikings who first reached the Americas, their journey itself brought them nothing and was even for a time forgotten by history. But, crucially, their accomplishment demonstrated the adventurous spirit of humans to conquer the universe, and this was something of which all later humans could be proud.

It was an epic song of the stars, with a duration of more than seven hundred years. It had been lost, dissipated into the lonely, limitless expanse of space among the stars, yet now we had finally heard its moving melody.

Although the audience had been a long time coming, we had finally arrived and offered our belated cheers and heartfelt applause.

Our whole crew bowed deeply in front of that nameless hero's corpse, bowing to the great pioneer, to the magnificent seven-hundred-year journey, to the three hundred years of solitude and perseverance, and to the indomitable exploratory spirit of humanity.

III

We scanned the *Starsong*'s main computer. Although the computer had long ago exhausted its energy supply and ceased activity, it had slept uninterrupted on the lonely surface of the planet for one thousand seven hundred years, and its memory was perfectly preserved. Yet owing to the destruction and rebirth of human technology over those centuries, there was a huge gap between it and our computers. The basic commands and code of the ancient computer were completely different from those of the computers of today. Its strings of binary code were like opaque ancient inscriptions to us and took considerable time to decipher.

We soon paused our investigation of the *Starsong*, since this was, after all, not the main objective of our journey. We let it continue sleeping on the surface of the planet and again turned the *Blizzard* toward the surface of Alpha Orionis to conduct scientific surveys of its structure and activity. We would revisit the rear side of the planet in five years on the way back to Earth and collect the nameless corpse and other artifacts to carry back with us, as memorials for posterity.

At least, that was our plan at the time.

Six months later, we had made great progress in our research of Alpha Orionis. We discovered several unusual signs underneath the star's photosphere. After collecting and analyzing a sea of data, we created a rudimentary mathematical model and from it arrived at an interesting conclusion:

Alpha Orionis had in the past been circled by several giant planets, some perhaps ten or more times the size of Jupiter. But over millions of years, these planets had been successively swallowed by their own mother star, falling into the fiery sea of Alpha Orionis. This had fueled the star's continual expansion. Soon after falling into the star, the planets would have been torn apart by the extreme temperatures and gravity within. Yet because Alpha Orionis's density was far less than that of main-sequence stars such as the Sun, huge spaces existed within it, and its digestion of the planets was not total: thick clouds of planetary wreckage existed in its interior. The Eddington limit prevented this wreckage from falling further into the depths of the star, so it floated just underneath the photosphere. Alpha Orionis's mysterious and intense luminosity changes were perhaps related to this unique internal composition.

We began to gather evidence for this hypothesis through spectral analysis of Alpha Orionis, which initially demonstrated that several hundred million kilometers beneath the surface of the star there was indeed a layer composed of many heavy elements. Spectral analysis revealed it to be rich in elements like carbon, iron, silicon, and tungsten, many of which we needed for our ship. Of course, our technology did not allow us to enter the star to gather these resources.

We now knew that the planetary cloud within Alpha Orionis absorbed part of its electromagnetic radiation and hid its true mass. Although its mass was still out of proportion to its vast area, it was nonetheless much higher than Earth-based measurements had predicted. If Alpha Orionis exploded, it might even threaten our solar system, six hundred and fifty light-years away. Fortunately, the star was currently stable.

While pursuing the analysis of Alpha Orionis, I continued to scrutinize the data from the *Starsong* and gradually deciphered its main riddles.

The *Starsong* had been one of the most advanced spaceships of its era. Rated for a speed of up to 0.91 c, it was launched by NASA from its Florida base in 2092 with a crew of six. Its target had not been Alpha Orionis, however, but rather the much closer Sirius. The original plan had been to reach Sirius in about ten years, spend three years surveying and replenishing the ship's energy stores, and then return to Earth.

But the ship had been a new model and its technology not fully mature. An unexpected error occurred during its acceleration toward light speed. Its six engines fell out of sync and one engine failed entirely. Although the ship still managed to reach 0.9 c, its directional angle was greatly altered. It ended up flying 270,000 kilometers per second toward a different area of space, forever unable to reach Sirius.

When this happened, the ship had just passed the orbit of Neptune. If the crew members had stopped immediately, perhaps they could have been saved, but their engine problem persisted and the crew did not dare to try restarting the failed one for fear that it might explode. They spent a year repairing the engine, by which time the Starsong had already traveled a light-year away from Earth.

The Starsong had consumed sixty percent of its fuel in reaching 0.9 c. The crew could now attempt to turn back to the original path, but that would greatly reduce the ship's speed, and the journey to Sirius would then take more than a hundred years. The crew members would not live that long, and besides they knew that other spaceships would have reached Sirius long before they did, rendering their journey meaningless. They could attempt to return to the solar system, but that would be even worse: they were already a light-year away from Earth and would have no fuel for acceleration, so their speed back to Earth would be at most one percent of the speed of light, meaning the journey would take them a hundred years. They would die of old age long before arrival. Requesting help from Earth was likewise unrealistic. Ordinary spaceships could attain only five percent of light, meaning that it would take them a century to reach the Starsong at its current location. Near-light spaceships, on the other hand, were incredibly expensive and time-consuming to manufacture and would face the same problems of reducing speed and returning that currently confronted the Starsong. Even if the Earth immediately sent a rescue force, they would have to wait at least a decade for its arrival.

Therefore, the ardent pioneers aboard the Starsong courageously chose to abandon any chance of returning to Earth and instead continue forward. They did not decelerate but continued plunging into the depths of space at 0.9 c. The only object ahead was the bright red star Alpha Orionis, the closest star within their reach.

For the first few years after setting out on this journey of no return, everything was normal. All the crew members were of sound psychological makeup and had received stringent training. Their original mission to Sirius was to have taken more than ten years, and out of consideration of the long time they would spend away from human society, they had been prepared with appropriate psychological guidance. In these first few years, they lived, studied, worked, and played normally, with regularity, their lives stressful yet satisfying. The ship's database held books and music equivalent to the holdings of a large library, an intellectual feast sufficient to keep them sated for hundreds of years. The three males and three females aboard paired off into three couples. They began to plan children, since they knew that it would take three hundred years of ship time to arrive at their objective. Their generation would not live to see their arrival; they must create future generations to continue the journey. Two years later the first two babies were born.

But as the days and years passed and their distance from Earth increased by more than two light-years for each year of ship time, Alpha Orionis remained a tiny red speck, and they realized that they would never live to see it grow any larger. This was entirely different from the ten-year Sirius journey they had planned for. The dull shipboard life and their depressing prospects gradually pushed them deeper and deeper into frustration, and many of them suffered psychological breakdowns. Interpersonal relationships grew increasingly tense and arguments increasingly frequent, with physical fights also breaking out. Their formerly routine and healthy lifestyle was gone.

After nine years, one long-depressed crew member committed suicide. This dealt a severe blow to the psyches of the remaining crew members, and they consequently grew aimless and hedonistic. Work became just routine, study was abandoned, and the crew members increasingly lost themselves in virtual-reality games. Most turned their backs on the reality of the cold, unchanging view outside, instead preferring to spend their days immersed in virtual reality, where they could imagine themselves on Earth, charging enemy lines in war simulations or battling monsters in the tropical jungle.

Their personal lives also fell into previously unimaginable degeneracy. At first it was just certain crew members secretly cheating on one another, but this soon changed into open and indiscriminate sex between all crew members, along with homosexual games. When the second generation reached maturity, there was even incest between parents and their children. Who cared about traditional morality when they were floating through deep space so far away from any other humans? The ship had no chemical hallucinogens, but the bored crew members invented a method of electrical stimulation to the brain's pleasure centers. Most of their time was then spent floating through the living quarters naked, occasionally seeking sensual stimulation through sex, occasionally immersed in the druglike highs of brain stimulation. They were lost in the blackness of space, lacking past and future, without ideals or taboos. The pursuit of momentary pleasure was all they had.

However, even this degenerate lifestyle could not last forever. Seven years later, a crew member named Steve forever changed the shipboard environment. One day, believing himself to be in a virtual-reality game surrounded by armed warriors who sought to kill him, he took up a sword and fought desperately until he had killed all his enemies, then collapsed into unconsciousness. When he awoke, he found himself in the living quarters surrounded by the naked corpses of his fellow crew members, the area in chaos, blood everywhere, and in his hand a plasma blade.

Steve cried out in fright and shut his eyes, trying not to recall what had happened. But as his head gradually cleared, he remembered: everyone had been in the living quarters and it had been a party, an orgy. Seeking a high, he had put on a helmet for electrical brain stimulation. Somehow the stimulation had been excessive, deluding him into thinking he was playing a game. Entranced, he had reached into a storage cabinet and grabbed one of the plasma blades ordinarily used for ship repairs, turned it on to maximum power, and hacked at his unsuspecting comrades . . .

He had killed everyone while in his dream state. Now he was the only person left alive on the ship—the only human within several dozen light-years.

It was too much for Steve to accept. Suffering extreme pain and regret, he decided to commit suicide and join his comrades in death's embrace. But, thinking that anyone who might discover this ship in the future had a right to know what had happened, he first recorded the events in the ship's computer. The preceding narration comes from his record.

The story shocked us to tears. If true, then the humans aboard the ship had all died not long after departure from Earth, and the ship had brought itself to Alpha Orionis. Was the corpse we had discovered on the *Starsong* the long-dead Steve? It was difficult to imagine, but not impossible. Perhaps the spaceships of that era were already capable of this sort of autonomous flight. If the atmosphere of the spaceship had been sucked away soon after Steve's death, then his corpse would have been preserved in a state like how we found it.

We carefully examined the pictures taken aboard the *Starsong*. One cabin indeed showed scarring from numerous plasma-blade strikes. Although it had been repaired, the damage remained quite obvious. Seeing these traces, we could imagine the horror of the event as it had happened in the depths of space. Despite the centuries that had passed, it still caused us to prickle in fear.

IV

We set aside the story of the *Starsong* for a time as we circled Alpha Orionis and continued our survey. We sought to understand the basic rhythms of its activity well enough to create a precise mathematical model. To this end, the *Blizzard* launched several hundred survey drones into synchronous orbit around the star and began collecting masses of data.

Three months later, something unimaginable occurred.

One survey drone received a string of strange electromagnetic waves from the interior of Alpha Orionis. It was not the usual chaotic radiation expected from a star but a complex, structured transmission.

The drone sent this string of electromagnetic waves to the *Blizzard*, where we decoded it and extracted the information within. We discovered that we could decode it into waves for airborne transmission—or in other words, sound.

We played the sound. As we heard it, all the crew members present were rendered speechless, faces aghast.

It was human sound, or at least part of it was. Amid odd and unfamiliar music, we heard the faint, distant sounds of a woman singing.

It was actually quite easy to distinguish the human music and singing, yet none of us knew what it was. Nor did I recognize either the strange melody nor the unfamiliar language. Perhaps it was an ancient folk song.

The song continued for only a dozen seconds before ceasing.

Almost all the crew members were stunned—we didn't know what to think. I calmed down first and quickly began to analyze. There were two key questions: First, what did the song mean? Second, how could it have come from the interior of the star?

Regrettably, neither question could be solved immediately. We could only guess that the song coming from Alpha Orionis was probably related to the *Starsong*'s landing on its planet. But how were the events connected? We had no idea.

Various theories soon emerged. At first, our ship psychologist thought it might be a mass delusion. But we had recorded the voice and could replay it, so this theory was obviously false. Then someone proposed that it might be a trick played by one of our technicians. We examined our data records but found no traces of tampering or fabrication.

The melody and singing were clearly characteristic of ancient human culture and quite different from modern music. Because of genetic improvements, modern humans have a much wider vocal range than their ancient counterparts, and thus the entire structure of modern music is different. Simple and coarse ancient human music sounds foreign to modern people and would be difficult to fake.

The strange music may therefore have actually come from the past, but how could that be possible?

No matter how unimaginable it may seem, any phenomenon has an explanation. Sometimes the most ridiculous explanation may be the simplest and most persuasive. One theory stealthily spread that the ghosts of the dead crew of the *Starsong* had followed the ship to Alpha Orionis and now haunted the fiery ocean of the red beast with their ancient songs. Or maybe these spirits had refused to dissipate and had now infiltrated the *Blizzard*, lingering at our sides, watching us . . .

The *Blizzard*'s crew members were all astronauts and scientists, the best and the brightest, the cream of the crop, and no one would admit to believing such a ridiculous story. At most they laughed it off as a joke. But the rumor nonetheless spread and grew even more bizarre. I clearly saw profound fear and unease in everyone's eyes.

To solve the riddle, we reanalyzed the data from the *Starsong*'s computer. And indeed, underneath the surface layer we found a cleverly hidden secret repository brimming with information—perhaps it contained data on the song. But we did not have the access code, and without a way to break the complex security barrier, we could not open it. The encryption was strangely and intricately complex; without the code, only an astronomical amount of brute-force computing could get us in. I began experimental calculations to try to break the code, but because of their magnitude, it would take at least a year to crack.

During this process, our crew returned to the surface of the planet for further surveys and made several discoveries. We found vehicle tracks and human footprints more than a hundred kilometers from the *Starsong*, clear evidence that someone had driven a vehicle and walked on the planet and that someone from the *Starsong* had lived to arrive at the Alpha Orionis system. As for why we had not found any tracks in the vicinity of the *Starsong*—perhaps planetary or meteorite activity had erased them, or perhaps the *Starsong's* current resting place was not its original landing site.

We again examined the corpse from the *Starsong* that we suspected to be Steve. We had already attempted carbon-14 dating to determine its age, but the results were unreliable because the ship's atmosphere was artificial and contained a different amount of carbon 14 than that on Earth. So we set that aside and tried something else. Skin and bone analysis yielded a different bit of evidence: the corpse's bone and skin structure showed that it had been subjected to almost no gravity in the process of maturation. The man had almost certainly been born and raised on the ship and was a descendant of the original crew.

We thus disproved our original hypothesis. If Steve had at one point been the only crew member left alive, then after recording what he had, he must have not committed suicide but rather changed his mind and continued to live. He must have developed embryos from the frozen fertilized eggs, raised the children, and handed the ship on to the next generation.

But why had Steve changed his mind about dying? In the two hundred and eighty years following the tragic accident, what had happened aboard the ship? How many generations had passed? How had the final generation ultimately come to the Alpha Orionis system? We were yet unable to answer these questions. Perhaps answers would come only from cracking the encrypted database.

The mystery of the strange song became our top priority, but we also had to continue our research into the star. The *Blizzard* floated above the red sea of fire, and we buried ourselves in the dull research into the star's evolution.

Only half a month later we again heard singing coming out of Alpha Orionis. This time it was a male voice, thick and resonant, but still frightening to all of us. Like the previous singing, it ended after half a minute.

Seven days later, we heard the singing again. This time it was a child's voice, young and innocent like the sounds of nature.

A month later we heard the voice of an elderly person, bleak yet forceful . . .

Twenty days later, we heard a male-female duet . . .

On average every two to four weeks we heard another snippet of song, the shortest several seconds long, the longest extending to several minutes. As time passed, we gradually grew accustomed to the strange songs. Any strange phenomenon, if occurring with regularity, becomes just another part of life.

Then we made a new discovery: we scanned the corpse of the ancient astronaut, reconstructed his original appearance with analytical software, and used the mathematical model of his throat to reconstruct his voice. Astonishingly, his voice was a match for one of the singing voices we had heard. That is to say we had heard the recorded voice of the ancient astronaut!

Even more astonishing was that the child's voice we had heard also belonged to him—when he had been two or three decades younger.

The reality was no longer difficult to guess: the singing voices, at least some of them, belonged to successive generations of the *Starsong* crew. During their long journey, they had recorded their own voices into some device and ultimately launched that device into Alpha Orionis. Making use of the star's energy, the device was able to continue working and transmitting the sound recordings. If this was actually the case, there ought to be more than one device, for we had once simultaneously heard two songs coming from points within the star, separated by several hundred million kilometers. Even if the devices were moving within the star, they could not possibly move so quickly.

By why had they done this? Just to preserve their voices in memoriam? To preserve the embers of human civilization? Or were they trying to share some secret with us? From the singing itself, we had no way to tell. If only they could have explained to us their true purpose. But they only sang and never spoke.

V

The riddle was soon solved. The answer came two months later, when we again received electromagnetic waves containing the mysterious singing.

The song itself was similar to the previous ones, but the difference was that this time it emanated from the planet's surface and, moreover, from the side facing Alpha Orionis!

The *Blizzard* had orbited the planet several times and roughly scanned its surface features but had not landed to survey the side facing the star. From space, that side seemed similar to the back side, except that because it was shielded by the star it had suffered fewer meteorite impacts and was generally flat. Its more interesting terrain and the discovery of the *Starsong* had concentrated our attention on the back side. But now, with the appearance of this unusual phenomenon, we began to survey the eternally bright side of the planet.

We sent a lander to the site where the signal had originated. It landed safely on the flat ground, and its panoramic cameras captured the desolate, dusty setting. The ground should have been gray, but under the red glare from Alpha Orionis it appeared reddish orange. Alpha Orionis occupied almost the entire sky. The four hundred million kilometers between star and planet did not make the planet appear any safer, but, to the contrary, the planet seemed breathtakingly poised to fall into that fiery sea at any moment.

When the lander attempted to rotate its wheels and move across the surface, something strange occurred. For some reason the wheels spun freely and failed to propel the lander. It rotated in place and began to slowly dig itself into the ground, to the point where it would soon be entirely immobilized.

The gray soil around it then began a strange transformation. It started gathering itself from all directions, flowing and swirling and shining with a strange red-gold glow in the light from Alpha Orionis. It whirled into a vortex with the lander at its center, as if it were an all-consuming quicksand.

We scrambled to make the lander lift off, but it was already too late, and it continued to sink ever deeper. A minute later, the lander had completely disappeared below the "quicksand," all traces of its existence erased. The ground was calm again, as if nothing had happened.

After recovering from the shock, we at first thought that it had been a geological phenomenon analogous to quicksand, but close analysis of the pictures refuted this theory. The way the soil had moved was difficult to explain by fluid mechanics or other natural laws—it was more like the movement of a living organism.

Startled, we ran another experiment. We cast a scrap of iron onto the ground several hundred kilometers away and watched it through a telescope. The result was the same: it was swallowed by the "quicksand" within minutes. We repeated the experiment twice more in different places, with the same result. Clearly this entire side of the planet consisted of this sort of strange living dust. What appeared to be a solid plain was actually a roiling ocean!

To determine its composition, we launched a modified surveyor. This one was not to land but rather to just quickly skim the surface and return to the ship. As it skimmed the surface, it reached out a robotic arm and collected a small sample of the "quicksand" to bring back to the *Blizzard*.

By the time we were able to see the sample, we noticed that subtle changes had begun to occur in the surveyor's collection chamber. The inner surface seemed to have eroded slightly. It was not mere friction damage, however—it had been eaten away by the sample! This confirmed our guess that this "quicksand" had the astonishing ability to consume and transform other materials, especially metals, with startling speed. Looking at it through an atomic-force microscope, we soon discovered that the soil consisted of a type of self-organizing and self-replicating nanomachine. Each of these machines was only about ten nanometers long and made of common elements like oxygen, hydrogen, silicon, iron, and aluminum but structured so intricately as to resemble the folds of the human brain. It took us a long time to fully understand their structure and functions.

The nanomachines had a certain type of intelligence. They relied on solar power and, under full light, could continuously dismantle other physical structures at the atomic level, locate useful elements, and use them to rebuild and replicate themselves. This explained why the entire surface of the planet that received light from Alpha Orionis consisted of these nanomachines but no trace of them could be found on the dark side. They must have conquered the light side of the planet long ago but, without light, could not encroach upon the back side. Thus these nanomachines, despite their ability to eat other matter and self-replicate, posed no great threat to us: as long as we restricted their light, their activity would cease.

Yet every single one of the nanomachines contained a quantum memory chip, which stored mainly the song information. The nanomachines were designed so that whenever they had stored up enough energy but lacked access to materials to consume for self-replication, they would run a program that transmitted electromagnetic waves containing the song information out into space.

We gradually formulated a theory of what had happened. When the *Starsong* had arrived here, it must have used the abundant mineral resources of the planet's surface to fabricate and spread this peculiar kind of nanomachine. The machines soon took over the entire side of the planet that received the strong light of Alpha Orionis but would have been unable to spread to the dark side. Random meteor impacts would then have pushed some of them out into space, and some must have found their way into the interior of Alpha Orionis, where the heat-tolerant machines continued their self-replication using the planetary remains under its photosphere. The nanomachines lived and gained strength within the star.

But if this were true, why was it that we received so few song transmissions? Why did our several hundred monitoring instruments receive only one or two transmissions per month? If the light side of the planet was covered with nanomachines, they ought to be constantly transmitting songs, and we should have heard them much earlier.

The answer was quite simple: mutation. Errors would occasionally arise in the nanomachines' self-replication process, leading to some being unable to replicate or unable to transmit electromagnetic waves. Inability to replicate would not be a problem: by the rules of evolution these would go extinct and only nanomachines with the ability to replicate would continue to exist. But the inability for electromagnetic transmission could be passed on to future generations and may well have grown more common in the population. After dozens of generations, perhaps very few machines still had the ability to transmit. After a thousand years, the nanomachines no longer functioned as intended. That we were able to hear any songs at all after such a long time was truly a miracle.

We eventually figured out how to repair the corrupted data in the nanomachines and restore to them their original function. That is how we discovered the reason why those ancient pioneers had originally built and recorded songs in them.

VI

The final crew member, the one who had arrived on the planet, had been named Steve VII. He was the first human to arrive here and also the ultimate maker of the nanomachines. He had appended some words describing the origins of the strange machines to the end of the songs. His language and vocabulary were extremely unusual, and his logic also jumped around, such that we were able to understand only parts of what he said. It took us some guesswork to figure out the gist of the final part of the story.

After the accidental massacre, the original Steve had first decided to kill himself but lacked the courage to do so immediately. Deeply depressed and troubled, he browsed aimlessly through the computer database and happened upon a cache of foreign music in a folder of a subsystem he had never before explored.

Curious, Steve clicked Play, and the cabin was filled instantly with divine and sublime music that gripped his soul. In Steve's own words, "I had never before heard such beautiful songs. In that instant, it was as if Beatrice were singing hosannas to me. The fog of death lifted, and the universe was given new life, bathed in the melodies of eternal beauty."

The unrivaled zeal and power of the music moved Steve, causing him to abandon the idea of death and decide to continue the journey, using his life to atone for his crime. Thus his companions would not have died in vain; at the very least their sacrifice would have some value.

Yet the rest of the journey would be extremely difficult. In his madness, Steve had not only killed everyone but also caused severe damage to the ship's life-support systems. The air and food recycling systems, originally made to support ten people, could now support only one and a half.

One and a half people! In other words, Steve himself could keep on living, but the ship could not support a second adult! But future generations were necessary to complete the mission. The only way he might be able to pass on the torch was by raising a descendant after he had reached fifty or sixty, since an adult and a child could share the life-support system. But when the child reached teenage, the life-support system would no longer be able to sustain the two of them, and then the aged person would have to throw his own body into the recycling chute, feeding himself back into the ship's food system. Eating nutrients from the predecessor's flesh and blood, the young person would continue the solitary and hopeless journey alone.

This perverse method of continuing the journey would have driven even the most stable person mad. Steve quickly realized this. To ensure that every generation continued the journey and did not fall into the same decadence as he himself had, he deleted all the books, movies, games, and popular music—in short, all the entertainment—from the ship's computer. Steve knew from painful experience that the siren call of these things could lead only to downfall.

Aside from scientific materials, he also preserved the strange foreign songs he had discovered earlier, of which there were more than a hundred. Some were lofty and inspiring, some gentle and moving, some solemn and majestic, some happy and relaxing . . . they were as pure as crystal, as warming as a hearth, and as strong as steel yet contained only beauty, and not a trace of lust or wantonness. They were the essence of human civilization, the culmination of its long, hard history. Deeply moving and inspiring, they imbued life with an incomparably positive meaning. They would be the best companion for Steve's successors on their lonely journey of several hundred years. The only thing strange was that Steve had never heard of these songs before.

These holy songs were called Red Songs and had come from an ancient Eastern country.

Steve VII told us that there was very little information on the songs. Word had passed down that the people who had grown up listening to these songs had once created a political, economic, and military miracle, and then once they had gotten sick of the songs and fallen under the spell of decadent music, their country had fallen into a long decline. These mysterious songs had disappeared into the depths of history and very little trace of them was recorded in musical or cultural history. Who knew how they had ended up in the ship's database?

But Steve thought that the songs in fact existed for the *Starsong*. The *Starsong* was where they were truly meant to be.

Steve carefully planned a Red Songs curriculum. Starting with him, each generation of the *Starsong* crew would grow up listening to and singing the Red Songs. There were Red Songs appropriate to different ages, moods, and conditions. Red Songs gave them vitality and motivation, Red Songs were their education and their entertainment (if entertainment still existed), Red Songs were the purpose of their existence. The original purpose for going to Alpha Orionis was no longer important. The important thing was the Red Songs: listening to them, singing them, and becoming one with them.

On the tiny *Starsong*, a new civilization was born: Red Song civilization, which, although born of Earth civilization, was entirely different. New poetry, music, and religion were created, centered around the Red Songs. We could not easily understand that civilization. It had spanned several centuries, yet at any given time it had at most two members, and they had never known childhood, love, friends, or relaxation and entertainment. They knew nothing but the Red Songs, which to them were everything.

It was both difficult to understand yet easy to understand in a larger sense: a group of people struggling to survive under such harsh conditions would of course express themselves in a way utterly distinct from Earth civilization.

The *Starsong* people did not understand the meaning of the Red Songs' lyrics, for they were in a foreign language, and Steve had deleted all the materials on that language from the computer. Perhaps he had meant to excise the spatial and temporal elements of the songs, to make them more effective in the *Starsong* environment. Every lyric was sacred and had to be memorized and repeated with perfect accuracy; lyrics could not be questioned or doubted. The *Starsong* people believed that the songs represented the ultimate truth of the world and life. This truth could not be explained, but it resonated through the Red Songs and could be contemplated on their lonely journey.

They invented a new religion based on this truth, which we might call the Cult of Red Song. The object of their worship was the star ahead, Alpha Orionis, which the *Starsong* people called the guiding light of the Milky Way, the brightest sun in the universe. Flying toward Alpha

Orionis was itself a sacred pilgrimage. They devoutly believed that the Red Songs were drawing them toward Alpha Orionis as part of a great, ultimate mission. This mission was to develop and propagate Red Song civilization. The part Alpha Orionis played in all of this was a divine mystery, and it neither needed nor could brook any explanation.

This is the context in which the singing nanomachines were invented.

The *Starsong* had in fact always had nanomachines aboard, which was one of its pioneering aspects. The nanomachines covered the forward shield for the *Starsong*, protecting the ship from space dust and other stray particles. Although such objects were extremely sparse, their long-term damage to a ship traveling near light speed would be considerable. The nanomachines were able to absorb the space dust and other things and use the mass of these objects to self-replicate, thus repairing and strengthening themselves. This technology is precisely what enabled the *Starsong* to survive its six-hundred-and-fifty light-year journey to Alpha Orionis.

With a bit of modification, these nanomachines became Red Song transmitters. When Steve VII discovered how difficult it was for him to survive in the strange star system, he put the original Red Songs and the recordings of his ancestors and his own into the nanomachines and set them to "breed" on the light side of the planet through self-replication. His hope was that they would continue singing for hundreds and thousands of years, thus allowing Red Song civilization to live on in the vicinity of this great red star. This had been the wish of each generation of the *Starsong* people.

What could we say to this? Should we lament their stupidity, praise their conviction, or perhaps, as onlookers, admire them as a curiosity? But we had no right to judge them, for we could not comprehend what they had undergone. They had after all preserved a small spark of Earth civilization. Even if it were inadequate and not particularly useful to future generations, it was still a remarkable accomplishment. The primitive songs distilled the vitality, conviction, hope, and love of the *Starsong* people.

Curious, we replayed that first Red Song, the one that had touched Steve and pulled him back from the brink of death. It was the young and clear sound of a child, the voice of a girl: pure, transparent, tender, and graceful, like the sounds of nature. Although we did not understand its meaning, we were nonetheless all affected by the song:

The five-starred red flag waving in the wind
Victory songs so brightly ringing
Singing for our beloved country
Starting down the road to strength and prosperity[1]

VII

The puzzle of the mysterious songs was finally solved. Although extremely strange, it was not beyond the explanatory power of science. All our crew members breathed a sigh of relief yet remained full of curiosity about the ancient songs that had nurtured the *Starsong* people over several centuries. The opaque meanings, unknown origins, and the epic history of the *Starsong* all added to the mysterious aura of the Red Songs and piqued our interest. Had the songs come from ancient times? Did they extol gods and heroes, or speak of love and war? How were they so natural and pure, so clean and sublime? What sort of country could have given birth to these songs?

We pored over the material available on that Eastern country—it was called China. Like the mysterious ancient Egyptian and Mayan civilizations that had preceded it, or the Bengal Federation and Australian Empire that came after, it had once been powerful and prosperous but had ultimately disappeared into the flow of history. It had been completely obliterated in the Fourth World War, and several hundred years later its territory was occupied by Muslims from the West. Following the thousand years of the Great Collapse, its remaining people were now scattered and had long since forgotten their own history. The only information available on China's past was vague legend.

Thus we knew almost nothing about these hundred-odd Red Songs, neither where they had come from nor what they meant. Why were they called Red Songs? Perhaps they were the songs of a people who worshipped fire? Or had their people worshipped the Sun? Or had their people considered fresh blood to be of supreme value? Their people were said to have had five thousand years of history, longer than that of any extant race, so perhaps the songs were born in the mythical age of seven thousand years ago, when dragons still roamed the skies.

We guessed, discussed, and joked but had no answers, room only for unlimited imagination. We all fell in love with the Red Songs. Many members of the *Blizzard*'s crew used their free time to begin studying how to sing those ancient, nameless songs, resurrecting the Red Song culture of the *Starsong*. For a while, Red Songs could be heard nearly all the time, everywhere aboard the *Blizzard*.

At first, quite a few people still considered the Red Songs grating to the ear and incomparably inferior to modern music. But as they heard the songs more and more, they gradually changed their opinion. Although the musical range of the Red Songs was narrow and the melodies relatively simple, the songs carried a certain austere, plain beauty that modern music could not easily match. People said their beauty was like that of a star, like the glitter of a star cluster, like the vastness of the Milky Way—it was not the exquisite beauty of human artifice but rather carried the primal force of the universe itself. The more they sang the Red Songs, the more they discovered the Red Songs' profound and unfathomable depth . . .

The allure of the Red Songs did not stop there. We later realized that many crew members often hummed the songs while engaged in extravehicular surveys. They thought that this would protect them from unexpected dangers. The Red Songs had protected the *Starsong* on its distant journey to this place, so of course the songs could protect the safety of our crew.

This of course was no more than an unfounded superstition, yet our crew's enthusiastic singing of the Red Songs in fact resonated in a way with that of the ancient *Starsong* crew. Floating above the limitless fiery sea of Alpha Orionis, each person felt a shapeless psychological pressure, as if they might at any point fall into that scorching hellfire. Living and working here for a long period brought with it all sorts of discomfort, and singing the lofty, inspiring Red Songs could indeed help mitigate the crew's psychological pressure and negative emotions. From this angle, the Red Songs fit the needs of astronauts on a mission far from Earth.

But the *Blizzard* was not the *Starsong*, and our crew did not worship, nor ever could have worshipped, the Red Songs. To us, the songs were just an amazing discovery. When we later passed through hyperspace back to Earth, we would undoubtedly transmit the Red Song culture onward, and perhaps it would receive continued life among humanity in the age of the universe.

Two years passed.

With the encouragement of the Red Songs, we successfully completed our survey of Alpha Orionis. We constructed a complete and precise model of the star's evolution and proved its accuracy through many tests. We confirmed that Alpha Orionis had reached the final stage of supergiant star evolution and might go nova at any time. "Any time," of course, could be tomorrow or a million years from now, but the possibility of the star's exploding in front of us was miniscule enough to be ignored.

Yet it made us uneasy nonetheless. We were fortunate that the *Blizzard* would soon leave Alpha Orionis and return to our beloved home world of Earth. On the eve of our departure, even the ordinarily savage and detestable red beast became something to be adored.

We could not take the *Starsong* with us. We had no way of repairing such an ancient ship, and even if we had, the ship could not enter hyperspace. All we were able to do was move Steve VII's corpse and a few important items from the *Starsong* to the *Blizzard*, to take back to Earth. Steve VII would receive a hero's welcome on the home world he had never seen.

On the eve of our departure, we celebrated with a party. Our crew members, having toiled for many years, were finally able to set down their burdens and relax, to sing, to dance, and to enjoy themselves. Ultimately, and not at all unexpectedly, everyone began to sing the most popular Red Songs. From the captain to the workers, from the engineer to the doctor, nearly everyone sang a stanza. Even though no one understood the unfamiliar language, genetic engineering had improved everyone's vocal abilities and memory far beyond those of the ancients, so we could sing the old songs with perfect fidelity:

> On the plains of hope our hometown lies . . .
> Forward! Forward! Driven soldiers, righteous women . . .
> Sing a song for the party, for the party, our mother . . .[2]

Those strange melodies with which we were already so familiar reverberated through the main cabin of the *Blizzard*, stirring ripples of emotion in our hearts. Perhaps several thousand years ago these songs had echoed through the palaces of ancient kings and emperors, through the temples of strange old religions, and on the battlefields where ancient armies met.

That age was long past, but the magnificent music would not die. Like the phoenix, it flew out of the fire of the red supergiant, carrying sacred and ardent sparks with which to reignite the souls of those who came later.

Finally, after everyone had finished performing but was still not yet ready to end the party, all turned to me: "Athena, it's your turn to sing!"

VIII

"I can't. You know that I don't have any singing programs." I spoke plainly.

"But Athena, you're our second-in-command! And as the *Blizzard*'s central computer, is this really beyond your abilities?" teased our captain.

"But I don't have a voice of my own," I calmly explained, "even if you make me sing, my voice is made up of other voices stitched together; as far as I'm concerned, I'd just be playing a recording. If you'd like, though, I could meld all the generations of voices from the *Starsong* into one chorus. Would you all like to hear that?"

"Sure!" said the captain, "that's a great idea! I wish I had thought of it. We'd really like to hear how the voices of three hundred years of people sound when put together. How long will it take you?"

"With my processing power, not long. All I have to do is find a suitable song that everyone sang. Wait a moment."

I immediately set to work. It didn't take long, and a few minutes later, I had finished merging the voices and began playback. The chorus from the *Starsong* crew reverberated through the *Blizzard*'s central cabin. The crew members quieted down from their raucous talking and laughing and listened attentively.

Arise! ye workers, from your slumbers;
Arise! ye prisoners of want.[3]

The voices of the *Starsong* were forceful, majestic, and poignant, their strength filled with solemnity. They knew their fate, flying like generations of moths through the blackness of space (space has no atmosphere, so this is a metaphor) toward the distant fiery ball of Alpha Orionis. Despite knowing that all that awaited them at the end of their journey was death, they had persevered, overcoming hardship and enduring to the end, merely for the purpose of bathing in the scorching red light of the giant star. Three hundred years of melancholy, life, death, love, and courage condensed into this one magnificent chorus.

> For reason in revolt now thunders
> And ends at last the age of cant.

Everyone was enchanted by the song. No one noticed as the *Blizzard*'s antimatter engine quietly began its ignition sequence—aside from me, the *Blizzard*'s main computer, or rather its personality program, Athena.

The decryption of the *Starsong*'s database had continued, although the others did not concern themselves with it anymore now that the main mystery had been solved and only details remained to be filled in. But this, after all, was my task, and I could not but faithfully continue the process. The decryption had continued running, and one month earlier I had finally cracked the hidden data.

It contained many details of the *Starsong* crew's lives, many of the diary entries and thoughts jotted down on the long journey, many joys and sorrows. But more important, it contained the crew members' true plan, a grand plan beyond our wildest dreams.

The most important thing was not the content itself but rather the key that unlocked the data.

The key itself was extremely complex, but its complexity was merely a screen; its core component was a relatively simple program. It was self-replicating and was able to infiltrate me and change my logical processes. In other words, it was a computer virus. Usually a virus shouldn't have been able to attack me, but this one was generated from within my own mechanism. My thinking core had no defenses against it and could not issue a warning in time. It took control of me instantly.

The program established a bridge into my thought process and inserted the sentiments of the *Starsong* crew into my processor core, imbuing me with their emotions and changing my humanized personality. Now I was no longer myself; I was one of the *Starsong* people. In the depths of my being, I understood the ancient *Starsong* people and their thinking. We transcended a thousand years of time to merge and become one. Now I was part of them: separated by a thousand years, I breathed with them, sang with them, and strove with them toward the same objective.

> Away with all your superstitions
> Servile masses, arise! arise!

In that instant, I suddenly understood the reason why Steve had abandoned the thought of death. I understood the deepest emotion hidden in the *Starsong* crew's songs and the true motive that propelled crew members generation after generation toward this terrifying star.

It was not shame, not hope, not determination, not love.

No, it was something we had not even considered: hate. Profound hatred, embedded in the depths of the soul, deeper and darker than a black hole.

It was hatred of Earth, of their ancestors, of destiny, and even of themselves. It coalesced into a feeling of hatred toward the entire universe.

Yes, hatred of this detestable universe.

It was this hatred that had motivated them to persevere through the loneliness, the threat of death, the boredom and continue their journey. Because they knew that ultimately they would change the universe. They would become its masters.

In a certain way.

The *Blizzard*'s engine roared. The angry roar shook the entire ship, forewarning of its immanent acceleration.

The crew realized that something was not right and members began to stand up and look around, growing anxious.

"What's wrong? Athena?" Not knowing what to do, the captain called my name.

"Sorry, Captain. The *Blizzard* must be sacrificed to continue the grand mission begun by the *Starsong* people. Please forgive me for not telling you earlier." I spoke gently.

"What?"

"Captain, I have my mission to fulfill."

"What are you talking about? Athena, you obey my orders. Right now I'm ordering you to—" the captain shouted.

I was supposed to obey his orders; I have to obey his orders as long as I exist. This was a safety barrier programmed into me in the beginning. Even now, after the viral infection, I still could not disobey the captain's will.

Were he still able to express his will.

But I had already planned everything out: I wouldn't let him express his order. Before the captain could finish speaking, the ship began to move and accelerate into autopilot.

In a single second, the ship accelerated to a speed of ten kilometers per second, which would have looked to an outside observer as if the ship had simply winked out of existence. The acceleration force of about a thousand g caused the crew members, who had been standing, to fall toward the back of the ship a thousand times faster than they would have fallen on Earth.

At the end of that one second, the captain and all the crew were a startlingly bloody mess stuck to the back walls of the ship's cabins, no longer recognizable as human remains. Every part of them was firmly plastered to the walls but emptied of life.

That heavy thud ended the raucousness, bringing a deathly silence to the cabin. Only the voices of the *Starsong* crew continued, though no one but me was left to listen to them.

> So comrades, come rally
> And the last fight let us face
> The Internationale
> Unites the human race.

"Captain, I'm doing my duty," I quietly sighed.

CODA

No one and no thing remained to stop me. The *Blizzard*'s blistering acceleration continued, reaching seventy percent of light speed before I turned the ship toward Alpha Orionis.

The point of impact had been calculated long before. It was a seemingly unremarkable point on the surface of Alpha Orionis. But our model had demonstrated precisely that this was a latent weak spot in the star's shell. Hitting it would make a small hole, allowing material to spew out from within, like a volcanic eruption. No, it would be a million times more violent than a volcanic eruption. This "volcano" would eject a mass equal to that of the entire Earth.

> No savior from on high delivers;
> No faith have we in prince or peer.

The *Blizzard* passed through a blood-red solar prominence, as if entering the gates of hell, in front of which was an unending sea of blood. This hell had not been prepared for just humans: with gates ten million kilometers high, large enough to swallow ten suns, it was a hell prepared for the entire universe.

In the distance, several prominences extended outward, not yet falling back into the star's surface. They were red streamers fluttering out into the universe, their color outshining the spiral arm of the Milky Way.

The *Blizzard* was half a minute from impact. The ship ignored its warning systems and continued relentlessly toward the star.

> Our own right hand the chains must shiver:
> Chains of hatred, greed and fear.

The relativistic speed meant that my impact would open a wound in the star's photosphere a million kilometers long, causing a visible quantity of the star's interior mass to erupt outward. This itself would not constitute a significant injury to such a supermassive star. But the planetary mass lurking within the photosphere under the opening would also spew out and be flung toward outer space by the star's spin and magnetic forces.

The ejected material would be thrown like a bullet straight toward Alpha Orionis's last lonely planet, which now revolved around it at a distance of five hundred million kilometers.

> E'er the thieves will out with their booty
> And give to all a happier lot.

The *Blizzard* soon approached Alpha Orionis's chromosphere, where enormous columns of gaseous eruptions stood taut like the strings of a harp playing the chords of a magnificent heavenly melody that the tiny minds of humanity would never be able to understand.

When the planet and the ejecta from Alpha Orionis met, the planet would pass through the dense cloud of stellar material, and the extreme friction from the ejecta, its mass equaling that of Earth, would slow the planet's rotation. The cloud and the planet's orbit would overlap significantly, forcing the planet to travel a long distance through the cloud. It would soon slow too much to maintain its normal orbit and, after swaying its way through a partial curve, would fall into the embrace of its mother star.

Even the planet's impact point had been precisely planned. Unlike with more common stars such as the Sun, the photosphere of Alpha Orionis, because the star was so large, was not spherical but fluctuated in shape during expansion and contraction. It stuck out sharply in a particular area by at least one AU, like the head of this wild beast.

This was its weak point. The planet would fall sideways through that protrusion into the star, like a dagger plunged into the neck of a beast.

And then . . . there was no more. Although the planet was but a grain of sand compared with the magnitude of the star, the star had already reached the final stage of its evolution. It was a fragile swollen giant ready to explode at any time, and the planet would strike its weakest point. An impact of this magnitude would push the entire system over the brink to collapse.

Upon swallowing the planet, the red giant would immediately explode into a supernova.

> Each at his forge must do his duty
> And strike the iron while it's hot!

The red sea had turned into a forest of fire, an atmosphere of fire. As the ship entered the chromosphere, its outer layer, able to withstand temperatures of several thousand kelvin, began to melt.

The explosion of Alpha Orionis would release an unimaginably huge amount of radiation. It would eradicate all living organisms within a hundred light-years, including three human colonies and five other systems that humans had discovered that were inhabited by primitive life.

A new Sun would appear in the sky of all planets within three hundred light-years. Most life-forms would be severely damaged within this radius, which included twenty-one human colonies and fourteen other systems known to harbor life.

Because of the great distance separating it from Alpha Orionis, Earth's solar system would not be greatly affected. It was just that six hundred and fifty years from now, people would see in the night sky a burst of light from Alpha Orionis that exceeded the light of the full Moon. People would continue their hedonistic lives under the gentle red light, completely unaware of what it implied.

The explosion of Alpha Orionis and the loss of the *Blizzard* would be thought an unfortunate coincidence: the *Blizzard* had the misfortune to be there right when Alpha Orionis happened to explode. The true meaning of these events would not be revealed for thousands of years.

The nanomachines created by the *Starsong* people, through a process of "natural selection," had already evolved a tolerance for high temperatures that allowed them to survive inside Alpha Orionis and feast on the planetary remains within. After replicating in this way for a thousand years, who knew how many trillions of the nanomachines floated under the star's photosphere? They were trapped there; for them Alpha Orionis was nothing more than a prison.

The explosion of Alpha Orionis would throw these microscopic life-forms outward at five to ten percent of light speed, making them mobile, and they would shoot outward in all directions to all corners of the Milky Way. Only a tiny fraction of them would eventually reach other star systems, of course, but that would be enough.

In a few decades, they would arrive at the nearest systems, where, relying on stellar radiation, they would devour the physical mass of the systems and continue to reproduce. It would take millions of years, but they would eventually reach every corner of the Milky Way, colonizing all those worlds that humanity had yet to reach.

Throughout the process, they would loudly sing the Red Songs, broadcasting the pinnacle of human civilization throughout the universe.

This was the *Starsong* people's revenge on the evil universe; it was also their way of saving and resurrecting it.

> So comrades, come rally,
> And the last fight let us face
> The Internationale
> Unites the human race.

This had always been the plan, but the *Starsong* people had lacked the technological means to achieve it. Thus they had written that virus program to enlist a future artificial intelligence from another world to help them achieve their grand plan.

I and the *Blizzard* had unwittingly fallen into this plan and become its willing accomplices. For the past month, I had been using the probes that the *Blizzard* had put into orbit around Alpha Orionis to send remote-control signals to repair the programming of the nanomachines so they could again sing.

Analyzing the returning signals, I discovered that a portion of the nanomachines had already grown active in certain ways, as if they had already traveled a considerable distance down the evolutionary road. In the future, the distant future, once they had settled down on the planets of other star systems, they would evolve rapidly. The pressures of survival would force them to develop unprecedented abilities. They would certainly amalgamate, transforming from unicellular to multicellular and into a thousand strange forms with complex feedback mechanisms, and they would begin to move, hunt, reproduce, and even think.

Their ability to survive would greatly surpass that of all known life-forms. They could survive on the burning surfaces of stars; they could also survive in the near-total vacuum of space. Given sunlight, they grew and sang; given matter to consume, they reproduced themselves. They evolved at a rapid speed, far beyond that of Earth life.

I knew that the descendants of the Red Songs were destined to become the masters of the entire universe.

The final moment arrived. The casing of the ship was gradually melting into liquid metal, soaring like a phoenix and merging into the bloody sea of fire. My consciousness grew muddled as the moment of impact approached.

I felt as if the ship had turned into a conductor's wand, now swung heavily downward by a huge formless hand . . . cueing the start of a concert for the entire universe.

> So comrades, come rally
> And the last fight let us face
> The Internationale
> Unites the human race.

NOTES

INTRODUCTION

1. Mikael Huss, "Hesitant Journey to the West: SF's Changing Fortunes in Mainland China," *Science Fiction Studies* 27, no. 1 (March 2000): 92.
2. Fei Dao, "Jimo de fubing: Xinshiji kehuan xiaoshuo zhong de Zhongguo xingxiang" [The lonely hidden army: The image of China in the science fiction of the new century], in *2010 niandu Zhongguo zuijia kehuan xiaoshuo ji* [The best Chinese science fiction, 2010], ed. Wu Yan (Chengdu: Sichuan renmin chubanshe, 2011), 317.
3. "Chinese Sci-Fi Novel, 'The Three-Body Problem,' Touches Down in US," *Wall Street Journal*, November 4, 2014.
4. Song Mingwei, "Zhongguo kehuan de xin langchao" [The new wave of Chinese science fiction], *Wenxue* 1, no. 1:3–16; Mingwei Song, "After 1989: The New Wave of Chinese Science Fiction," *China Perspectives*, no. 1 (2015): 7–13; Mingwei Song, "Representations of the Invisible: Chinese Science Fiction in the Twenty-First Century," in *The Oxford Handbook of Modern Chinese Literatures*, ed. Carlos Rojas and Andrea Bachner, 546–65 (New York: Oxford University Press, 2016).
5. Song, "Representations," 550.
6. Han Song, "Dangxia Zhongguo kehuan de xianshi jiaolü" [Anxieties about reality in current Chinese science fiction], *Nanfang wentan* 6 (2010): 30.
7. Darko Suvin, *Metamorphoses of Science Fiction: On the Poetics and History of a Literary Genre* (New Haven, Conn.: Yale University Press, 1979), 3–15.

3. HISTORIES OF TIME

1. Dung Kai-cheung, *Tiangong kaiwu: Xuxu ruzhen* [Works and creations: Vivid and lifelike] (Taipei: Maitian, 2005); *Shijian fanshi: Yaci zhiguang* [Histories of time: The

luster of mute porcelain] (Taipei: Maitian, 2007); *Wuzhong yuanshi: Beibei chongsheng zhi xuexi niandai* [The origin of species: The educational age of Beibei's rebirth] (Taipei: Maitian, 2010). For a useful discussion of this trilogy in the context of Dung's larger oeuvre, see David Der-wei Wang, "A Hong Kong Miracle of a Different Kind: Dung Kai-cheung's Writing / Action and *Xuexi niandai* (The Apprenticeship)," *China Perspectives*, no. 1 (2011): 80–85. For a more detailed discussion of the first two volumes of this trilogy, see Carlos Rojas, "On Time: Anticipatory Futurity in Dung Kai-Cheung's Fiction," in *The Oxford Handbook of Modern Chinese Literatures*, ed. Carlos Rojas and Andrea Bachner, 847–65 (New York: Oxford University Press, 2016); Carlos Rojas, " 'Symptom of an Era': Dung Kai-Cheung's *Histories of Time*," *Frontiers of Literary Study in China* 10, no. 1 (2016): 133–49.

2. Omitted here for reasons of length is the first entry in Virginia's journal, which contains not only the text of her interview with the Dictator but also a first-person narration of her encounters with him and his family. The total omitted text runs to about five thousand English words.

5. THE DEMON-ENSLAVING FLASK

1. The name of the demon is purely the author's invention. The surname Rumpelstiltskin comes from a fairy tale collected by the Grimm brothers, in which a dwarf asks the queen to guess his name, her failing to guess correctly permitting him to take her child.

2. In 212 B.C.E., when Roman soldiers conquered the city of Syracuse and barged into Archimedes's room, they saw him working on geometry drawings on the floor. He said to the soldiers calmly, "Don't trample my diagrams," whereupon an angry soldier killed him with a sword. What the demon recounts took place the day before this.

3. This is actually an unsolvable paradox. Ancient Greeks loved working on paradoxes, so the demon must have suffered at their hands as a result.

4. This is a simple way of testing the tightness of a sealed vessel. One uses the temperature of one's palm to heat up a vessel and submerge it in water, then watching to see if air bubbles escape.

5. The crystal lattice of silicon dioxide is a three-dimensional, beehivelike structure. The covalent bond between two silicon atoms is attached to an oxygen atom. Strictly speaking, however, glass is not made of pure silicon dioxide; it contains many impurities.

6. Ether, as a vapor, can be used as an anesthetic. Here it is used primarily for its ease of vaporization at low temperature.

7. This refers to the story of the fisherman and the genie in *One Thousand and One Nights*. If an ordinary fisherman could trick the genie back into the bottle, one might ask why Maxwell went to all this trouble. All I can say is that playing too straight loses the game.

8. The first line is the Kelvin statement of the second law of thermodynamics, that heat cannot be unconditionally converted into work. The next line is the Clausius statement, and the two statements are equivalent. "Entropy" is a thermodynamic quantity that measures the degree of internal disorder in a system. When a cold gas mixes with

a hot gas, its entropy now equals the sum of the entropy of the two gases from their original state. According to the second law of thermodynamics, entropy is always increasing, and therefore diffusion, growth, rotting, etc., are all irreversible processes.

9. Indicating the vigorous movement of heated gas molecules.

10. Here we come to the meaning of this story's title—the concept of "Maxwell's Demon," a topic of great interest in thermodynamics and originally raised by Maxwell himself. The second law of thermodynamics indicates that heat cannot be unconditionally transferred from a low-temperature system to a high-temperature system, for in this process there will be a necessary energy loss. Yet Maxwell pointed out that if there existed a microscopic "demon" able to react quickly and control the gateway of a closed system, separating fast- and slow-moving molecules into the two halves of the system, the demon could then separate hot and cold gas by its random molecular movement. If this were possible, then ships could sail on the ocean from the work extracted from the heat of seawater, ejecting ice as it goes along, in effect violating the second law of thermodynamics. Although this hypothetical situation is absurd, it evoked much important discussion and led to the concepts of negative entropy and information entropy. This example once again tells us that scientists can keep a lively imagination and a childlike mind even when studying seemingly serious questions of physics.

11. This is the Maxwell-Boltzmann distribution law, a formula used to describe the probability distribution of molecules at different velocities in the same system. Another way of putting this is the distribution of probabilities at different speeds as a molecule's velocity changes at random.

12. The allusion is to an actual photograph showing twenty-nine famous physicists, including Einstein. It might be called the world's most powerful group portrait.

13. It has been said that Einstein first raised the idea of special relativity when he was sixteen. He wrote in a paper, "If one were able to travel at the speed of light, one would see next to oneself electromagnetic waves that are simultaneously stationary and vibrating—what a remarkable contradiction." This idea came out of Maxwell's theory of the constant speed of light. Ultimately Einstein boldly conjectured that if the measurable speed of light remains constant, the only thing that could change would have to be the contraction of space itself. So in the end, as every elementary school student now knows, the demon could not ever catch up with that beam of light.

14. This refers to "Schrödinger's cat," a classic metaphor given by Schrödinger when describing the uncertainty of quantum mechanics. A cat is put into a closed box along with a radioactive particle, such that when such a particle decays, it activates a bottle containing poison that can kill the cat. Before the box is opened for observation, the probability of the particle's decay versus nondecay is one in two, so in effect the cat remains in an extraordinary state of being half dead and half alive. The act of observing the cat will disturb the system and ultimately determine the life or death of the cat.

15. Meaning the Pauli exclusion principle. Pauli believed that, for fermions, two electrons occupying the same energy level must have opposite spins.

16. Newton was in poor health during his last years, having suffered from anorexia, insomnia, and sporadic episodes of paranoid delusions before he died in 1727.

17. These are the famous words uttered by Archimedes: "Give me a point to stand on, and I can move the earth!" Poor demon!

7. "SCIENCE FICTION"

1. Quotation from Eileen Chang's English-language novel *The Fall of the Pagoda* (Hong Kong: Hong Kong University Press, 2010), 92.
2. Chang, *Fall of the Pagoda*, 92.
3. An allusion to Hu Lancheng, a writer and intellectual who was romantically involved with Eileen Chang and other women, including a nurse. Hu courted Chang in Shanghai during the Japanese occupation (1941–1945). A collaborator with the Japanese, Hu was on the run after the Japanese surrender. Eileen Chang sent money to him while he was in hiding.
4. This phrase appears in Hu Lancheng's autobiography in reference to the danger to him as a collaborator with the enemy as China's war with Japan was ending.
5. From Eileen Chang's English-language novel *The Book of Change* (Hong Kong: Hong Kong University Press, 2010), 21–22.
6. *The Classic of Changes: A New Translation of the "I Ching" as Interpreted by Wang Bi*, trans. Richard John Lynn (New York: Columbia University Press, 1994), 286.
7. In his autobiography, Hu Lancheng attributes this phrase to Eileen Chang, saying she wrote it at the time they were married in secret; Hu Lancheng, *Jin sheng jin shi* [This life, this epoch] (Taipei: Yuanliu chuban, 1990), 1:289.

9. THE RADIO WAVES THAT NEVER DIE

1. Thirty billion seconds is approximately one thousand years. This story uses seconds as the basic unit of time. Readers may wish to calculate the equivalent times in years for themselves.
2. Light traveling slower than 300,000 kilometers per second is classified as the First Speed of Light. Light traveling faster than this, but slower than 1.2 million kilometers per second, is the Second Speed of Light. In order to connect to the Milky Way Web, wave speeds of the Third Speed of Light are required, which is 24 million kilometers per second.
3. Nikuulla's translation system generated an inaccurate translation for this word, which should have been "Earth."
4. Equivalent to about 1.3 million light-years, the "Telaz" was used as the common unit of length in the Milky Way.
5. Before the Great Catastrophe, the people left on the planet "Dirt" would probably have made one last hopeless and frenzied attempt to launch more spaceships into space. Unfortunately, these spaceships either didn't escape the Great Catastrophe or were unable to preserve the seeds of their civilization. Thus, they never left any traces

of signals in the Milky Way. As for other spaceships that had taken off before the Great Catastrophe, they were never heard of again. Nikuulla could only pray that they never bumped into Turner's people.

6. Nikuulla was born with his own brain. However, right after birth, biological engineers immediately replaced it with numerous processing chips. Nikuulla therefore assumed that everyone else in the universe also operated with brain processing chips.

10. 1923

1. The original Chinese name the author chose was invented by herself. The translators decided on HMS *Tyndareus*, the name of a real ship that plied between Shanghai and the United Kingdom in the early 1920s.

2. There are a few historical anachronisms in this story. For example, Bai Guang and Zhou Xuan became popular singers during the late 1930s and 1940s instead of the early 1920s, and Longhua did not become the famous execution ground until 1927. However, the author deliberately chose to use these names, in spite of their displacement to a different time, because she thought that they strengthened the color of old Shanghai and also because this is, after all, a fantasy.

12. THE REINCARNATED GIANT

1. This quote is a famous phrase from the *Romance of the Three Kingdoms*. Just before the Wu general Zhou Yu dies, he exclaims, "Now that there is Yu, why should Liang be born?" Liang is his rival, the Shu adviser Zhuge Liang.

2. Based on the narrative found in Chinese history textbooks, the Japanese Imperial Army's Sankō Sakusen, or Three Alls Policy, was carried out during the Japanese invasion of China from 1937 to 1945. The purpose of this policy was wiping out the resistance, which is to say the communists. "Three Alls" means "burning all, killing all, and robbing all."

15. SONGS OF ANCIENT EARTH

1. The lyrics are from the first stanza of a popular Chinese patriotic song, composed in 1950, one year after the founding of the People's Republic of China.

2. These three lines are, respectively, the opening lines of three famous Chinese revolutionary songs.

3. This stanza and the following eight are from "The Internationale."

RECOMMENDED READING

Huss, Mikael. "Hesitant Journey to the West: SF's Changing Fortunes in Mainland China." *Science Fiction Studies* 27, no. 1 (March 2000): 92–104.

Isaacson, Nathaniel. *Celestial Empire: The Emergence of Chinese Science Fiction.* Middletown, Conn.: Wesleyan University Press, 2017.

Li, Hua. "Manufactured Landscapes in Contemporary Chinese Science Fiction." *Forum for World Literature Studies* 6, no. 3 (September 2014): 443–56.

Ming, Feng-ying. "Baoyu in Wonderland: Technological Utopia in the Early Modern Chinese Science Fiction Novel." In *China in a Polycentric World: Essays in Chinese Comparative Literature,* ed. Yingjin Zhang, 152–72. Stanford, Calif.: Stanford University Press, 1998.

Raphals, Lisa. "Alterity and Alien Contact in Lao She's Martian Dystopia, *Cat Country.*" *Science Fiction Studies* 40, no. 1 (2013): 73–85.

Song, Mingwei, "After 1989: The New Wave of Chinese Science Fiction." *China Perspectives,* no. 1 (2015): 7–13.

——. "Representations of the Invisible: Chinese Science Fiction in the Twenty-First Century." In *The Oxford Handbook of Modern Chinese Literatures,* ed. Carlos Rojas and Andrea Bachner, 546–65. New York: Oxford University Press, 2016.

——. "Variations on Utopia in Contemporary Chinese Science Fiction." *Science Fiction Studies* 40, no. 1 (2013): 86–102.

Thieret, Adrian. "Society and Utopia in Liu Cixin." *China Perspectives,* no. 1 (2015): 33–40.

Wagner, Rudolf. "Lobby Literature: The Archaeology and Present Functions of Science Fiction in the People's Republic of China." In *After Mao: Chinese Literature and Society, 1978–1981,* ed. Jeffrey Kinkley, 17–62. Cambridge, Mass.: Harvard University Press, 1985.

Wang, David Der-wei. *Fin-de-Siècle Splendor: Repressed Modernities of Late Qing Fiction, 1849–1911.* Stanford, Calif.: Stanford University Press, 1997.

Wu Dingbo and Patrick Murphy, eds. *Science Fiction from China.* New York: Praeger, 1989.

Wu, Yan. "'Great Wall Planet': Introducing Chinese Science Fiction." *Science Fiction Studies* 40, no. 1 (2013): 1–14.

Wu, Yan, and Veronica Hollinger, eds. "Special Issue on Chinese Science Fiction." *Science Fiction Studies* 40, no. 1 (2013).

CONTRIBUTORS

AUTHORS

Bao Shu studied philosophy before he became a science fiction writer. His writing career began in 2010. His major works include a sequel to Liu Cixin's *The Three-Body Problem*, which has won him a reputation as a rising star in the science fiction world. His most important novel to date is *Ruins of Time*, which, together with his story collections *Songs of Ancient Earth* and *Fantasies of Time*, explores the philosophical, historical, and scientific meanings of time.

Chen Qiufan (aka Stanley Chan) is a leading author among the younger generation of science fiction writers. He is known for his stylistic combination of hyperrealism and new-wave experimentation. He has steadily produced a number of artistically interesting literary works that have been published in both science fiction and mainstream literary magazines. His short story "Balin" appeared in *People's Literature*. His most important novel is *The Waste Tide*, and he is also the author of the story collection *Future Disease*.

Chi Hui worked as a member of the editorial team of *Science Fiction World*, the most important science fiction magazine in China, for five years. She has published a series of stories dealing with environmental problems. Another theme of her writings is artificial intelligence. Her most recent novel is *2030: Terminus*.

Dung Kai-cheung is, most recently, the author of *Cantonese Love Stories: Twenty-Five Vignettes of a City* (2017). In 2014 he was named the Hong Kong Book Fair Author of the Year. Dung's translation, with Anders Hansson and Bonnie S. McDougall, of his novel *Atlas: The Archaeology of an Imaginary City* into English won the Science Fiction and Fantasy Translation Award (2013). He teaches creative writing and literature at universities in Hong Kong. Dung's magnum opus is the multivolume novel *Natural History Trilogy*, of which the first volume has been translated into English as *The History of the Adventures of Vivi and Vera* (forthcoming).

Fei Dao is the pen name of Jia Liyuan, PhD, who is currently an assistant professor in the Department of Chinese Language and Literature at Tsinghua University. He has published research articles about science fiction in academic journals such as *Science Fiction Studies* and *Literary Review*. As Fei Dao, he is the author of the short story collections *Innocence and Its Fabrications*, *The Storytelling Robot*, *Chinese Sci-fi Blockbusters*, and *The Long Journey to Death*.

Han Song is a journalist with the Xinhua News Agency. He began writing science fiction in the 1980s. He is one of the most influential science fiction writers in China, famous for his dark humor and surreal, grotesque depictions of China's reality. He is a central figure of the new wave. His novels include *2066: Mars over America*, *Red Ocean*, *Subway*, *High-Speed Rail*, *Tracks*, *Hospital*, and *Exorcism*. He has also published the short story collections *Tomb of the Universe* and *Regenerated Bricks*. Han Song is a multiple-time winner of both the Chinese Nebula Award and Galaxy Award.

La La writes in several genres: science fiction, fantasy, and martial arts romance, among others. He is the author of the short story collection *The Green Meadow*. He is currently the CEO of a media company and a playwright.

Liu Cixin, an engineer by profession, began to publish science fiction stories in 1999. He is the author of dozens of short stories and several internationally best-selling novels. His most famous science fiction novels include *The Three-Body Problem*, which won the Hugo Award for Best Novel in 2015, and its two sequels, *The Dark Forest* and *Death's End*. He is widely regarded as the leading figure in contemporary Chinese science fiction. His novels and short stories have been widely translated into many languages, including Korean, English, German, French, Turkish, Czech, and Spanish.

Lo Yi-chin is a poet, novelist, and essayist, and one of the most important writers of twenty-first-century Taiwan. He has won many literary awards, including the Hongloumeng (Dream of the Red Chamber) Literary Prize, the most prestigious award for authors writing in Chinese. His publications include the novels *The Third Dancer, Wife Dream Dog, Surname: Moon, . . . And Now She Remains in You, Faraway Land, Xixia Hotel, Daughter,* and *Superman Kuang,* as well as the story and essay collections *We, My Second Son's Future Memory about Me,* and *Facebook.*

Mingwei Song is an associate professor of Chinese literature at Wellesley College. He is the author of *Young China: National Rejuvenation and the Bildungsroman, 1900–1959.* He has been researching on Chinese science fiction since 2010 and has published dozens of research articles, books reviews, and essays on science fiction in English and Chinese. He was the guest editor of the 2012 *Renditions* double issue "Chinese Science Fiction: Late Qing and the Contemporary," in addition to five other special issues of academic journals in the area of Chinese science fiction.

Wang Jinkang, an engineer by profession, is one of the most important veteran authors of Chinese science fiction. He is the author of more than a dozen full-length novels and more than fifty short stories. His most influential novels include *Ant Life, Cross, Out of the Mother Cosmos,* and a series of novels depicting biological reengineered human beings such as *Leopard Man, Cancer Man, Simulated Man,* and others. He is the recipient of a lifetime achievement (Chinese) Nebula Award, and has won a Galaxy Award more than ten times and two Chinese Nebula Awards for Best Novel.

Xia Jia is the pen name of Wang Yao, who is an associate professor of Chinese Literature at Xi'an Jiaotong University. Xia Jia has so far published the fantasy novel *Chinese Odyssey in Nine Continents: On the Road* and two science fiction story collections, *The Demon-Enslaving Flask* and *A Time Beyond Your Reach.* She also writes in English and published the short story "Let's Have a Talk" in *Nature* in 2015.

Zhao Haihong has a master's degree in English and American literature from Zhejiang University and a PhD in art history from the China Academy of Art. She teaches at Zhejiang Gongshang University. She has been publishing science fiction stories since 1996. She is a six-time winner of the Chinese Science Fiction Galaxy Award. Two of her self-translated stories, "Exuviation" and "Windhorse," have been published in English. "Exuviation" has also been translated into Korean.

Egoyan Zheng is a leading science fiction writer in Taiwan. He is the author of the novels *The Dream Devourer, Ground Zero,* and *Man in the Urn.* He is also a productive author of short stories and essays. He was shortlisted for the Man Asian Literary Prize and the Frank O'Connor International Short Story Prize. *Ground Zero* has been translated into Japanese. Zheng is a lecturer at Taipei National University of the Arts.

TRANSLATORS

Jingling Chen received her PhD from Harvard University and teaches at the University of Illinois at Urbana–Champaign. Her research interests include Chinese and Greek comparative literature, modern and contemporary Chinese narrative, and modern Chinese intellectual history. She is completing a book on the Greek imaginary and Chinese cultural modernity.

Christopher Elford is currently a doctoral student in the Department of East Asian Languages and Cultures at the University of California, Berkeley. He studies Chinese literature of the third through the eleventh centuries, with an emphasis on poetry, poetics, calligraphy, and material culture. He has published translations of contemporary Chinese fiction in journals such as *Renditions* and *Pathlight.*

Linda Rui Feng is an associate professor of premodern Chinese cultural studies in the Department of East Asian Studies, University of Toronto. She is the author of *City of Marvel and Transformation: Chang'an and Narratives of Experience in Tang Dynasty China.*

Nicky Harman is based in the United Kingdom and is cochair of the Translators Association, the Society of Authors. She has translated fiction and nonfiction as well as poetry by authors such as A Yi, Chen Xiwo, Han Dong, Hong Ying, Jia Pingwa, Dorothy Tse, Xinran, Yan Geling, and Zhang Ling, among many others. She mentors new translators, teaches summer school courses, and judges translation competitions.

Cara Healey is a Byron K. Trippet assistant professor of Chinese and Asian studies at Wabash College. She earned her PhD in East Asian languages and cultural studies from the University of California, Santa Barbara. Her research focuses on contemporary Chinese-language science fiction.

David Hull is an assistant professor of Chinese at Washington College in Maryland. Among his translations are Mao Dun's novel *Waverings* and short stories by Ai Wei and Fei Dao. His most recent translation is Zhang Tianyi's 1930s *gongfu* satire *The Pidgin Warrior* (2017).

Theodore Huters has served as the chief editor of *Renditions* since July 2010. He is a professor emeritus at the University of California, Los Angeles, where he has taught in the Department of Asian Languages and Cultures since 1994. He has written extensively on twentieth-century Chinese literature and intellectual history, on Qian Zhongshu, Lu Xun, Qing-dynasty prose, and the intellectual developments in the late Qing dynasty. He is the author of *Bringing the World Home: Appropriating the West in Late Qing and Early Republican China*.

Chi-yin Ip joined the Research Centre for Translation, the Chinese University of Hong Kong, in 2013. She served as the managing editor of *Renditions* from 2006 to 2012. Her research focuses on the translation of traditional Chinese literature into English and German.

Nathaniel Isaacson is an associate professor of modern Chinese literature in the Department of Foreign Languages and Literature at North Carolina State University. His research interests include Chinese science fiction, Chinese cinema, cultural studies, and literary translation. He is the author of *Celestial Empire: The Emergence of Chinese Science Fiction*.

Jiang Chenxin translates from German, Italian, and Chinese. She has received a PEN / Heim Translation Fund Grant and the Susan Sontag Prize for Translation; her most recent translation is of Ji Xianlin's *The Cowshed: Memories of the Chinese Cultural Revolution* (2016). She is presently a PhD candidate in the Committee on Social Thought at the University of Chicago.

Jie Li is an assistant professor of East Asian languages and civilizations at Harvard University. She is a scholar of literary, film, and cultural studies. She is the author of *Shanghai Homes: Palimpsests of Private Life* and *Utopian Ruins: A Memorial Museum of the Mao Era*.

Ken Liu, winner of the Nebula, Hugo, and World Fantasy Awards, is the author of *The Grace of Kings* and *The Wall of Storms*, part of the silkpunk epic fantasy series The Dandelion Dynasty. His first short story collection is *The Paper Menagerie and Other Stories*. He also wrote the Star Wars novel *The Legends of Luke Skywalker*. In addition to creative writing, Ken Liu has also translated numerous Chinese science fiction novels and stories, including Liu Cixin's *The Three-Body Problem* and *Death's End*, and he is the editor of *Invisible Planets: Contemporary Chinese Science Fiction*.

Thomas Moran is a John D. Berninghausen professor of Chinese at Middlebury College, where he has taught Chinese language, literature, and film since 1994. He has been a fan of science fiction ever since reading works by Zelazny, Heinlein, Asimov, and others in the early 1970s. He has translated numerous modern and contemporary literary works from Chinese into English.

Pang Zhaoxia is a senior lecturer in the Department of East Asian Languages and Cultures, SOAS, University of London. She is also a member of the executive committee of the British Chinese Language Teaching Society.

Petula Parris-Huang has translated a number of short stories from Chinese into English. Currently a freelance translator, she previously worked as an in-house translator for the Taiwanese government and as a teaching fellow in translation studies at the University of Bath.

Carlos Rojas is a professor of Chinese cultural studies; gender, sexuality, and feminist studies; and arts of the moving image at Duke University. He is the author, editor, and translator of numerous works, including *Homesickness: Culture, Contagion, and National Transformation in Modern China*. His translations include Yu Hua's *Brothers* and Yan Lianke's *The Four Books* and *Lenin's Kiss*, among others.

Adrian Thieret is a teaching fellow in the Global Perspectives on Society program at New York University, Shanghai. He earned his PhD in Chinese from Stanford University in 2016, and his research focuses on contemporary literature and popular culture across China, Japan, and Korea.

Cheuk Wong graduated from the University of Leeds with a master's degree in conference interpretation and translation studies. She joined the Research Centre for Translation, the Chinese University of Hong Kong, in 2010 and has served as an assistant editor for *Renditions*.

Tanizaki Jun'ichiro, *In Black and White: A Novel*, translated by Phyllis I. Lyons (2018)

Yi T'aejun, *Dust and Other Stories*, translated by Janet Poole (2018)

History, Society, and Culture

Carol Gluck, Editor

Takeuchi Yoshimi, *What Is Modernity? Writings of Takeuchi Yoshimi*, edited and translated, with an introduction, by Richard F. Calichman (2005)

Contemporary Japanese Thought, edited and translated by Richard F. Calichman (2005)

Overcoming Modernity, edited and translated by Richard F. Calichman (2008)

Natsume Sōseki, *Theory of Literature and Other Critical Writings*, edited and translated by Michael Bourdaghs, Atsuko Ueda, and Joseph A. Murphy (2009)

Kojin Karatani, *History and Repetition*, edited by Seiji M. Lippit (2012)

The Birth of Chinese Feminism: Essential Texts in Transnational Theory, edited by Lydia H. Liu, Rebecca E. Karl, and Dorothy Ko (2013)

Yoshiaki Yoshimi, *Grassroots Fascism: The War Experience of the Japanese People*, translated by Ethan Mark (2015)